The English Rogue

Continued in the Life of Meriton Latroon, and Other Extravagants, Comprehending the most Eminent Cheats of Both Sexes

The Third Part

Richard Head, Francis Kirkman

Alpha Editions

This edition published in 2021

ISBN : 9789354841866

Design and Setting By
Alpha Editions
www.alphaedis.com
Email - info@alphaedis.com

As per information held with us this book is in Public Domain.
This book is a reproduction of an important historical work. Alpha Editions uses the best technology to reproduce historical work in the same manner it was first published to preserve its original nature. Any marks or number seen are left intentionally to preserve its true form.

Contents

The Preface.	- 1 -
PART III.	- 3 -
CHAP. I.	- 5 -
CHAP. II.	- 10 -
CHAP. III.	- 17 -
CHAP. IV.	- 22 -
CHAP. V.	- 28 -
CHAP. VI.	- 42 -
CHAP. V.	- 57 -
CHAP. VIII.	- 63 -
CHAP. IX.	- 68 -
CHAP. X.	- 74 -
CHAP. XI.	- 80 -
CHAP. XII	- 86 -
CHAP. XIII.	- 93 -
CHAP. XIV.	- 100 -
CHAP. XV.	- 108 -
CHAP. XVI.	- 118 -
CHAP. XVII.	- 127 -

CHAP. XVIII.	- 137 -
CHAP. XIX.	- 145 -
CHAP. XX.	- 156 -
CHAP. XXI.	- 164 -
CHAP. XXII.	- 168 -
CHAP. XXIII.	- 172 -
CHAP. XXIV.	- 179 -

The Preface.

Gentlemen!

In the first impression of this third part, a large and as I thought a sufficient Apologie was made, for the Writing and publishing thereof. Wherefore I shall not enlarge at this time, onely tell you that you have here laid before you, a large Catalogue of all sorts of notorious Rogueries; your own consciences may serve as a finger in the Margin, pointing directly to the Guilt with which you are principally concern'd; to deal plainly with you, had I lived in a less wicked Age than this is, this Book had ne're been extant; it was the vicious practices of these corrupted times, that gave it matter and form, life and being: had the evil inclinations of men extended no further, then to some wagish excursions, I should have been silent; but since Villany improves it self daily, notwithstanding the many lamentable examples monthly attending the commission thereof. I thought good to erect this Monument of their shame and wickedness, which may serve instead of a continuall Sessions, an ever-lasting Tyburn, to fright these vile miscreants from their enormous practices: I know not with what faces they can perpetrate that again, which is now so notoriously laid open to the view of the whole world; the beastliness of their debaucheries stinking above ground. But I have heard some men say, that the writing of this is not the probable way of reducing, but increasing the number of such persons whose enormities I have just cause to complain of: I would not have you to be so rash in your Judgments, as uncharitably to believe me to be a Seminary of Vice, and that I erected a Nursery for its propagation, for I must assure you I am of better principles, and that no profit whatsoever shall buy out my interest in a good conscience. What I have done is well intended, and is the product of a painful Experience, Travel, and Expence; and if you will have a little patience, you shall find (in the winding up of the bottom by the conclusion of this Story, in a fifth and last Part, which is very suddenly intended) that no crime shall go unpunished, no particular Person who hath been guilty of these vicious Extravagancies but shall have a punishment suitable to their crimes: and then I hope all persons who make use of this Book to practice debaucheries, will be induced to forbear and decline their wickedness, lest a just judgment overtake them, as they will find it hath done these Extravagants. This is the true design and end of this Book in generall, and whoever makes any other use or Construction do's greatly abuse the real and true intents of their honest Monitor.

Fra. Kirkman.

PART III.

CHAP. I.

Mrs. Dorothy *rehearses how she cheats her Lovers; who being with Child, made all that had to do with her contribute to her expence in lying in, and recompence her lost honour. She goes into the country to lay her great Belly; in her Journey she falls into the acquaintance of a crafty Old Woman* (alias: *a Procurer.*)

Mrs. *Dorothy* having thus given me an account of her first Adventure, I received much satisfaction in the Relation; and told her that I found she was much improved in cunning since my first acquaintance with her; for I had enjoyed her without much advantage to her self, for she had a great Belly, with little profit, not knowing who was, or were to find a Father: whereas now she had her choice of three, and money enough to boot whereby to purchase a handsome provision for her self and child. Yes, reply'd she, I did not intend to be caught again; for then it would have been my own fault, you having experienced me in the fallacies of your Sex; and therefore, as I told you, I made my bargain with all my three Friends as politickly as I could; and upon second thoughts, altered somewhat of the terms I had formerly agreed upon: for whereas my first Customer had given me twenty pounds in hand, to provide me with necessaries during my time of lying in, and had agreed to provide for the Child, when it should be born: I told him I had provided a Nurse for it already that was willing to take all the charge, and discharge him from any further trouble, upon payment of fourty pounds more; to this he easily consented, and gave Bond in to me, in the name of a Friend of mine; whom I told him was the Party that would make provision for the Child.

Thus did I settle matters with the first: and with the second I continued my bargain, of having twenty pounds down, and fifty pounds more at the birth of the Child. And my Masters Brother and I continued our old bargain of the like sum, of twenty pounds down, and fifty pounds more, to be paid at 6 moneths; neither did I discontinue my familiarities with any of them; for I managed my affairs so cunningly, that some nights I lay with my first Customer without the knowledge of my Master's Brother, from whom I endeavoured only to conceal it, and not from my second for he, as I told you, was privy to my dealings with him, and by that means only first gained his ends upon me: sometimes I lay with my second Customer, but it was with some regret, for I had the least affection for him of the three; but now he since he had bled some of his yellow pieces, and give me what I desired of him, I could not well refuse him his desires of me, neither was he so shy as formerly; for he valued not though my Masters Brother sometimes discovered us, for he knew that our dealings were not concealed from him, and therefore he was the bolder. But with my Masters Brother I was more free than ever; he having as much again for his money as either of the other, neither was it perceived by either of them; for he having the command of the house, so ordered it, that my Lodging was nearest to his; and therefore we had the more conveniency to come at one another.

We drave this trade for some Moneths, till in the end my Master's Brother gaining the goodwill of his Sweet-heart, he was married to her, and then he for some time fell off. But he had not lain with his Wife above a fortnight, but he became weary of her embraces, and renewed his love again to me; I at first withstood him, and used Arguments to disswade him from any such course; but all would not do; for he told me he found but little pleasure in the cold embraces of his Wife; neither had he married her, but for her Estate, which was considerable; many other Arguments he used to perswade me, who was not altogether unwilling; and so we again renewed our former pleasure; but we were necessitated to be very private, and only now and then to have a private meeting in the day time, for he was to accompany his Wife in the Night. But as privately, and craftily as we carried our selves, we were at length discovered; for my second Customer, after he had paid for his pleasure, was more desirous to have his penny-worths out of me, and still importuned me to interviews so often, that I much grumbled at him; and he being a weary Fox, still dogg'd and watch'd me, and that so often, that at length he found me and my Masters Brother in our strict embraces; he being both glad and angry, without any [by your leave] entered the Room where we were (the door being only carelesly put to) and without any words approaching the Bed whereon we lay, drew the Curtains, and said; well, Master *John* (for so was his name) that sawce which is good for the Goose, I hope will be good for the Gander; self do, self have; I hope, Sir, since you have put in for your share in the pleasure, you will be share, and share like in the charge. Well, replyed Mr. *John*, it shall be even as honest Mrs. *Dorothy* will have it; and thereupon removed, and sitting upon the Bed, I began to give him bad words, calling him jealous Coxcomb; and he again flew at me, telling me that I was insatiate, and that twenty would not serve my turn; and that now he found the reason of my slighting him, for Mr. *John*; but if we would not do him Justice, he would be revenged on us both: to that Mr. *John* replyed, asking him what he would have? I would, said he, have my money, and my Bond again; for I see, and find, there is little reason that I should pay for other mens Leachery; you make me provide for a Child, that, for ought I know, hath twenty Fathers; well, said I, you have had too much for your money; and if you are grieved, amend your self; so I will, said he, furiously going away out of the Room. He being gone, Mr. *John* and I fell to consulting, what was to be done in this affair; and after many propositions, we at length agreed, that it was most convenient for me to be gone from my service, and to leave *London*, for some Country Habitation; lest this angred Coxcomb should mischief us, by discovering our practice to Mr. *John's* Wife, or some else, that was worse: I was willing, and ready to take this course; but I told Mr. *John*, that moneys would be wanting, to make a handsome provision for me; for as affairs now stood, there was no expecting any mony from my angred Customer, but what should be forced from him. That is true, replyed he; but so soon as the money is due, for which he hath given you Bond, I will take course with him, and compel him to pay it; and in the mean time I will furnish you. This was that which I aimed at; and I knowing that he had lately received a large sum of money for his Wifes portion, with much ease gained him to pay me the fifty pounds down, for which he had given me Bond, and being thus provided with moneys, and making up my pack (which was much improved since my coming) I prepared for my departure. I as yet knew not what Country to retire to, but was resolved not to go back into my own; and therefore consulted with Mr. *John* about the place; who still hankered after me, resolving I should not go far, but that he might easily visit me; appointed me a place about ten Miles from *London*: and because he would not be suspected of going with me, nor of being any wayes privy to my departure, he permitted me to take my Journy without him; he promising in a few dayes to take the opportunity of giving me a visit.

Thus did I leave his Brother's House; but not so abruptly, but that I had the leave of my Master and Mistress; whom I told, that my Father being sick, had sent for me immediately; and to that end, a Letter was framed by Mr. *John*, and brought me by a Porter.

Being now Coach'd for my Journy, I in short time arrived at the Inn, where I was appointed to stay, till Mr. *John* should arrive, and make better provision for me; where an Adventure befell me, which is worthy of your hearing: For among the rest of the Travellers, there was an Antient Woman, who took great notice of me, still looking towards my Apron, and eying very diligently my belly; which although it was now somewhat greater, being about three Moneths gone with Child; yet I had endeavoured, by busking it down, and using all other means to hide it; but the Old Woman was not so dim-sighted, but she discovered the fraud; and having been a good one her self in her time, quickly smelt out the matter; and believed, and guessed the cause right, as it was; for my thinn Chops, and sharp and whitely looks gave evident testimonies of what disease I was sick of; and looking more throughly upon me, and examining the features of my buxome Countenance, she conjectured right, that some good Fellow had got up my belly at *London*, and I was going into the Country to be lightned of my burthen: she having a while considered with her self, that I might be very useful for her in an affair she had then in hand, was very pleasant with me, desiring my further acquaintance. I was not shye for the matter, but knowing that I had money enough to bear me out in any cross adventure that might happen, was resolved to see what the Old Woman meant by her familiarity. She first gave me Joy of my great Belly; to which I replyed, she might be mistaken; well, well, said she it matters not, whether I am or no; but if it be not so, I wish it were; and methinks it is a pity that you should be sick of any other disease; for I have so much skill in *Physiognomy*, that I can tell that you are of a more Jovial Temper than now your countenance shews for, and it is very unfit, that one of your years and complexion should want the pleasures of a fit Bed-fellow; but I suppose you are not ignorant of those enjoyments, and have a Husband, with whom you have experienced the sweet of a Married Life. Truly, Madam, said I, you are much mistaken; for I never yet entred into that honourable Estate of Matrimony. Well, that matters not much, replyed this good Old one; but I have miss'd of my aim, if you are ignorant of what I have told you; and although you may have no Husband, yet I believe you have a Friend, who has been dabling with you, and swel'd your Belly; if it be so, you are not the only she that is guilty of that pleasing Crime; for I my self have been good in my time; and still have a Colts tooth in my head.

Thus did the Old Dotterel initiate her acquaintance with me; and had well near put me to the blush, but that I turned my face aside, and gently wip'd it with my Handkerchief; and then I told her she was very pleasant, and that a little in the extreams, considering the publickness of the place (there were more Guests in the Room) and our small acquaintance. As for the place, said she, I must confess, as we are not all one Womans Children, so we ought to be somewhat careful; but I shall make amends for that, by desireing you to withdraw into a more private place; and as for the short time of our acquaintance, I question not, but we shall quickly set our Horses together, and I hope our present meeting may be advantagious to us both, especially, if it be as I yet expect it. What do you mean, said I? That is, replyed she, if you be with Child, and such a Gamester as I wish you. I was much amazed at this Womans confidence; but however, she having been so open with me, I resolved to be as free with her: hoping her words might prove true, and that some benefit might be made out of her acquaintance; and therefore advising her to leave that Room, for another more private, she soon obey'd me; and having entred, and causing a good fire, and Wine to be brought, we sat down together, not without my receiving some salutations, and strict embraces from my Antient, but to me new acquaintance. After we had each of us washed away sorrow with a Cup of the best Canary, the Old Woman being now more bold than before; again took me in her arms, & laid her hand hard upon my Belly; when it so fortuned, that at that very instant the Child gave a gentle turn in my Belly; which she quickly felt; and then cryed out, Well, Daughter, you see I was in the right; therefore since I have discovered somewhat, I pray tell me the rest of your condition; and I question not but you will receive much profit by your discovery: I was resolved to be very free with her, and acquaint her with the chiefest of my Adventures; still concealing so much thereof, as should, or might be convenient to be made known; whereupon I thus began.

Mother (since you will have it so) I shall make a free confession of my Crime; hoping you will be merciful in the pennance you shall impose; seeing, as you say, I am not the alone guilty party; and thereupon I recounted to her, how that I being born in such a Country, and desirous to see fashions, went up to *London*, and there happened into a Service; where my Masters Brother falling in love with me, after some Courtship (he promising me marriage) we came to enjoyment; that he, notwithstanding his promise married with another; who indeed exceeded me in Fortune, as I her in beauty; but my sweet heart soon after marriage came to me, and repented of his bargain; but since that was past could not be remedied, I was forced to be contented; and indeed, I having a great love for him, permitted him still to lye with me, that in the end, I was with Child by him; and then we consulting what was most necessary to be done, it was at length concluded, that I should leave my service, and retire into the Country, till I were rid of my great Belly; and to that end and purpose, I was now come into the Country, expecting him in short time to follow me. Thus did I give her a short, though somewhat true, account of my Fortunes; and when I had done, she thus replyed.

Well, Daughter, since your condition is as I judged it, and indeed hop'd it to be; I shall play the Chymist, and extract Golden Fortunes to you out of your own desperate misfortunes; for I doubt, as your Lover hath once been false to you, so he may prove the second time; and now he hath sent you a journey, he may leave you to shift for your self; and to look for another Father for your Child. But, Daughter, (continued she) if you will be rul'd by me, you shall not only have a rich Father, but a great fortune for your Child: and perhaps, so much ready money for your self, as you will not only give me thanks, but reckon this our meeting to be the most fortunate Accident of your whole Life. I thank you very kindly, replyed I, for your fair offers, but I shall desire you to explain your self further; and I suppose I shall put so much confidence in you, as to be rul'd by you; although I do not in the least doubt that I shall be put to those extremities you imagine. So much the better, replyed she; but however, that I may fit you for those purposes I have designed, and partly propounded to you; I shall give you an account of some part of my Life and Adventures; and thereupon she thus Began.

CHAP. II.

The Old Woman relates to Mrs. Dorothy, *where she was born, in an Ale house; how educated in all manner of debauchery; how she had a Bastard, which she murther'd, is after marriage gotten with Child by a* Moor, *and perswades her Husband it was his, notwithstanding, it being conceived so by the strength of imagination. Her Husband growing jealous of the Black* Moor, *fights him; and they kill one the other. A strange adventure between her Lover and a* Frenchman, *with a Wind mill.*

I was born (said she) at *Portsmouth*; a Sea-Port-Town, very well known, not only to most *English* Men, but also to many Strangers. My Parents were of the ordinary ranck, keeping a fudling School, or House of good fellow-ship. I was educated, according to the Custom of the place, to learn to read, and Sew; in learning of which having spent two or three years, at the Age of eleven I was taken home to sit in the Barr and keep the scores; I was well pleased to be at home, because there was great variety of Guests; especially merry drunken Saylors: who, when they had liberty to come ashore, would lustily booz it; and sing, and dance, all weathers. And to that end, our House was still accommodated with a blind Harper, who pick'd up a merry living: I taking pleasure in Musick, and my Father thinking it would advance his trading, bought for me a pair of Virginals; and hired a man to teach me: I giving my mind to it, soon learnt some tunes, which I played to the merry Saylers, whilst they pull'd off their shoes, and danc't Lustick; and sometimes I gaining a Teaster, or Groat for my Musick, was so encouraged, that I quickly took all the instructions my Master was able to give me; I likewise learned some songs of him, and some of the Saylers; so that in little time I was well furnished with fat and lean Songs; so we term'd the bawdy and others. Although I soon understood what was meant by bawdy Songs; yet I was yet to young to have experience of them: however, when my Auditors laugh'd, and sometimes hug'd and kiss'd me, I had some kind of Notions that were very pleasing to me; and although my Mother sometimes told me of the hateful name of Whore, and how much it concerned me to keep my Maidenhead; yet I resolved that if it were long ere I were married, yet it should not be so before I tryed what it was to lye with a Man: however I followed my Mothers directions, in frowning, and scouling on those who forc'd a kiss from me. But, as I had designed, so it came to pass; for at the Age of fourteen years, a Sayler, who of all other sort of People, I liked best, gained my good liking: he newly came home from a boon Voyage, and was full of half Crown pieces, and took up his quarters at our house; my Father seeing him so flush, was resolved to milk him; and therefore permitted him to keep me Company, though he saw he was very familiar in hugging and kissing me; I likewise had a great mind to some of his money, and therefore begg'd some of him to buy Ginger-bread, Sugar, Plumbs, Figgs, Fruit, and such like liquorish things; he believing, that as I had a liquorish tooth, so I might have a liquorish Tail, refused me no moneys I desired; but I being somewhat modest in the smallness of my demands, had but little that wayes by fair play; therefore I bethought me, how I might be Mistress of more; therefore was resolved, at the next opportunity, to pick his pocket, which I guess'd would be no difficult matter to do; in regard he was oftentimes much overtaken with the Creature; and therefore, to the end I might effect my desires, when we were met next together, I drank pretty smartly with him, and conveyed some strong waters into each cup of his Beer; and so in short time he being somewhat tipsie, desired me to sing him a song, which I performing, he was quickly, as I supposed fallen asleep; I sat in his lap, and as cunningly as I could, slipt my hand into his Pocket; where I gathered up three or four half Crowns; as sleepy as he was, he observed me, and while I was at my work, he was at his; and as slighly he conveyed one of his hands into another place, having not as yet been at that sport; I squeek'd out, which made him rise, and me withdraw my hand, and both of us leave our Prizes; and I blushing for anger, that I was so doubly catch'd, would have left the Room; but he taking hold of me, desired me to be quiet, and told me, what was done on his part was but in jest, as he supposed what I did was; and that it was but *quid* for *quo*. I having by this time gained some confidence, was, at his entreaty, content to stay longer with him, and sung another song; which when I had done, he gave me four half Crowns (a greater sum than I was ever till then Mistress of) and told me, since he knew what I would have, he would give it me, as he hoped I would do the like. To which I replied, I knew not what I might do in time, if he continued his kindness to me. Thus did I encourage him to be liberal to me, in hopes of his desired reward: and thus neither of us (knowing one anothers minds) was long backwards, without enjoying our desires; he giving me some money and a Ring. I permitted him to enjoy me as fully as he could wish or desire; and many rancounters we had together, both at home and abroad, as time and place would permit: but as the longest day will have an end so had his money; and then my Father perceiving that it was low ebb in his Pocket, began to be more wary and circumspect of him, and to watch him, and slight him, lest he should gain anything upon me, and run into his score; and so he might lose as much in the shire, as he had got in the hundred; the Old Woman, my Mother, being somewhat suspicious of me, still watch'd us with much wariness; and he not having money to treat me abroad at other houses, as formerly, we were fain to have all our sports at home when we had conveniency; and there we were so narrowly put to it, that we were oftentimes in danger to be catch'd.

When my sweet-heart could get any Moneys he would treat me abroad; and one day having been walking with me, he committed one of the greatest extravagancies I ever heard of he had drank very hard and was now almost fluster'd, when coming by the Wind mill which is near our Town, the wind blowing somewhat moderately, there was a *French man*, who challenged some *English* Saylers to shew some feats of activity; among other exploits, he took hold of one of the wings of the Wind-mill, and holding fast, was carried round therewith, lighting very orderly on the ground upon his feet. This was a wonderful, and we thought desperate attempt, and he much bragg'd of it daring any *English man* to do the like: my sweet-heart being with me, and desirous to gain my esteem, and being somewhat pot shaken, makes no more ado, but likewise takes hold of one of the wings of the Windmil; which by reason the wind blew more freshly than it had done lately, caused the Mill to go more swiftly then ordinary; and he not being able to hold fast, was thrown off: but though it was a pretty way off, yet to his good Fortune, he was not thrown to the ground (which would have broken his bones,) but into a pond of water; and there he being very skilful in swimming, soon recovering himself, swam to the shore; and not forgetting what he had done, cryed out, *Now let any Mounsieur of ye all do the like*. All there present did much applaud him; some attributing that to his design and skill, which indeed was by chance; and truly, it was a good chance for him, that he broke not his neck: but he then escaped any further danger: and some Merchants being there present, were so surprized with the manner of the action that they gave him ten shillings to drink; he being thus rewarded for his folly, thought it his best course to go home; where we being come, and my Father made acquainted with the matter, and that he had money in his Pocket made much of him, and perswaded him to go to bed; and my Mother procured him a Sack posset, which we all eat of at his beds side; but little did they think that this was a kind of a Bride-posset: for, although we were not married that day, yet we lay together that night; for when they were in their bed, in went I to his; where he expected me, having before enjoyned me to make use of that opportunity, which I did, to both our good intents: for we enjoyed one another in full freedom of all dilights: this being the first and last time I ever lay with him: for not long after, his coyn being spent, and a Voyage presented it self, he Shipp'd himself, and away he went for the *East Indies*; we promising a constant continuance of our affections. But he being gone, it was not long, ere I found a strange alteration in my body, being taken with pewkings, and vomitings, such as young Married folks are used to have; whereupon I concluded, that I should soon have a great belly, which so fell out; but before that, I had a Husband to Father it.

Our House being publique, we entertained all Comers; amongst the rest, there came a Sayler, who had had the Fortune to meet with a prize; and he for his own share had two hundred pounds Sterling. This was so tall a Fortune as was unusual to be the possession of an ordinary Sayler; and he chancing in at our house, my Father was very desirous to rid him of his mony: he acquainted my Mother with his purpose, and told her, that this Fellow would make a very good Fortune for me their Daughter; and they might by means of this live more plentifully then ever. The Fellow soon expressed a great deal of love for me, which my mother taking notice of, told me of her own and my Fathers intentions, and bid me prepare to entertain his love, for they designed him for my Husband; she advised me to be free and courteous to him, but by no means to let him proceed further then the ordinary civility. I promised her all obedience, and she was very diligent and watchful over me. My sweet heart was very sweet upon me, and would fain have been dealing with me, as Merchandize, bidding very fair for me, but I resolved to have all or none; would not let him have a bit, but what was lawful: he being thus stopt, was the more earnest; and at length, rather than lose me, agreed to have me at my own terms which was marriage; which at length was fully agreed upon. But my qualmes encreasing as did my belly, my Mother suspected somewhat was the matter, and therefore took me strictly to task; and so wrought with me; that I confessed I had been sporting with my former sweet-heart; this news much startled her; but she who had passed many such brunts, soon found out a remedy; and told me that if I would be wholly ruled by her, she would still warrant the business should go on prosperously enough; for, said she, I will direct you to carry your self, so as the loss of your Maiden-head shall not be discovered; and as for your great Belly, we will when you are marryed, send your husband to Sea before your time of delivery: and in the mean time, we will manage all matter cunningly enough. My Mother having thus encouraged me, I prepared for the wedding day, which was soon after appointed; which being come, and night also, we went to bed; and there my Bride-groom going about to enjoy me, I counterfeited all kinds of simplicity; I cryed, sob'd, and screeked out; and he had much ado, with puffing and blowing, and sweating, to possess himself of me. I had all the marks and symptoms of untouch'd Virginity; and the more to beguile him, notwithstanding all his fair words, and endeavours, I made so great a noise as raised my Mother; who coming into our chamber, found me in swound; from which she soon brought me, by rubbing me with Vinegar, and other Remedies; and she perswaded me to be patient, and desired him to deal kindly with me, using this Proverb; *Gently*, John, *the Girls Young,* She left us, and then with somewhat more Patience I permitted him to take his pleasure with me.

Thus was I marryed, and came off with all Credit imaginable; but afterwards it did not proceed as we expected; for my Husband being very fond of my company, would not by any means be perswaded to leave me for the Sea; but intended, now he had gained money enough, to live on shore. This resolution of his was very unpleasing; but I was forced to be contended, and to provide against the time of my delivery of my great Belly, which now came on a pace, and indeed was somewhat sooner than I expected; for I was taken one day with a suddain pain, which much surprized my Mother; for my Husband was in the House, and hearing my cryes, would needs force his way into my Chamber; where I was accompanyed by my Mother, who was instructing me what to do; on his approach to the Bed, my pains encreased, and a Child was born into the World; but, that he might not discover the fallacy, by the crying of the Child, I smothered it; and lying still for some space, my Mother perswaded him to depart; he being gone, my Mother fell to work; and removed the Child, playing the Midwife in the best manner she could; and all being buried, and *I* put into order, she told her Son in law, that these were extream fits of the Chollick, and would now they had begun, continue for some dayes; wherefore she desired him to take another Lodging, and let her lye with me: to this he hardly consented; but at length, at both our importunities, he was content, and in ten dayes time, I still every day counterfeited fits of groaning, but he seeing I sensibly amended, would no longer forbear lying with me.

Thus did I escape this misfortune, and came off with flying Colours, without the least suspition; so that I was encouraged to proceed in further Roguries; which was the ruine of my Husband, and in which I had like to have been involved. I told you our house was for all Guests; and now by the addition of my Husbands money, which was employed in my Fathers Trade, to encrease his stock, our house the best furnished, was the best customed house in the Town; amongst the rest, there came a Person of Honour, who had been a Traveller, and among his Attendants a Negro, or Black-man, which he had brought from *Guiana*. This Black-more was reported by his Master and others, to be the Son of a Prince in his own Country; I look'd on him with an affectionate and smiling countenance; which he perceiving, and also that I was handsome, much desired my company; and being Master of money enough to spend on me, he had many opportunities of courting me; at the first, I examining what I was about to do drew back, thinking it a very strange thing to be kiss'd by a Black-more, but use brought it into Custom; and I endured not only that, but also methought I had a minde to taste of his flesh, perswading my self, that there would be more than ordinary satisfaction in that enjoyment; and he finding me coming, so prosecuted his suit, that it was not long ere I enjoyed him: I must confess much to my content, for nothing but his sparkling eyes was to be seen in the dark, which indeed were as shining, as two stars in a clear night; and he was as much delighted with me: so that we promised to take all opportunities for enjoyment. The Lords business kept him there so long, that we had so much sport in jest, as turned to earnest; for I found my self to be with child, and I did absolutely believe that my Black-friend was the Father of it: this consideration put me into a deep melancholly; for we carried our business not so privately, but that we were taken notice of, and suspected by my Mother; but much more by my Husband, whose extreme love to me was converted into as extreme a jealousie; and he looked on my Black-friend with a great deal of horror.

I finding my self with Childe, and doubting it was by him, a fancy possessed me, that I should bring forth a Black-More like the Father: this, I say put me to a very great *non-plus*; and I endeavoured by all means to blind my Husband, and take all suspition from him: I told him, I believed I was with Child, this pleased him; but I also added, I doubted, I should not render him compleatly satisfied: for that I had a very great fancy that the Child would be black, and I could give no reason, but that the sight of my Lords Black-More was deeply imprinted in my fancy: I told him, I had read the story of a Black Queen and King, who had a Child that was white; and being so born, was thrust out of the King his Fathers Dominions, for no other cause but because he was white; and the Queen his Mother hardly escaped the fury of her Husband, who shrewdly suspected her guilty of Adultry with some white-man, because the Child was so. This said I, was the Crime laid to her charge; and it seemed so reasonable to him and all his Nobility; that notwithstanding the Queen was alwayes esteemed to be a vertuous woman, yet she hardly escaped with her life. But at length, a wise man of that Kingdome coming to the Court, and hearing of the matter, and that the Queen was banished as well as her Son; he, said I, walking about the Court, and coming into the Kings Bed-chamber, there saw the Picture of a fair white-woman, which had, as great rariety, been presented to the King he then remembring the unfortunate case of the Queen, did really believe that the sight of that white Picture had occasioned the Queen to conceive and bring forth a white Child. Being thus convinced, and perswaded in his own opinion, he was not long before he perswaded the King to the same; and the Queen having been alwayes of an unblemisht reputation, it was concluded by the King, and all the Nobility, that the Queen was innocent: and thereupon the banishment was repealed, and both received home with great joy, state, and honour; and this Son, after his Fathers decease, was crowned, and reigned King of the Place. Now sweetheart, said I, this being so, and fancy having so strong an operation in the womb by the only site of a Picture, I cannot but imagine that the real presence of one may work much more and greater effects, especially since I find a very great inclination not only to love, but long for black things; black cherries, I affect extreamly, as also damsons, sloes, & black-bullies; I chiefly feed on black puddings; and it is not very long, said I, since I longed for a black hat, and did eat it up every bit: and now I have lately had a great desire to a dish of butter'd char-coal.

This discourse wrought variously with my Husband, who, although he did somewhat suspect me, yet would he take no great notice at present, but told me, that surely this was but fancy, and would in the end amount to nothing: I was content with his answer; but knowing his mind stood thereto bent, I first propounded, that the Black-more should depart our house, or else that I might remove from home to some other place, to see, if by his absence the fancy would leave me: to this he willingly agreed; and in regard to move for the Black-more's departure until his Lord went also, would not only raise suspicious Discourses, but turn to our disadvantage, by reason they were good Guests; we therefore resolved that I should remove four or five miles from home; the which I did the next day; but my departure was not so secret, but that I gave notice thereof to my beloved Black-more, who promised not to be long before he took the opportunity of giving me a visit; the which he did unseen of any, I letting him in at a back Garden door; and thither he usually came to me once in two or three days: we sometimes spent some hours together in a Banqueting-house in the Garden; and at last grew so bold, as to spend whole nights in bed together; so that my Husband, who sorely suspected me, was resolved to watch my waters; and one Evening missing the Black-more, who was then come to me, he at midnight departed; and coming to the back door whereat the Black-more entred, he finding it open, entered, saw the Candle in my Chamber, and I believe could hear our voyces, but knew not how to enter without great noise; wherefore, now resolving in his mind what to do, he waited till the morning, walking about the Garden; but in regard the Black-more had some affairs of his Lords that morning to dispatch, he arose early, and left me; I shut fast the door, and left him; no sooner was he down, but my angry Husband with a drawn sword meets him; he seeing and knowing him, guessed his purpose, likewise quickly draws; and they running upon one anothers swords, soon bereft each other of life.

CHAP. III.

The Old Woman relates, that her Husband and Black-friend having killed one another, she removes her lodging; and is brought to bed of a young Black-more, which she likewise murthereth; and then again removing her quarters, and passing for a maid, is married to a young Inn-keeper; who, instead of her, had a maid servant for his Bed fellow; who being both sleepy, she sets fire of the House; and then pretending to fetch water at the Well, tumbles her in, where she is drowned.

Thus, said Mrs. *Dorothy*, did the old Hagg give me an account of her mischievous beginning; and indeed, in the prosecution of her story, she acquainted me with so many horrible actions, that I was agast; and wondered that the Earth did not open, to swallow up a wretch so monstrously wicked; but I think, said she, by what I have said, I have told you enough to know her, and therefore shall pass over the rest of her actions in silence: nay, said I, Mrs. *Dorothy*, since you have begun to give us so fair an account of the foul actions of this your wicked acquaintance, I shall desire you to take the pains to proceed therein. Truly, said Mrs. *Mary*, although I have known many wretched People in my dayes, yet I never heard of the like; and I suppose by what you have already recounted, that all you have further to say will be both remarkable, admirable, and pleasant (if we may account that pleasant which is so mischievously, and wickedly witty;) and therefore I, as well as our friend here, desire you to continue your relation; and if you will take the pains, we will have the patience to hear you to the least particular. Mrs. *Dorothy* being thus requested by us both, replyed, that she should be content to grant our desires, but then we must have a great deal of patience, and pardon those impertinent ignorances that she should be forced to recount, in relating so many notable and various adventurous actions of another: We told her, we should willingly attend, and excuse her in all; and thereupon she thus continued.

Although (said this old Trot) my Husband, and my black friend had quickly dispatch't their business, by thus dispatching one another, yet they were neither so sudden nor so silent, but I both heard and saw them tilt at one another with their swords, which were bathed in each others heart blood; and so they fell, grinning at each other with horrible Countenances and they lay so close together, that they could catch hold of one another, and fight with their hands, their swords being sheathed in one anothers bodies; but this contest could not, neither did it last long, their hearts being suffocated with Blood, and so in short time they both expired; which I discovered by the noise of hollow groans: and thus continued she, was I deprived of a Friend, and a Husband. I was startled at the present, but considering what was to be done, went to bed, and lay there till some of the house came and bounc'd at my Chamber door; I suffered them to continue knocking for some time, as if I had been asleep; but they growing more furious by reason of my silence, were ready to break open the door, when I jumped out of my bed, and in my smock opening the door, asked them what was the cause of their violent knocking; they replyed, they were glad to see me alive, which they much doubted, by reason of my silence, and having seen such a doleful sight as was then in the Garden: I seeming ignorant of all, desired them to explain themselves, and acquaint me with their meaning; they were not long then ere they had told me, that my Husband and the Black-more who quartered at my Fathers, were both dead in the Garden: I was amazed, ran then to the window, and there beheld what I too well knew already; and then cryed out, and in lamentable and furious manner threw my self on the floor, tearing my hair, and making great lamentation; by this time the Constable and other Neighbors were come, but could not get any thing out of me to discover any knowledge of the fact. I seemed a stranger to all; and so the Bodies being removed, word was sent to my Father and Mother, who quickly came thither; but finding me, as the rest, to pretend ignorance, nothing could be done; but the People conjectured variously, and though they could not accuse me as the murtherer, yet I was shrewdly suspected to be the cause; they judging the truth as it was: but however, I was without the compass of the law, and therefore escaped all trouble.

Their Bodies were soon after buried, and I thought it absolutely necessary to abscond my self, lest (the time of child bearing being near approaching) I might be further discovered by the Complexion of the child, which I did verily believe would be black; and therefore I left my Fathers house, and went to an obscure Village about ten miles off; I took up my lodging with an old Woman of my Mothers acquaintance, pretending a great melancholly since the death of my Husband, and therefore avoided all Company: I had all along attempted to destroy the Child in my Womb, and to that end I had taken *Savine*, and many other drugs and potions, and using to jump, and leap, and wrastle, to cause my self to miscarry, but all in vain; so that in fine, I was forced to use the same remedy I had done, and smother the Child so soon as it was born; I had all possible conveniences to do it, whilst the Midwife, who lived at some distance, was not much looked after, although it was somewhat black, which was now taken to be so, only by reason of its strugling for passage; and wanting a Mid-wife, I caused it to be quickly nail'd up in a box, and so with little trouble passed over the difficulty of this affair: my Mother soon came to me, and accommodated me, with every thing fit for my condition, so that it was not long ere I perfectly recovered; and I having no mind to return to my Fathers nor to stay in that place, caused my Mother to provide me with a gentile habit; and money in my pocket, and being thus fitted, went twenty miles further, to the house of another of my Mothers acquaintance; and having been so unfortunate with a Husband, was resolved not to own that ever I had been married, but to pass for a maid;

which I might well enough do, not being yet above eighteen years of age. My beauty then was so charming, that I quickly gained many adorers; and it being given out that I was a Virgin, and of a good fortune, had many Sutors in earnest, that woed me in the honest terms of marriage. Having the choice of several, I was the more coy; but in the end, there was one, who was an Inn-keeper, whose Father being lately dead, and left a handsome competency, him I accepted of, but with great jealousie and suspition of my self; lest he was a cunning youngster, should discover the want of my Virginity. I was sensible it would be no difficult matter for him to finde me out, but I was resolved to try my Wits, and prevent his discovery: to this end I delayed my marriage for some time, till I could bring my matters to pass; which (said she) I did in this manner.

There was a Servant-Maid in the House, whom I usually had for my Bed-fellow, and with her I was very free in all my discourse, acquainting her with all passages between me and my Sweethearts; and many pleasing discourses we had upon those occasions, and commonly we spent some hours every night when we were in Bed, in these Conferences: I asking her which of my Sweet-hearts was the best, and likliest to prove a good Husband; she and I both jumped in one mind, and she seemed to rejoyce at the good Fortune I was likely to enjoy, in having so handsome, and accomplish'd a Person, as he was with whom I was to be Married; saying, that of all men breathing, she never saw one whom, she thought, she could love better; and adding, that she would give all the money in her Pocket to have my place on the Wedding Night. Well, thought I, are you there? I'le be with you anon. Truly said she, I am a perfect Maid, not having yet had to do with any Man; and for deed, nay, for thought and word, untill this time, was a pure Virgin; but methinks, since I saw your Sweetheart, I have such pleasing imaginations, that I could willingly experiment the effects; but, continued she, I hope you will take all this in good part, and not be jealous of me, for I shall not in the least injure you, no, though your Sweet-heart should desire it; besides, my Quality and condition is so much beneath yours, that it would be but a folly to expect it: but shall wish you all happiness with your beloved Bridegroom. She having opened her mind thus freely to me, it was the thing I only aimed at, and above all things wish'd for; and therefore, that I might now stricke while the Iron was hot, I thus replyed; come, come, do not counterfeit more Modesty than needs, but tell me truly, and sincerely, if I can find a way to compass your desires; and be therewith content, and willing, will you obey me in what I shall desire of you? This is a strange proposition, said she, and I believe far from your heart to do, and only to try me farther; but I pray let us talk no more of this matter.

I quickly answered, that I was now in earnest, and would (if she would swear to me to be secret) discover a secret that was of the highest importance, and that then all things would be as she had wished; she wondring what I meant, and being desirous (as all women are inquisitive after secrets) to discover mine, soon made many protestations and vows, to be secret in what ever I should impart to her; and thereupon I told her, that indeed about twelve moneths since, being in my fathers house, a Gentleman of quality lodging there, and having divers times courted me; and I always refusing to hear him; and being very obstinate, notwithstanding all his endeavours by Presents, and otherwise; he, I said being wholy impatient, and resolved to venture all for my enjoyment, took his opportunity, and came to bed to me; I feeling him near me, cry'd out but in vain, for my Lodging was at too great a distance from any bodyes hearing; and so in the end, notwithstanding my striving, and strugling, he had his will of me; and indeed, to tell you the truth, the danger of the brunt being over, and I well knowing that what was past could not be recalled, was, in the end, willing a second, or third time, to permit him the same enjoyment; and so he went away in the Morning well satisfied, and I better pleas'd than when he came to me. I was resolved to keep this from the knowledge of my Parents, and did so, though he offered me Marriage, which would have been advantageous enough for me, he being, as I said, a Person of Quality; but however, he continued his practice with me all the time of his stay at my Fathers, which was two Moneths; and then he departing, promised a sudden return, and that he would then discover himself to my Father, and request me in Marriage; I trusted to his fair words, and permitted his departure; but he had not been long absent ere I perceived my self to be with Child: I kept this from the knowledge of all, so long as I could; but in the end, my Mother suspecting me, charged me so roundly, that I confessed the Fact; she thereupon took the best remedy she could, and unknown to my Father, sent me away to a Friend of hers, where I lay in of a Child, which soon after dying, and I recovered, I again removed hither, where what hath befaln me you already know as well as I; and now, my dear Friend, said I, the case being thus, you may do me a great kindness, and please your self, as you say, by taking my place on the Wedding-night; and he lying with you in my stead may be deceived, and take me for a pure Virgin; whereas otherwise I am in much doubt to be discovered, in regard, that not only I have lost my Maidenhead, but have also lately had a Child.

My Bed-fellow gave diligent attendance to what I had related, and after I had satisfied her how she should behave her self in every respect, she consented to take my turn. My business being in this forwardness, I quickly consented to clap up the bargain with my Sweet-heart; and the Wedding-day being come, we were accordingly Married; and at Bed time I went to Bed with my Bride-groom, but feigning Modesty, commanded all to depart the Room; which they did, leaving one Candle burning; I seeing the Company gone, leap'd out of the Bed to put the Candle out; which I did, and then, according to appointment, the Maid, who was ready in her smock behind the

Hangings, quickly got into the Bed, and enjoyed my place; I staid in the Chamber, and could well enough discover all passages between them, and how she made some faint resistance; but not long it was ere they fell a sleep, and slept so long, that I was at a very great stand what to do, lest day-light should come ere she should awake, and then be seen by my Husband, and I disgraced and lost for ever; I ruminated in my mind many wayes; at last I was resolved to proceed to violence, and hazard all, rather than lose my credit; and therefore seeing they still slept on, I went out of the Chamber into the next; where with the help of a Tinder-box, I struck a light; and getting a Torch, and lighting it, set fire on some part of the house, which soon encreased to a great flame; I then made no great difficulty to make a noise, and cry out fire, fire; this was soon seen, smelt, and heard by my drousie bedfellows, who both arose; and I being there, caught hold of him, as if I had lain with him; and his bedfellow being now a little come to her self, and seeing me, began to consider what she was to do; and ran where her cloaths were, put them on, and then came to help me to mine.

My Husband, and all the rest of the Family being thus raised, ran about for water to quench the fire; I being left alone with my Husbands Bed-fellow, could have found in my heart to have killed her with a Sword there in the Chamber: because she had been the occasion of all this mischief; and the thoughts of that, and remembring what hurt she might do me hereafter, in discovering my secrets or, at least, in being my Co-rival; these Considerations made me resolve to dispatch her into the other world; and there-fore desiring her to go down with me into the Yard to fetch water at the Well, she did so; where I spying my opportunity, in the absence of the rest of the Family, as she was stooping to draw Water, I turned her head forwards into the Well; where, before any came to help her, she was dead. I pretended to bewail her misfortunes; but the fire, by the asistance of some Neighbours, being now quench'd, we all retired into that part of the House that was unburn'd; where every one lamented, not only the misfortune of the fire, but that of the Maids death; in which I alone was principally concerned.

CHAP. IV.

She being at home with her Husband, is Courted by Gallants; one of which Cuckolds him; She is out witted by her Gallant, and cheated of a Gown, and three Rings; she is Courted by another Gallant, and they study a Revenge on the first; which she executes, by appointing the first to come to Bed to her; where her Husband, by her appointment, was in her stead; who taking him in the manner, soundly whips him; in the mean time she is in Bed with her new Gallant.

The next day after our unfortunate Wedding-night, all Persons concerned began to reckon up their losses; in which, neither I, nor my Husband suffered but little; for he had nothing there but the Clothes on his back, and I only had mine, and a Trunk of Clothes, and Linnen, which were safe. Our Landlord lost some of his Goods, and an hundred pounds would not repair the damage the House had sustained by the fire; he therefore complained much of his losses: but his lamentations were not equal to those of an Old Woman, who lived in the Town, and was the Mother of the Unfortunate Maid, whom I had so treacherously, and ungratefully murthered: I was almost as joyful as she was sad, that I was rid of so dangerous a Corrival, whom I had entrusted with my greatest secrets.

The disorders of this House caused us to quit it sooner than we intended; for that very day we removed to my Husbands Habitation, which was not above four Miles distant, and there we Lodged, where that night I received those imbraces from my Husband which were very pleasing to me, and then all things were as well fixed as I could desire; only my Mothers coming was every day expected, I having given her notice of my Transactions by Letters: She came in few dayes, and that not empty-handed; for she brought an hundred pounds in ready money with her: this, she told her new son-in-law, was but part of a greater Sum, my Father and she intended for my Portion; although my Husband expected five hundred pounds with me (I having given out that I should have so much) yet he was content with this for the present; and this money was part of what was left me of my first Husbands. During the stay of my Mother, we kept open House; and giving up our selves to all manner of mirth, I found my Husband to be but an easie Coxcomb, and one whom I thought I should out-wit, and over-rule; he was much inclined to gameing; and, as the fortune of the Dice went, he sometimes won, and lost again as often; at which he would be somewhat waspish and griping: and what he lost by gameing, he would get up again out of large Reckoning, and tricks he would put upon his Guests, who now were more in number than formerly; for it being given out, that he was Married, and that to one that was handsom, all the Countrey came in upon us; especially all the roaring Lads, who spent highest, came all to see, and present their service to their Landlady; and as a Citizens shop is never so well furnished, as when a handsome

Wife is placed in a varnisht seat; even so is an Inn-keepers Barr; and doth draw in Customers, all in hopes to have a lick at her honey pot; and although a Woman be never so chaste, and the Guests finde it so, yet if she be but handsome, her company is still desired; but you know my temper so well, that you may guess I should not hold out a seven years siege, if I were but once bravely assaulted; but withall, I resolved to be as cunning as all my Observations had taught me, and not be like a Glove for every ones drawing on. If I had any Servants, I resolved they should be of the best; and those I counted so, who wore most money in their Pockets, I had my choice of several of that kind; and though I still counterfeited a great Modesty yet I was treated, and regalia'd both at home and abroad; there was no sport, or divertisements, but I made one of the Company; no fair near our Town but I visited, being conducted thither by one Gallant or other: where I had several Fairing presented me. I had my Husbands consent to all my actions, for I still acquainted him with all; and when I was carried to any place, I told him every particular, and caused him to meet me at the place and time appointed; without which I pretended a mighty unwillingness; and this I did, that he might put the greater confidence in me.

 This trade I did drive for a long time, without joyning issue with any of my Gallants, and they gained no more upon me than a kiss, or a languishing look, which I sometimes cast upon them to cause them to believe that in time they might arrive to the height of their desires; and for these my kind looks I was as kindly rewarded; they presenting me with Gloves, Scarffs, Hoods, Rings and Cabinets, and such like Womanish toyes, and all in hopes that they might toy with me, as in fine they did: I had several of these Gamesters, but one above all the rest was most in my favour, he having been the most prodigal in expences upon me; I gave him full freedome with me, and I cornuted this as well as I had done my other Husband; he spent much of his time in gaming, and was very earnest at it with his Guests: and while he was at his game, I and my Gallant were at ours. My friend for his greater pretence of freedom in our house, would humour my Husband, and Game with him, and lose his money; for indeed my Husband was at that sport the better Gamester, although my friend pleased me better at the other; by these extravagancies of his, and his losses at Gameing, he in time came to a low ebb of money in his pocket, and was necessitated to withdraw, and lessen his expences; so that he was not so welcome to me or my Husband as he had been: for I was of the Old Womans Opinion, *No longer Pipe, no longer Dance*: as he avoided expences I shunn'd his Company; and having Friends enough who desired to be my Customers, I endeavoured to be rid of him. He still continued his wonted freedome, and desiring my Company abroad; and so confident he was grown, that he would ask my husbands leave, who had not yet refused him; and therefore a Comedy being to be acted at a Town not far off, he gained my company to go with him; I had other company that I liked better than his, but I could not shift him off, although I very much endeavoured it.

The Play being done, he desired to treat me privately, which I accepted of, having a design to manage that was newly come in my head, and which was this: I had seen a Gentlewoman at the Play, who had a new silk Gown, of a pretty colour and fashion, I was resolved to beg such another of him, and in case of refusal, to break with him totally: I therefore took my opportunity, and when he desired his wonted freedom with me, I told him he was mistaken, and I absolutely refused, and forbid him turning up any more Coats then he was willing to pay for: he asked what I meant by my discourse and refusal: I told him unless he would give me such a new Gown as I prescribed to him, he should have no more to do with me: my Gentleman was as blank as a Bell founder, and his courage was somewhat cooled at my demands; so that he soon arose, and walked up and down in a musing posture; at length he spake, and made some excuses and pauses: but I being resolved on the question, told him, that he had forborn his Pension a great while, and therefore I was resolved he should be the more liberal, and that I would to try his love by performing that request; if he would not grant my desires, I would also refuse him his; but if he would give me such a Gown, he should still oblidge me, and have the first taking of it up. Come, come, said he, you and I will not fall out for such a matter as that, and you shall have it, or any thing else that is in my power, or indeed that you can wish for; and within these three dayes I will send it you, on condition that I may have a full nights lodging with you, well, replyed I, be you so good as your word, and I will order the matter so, as you shall have your desire: and thus we having clapt up a bargain, concluded the discourse with two or three kisses; and so after a considerable repast, we returned home, and there we parted; he to contrive how to be so good as his word, and I to order my Husbands absence, that we might lye together, as I had promised.

My Gallant examining the matter, found that at present the strength of his Pocket would not be sufficient to accomplish his desire, and therefore he supplyed that defect by the strength of wit; he visited the Gentlewoman who was owner of the Gown, and being of her acquaintance, he requested her to let him have her Gown to shew a Taylor to make such another by for a Sister of his; his desires being modest were the sooner granted; and a Taylor of his acquaintance receiv'd it of her, and immediately at his commands brought it to me, I accepted it with a smileing countenance, and giving him a small piece of Money for his pains, dismiss'd him; when soon after my friend likewise followed; and my Husband being absent, we concluded that night to devote our selves holy to *Venus*; and he being us'd to lye at our house, it was no great difficulty for him to quit his bed and come to mine, where we spent all that night in all those amorous enjoyments that we could devise: but he thinking he had paid dear for his nights pleasure, was resolved to have something more into the bargain; and that he might engage me another time, if I fell out with him, as he foresaw I would; wherefore he taking his opportunity when I was asleep, slipt no less then three of my Rings off from my fingers, and put them on his; and early in the morning he left me and my Bed, and went into his own: and having before contrived now to play his Cards, he went to the Taylor, and advised him to come to me, and tell me he had forgot to finish somewhat that was very necessary, and had been omitted to be done in the Gown, and therefore he was come to fetch it, that it might be mended, and he might have no disgrace by his work; I being without all suspition, and seeing indeed there were some defects, which he shewed me, delivered it to him, desireing him to make haste with it, because I intended to have it home before my Husbands return, and then to tell him that my Father had sent it me; but I reckond before my Host; for although I waited two or three dayes, and sent to the Taylor, and asked my false friend, yet I could have none, but idle excuses and flashes; so that in conclusion I found my self cheated; for as I understood afterwards, the Gown was presently sent home to the right owner; whom I saw wear it the next sunday; and then knew it, by some particular marks to be the same. This passage vexed me to the heart; but I was three times more angry when I missed my Rings, and upon examination found that he had beguil'd me of them; and indeed for further confirmation, I saw them upon his fingers; this (said she) extreemly perplexed and inraged me; so that then I converted all my love into (its contrary) hatred, and studyed nothing so much, as how to compass revenge. He finding that I was angred, refrained my Company at present, and that gave opportunity to another, who had long time courted me at a distance, to lay a closer siege to me; and he so far prevailed with me, what with gifts, treats and presents, that I promised him that in short time he should reap the fruits of his desired Harvest; but I was resolved to make him instrumental in my revenge upon my abuser; and to that end I thus broke the matter to him.

Sir, your friendship and love I very much esteem; and believing you to be sincere, and one in whose breast I may repose trust and confidence; I shall discover somewhat to you, that may for the future be of good consequence to us both; and it is this: I believe you have not been so dim sighted, but you have observed more than common familiarity between me and Mr. such a one, naming my abusive Lover; some presents he hath given me, for which he expected more freedome with me than I was willing to impart; but I still kept him at a distance, although he pressed hard upon me to enjoyment; which I not thinking fit at present to permit, he began to clamour, at length through his importunities, I consented he should lye with me at such a time, on condition he gave me such a silk Gown as I named; to this he agreed, and sent in the Gown accordingly: now it so fell out, that I could not perform what he expected, and therefore delay'd him for a few dayes longer, till my

Husband should be absent, promising then to keep touch with him; but whether he not believing me, or else the necessity of returning the Gown, which he had but borrowed, as I since found; one or both these reasons induced him to be false to me, and by a while he got the Gown out of my hands; and he was not content with doing that only, but he also intending to abuse me further, when we were toying together, cheated me of three of my rings; which he as a Trophy of his Victory, and my weakness and shame, still wears on his fingers; and I fear he is so prodigal and lavish of his tongue, as to bray to his acquaintance, that he had those as my gifts for unhandsome service done me.

Thus did I disguise the truth of my dealings with my abusive Lover, and having given my new one this account, desiring his assistance in a revenge: to this he quickly answered, that as for the Gown I had been so out-witted in, he would make up that loss, by giving me another; and so he would also for the rings, if I pleased; or else compel my abusive lover to deliver them; and in all things else he would vindicate my credit. I replyed to him, that I would not have any compulsion, for that would make too much noise; but rather have his assistance in my revenge, which I had thus contrived.

I would have him possess my Husband with jealousie against my abusive Lover, and leave the rest to my ordring, which I managed thus: I gave my abusive Friend more freedom, & shewed a kinder Countenance than I had done of late, & that only to draw him on, which I did with much ease, for he had a great desire to be friends with me, and upon our first convenient parley, he confessed himself guilty, & made some trivial excuses, which I admitted of, as I did his love, in hopes to gain my rings, and a revenge; as for the rings, he presently returned me one, and promised the other two the third night following, when I agreed to lye with him, promising so to order the matter, that my Husband should be then out of the house; we after this parley parted, and my new friend had so dealt with my Husband, in discovering my abusive Friends freeness and privacy with me, that he now became absolutely jealous, and intended to make me sensible of his anger; but I knowing where the shooe wrung him, was before hand, and the next night told him, that if he did not take some speedy course, I was in danger, and he too, to be abused by my abusive Lover; for said I, he hath gotten two of my rings, and shews them abroad, reporting he had them of me, as tokens of my dishonour; and to me he will not deliver them, unless I will promise him a nights lodging: now said I, if you have a mind to save my honour, your own, and revenge us both on him, I will thus do; I will seemingly consent that he shall come to bed to me to morrow night, and to that end, I will have you pretend to go out of Town; but instead of your going, I will go to such a friends house, and there I'le stay; you shall lye in my Bed, and at the hour I will appoint him he will come to bed to you, when you and your friends, and servants, I hope taking him in the manner, will so handle him, as he shall have little cause to boast of his nights lodging; and you and I shall be sufficiently revenged on him for thus attempting my Chastity.

To all this discourse my Husband gave very good attention; and it corresponding with what he suspected, he now wholly quitted any suspicious thoughts of me, and agreed to execute all I had propounded; so that when the time came, my Husband pretended to lye out, took his leave of me, and my abusive Friend, who was glad of his absence: I made haste with him to bed, telling him about ten a Clock he might come safely into my Chamber, and bed which he knew well enough, not to mistake the way. I then left him, and taking horse, went to my new friend, who expected me at our appointed Rendevouz, where he presented me with the desired Gown, and I according to my promise, gave him a nights lodging with me, which was much more pleasant to us both, than was that of my abusive Friend; who at the hour appointed, went to my Chamber, and into the Bed where my husband was expecting him; he believing it was I, began his embraces, and other actions, declaring his intent; with that my husband leap'd out of the Bed, and four good Old Women of my Friends, who were hid under the bed, discovered themselves, and having a dark Lanthorn, lighted the Room, and fell to work: first, they tyed his hands and feet to the posts of the Beds Head and feet; and then each being provided with a good handful of Birch laid on lustily, till he roar'd sufficiently; my Husband making offer to geld him: but when it came to that point, he begg'd so heartily, that my Husband consented to his desire, only he paid the two rings he had of mine, as ransome for his Jewels.

CHAP. V.

Her abused and whipt Lover vows revenge, which is done in part; afterwards he is kill'd, yet kills his Corrival: the manner how, with other things very remarkable.

Never did the Canicular dayes infuse into Dogs a greater madness and fury, than did this whipping in Loves School inrage the minde of our sufficiently jerkt Amorist; which for the present (whilst under his Chirurgions hands) he durst not express; for all that he could do, was to supplicate them not to deprive him of what would make him stand as a Neuter between the Sexes of humane Generation; which they granted him.

With much hazard, and greater fear, escaping their hands, only in his shirt, without shooe or stocking, he got out into the streets; and being overjoy'd that he was secure, but had the black mantle of night to conceal his shame, and convey him home, without the knowledge of the Town inhabitants, ran through the streets with all speed imaginable; but, by the way, meeting with a sharp stone, it so hurt his foot, that he was compell'd to slacken his pace, and lamely limp to his lodging. The Clock had then struck twelve (an hour wherein supposed Bugg-bears walk, to frighten Children) as he could see just before him two women, whom a third had raised from their warm beds by her incessant cries, proceeding from the intollerable pains she then indured, being ready to be delivered, to hasten to call up a fourth, *viz*. a Midwife. Haste on both sides had made them so carelesly heedless in their way, that they were within a spit and a stride of each other, before they could discern one the other. My cheating, and cheated Leacher perceived the women first, which put him to a stand, what he were best to do, either to go forward, or backward; they, on the other side, seeing a thing all in white stand opposit in their way, judged it to be the troubled spirit of the lately diseased Husband of this woman they were going to fetch the Midwife for. He, on the other hand, resolved to go forward; and they seeing him approach them (skreeking out) ran back as fast as they could; who being stopt by the watch, and demanded why they made that hideous outcry, made answer, they had met the Devil, or some thing like him. Condemning the womens idle and causless fears (as they judged) they advanced forwards, armed with Bills, Halberts, but principally with an unparallell'd resolution. My Gallant had stept into a by-corner, when the woman cried out to secure himself from what might ensue that unexpected allarum, fully resolved to run home to his lodging directly, with what speed he might; he started out just as the Watch were advanc'd within half Pistol-shot of him; the sudden surprize confirmed them in the womens report, so that, without consideration there was not one of these desperate Kill-Devils to be seen, but such as with a too precipitate haste, lay tumbling in the Kennel, one over the other. This accident gave new wings to my Lovers feet, which were so benumm'd with cold, that he very much stood in need of such *Icarian* practices, *Dædalian* inventions.

In conclusion, with much knocking, he made a shift to get in. His Landlady (who was a Widow) seeing him in this condition, charg'd him home, asking, Where he had been, how he came thus to lose his skin? Whether he had been robb'd? Though wanting Garments, yet he would not be without a Cloak to hide this Venereal enterprize of his, and therefore replied, That falling into ill company, it was his ill hap to fall into that damn'd itch, that tickling humour of playing; that having won something, and like to win more, they would not let him play longer, but seizing him, stript him, and would have done, I know not what, had not his flight procured his safety.

His loving Landlady believing that he was thus really abused, conducts him to her own warm bed, and like a kind friend would not let him lie alone, for fear of catching cold. But his Breech was so sore, he could not lie on his back; and so troubled were his thoughts, he had no mind to lie upon his belly. His Landlady finding him so backward, imagined the cause to proceed from his being too forward abroad with others, and gathered by too many apparent symptoms, that she was much deceived in his pretended continencie at home; and being hartily vext to be thus disappointed of her expectations, she leapt out of bed, telling him angrily, she had more lodgings and Lodgers in her house, and would not be beholden to him for either; and had she known so much before she did let him in, as she hath done since, she would have tried how the cooling Julip of standing in the street all night in his shirt, would have wrought with his feaverish concupiscence.

Netled he was to the purpose to hear his Landlady (who had ever since their first acquaintance born him a more than common kindness and respect) thus taunt at him; but his thoughts were so absolutely taken up with a subject of another nature, that he returned her not one word; which so exasperated her spirits, not to be replyed unto; that laying aside discretion, with her modesty, she was resolved to ring him a peal in the *ear-ratling-Rhetorick* of *Billingsgate*. How now, (said she) is it not enough that my Servants, from time to time, have sate up late, or rather early, but that I must be disturb'd from my rest, to give repose to a restless *Stallion*? Shall my roof prove the *Protector* to such *Caterwawling Night-walkers*? Is it not enough, that I have furnished you continually with money, but you must ungratefully make that the *Common-procurer* of your private Veneries abroad, and those gawdy Clothes I gave you must be the *Gentleman Usher* that must lead you to them? Are all your former respects come to this? are your hot pretences grown so cold at home, that nothing can warm them, but a fire in another mans Chimney, made there at my expences? She would have proceeded, but that her clamorous tongue interrupted her, by raising one of Her Lodgers, who came down at that instant, to know what the matter was; when my Come-Rogue, not induring her rallery longer, rudely bid her, rather than gently desired her to go to bed; begging that she would not trouble him after that manner, charging her with incivility, for disturbing him from his rest.

The Gentleman, that came down the stairs, hearing this; and judging she had prostituted those kindnesses to one that scornfully refused them, which he had so frequently sollicited her for partly for pleasure, but principally for profit, had not the patience to check her for it in any other place, than these down-right; outragiously bellowing forth, Am not I the oldest Guest in your house, and not a penny in your Debt? Have not I pamper'd you at home, and Coacht you abroad, till I have not had a wheel in my pocket for your extravagant delights to move further on; and have afterwards stab'd my Credit, that you might deliciously feed, and satiate your self on the blood of the grape: then (when few refuse to give themselves satisfaction) I have attempted to enjoy what you now prostitute; but you kept me at that distance, I knew not whether your breath stunk or not. Nay, I have made use of Critical minutes to purchase my desire, more especially then, when I could see by the flaming of your eyes, what conspiracies wine and wanton discourse had formed within you, to fire the Fortress of the most resolved Chastity. And shall you now be bid to go to bed? be begg'd to retire from your satiated Lovers embraces? how can you stand thus impudently in your smock in a mans Chamber, and yet commanded to be gone? Come, you forget your self; your *dark-Lanthorn delights* have dazzled the sight of your Reason; and let this (kicking her with his foot) light you to your own Chamber; and withal laying hold on her, would have forcibly thrust her out; which rude carriage of his made her cry out aloud, fearing some further mischief.

This out-cry so startled my Gentleman in bed, that not enduring to hear his Land-lady so grosly abused, got up, and closing with him, threw him; and having no other weapons, but their fists, pounded one another to some purpose. The Woman fearing what mischief might ensue, put her head out at the window, and cryed Murder as loud as she could bawl; the Watch (hearing murder cryed out) came running to the house with all speed (not dreaming they should see again that Spirit which had so lately frighted them) and perceiving a great bustle in the house, and the same horrid noise continuing, they broke open the doors, and entring, found two men scuffling in their shirts, having blooded one the other sufficiently (this bleeding excused very well the other blood that came from the firked-back and breech of my Gallant) I say, finding them in this bloody condition, they doubted they had injured one another with some sharp instrument; they needed not to search farther than their hands, having neither of them more cloathes to conceal anything than what modesty commanded. Notwithstanding they were parted by the Watch, yet they could not hold their hands off one another; which caused the Watch to interpose again, and now they resolved to secure them that night (from further mischieving one the other) at the Watch-houses, and so commanded them to put on their Cloaths; which the one quickly did, but the other could not. It would have been worth all my revenge to have seen in what confusion he stood, at that word of command, or to have known what the watch-men thought when they saw their Prisoner could finde no Cloaths.

Though their wonder was great, yet they resolved to have their curiosity resolved; and therefore askt him, where were his cloaths, and how he come, or how he could be without them? by the way, surely there was not much wit in that Constable and his Watch: for had they had any, they might presently have concluded (from the posture they found those Gentlemen in) that they were a couple of mendicant Poets, who had but one suit of apparrel between them, that when the one went abroad, a wheedling, the other was forc'd to lye a bed a staring; and disputing who should next scout abroad to find out the Enemies of famine, and not agreeing upon the point, fell together by the ears. But to return where I left of, the Constable having interrogated him as aforesaid, he (endeavouring to excuse himself, and palliate the scuruy usage of his revengeful Mistriss) answered him, that walking that after noon, it was his mischance, by a push of that Gentleman they found him fighting with, to fall into a *Common-house*, (Pox on his witty allusion) and that having no suit than that, he intended to have lain in bed till it had been cleansed and dried. That the Gentleman aforesaid would not let him rest, but came into his Chamber, and with scoffing and irritating expressions, provok'd him to rise, and endeavour to be rid of his trouble.

The other told the Constable, that what was said was a greater lye than the Devil could invent; that the cause of the Quarrel was his endeavouring to hinder his Leachery that night, by preventing his Landlady from going to bed to him. The Woman hearing this, replyed, they were both of them a couple of confounded lyars, and (that she might make one of the number) told them; that they intended to have ravisht her, and that the one breaking up her Chamber-door, the other followed, and fell together by the ears, who should be the first Actor in their damn'd design: to prevent which, she was compell'd to cry out Murther, upon which they withdrew out of her Chamber, and went into one of their own, where (said she) you find them like a couple of malicious dogs, fighting for that morsel neither of the Curs is ever likely to taste of.

This Forgery was more semblable to probability in the Constables opinion, than any thing else he had heard. Wherefore not to spend further time in examination, he charged his Watchmen with my two Gentlemen, and so inconsiderately rash he was, that he vow'd they should go with him; and had carried them in that very condition, had not the Woman of the house interceeded, that she might cloath his nakedness as well as she could for the present; hereupon she furnished him with a Peticoat of her own, having no other Cloathes that would fit him: instead of a cloak, she helpt him to a red Rugg; and to crown all, she clapt upon his head her straw-hat. Had it been day-light, it would have been worth twelve pence a piece to have seen this *Slavonian*, whose garb, for strangeness, the barbarous World might admire, but never imitate. I do not hear that he over-slept himself that night; nor can I believe that the morning gave his eyes no great satisfaction, in viewing the preposterousness of his habit; and his Twinklers lookt, as I am inform'd, as if they had been imployed in nothing all that night, but on looking on the phantasms of some of his dead and damn'd acquaintance.

I slept but little my self, that night, partly, by thinking how this revengful plot of mine would take effect, but chiefly, by reason of my unsatisfied Bed-fellow, who kept me waking, in spight of my teeth. However I arose early, and being but a little way distant, soon got home; where arrived, I understood from my husband, that my Rings were restored, that he had left me his Breeches, as owning me his Master; and so he might well acknowledge, for he was never so whipt for being a naughty Boy, as I caused him to be; and well he escap'd so, having like to have left behind him a most pretious remedy against several female distempers; a *Recipe*, as infallible against all manner of obstructions, as ever was applyed to any *Chalk*, or *Oatmeal Eater*, since *Eve* lay in with *Cain* in her first *Child bed*. Immediately after I heard of the rest of that Knights incomparable Adventures, and how he was secured; and had a particular account of the pleasant dress he was in: never did any thing tickle me more, than the Relation, how amply and fully I was, revenged of him; yet I could not but entertain a thought that might incline to pity him; but it would extend no further then than to send him his Cloathes, and withall a Letter, to give my self the plenary satisfaction of laughing at him; and those sufferings he underwent by my procurement; the words and sense were to this purpose.

The Letter.

Sir,

I am much troubled that one of your age and experiance should prove so meer a Novice *in* Loves-School, *as to be guilty of an amorous* erratum, *that should deserve the lash: I see now you are a meer* Baby *in our Sex, and ought to be whipt again into a better understanding. What, trust that Woman whom you have abused! Why, a Child of the* first head, *in the* nonage *of Amorous matters, in the* Hanging sleeves *of Courtship, knew this as a* Maxime--*that if Love, though never so fervent, be once by abuse converted into hatred, the woman is indefatigable in her revenge, till* Death *hath put an end to the Controversie. Henceforth be better advised from me, how you behave your self before your little* Sparkling Goddesses *(as wantonly you are pleased to call them;) if you will preserve your good esteem and be dayly cherisht with their Soul-winning and ravishing Smiles, you must not be relax in your offerings; but if by slighting, cozenage, &c. you instigate their incest* Deities *to revenge, nothing but an absence, as distant as the two Poles, shall protect you from their subtle and speedy revenge. And now, thank me Sir, that mine hath fallen so slightly on your Shoulders, having given a stript Simmar, for the Gown I should have had: I am sorry though, I had not secured you* witnesses of manhood, *that they might have been* Testimonies *continually by me, to assure my self you will not for the future abuse my love, by fondly affecting an other. Lastly, hearing that you are clad, as if you were sent* Embassadour *from the* Northern Witches *to their* Emperor *the* Devil, *I thought fit to send you some Cloaths (in lieu of those Rings you left with my Husband) which are more sutable for humain conversation. But let me advise you, haunt me no more in them, lest I conjure you out of them again, and the Devil into you. Be wise, and have a care of being amorous, when pennyless.*

Your abused, in part

revenged, &c.

I commanded the Messenger to observe his carriage in reading the Letter; who told me, all the mad-men in the World, put them altogether, could not in their most extravagant gestures, have exprest madness so to the life as he did. However, he was not so mad, but that he did put on his Cloaths, which upon old acquaintance so complyed, as to fit him to a hair. Soon after he was discharged; and now invoking the Devil to be of his Cabinet Council, he walkt into a solitary place, that he might hatch mischief, that is, be revenged on me, my Husband, or any else that he supposed might be his rivals. He was quickly furnished with a mischievous design, agreeable to his desire; and how could he otherwise, for there are millions of hellish imps of the worser sort, who continually attend the motions of the malitious and revengeful, to execute the commands of such who care not how they precipitate others and themselves into ruine and destruction.

This stratagem he contrived, by the help of a little credit he had yet surviving, he puts himself into a new riding garb, mounted with sword and pistol; having gotten a Perriwig of a colour clean contrary to what he usually wore; having for the better carrying on his Plot, procured a false beard, with a black patch on one of his eyes; in this disguise, the most discerning eye of his most intimate, and familiar friends and acquaintance, could not have discovered him who he was. In this equipage he rides out of town, some half-score miles, only to dirty his horse and boots; and leaves a Letter with a Friend to be delivered to my own hands, in these terms.

The Answer to the former Letter.

Madam,

Or rather Mad-dame, for she that is madder that you was begotten in Monte Gibello, *where troubling the Sulphurous wombe of that burning Mountain, was belcht into the World, and carried on the back of a whirlwind, to disturb the inhabitants thereof. Think not I will trouble my self to answer particularly every flouting invective, the which your letter is stuft withal, but shall tell you in general, you are too dangerously wicked for my acquaintance; and he that intends to contract a friendship with* Hell, *must first shake hands with you; your eyes will be his light, to guide him; your cheeks, and breasts, are his highway; and your mouth the gate or entrance thereinto. I do not intend to buy repentance at so dear a rate, as ever to see you again; therefore your threats were needless. I am not yet fallen in love with my winding-sheet, that I should court Death, or hug a Contagion. My sense of smelling is indifferently well recovered of its late distemper, and can now distinguish the scent of sound Bodies from putrifaction. My eyes too have regained their sight, and can plainly see the she-devil in you, maugre all the paint, and* fucus, *that is on that daub'd face of thine. Prithee name me not at any time, lest thy breath for ever poyson my memory; and to that intent, forget that ever I had a being; and so wishing thou never hadst one, I take my eternal farewell of thee,* &c.

This Letter he sent me, to the intent I might believe he was so far from revenging himself on me, that he never intended to see me more; by which means he facilitated his purpose. In prosecution thereof; late in the evening he came to Town, and directed his course to our house; upon his alighting, he seemed much tyred, which we verily believed, his horse being all of a foam; and desiring his Chamber might be shewn him, it was done accordingly; and order being taken for a Sack-posset, he supt it up, and laid his head to rest; he lay abed somewhat long the next day, pretending indisposition by reason of his long journey, but getting up; he seemed somewhat pleasant, calling for a pint of Sack for his and his Land-ladyes Mornings draught, assuring me, that as a stranger he would not be indebted for any civilities he should receive in my house. I on the other side, seeing him so forward to part from his money, gave him a considerable lift by my usual way of spunging. Dinner time approaching I askt him what he would have; who ordered me to provide variety of what was in season; not imagining that Table, on which this meat should stand, should so soon prove the Stage on which a bloody Tragedy must be acted. A little before we sate down to dinner, I sent for my friend (that lay with me that night I acted my revenge) to participate in our good cheer; who coming, we sate down together, there being no other, than this disguised Gentleman, my Husband, my Self, and Friend. We did eat, and drink freely; about half dinner this Gentleman seemed to be very officious in helping me, at last, Madam, said he, I will help you to one bit more, which you shall not refuse for my sake; I returning him thanks, in an instant he whipt off with his knife, my Husbands ear, and laid it hastily on my Trencher; and turning his head quick about, be not angry, Sir, (said he) you shall have bitt for bitt; and thereupon endeavoured to cut off my nose, but I was to nimble for him, and by running out escap'd the danger; my Friend observing what had past, being too suddenly done to be prevented, stept from the Table, and drawing, bid the Rogue disguised draw too, or he would pin him to the wall, for this matchless piece of villany; whereupon he did, but behaved himself so ill, that my friend wounded him desperately in the body at the first pass; concluding he had received his Mortal wound, he resolved not to die alone, wherefore he made a full pass, and so running upon his Adversaries point, each dyed at once by the swords of one another. I soon returned with a long train of *Mirmidons*, whom I had instructed how to chastise this insolence; but Lord! what a confusion was I in, when I saw the two combatants lye dead on the floor, and my Husband gazing on them motionless, like one converted into a Statue for the loss of his ear; which he should have lost, by right, long before that time.

Some more busie then the rest, stirring their bodies, the false beard of the disguised fell off, by which he was presently known who he was; and because it was every where known through the town, how this Gentleman had spent what he had on me, and was abused for his pains; I was immediatly cryed out upon, as the Authoress of all this mischief, I endeavoured to excuse my self, by relating what he had done; *viz.* the cutting my Husbands Ear off and the endeavouring to cut off my Nose; but this allegation signified little. Searching his pockets, they found a note, or letter, sealed, & seeing it was directed to me, they then, without my consent, break it open, imagining they should find therein the mystery of this tragical encounter but all they could discover was only his intention of cutting off my Nose, and my Husbands Ear: the Lines were these which follow.

Insatiate Strumpet; perjur'd-painted-Whore,
Who hast the vice of all thy Sex, and more,
Devil, nay worse; for thou canst by thy face
Make Men Apostate in the State of Grace.
By thee I fell; then did my Pagan *knee*
Oft render Worship to thy Devilree.
I (being converted) Idols won't allow;
Down must the Dagon *of thy face I vow.*
See where it lyes; that Idol, once ador'd,
Must be for want of it, by all abhor'd.
Thy Husband lends an Ear, then let thy Nose,

To Sister-Sense *her wretched State disclose.*

And then consult thy Glass; See thy fare face

Is vanisht, and Deaths-head stands in the place.

Thy lips some Nectar *sipt from I suppose*

Will be exclaim'd on, fogh, they want a Nose.

And may thy sparkling eyes, which me did win,

Be thought to kindle from a fire within.

May ulcers seize thee, for the wrong th'ast done,

And living rott, without compassion.

The rumour of this sad disaster ran swifter than a Torrent through the Town; insomuch that our house was so cram'd with People, that our servants were forc'd to acquit their imployments, to give room to the inquisitive Incomers, a chirurgeon was sent for to dress my Husband; & a Coroner to sit upon the other two that were slain; glad I was, that I had the opportune excuse to leave the Company; and attend my Husband; by which means I avoided the hearing so many thousand accrimations that were laid to my charge. In the meantime the Jury found their Deaths hapned by Man-slaughter: and so thereby though we were present, we could not be found accessories.

The noise of this accident did also flye into the Countrey, not escapeing the ear hardly of any one Guest that frequented our House; report had rendred the Fact so horrible, and my Husband and Self so notoriously accessory thereunto, and now all our former wickedness, and roguery was drawn up in a long Scrol, and this last added in Capitals, to make up a compleat Sum of Villany. By which means we had little resort to our House; and our House-rent being great, and our Trading small, my Husband and I were now necessitated to put our heads together, by some other means to patch up a future lively-hood. Thou seest, said he, the more serious, and reputable sort of People, shun our house, as if old *Belzebub* were there sitting abroad to hatch those diseases which should be the destruction of the Universe. And therefore to be revenged of their thus slighting us, I will meet them abroad, and what moneys they forbear to spend with me, I will compel them to lend, and more. Though I am not stout and resolute enough of my self to do this, yet thou knowest *Humphrey* our Tapster, is a strong Fellow, and hath a good heart; he and I, fear not, will do the business.

For my part, I must needs confess, I question'd not *Humphrey's* performances, having made tryal again thereof; I ever fancyed to try experience, and marking what a rough-hew'n Fellow he was, all Bone and Sinew, with a face like a tann'd Bulls hide, I could not be at quiet, till I had found the difference between this Man, nerv'd with wire, and others, that were clean limb'd, and streight slender bodyed joynted like *Bartholomew Babies*, with quaking Custard faces; but so vast a disproportion between them, that were I Widdow; and were courted by a Knight worth five thousand pounds a year, with a handsom fair whitely face, I should hardly be perswaded to accept of a Lady-ship, but for the sake of his revenew.

To be short, Sir *Philip Sidney's* Cowards were not much ranker than my Husband; but, thought I, if he hath courage enough to look a Man in the face, and bid him stand, *Humphrey* hath strength, and valour enough to compel them to deliver. Wherefore I perswaded my Husband by all means to go forward with what he had propounded: I was the more willing to it, in hopes that he would be taken some time or other; and as he was marked for a Knave, so he might be hang'd for a Thief; and so be freed from an impotent Husband. He seemed well satisfied that I assented to his proposal, and look'd upon it to be a good Omen, and promised success to his undertaking. On the other side (said he) you must not be idle at home; you know there is now none but the debauched that resort to our house, and therefore suit their inclination, if ought can be gotten by so doing. Your daughter is young, and handsom, let her be the sign to attract; but pray let me have you furnish your self with other Utensils. The Boy too is no fool, who, by observing your carriage, and direction, hath very ill spent his time, if he cannot tolerably pimp as well for others, as his Mother. Well, well, (said I) husband, you are merrily disposed; look after your business, I shall manage my own well enough, I warrant you. My Husband and his Tapster, committed many robberies in a little time: and very few but what were on our Guests; who freely discoursing their affairs over a glass of Wine after Supper, many times discovering what store of money they carried with them, and for what purpose, gave them a fair opportunity in the Morning to set on them, and deprive them of it. Nay, so little suspected he was of robbing, that several have returned to our house after he hath robb'd them, and made their complaint to him, how basely they had been abused; it was always his care, and indeed therein he shewed the utmost of his prudence, to return home with all the speed he might possibly, after he had rob'd any; by which means, he and his Man rob'd a long time secretly.

It was generally their good fortune to meet with such as durst not fight them; a thing that Travellers generally, and justly, are to be condemned for; who, with easie parting with their money, they not only shew how meanly spirited they are, but encourage the Thief in his robberies. Whereas, on the contrary, would they shew themselves as desperate, and as resolute as their assaulters, it is my opinion they would quickly turn tail, as not daring to venture the hazard of the dispute. But to return, though my Husband succeeded so well in his attempts, by meeting with none but Cow-hearted fellows; yet once, waiting with his man in a thicket, earely in the morning, for the passing by of a Gentleman that had lain the night before in our house, who had a considerable Sum of Money, in his Port-mantle, there travelled by another in the dawning of the day, whom, by a mistake, my husband assaults; the other drawing a Pistol, fired it at him, but mist him; however, the report had like to have done as much mischief, as if the bullet had past through his body, for with fear he fell from his horse; and had like to have saved the Hangman a labour, by breaking his own neck. Our Tapster seeing his Master fall, and verily believing he was kill'd by that was resolved to revenge his death, had not he seen another come Rideing to him (which was the Gentleman they lay in wait for) which made him altar his purpose, and ride away, for the preservation of his own life. The Gentleman supposing too, that he had really dispatcht this Pad, not seeing him move all this while (which he confest to me afterwards, he politickly did, to the intent he might be exempted from fighting, and securely see the event of the Combat: the other two that came to his assistance judg'd the same, and advised him to ride away with all speed to the next Justice; not only to avoid the present danger, for (said he) this other Rogue is rid away but to get some more of his fellows, to make a further attempt) but you will also receive the thanks of the Country, for destroying such Caterpillars, that eat up the Fruit of their Land. Setting Spurrs to their Horses away they Gallopt, to find out the next Justice; my Husband perceiving they were gone, got up, and mounting rode full speed home, without so much as once looking behind him. Coming home, he found me almost drown'd in tears, and half frighted out of my wits; not so much for sorrow of his death (which news I had privately sent me by our Tapster) but for fear, as soon as it should be known who this slain Thief was, I should have my goods instantly siezed on, and my doors shut up. I was in a Room by my self, getting some Plate together, with other choice portable things; and coming to the stair head, with an intent to convey them out of the house, met with my Husband full butt; whose face being pale and wan, by reason of his late great fear, possest me with so strong a conceit, that this was his Ghost, that the fright made me skreek out, and letting fall what I had in my Apron, I retreated. This sudden surprize so amazed him, that he stood indeed like an apparition at the Chamber-door, and had not the power to come in: this increast my belief, however, I pluckt up my Spirits, and boldly askt him, what he was, and what he came for? He sneakingly, in a low voyce, (for he was more than half dead) answered, he was my Husband, and that he came to see me. My Husband, said I is dead; and if thou be his damn'd Ghost, I conjure thee, by all that is good, presently depart, and trouble me not now, since whilst living, I could never be content, nor at quiet for thee. Not speaking one word, he turn'd his back upon me, and went down stairs. I never believed my self a Conjurer till now (although I have been called Witch a thousand times) and indeed I knew not what to think of it, (comparing altogether) whether this was a phantasm, or not, but troubling my thoughts no further about that matter, I took up what I had dropt, and getting into the yard, would have march'd off with what I had in my lap, had he not hastened after me, and holding me fast by the arm, told me, that he was not quite dead, though almost frightned out of his life, and therefore begg'd me I would not remove any thing that might tend to his prejudice; and if I would walk in, he would tell me his whole morning Adventure.

The two Gentlemen coming to the Justice, amply declared what an eminent piece of Service they had done their Country, by killing on the place one Padder, and putting to flight another; and that if his Worship pleased to Summon a quantity of the Parish, to defend them if occasion should require, they would shew them the place where the dead lay. Hereupon there were a great many that offered themselves freely to go along; but coming to the place, found neither man, nor horse, nor the sign of one drop of blood. The Countrey People finding themselves thus abused, and not knowing what the design of these two Gentlemen might be, in putting such a trick upon them, laid hold on them, and carried them back to the Justice; who being informed that there was not the least appearance of what had pretendedly been done, askt them the reason, why they thus abused themselves and others, with meer forgeries: to which they both replyed, that their eyes had seen what their tongues related, and concluded, that other padders, confederate with this, had carried off the Body of their Brother, that they might avoid suspition. The Justice and others were of the same opinion, and so the Gentlemen were dismist.

Our Tapster hearing that his Master was in health, returned home, resolving for the future, never to hazard his life with so great a peice of cowardize; and to speak the truth, it was high time to leave off, since they were shrewdly suspected by the whole Town to be High-way men, they being seen so often together on Horse-back, both early and late. My Trade however diminisht not, for I was taken notice of, all the Country round, to be a dealer in secrets, and ready money commodities; nay, there were not a few honest mens wives, that would not stick to trust me in the disposal of the whole *Cargo* of their reputation. Nay, I was so excellent at my art, that neither Privateer, nor Publican would act any difficult matter without my advice. I could Pimp, if occasion served most incomparably; and I was lookt upon as the best *Procuress* in all our Countrey; which I would not have been, but that I was so much tyred with my daily, nay, hourly Visitants; for though Age and Time have conspired to ruine the glories of my face, I can assure you, the remains may inform any they were good. Being so generally noted not only for my beauty, but my art in *Pandarizing*, a Song was composed on me by some riming *Doggril* or other, which I will sing you thus, and so finish the Story of my former lifes actions,

1. *At the Sign of the* Swan
There liveth a man,
I go not about to deceive you;
Ten thousand to one,
If you come, he is gone,
That his Wife may the better receive you.

2. *Lovely brown is her hair,*
Her face comely fair,
Her waste you may span, 'tis so slender;
Negro black are eyes,
Passing white are her thighs,
All the allurements of Venus *attend her.*

3. *Her Twins of delight,*
(Which are alwayes in sight)
Her breasts which are whiter than snow,
By their panting do beat
An Alarm to the feat,
To combate her Lovers below.

4. *With her smiles she invites*
To taste her delights;
Which I would, if I durst so presume;
But I fear she hath fires
Which will quench my desires,
But my body to ashes consume.

5. *She's an excellent* Pimp,
The Devils *best* Imp;

She's a Bawd, *she's a whore, that's too common*
If you intend for to fly
Hells flames, come not nigh;
She's a thing, that is worse than a Woman.

CHAP. VI.

Mrs. Dorothy goes with her new Acquaintance, who perswades her to accommodate a barren Gentlewoman a friend of hers, with her child, as soon as born. A character of this Gentlewoman, and her amorous practices: the manner of her being rob'd by one of her Gallants; he is apprehended and executed. Mrs. Dorothy is delivered of a Boy, who is made Heir to a great Estate, and she highly rewarded for her consent.

The Old Woman having thus finisht her Story, she addrest her self to me, saying, Dear Heart, you see how free I have been with you, not concealing from your knowledg any one remarkable passage of my life, though never so infamous or scandalous. I, and though our acquaintance is very young, yet put your confidence in me, and question not, but that I shall so assist you in the management of your concerns, that you shall have cause to thank me as long as you live. Hereupon she acquainted me, that there was a Gentleman (not far off) well known to her, that had been married a dozen years and upwards to a very beautiful, and well proportion'd Gentlewoman; yet had no issue by her; that for want of an Heir, the Estate after his decease would fall to the younger Brother; that it was a very great grief to the Gentleman, but especially to his Wife; and (said she) this Gentlewoman knowing me to be a person fit to be advised withal about matters of this nature, often sent for me to her house, where some years since, I counselled her to make trial, whether she or Husband was in fault; in order thereunto I have helpt her at times to the enjoyment of at least a score of several lusty young Persons. And because I would take the surest way, she never had more than one at one time, and him neither not above a quarter of a year together; he then frustrating our expectations, I counsell'd her to make tryal of another. The first I made choice of for her, was a proper young flaxen-hair'd man, tall and slender; a delicate young man he was indeed, whose complexion (being Sanguine) furnished him with more heat than is in any other temperature; which made his hair like fine threads of Gold, twirl in rings, or rather you might call them the lines and hooks with which the little wanton God of love did usually angle for female hearts; had you seen them, you would have sworn that they were sufficient to catch the heart of a *Vestal-Maiden*, or the most resolved *Votaress to Chastity*, that ever had a being. His eyes, quick and nimble, and penetrateing; he had a strong fancy, a quick invention, and a most incomparable utterance; and his carriage and deportment was incredible winning; whose single touch of the hand was sufficient to have thaw'd the most congealed-frozen temper in the world into affection. Notwithstanding all these allurements, and feir promising properties with near upon an half years mutual converse with each other, she found her expectations frustrated.

Being resolved to make further tryal (for she would not be convinc'd that she was either defective or barren,) she consulted me, how she might be rid of this her amorous Hot-spur, and have some other in his place, of a different constitution; alleadging that she being of the same complexion, she verily believed her impregnancy proceeded thence; saying further, that she had heard several, as Well Physitions as others strongly affirm, that the grand reason, why several Women have no children, was the too near affinity of their husbands complexion and constitution to their own; and that on the other side, none more infallible enjoy'd the fruits of their labours, the offspring of their bodies, than such, whose corporal temperaments were dissimilar or different.

Understanding her humour, I was resolved to comply with her in whatsoever she desired (being so profitable a friend to me) but I knew not how to displace her Sanguine complexion'd Gallant, who grew by this time a most passionate Lover; at length I bethought me to perswade him to sollicite her waiting Gentlewoman, making him believe that she was ardently in love with him, and that she had a good Sum by her, which would infallibly be at his devotion; my credulous young Gamester greedily swallowed my advice, and followed to a hair my dictations; having won her (for I know not who could withstand him) he came to me, and informed me of the time, and place, that he should commence those delights they intended to continue as long as life lasted; being joyful of this opportunity, I presently addrest my self to my Mistris, giving an account to her of her friends new courtship, and when it should be consumated; advising her to watch them, and catch them in the act, by which means she should be freed from his future addresses, and likewise confirm her Maids secresie and fidelity to her. All which she performed, by threatning her Maid to turn her away, and shame her to boot, if ever she associated her self, or entertained him again in her house; and calling him false, faithless man, and I know not what, banisht him for ever from her presence for his unconstancy.

The next Dick I pickt up for her was a man of a colour as contrary to the former, as light is to darkness, being swarthy; whose hair was as black as a sloe; middle statur'd, well set, both strong and active, a man so universally tryed, and so fruitfully succesful, that there was hardly any female within ten miles gotten with child in hugger-mugger, but he was more than suspected to be Father of all the legitimate. Yet this too, proved an ineffectual Operator. She now began to suspect herself of barrenness; but being prompted with hopes, and strangely induced by the sense of pleasure which she reapt in the variety of her amorous Confidents, she resolved on a third, a Gentle-man of her own election, who having been a considerable time a Student in the Inns of Court, was returned into the Country, to enjoy that plentiful estate his lately deceas'd father had left him, the antient Seat of his Ancestors; of stature so low, that he could but just take the upper-hand of a dwarf, being only elevated by the pole above him. She was fain at first to Court him, instead of his courting her: and indeed, I could not see how he could presume (without her encouragement) to caress a Gyantess, so much taller than himself.

There was not so great a disproportion in their bodies, as there were conformity and agreeableness in their wills; and that the Soul of his which was coopt up, and confined within too narrow limits, became more active and vigorous; so that attacking her with a lively and sprightful courage possessed himself of the garrison without a tedious siege of a 12 months courtship, his hair was of a darkish brown, or chest-nut colour, not handsome enough to be a woman, yet too fair to be a man. Though he was not tall, yet nature exprest no irregularity in his formation: being symmetrical, or proportionably composed from the lines of his face you might have collected Capital Letters enough to have spelt a Gentleman; and not an action, or expression of his (excepting this of his too intimate familiarity with another mans wife) which did not largely declare the immensity of his Soul, and the virtues that thereunto belonged.

So dearly she loved him, (that notwithstanding he did not answer her expeditions in making her Belly swell) she so doted on his Company, and converse, that she gave her husband too many palpable causes to suspect her honesty, and integrity towards him. Not, but that for the sake of an Heir, (which he question'd whether he should ever get himself) he would be content to wink (as he hath done several times) at the freedome his wife hath taken with several others besides himself. But looking on my little dapper squire to be to little for that purpose, and that would come short home, as to that business, took an occasion to affront him, that it might produce a quarrel, that should eloign him from his house, and further intimacy with his wife. However, though he had low and undervaluing thoughts of this Gentleman, by reason of his stature, yet he found him in field, full as tall as himself in true valour, being (as we say) mettle to the back. It was the hap of this Gentleman to be desperately wounded by the lesser, and so dangerously, that it was supposed his wounds would end all the future differences between them; however recovering this Combate separated them eternally.

My Mistris was so well acquainted with the loss of her Gallants, that she was not much troubled to be deprived of the society of this last; but all her trouble was, to get another in his room. Shee applyed her self to me again, her undeceiving Oracle, and received her accustomed comfort, that in a little time I would procure her another, that should out-throw the rest, at least a Barrs length; I was not long in the procuration; for there was a Gentleman that frequented our House, who spent his money very freely, yet had not a foot of land, neither had he any trade, or tools, but the high way, sword and pistol to bring him in a lively hood. He was a lusty well set man, and red-hair'd; a complexion that hath often gone through-stich. I had often tryed him my self, and therefore I could the better recommend him to a friend.

One day (his stock being low, and he at that time in our house) he desired me to lend him half a peice. I being glad of this opportunity, told him I would, and withall desired to confer with him in private; he joyfully accepted my motion, thinking I had some secret design to take my accustomed use for the loan; but he was strangly surprized, and even distracted with excessive joy, when he heard me tell him, what a Mistris I had provided for him; that he should have his belly full of sporting, & be liberally paid for it too. We appointed the day when I should introduce him into his new Mistriss's acquaintance, but with this condition, that I should share with him in his gettings. It was concluded on, and he possest of his Treasure, to the full content of them both. My House was now his constant receptacle, or dormitory, but when he was in the embraces of his mistress; and he was very honest in giving me my share, my half part, and commonly spent the rest (to my advantage) of what he had received; and to the intent the more might come into my pocket, I advised her by all means not to starve his service, but incourage him often with sums of money; urging moreover, that the poor Gentleman could not but be at great charges in maintaining himself in a strange place, exiling himself freely from his own habitation, to be near at her Command; beside the great expence he is daily at in costly broths, jellies, with other provocatives, or restorers of decai'd nature.

I needed not to have tempted her to liberality, she being naturally prone thereunto; always extravagantly rewarding kindnesses of this nature. She began now to grow very pensive, and unusually melancholy, to see all her swelling hopes thus dasht; and was not so sociable as she used to be with her friend; which gave him some cause to suspect her inconstancie, or that she would speedily desert him, and accept some other; which put him on the contrivance to save something, that might be a support to him, if his sallary should fail, or at leastwise keep him alive, till his Country-Contributions, or padding incomes should supply his profuse, and unnecessary expences.

When ever he came, she entertain'd him with such an undeserved franckness, that she concealed nothing from him, that might either please his fancie, or satisfie his curiosity. Understanding she was admirable at her Needle, he desired her to shew him some pieces of her art, that he might by the applauding of the one admire the other. She readily condescended to what he propounded; being glad he had demanded a thing which came within the verge of her power to please him withal. Opening a large Cypress-Chest, she shew'd him great variety of excellent pieces of her own hand-working; and withal he discovered several bags cramm'd with other pieces, which he had a greater minde to handle; which I conceiv'd she shew'd him out of meer ostentation, telling him withal, that as long as one penny was in them his pockets should not be unfurnisht with money; and that when all those bags were emptied, her Husbands annual estate would quickly fill them again, and six times as many.

This assurance of having his constant stipend continued, prevailed not in the least on this Caret-pated villains ingrateful designs; but he resolved, with the first opportunity, to make himself Master of those sums, although he knew he must unavoydably lose his Mistress thereby; the next morning she sent for him, to acquaint him, that her Husband was gone some twenty miles off, and that he would not return in five days, having 300 *lib.* to receive of such a man, naming the place where he lived. This damn'd Dog, hearing this, caper'd for joy, which the poor Innocent believed, proceeded from his thinking what a long time he had to enjoy his Mistress uncontroulably: whereas it was otherwise, for now he knew how to kill two Birds with one stone.

However, that she might not mistrust him as guilty of any treachery, he behaved himself so pleasantly and his Caresses were so agreeable, that his Mistress esteem'd her self the happiest woman in the world, in the enjoyment of the person of so facetious, and most accomplisht Lover; nay, so fond she was of his company, that she was resolved to make the most of him in her husbands absence; and therefore caused him to lie in the house, not induring him out of her sight, till the day before her husbands returne; at which time he walkt out: what feastings, junketings and jollitings together there were in that time, none are better able to conceive than such who, with their large purses, have inlarged hearts, caring not how dear the purchase is, so that the pleasure be great, though not of two minutes lasting. You must understand, that I went snips with him in these delights, as well as in his profits; I had a liquorish tooth still in my head, and therefore would not be out of call, to participate with them in their Viands, and Banquetings; Indeed, I was ever an excellent smell feast.

The day (wherein he went abroad, as I told you) was the cursed time in which he procured assistants, to carry on his hellish plot, which had like to have proved my utter ruine. It seems he appointed them about four of the clock in the evening to come to the Gentlewomans house, where (as before) we were all making merry; and knowing the strength of the house, there being never a man at home, the Groom being gone with his Master, and only a foot-boy left, he appointed only two that should manage the design beside himself; who knocking at the gate, and the foot-boy opening it to them, they instantly seiz'd him, both binding, and gagging him. Having bolted the Gate, they advanced into the house, and seemingly very peaceful, they mounted the stairs, having secured those who were below in the same manner, as they had done the boy; as soon I saw two men now entring the Chamber, where we were, I then concluded that we were betrai'd, and that the principal Traytor was our supposed friend; I hereupon opened as wide as my jaws would give me leave; which one of the rogues perceiving, clapt a gag within my mouth, and so kept them at that gaping distance, the Rogues might have had some consideration before they had served me thus, as knowing I had few teeth to barricadoe my gums from the injury they might receive from that confounded instrument which stretcht my mouth asunder.

The good Gentlewoman, seeing how barbarously they handled me, did not question they would exercise the like cruelty next on her; to prevent which, she fell on her knees, beseeching them not to abuse her, and throwing them the keyes of what they lookt for, bid they take what they pleased. Her accursed Villain had the impudence to view the tears run down her lovely cheeks, without the least remorse, or pity on a soul so dearly loved him, he only raised her with his hands, assuring her, she should receive no other injurie than the loss of what money she shewed him, and his eternal happiness; for I know Madam (said he) how insatiate you are, how variable, how changeable upon the slightest occasion; I am not insensible what variety you have already tyred (the more to blame me that imforced him;) and how many more you intend, may be sufficiently drawn from your unsatisfied humour, and inconstant nature. And now if you love your life, stir not till we are gone; and thank our lenity, that we have not secured you other-wayes. Taking up the money, every one carrying a part; hold (said one) we have forgot something yet, that Ladies hands must be tyed, least she ungag that serious and now silent Matron there: her hands and legs must be tyed too, lest she talk or walk to fright us. Having so done, come now let us go (said the Red headed Traytor) it is high time, lest that old witch swallow on of us; don't you see how she gapes? God b'you (good Madam) you are bound to be constant now; dear Partner (pointing to me) farewell, I thank you for your procuration money, and so away they went; in less than half an hour the Gentlewoman had with her teeth set her hands at liberty, which soon gave my hands, feet, and tongue the like, and discending the stairs, we found the maids, and boy bound, and gagg'd; having loos'd them she whisper'd her boy in the ear, I knew not what, but it was to fetch a Constable, which he did in an instant; and whilst I was condoleing my Friends loss, and misfortune, I was apprehended by her command, and conveyed to Goal, there to bewail my own too rigid fate.

I cannot much blame her suspition of me, since there were arguments too many, and strong enough to perswade her I could not be innocent, and therefore what ever I alledged in my justification stood for a Cypher. I sent for my husband, with many other friends, but none of them could prevail with her from sending me to Prison; seeing there was no remedy, I was resolved to endure my confinement as patiently as I could.

These three rogues had their horses not far off, ready sadled, which they mounting, rode directly in that road where they were sure to meet their prize;

and as the Devil would have it, they waited not two hours, before they could perceive two riding directly towards them, and soon after could discern them to be the Gentleman and his groom; the first of an undaunted resolution, but weakly, by reason of a Chronical distemper, that had a long time afflicted him; his man, by his bulk, shape and looks, appeared like one that could teach a *Guy of Warwick* to fight, and give a president of such a valour, as only became a *Royal Champion* to own. The Gentleman was first commanded to stand and deliver, which he did, but it was a Pistol, which he discharged without any execution; they fired at him again; and wounding him in the sword arm, he dropt his sword, and whilst he was submitting to their disposal, his man sets spurs to his horse, and most valiantly ran for it; getting to the top of a little hill, not far distant, where turning his horse head, most manfully about, he had the confidence to look on, whilest the Thieves robb'd his Master.

The gentleman seeing himself thus deserted by this lubberly-cowardly Hog driver was ready to burst with anger; but knew not how to come at him to be revenged; and therefore begg'd the robbers, in lieu of what money they had taken from him, to do him the kindness, to baste his man soundly that stood on yonder hill, as a meer looker on. I, *I*, said the one, *I* will give you that satisfaction presently my self alone, and so setting spurs to his horse, rode up to him, and complemented him no otherwise at first, than with the flat of his sword, which notwithstanding made his sides and shoulders smart to some purpose; this great looby took all this with incredible patience; but the Pad by chance cutting him; nay, now said he, flesh and blood is not longer able to endure; and with that drew a broad two egg'd Scotch-sword, and handled it so well, that he cut this fellow off his horse presently; the other two seeing their fellow over-matcht, advanced with all speed, and both assaulted him at once: but he seeing them approach, and being now blooded, made ready to receive them by drawing a Pistol, which he fired so luckily, that the shot deprived him of one of his enemies more, and he had now no inequality of number to oppose him. Success had so flesht him, that he fought more like a Devil, than a man, laying about him backwards, and forwards; so that he disinabled the third, which was the first Plotter. Had his Master been able to fight, and there had been as many more against him, he so behaved himself, that there was no work for any to do but himself. Thus did this one man, who had never fought before (and therefore like an horse, knew not his own strength till it was tryed) conquer three, that were accounted Cocks of the *Hectors*.

The Gentlemen searching their Portmancicks, and finding 400 *lib.* was amazed at so considerable a purchase; and securing it, with this surviving Rogue, and their Horses, rode directly to the next Justice; where leaving the Booty in his hands for the present, the Prisoner had his *mittimus* drawn up, and was sent to the same Gaol his Landlady, the Hostess was in. Notwithstanding all those disguizes he made use of to seem another man, he was known by me, and received from me a whole broad side of just reproaches; which had like to have sunk him deeper, than the pressures of his present misfortunes could do. What (said I) did you not live too much at your ease? had you not but too much plenty, which took you off those desperate courses, or might have done, which would without doubt have brought you to the Gallowes in the end; but having so little regard to your own wellfare, I could not expect much from you as to mine; though gratitude might have commanded you to have studied my preservation, although you should hourly hazard your own. Instead of applying smooth, and soothing answers (which might have been as Cordials, or Balsom to my wounded mind) he gave me this corrasive, this Choak-pear, that if I would not hold my clack, which dinn'd his ears worse than the Cataracts of *Nile*, he would declare before the Bench, upon his tryal, that he would never have done so foul a fact, but by my instigation; and that if I held not my tongue, he assured me, that (since he knew that it was impossible for him to escape with life) he loved me so well, that I should dye with him, to bear him company in the other world.

Perceiving what his desperate resolution was, I thought good to alter the Scene of my chat, and beg him to be patient; assuring him, that what I had said was not out of any ill will, but to make him sensible how much I was his friend at all times; and that my own imprisonment (for his sake) troubled me not so much, as the danger that he was in; and that he might accuse me, if he pleased, and so endanger my suffering with him; but I charged, withall, his Conscience with my innocencie in, and ignorance of what he and his accomplices had acted, contrary to my privity. It was some comfort to hear him then acknowledge before a great many witnesses, that I was no way accessary to his guilt; and when the Assizes came, he acknowledged upon his Arraignment, that none abetted, or were concerned in what he had done, and there stood arraigned for, but himself and two others, which were slain in the contest. Whereupon I was discharged by Proclamation of Court, none coming in against me; and he received sentence of death, which was accordingly executed three dayes afterward; he then again at the Gallows declaring to the spectators my innocencie in his robbery.

This Confession of his, I thought, would as well reintroduce me into the favour of the abused Gentlewoman, my former friend, as by his suffering death give full satisfaction to her inraged revenge. In order thereunto, after my Gaol delivery, I sent her several Letters to pacifie her passion, and imployed several friends to acquaint her with the reallity of my former fidelity, and present integrity: at length they so far mediated with her in my behalf, that she sent for me (when her Husband was abroad) and in the walks of her Garden, discourst me largely, as to whatever had past between us, or anybody else by my means. And now, said she, this last unhappy and unexpected villany from a friend you procured me, and one I dearly loved, hath tyed up my hands from ever enjoying the like opportunities again. For my Husband finding that the purchase he took from the Thieves was but a Pig of his own Sow, his own money, and knowing the principal Robber to be the Person I often treated at our house with much civility, shrewdly suspects, that I not only consented to the Robbery, but would be easily induced to believe to his death too, were it not for the great loss he knows I should receive by his death if he should dye without issue. However he is much more cautious of me than he used to be, taking his money into his own custody, and he sets a watch over me to observe what company I keep abroad, or entertain in our house: and therefore, if ever you intend to redeem your former credit and estimation with me, study some project how I may carry on the design afore propounded, of having an Heir, that the Estate may not pass to the next Brother. A man I cannot but hate, for several weighty considerations. The crookedness of his disposition, and the unsuitableness of his humour to mine, were sufficient to make me not love him; but his insufferable wicked practises, both against me, and my Husband, make me absolutely detest the very sight of him. When I was first married (quoth she) I thought my self as capable of conception as any she that ever wore a head; & my husband being then healthful, & actively vigorous, soon confirming me, in the opinion of being a teeming woman: It seems I was with child, though I knew it not; and finding a great change and alteration in my body, I was so ignorant, as to believe I was breeding some ill humours, which, if not timely purged away, might ingender a disease that might prove my death. My Husbands Brother (which was wiser than my self in that point) knew very well I was breeding young bones, the growth of which would infallibly lift him out of all his flourishing hopes of enjoying his Brothers Estate; therefore out of a seeming tenderness, and vigilant care of the presevation of my health, followed my own perswations, with his damn'd advice; and at the end I was induc'd to take a vomit to clear my stomack, he telling me, for certain, it might be very foul, since I was so frequently troubled with puking in the morning, and vomiting after Dinner. An Apothecary of his own procuring (with his Devilish instructions) made up the Composition, which, without imagining the least harm, I easily swallowed, which wrought with me so strongly, that, having nothing left within my stomack for it to work on, I thought it would have brought up my very heart within its appurtenances; the Devil of a Physitian all this while seemed to comfort me, by saying, be cheerful, Sister; this will clear you (and so it did of what it should not) and clense you of those malignant humours which so much prejudiced your healthful constitution; and that he might make sure work of me, counselled me to take a purge, and that would carry all downwards, and then my business was done; I poor easie fool, was quickly drawn to it, and the second time swallowed that, which the next day made what I went withal prove abortive.

I had often seen, but more especially heard, that this Doctor was no sooner gone from his Patient, but he was immediatly in the Company of my brother, which made me, with a great deal of good reason, conjecture, they plotted no good together; wherefore I got two Doctors more to visit my Husband, who plainly told me, at the first sight (both agreeing in one opinion) that he was poysoned. Hearing them say so, I could not forbear; but, in the agony of my Spirit, cryed out, I know the Murderers; and their lives shall here, for the loss of his, make satisfaction in part, and in full, by their damnation hereafter. They desired me to be patient, assuring me that they would use their utmost skill to over-power the poyson; and doubtlessly he had dyed, had not these two eminent Artists bestirred themselves to purpose. In a little time they raised him on his feet (which made his former Doctor betake himself to his, having not been heard of by us since;) but they could not assure me how long it would be ere he would be down again; for (said they) he will be an infirm, impotent man, as long as he lives.

If now my hatred to my Husbands Brother be not justly grounded, do you judge; and I hope Heaven will not be offended with me, in finding out some way to dispossess him of his hopes, in having the Estate, who rob'd me of my fruitfulness, and would have deprived my Husband of his life.

Madam (said I) there is just now a plot come into my head; which if you please, shall be put in practice, and that is this. Since your Husband is thus infirm, and you barren, this must be the only way, which must crown your desires. I will immediately go upon the search for some young thing with Child, whether she be Wife, nor neither Maid, Wife, nor Widdow, it matters not; whom with large gifts, and larger promises, I will perswade to part with her Child, when born, and you shall lye in with it; let me alone to the management of all; but first, let me find out a Person suitable to our purpose, and I will warrant you to carry on the rest to your full satisfaction. I will instantly for *London* where I cannot miss of Subjects enough of this sort, out of which I may pick and choose. She liked this proposal so well, that she would not suffer me to stay a minute longer with her, but that I should instantly leave her, and make my self ready for my Journey; and thus far have I travelled in order to the finishing thereof, when I met with so blessed an opportunity, of falling into discourse with you, Dearest Madam, which I hope will tend to both our happinesses, if you will be ruled by me.

Thus, said Mrs. *Dorothy*, I heard the whole relation of her self, and others, with great attention: and thought it was now my Cue to speak, which I did in this manner, not only cautelously, but with much seeming reservedness. Mother (for so, by the disparity of our Age, I make bold to call you) the account you give of your self is so monstrously wicked that I know not whether, with safety, I may interchange any further discourse with you; neither can I but take notice of your subtility, and matchless craftiness, as well as your unparallel'd debauchery, and wantonness; you may very well excuse me, if now I stand on my guard, and wearily entertain a parley with you; since you are known to be an old Souldier in the Wars of *Venus*, and so may fight too cunningly for me, that am but a stripling upon any such account. However make your proposals (and if I may be assured you pump me not to intrap me) as I find them faisable, and profitable for the future, I shall accept them, and be ready to be servicable to you, and your design.

The good old Gentlewoman, as one transported, by hugging me in her Arms, interrupted me, saying; Daughter, mistrust me not in this affair, and try whether I will not in a little time make you as happy as your own wishes can make you; and thereupon asked me how long I had been with Child, and whether I could be content, that, by anothers owning it, the Child hereafter might be owner of an Estate (it seems born to) the tenth part whereof none of my Ancestors ever yet enjoyed.

It is confest, said I, my own weakness, and Female frailty betraid me to unlawful embraces of a handsom young man, whose subtle sollicitations could not be withstood by a Nun, much less by me; and yielding, I now carry both the Sin and the shame of those stolen delights about me, where ever I go. That though it was my ill Fortune thus to lose (by one throw at play, inconsiderately) a thing of that value, my Maiden head I mean, yet it was some comfort to me, that it was a Gentleman of no mean worth that won it; and I question'd not but the off-spring would be like the Father, as well in the comely proportion of the Body, as Gallantry of Mind; being thus fully perswaded it will prove so goodly a Person, it will the more trouble me to part with it to another; that if I should do any such thing it is not for necessity; for, as I had money considerable of my own, before my deluding Lover came acquainted with me; yet, to compensate that single kindness, he hath so showred his Gold and Silver on me since, that my Wealth may procure a Match considerable enough, though my face carryed in it no other invitation. Come, come, Daughter (said the Old Woman) Something hath some savour: and although you have enough, yet more will do no harm; besides your Child will be well look'd after, well provided for (which you may see when you please) and you rid of that incumbrance, will be in a better condition for any one to sollicite you in Marriage. Being thus convinc'd by the subtle Arguments of this cunning Matron, I condescended to whatever she would have me to do; and so without further delay, the next morning we rode together to the House of this old Gentlewoman; where alighting, she had no sooner provided a necessary Room for me, and given order for my Supper, which was extraordinary, but her impatience immediately hurried her to the

Gentlewoman, her Friend; and being out of breath, told her, as well as she could, that she had effected the business beyond expectation; but because she would not leave me too long, begg'd her excuse, promising the next morning a full account of all her proceedings. That night was spent in all the jollity imaginable; Fowles of all sorts, and the choicest of the season were provided; Wine flowed so plentifully through every room of the House, that I wonder it did not reel into the streets. I am sure the servants would, had not a noise of Musick held them by the ears, whil'st their Legs caper'd like a pair of Drum-sticks. Although they took but little repose that night, yet my Hostess got up early to wait on her Correspondent, who had not slept that night, for the eager expectation to hear how her desires were accomplisht.

But overjoyed she was, when she saw the old Woman approach, who taking her aside in one of the walks of the garden, askt her how she had sped, and in what manner. The old woman (as much transported with joy as she) have patience, and I will tell you, said she; In my way to *London*, I met with several that had nibled on the bait of concupisence; but they were such flounder-mouth'd, draggle-tail'd, dirty Pusses, that I would not venture upon any of them; but at length comming to an Inn on the road, I accidentally fell into the Company of a Gentlewoman (which is this that I have now brought with me, to be serviceable to you) who by her deportment informed me, that she was not meanly extracted; and by those wanton torches in her face, which Nature had drawn to allure, and captivate hearts, I guest she was not unacquainted with the Masculine gender; and as I imagined, so it proved; for I have so rigled my self by discourse into her concerns, that I soon made her unravel the bottom of her secrets. To be short, I found her every way fit for our purpose, and by an extraordinary device, I have made her ours; and that you may satisfie your self farther, I will bring her to the Park, a mile from your house, where I shall desire you to meet us in the afternoon. Hereupon she departed, and acquainted me how she had opened the way to consummate what we had agreed on; and so having dined, we went to the place appointed, where the Gentlewoman was already come to meet us.

The Gentlewoman seeing us at a distance, made up to us, but was strangely astonisht when she saw a person so unexpectedly handsome, and in a Garb which as much exceeded that which she wore, as the face she saw excelled most others that she had seen before; and therefore thought it requisite to make her address, as to a person of no mean Quality; yet thinking again, should she do so, I might think she mockt me; (for had I been nobly born and bred, I would never have condescended so low, as to prostitute my body to the unlawful embraces of some hot-blooded Gallant, and afterwards mercenarily expose the Infant to the disposal of a meer stranger;) therefore familiarly thus she spake; Sweet-heart, Though I never saw you before, I am not unacquainted with your affairs, and am much troubled, that so good a face should be so deluded, and grosly abused by any Promise-breaker of them all; but since what is past cannot be recalled, I shall endeavour to redress your misfortunes, after this manner; you shall lodge with a good old Gentlewoman, not far off, a friend of mine: but be sure you keep your self private; and when you have a mind to take the air, and enjoy your self, you shall not want a Coach to carry you whither you list, so it be far enough off: your provision at home, with all things necessary, and your expences abroad, shall be at my charge; all that I shall require of you is, that when you cry out in labour, your Childe may be at the dispose of your Landlady, whom I constitute your Guardian. If in the interim you want any thing, let me know it, and you shall be supplyed, and enjoy your self as freely, as if you were Empress of the whole World; and when you are discharged of your great belly, you shall not want a sum to make you a good portion for any honest man. Be not seen in the Town, and do not come to our house, but be ruled by your Guardian; and assure your self this, your Child shall be my Child, and what estate I have, or my Husband, shall be his: and so she took her leave of me, cramming my hand full of *Jacobusses*, as the earnest of a better penny.

I was forthwith conducted to this house, which was intended for my lodging privately, where I was entertain'd, according to instruction, with much respect and gallantry; a Maid was there ready provided to attend me, and there was nothing wanting in my entertainment to make my life comfortable, and my looks cheerful. Here did I merrily pass my time away, being often visited by my old Hostess, daily puzzling each others invention, what we should have for Dinner; what recreation in the afternoon; what for Supper, and what divertisement afterwards; how to make our pleasure more poyant by their diversity, and variety; but the greatest difficulty lay in our cunning projections of going abroad, which we knew we must carry with a world of secrecie, or spoil all whatever we intended to do.

In the mean time, the Gentle-woman (understanding my true reckoning, which was three moneths gone with Child) calculated her time accordingly, and gave out, she was with Child: every one admired at the news, having not had any in so long a time of marriage, and knew not whether they had best give credit to the report; her Husband would not be induced to believe it by any means, looking upon it as incredible, nay, almost impossible; but that which most of all favoured what she would have credited was her being troubled at that instant, with some hydropical humours, which had so swelled her belly, that she had much adoe from perswading her self, that she was really with Child. Her Husband perceiving this, from an Unbeliever became a Convert, and by his belief wrought all the Neighbourhood into the like perswation: but that which knockt the nail on the head, was the opinion of the Midwife (a Creature of the Gentlewomans, made absolute to her devotion by gifts, and promise of future rewards) which proclaimed it every where as a wonder, that one after so many years, having never born a Child, should now at last conceive. Neither was the kind, and over-indulgent Husband, backward in spreading ostentatiously, his glory, that he should at last be called Father, when all the glimmerings of those hopes were quite extinguisht. His joy made him so rash and inconsiderate, that he bespoke Gossips, and concluded upon a name for it, though he knew not whether it would be born alive, male or female. On the other side, the seemingly over-joyed woman provided clouts for the bantling, and all other things necessary, which an over-busie Lullaby could invent. So many wet Nurses were sent for, that they came tumbling to the house by dozens; and so many faults were found with them, that they Troopt off again as fast; one was dislik'd for her Hair, it being of a red colour, and therefore her milk was lookt upon as too hot, rank, and venemous; every one giving in their Verdict, that she should not be wholesome, since the *Turks* were accustomed to make the rankest poyson of the flesh of slaves that were red-hair'd. Another was too tall, and therefore slothfull, and unactive, being not talkative enough; a third not clear skinn'd, nor well featur'd, having a cast with the eye, which might be the ill pattern of directing the Childs eyes amiss: a 4th. had a too indulgent husband, whom they feared one time or other might curdle the Child's milk, and so endanger its health: a fifth had had formerly sore Breasts, and they doubted from thence the Milky-way might be polluted: a sixth was too melancholly enclin'd, which they judged would not only prejudice her suck, but deprive her of the talking qualifications of most Nurses, who look upon the impertinent nonsensical tittle-tattle to their Children, to be the basis of all their future learning. With much adoe, they at length pitch upon a lovely brown woman, full grown, well featur'd, quick sighted, clear skinned, middle statur'd, with breasts little and round, her blood cirkling them in the pleasant blew *Meanders* of her veins. Now lest they should loose her, if she went out of their sight, she was hired, and entertained into the house immediatly, although her Mistriss had five moneths to go of her supposed time.

Though her Husband was extasied with joy, his Brother was moved by a contrary passion, his folly making him shew it, in so unseemly a way, that every one now concluded him that, which they only surmized before, a villain, that had both studied and practised the ruin of his nearest relations; & he was often accused & upbraided for so doing, that he was forc'd to leave the Town, and since is gone to a Cozen of his living in *Barmudus*.

My time began now to draw nigh, being groan so bigg I could not with convenience stir abroad, and too restless to stay at home. As I felt any pain, I caused my Mistriss to be acquainted therewith, that she might be so too; if I felt my self much disordered, I sent away her confident presently to allarm her; who acted her part as artificially, as I did it really. These out-cries of hers made the whole Garrison continually stand to their arms; there being about her continually the Midwife, Wet-Nurse, Dry Nurse, with many Neighbouring assistants: the Maids below ready at command, and a *Man Midwife*, if need should require with so many instruments ready fixt, as would with the very Iron set up a Black-smith: and all for the strangeness of shape, surpassing any rarity in *Tredescants* Collection.

After so many false allarms, a true one came at last, carried by our Confident aforesaid, with my Child in her lap; whose very appearance was watch-word enough for the Gentlewoman to express the pangs of Child-birth, which she did then in a more violent manner than before, imagining something more than ordinary: she approaching the bed askt her lowdly how she did, and how she felt her self, and at that very instant clapt the Child into Bed to her; who immediately skreeking out, the Midwife ran to her, where seeming to be busied about her a while, at length takes the Child from her, and doing with it, and her, as is usual; the news of this her happy delivery was conveyed to the Husband, who was near at hand, attending, and with tears lamenting the sad pain his poor wife underwent for him; but the joyful tydings of having a Son born, wip'd away all those tears, and so animated his feeble Carkass, that he would have entred the Room, before it was either Civil, or Convenient, had he not been stopt by meer force. I shall not trouble you by relating what an Universal rejoyceing there was through the whole house, but only inform you, that before the expiration of a moneth the Child was Christened, being as lovely a Child as could be born of a Woman, not any limb or part of his body, which did not promise to exceed his true Father in every thing. The Gentlewoman being up, as soon as she understood I was well and fully recovered, appear'd abroad in publick, whose happy delivery was by all congratulated. And to gratifie me, she sent me an hundred pieces of old Gold, desiring me to remove my Quarters, and to engage my tongue eternally to conceal the secret.

I now thought it high time to send to my two Gallants, who were obliged to me in bonds, the one to pay me fourty pound, and the other fifty, upon my delivery; they being both assured of the truth thereof, delayed me not, but sent me my moneys by the first conveniency, which added to my late purchase; and what money I had before, made up to weighty a portion, for so light an Houswife as my self.

CHAP. V.

Mrs Dorothy *relates several passages in the Inn: as, how the Host drew Guests to his House, and then cheated them: the Boy by his Example, attempts to cheat, but is taken in the manner; is beaten by his Mistris, but is revenged of her and his Master; is turned over to be corrected by the Under Hostle, but is wittily, and pleasantly revenged on him.*

I was now (continued Mrs *Dorothy*) rid of my great Belly, and instead of that, had a great Bag of money; and my Child being thus provided for, as I have told you, I retired from the place where I had lain in private, now to appear in publick at the House of my very good friend, the old *Crony*; part of whose Adventures I have already related to you: and since you have not thought me tedious in the discourse I have already made you, I shall give you an account of some such Transactions in her House, during my stay there, which, I believe, will be no less pleasant than what you have already heard: and then having made a short pause, we thuss proceeded.

The whole Family, consisting of her self, her Husband, a Son of about twenty four years of Age, and Daughter about nineteen, a Chamberlain, a Tapster or Winer, an Hostler, Cook-maid, Scullion, and two or three boyes; who were imployed under the others, were all alike, knavish enough, all guilty of such unparallel'd Knaveries as I have rarely heard of; and knowing of one anothers tricks, they out-vyed one another, striving and contending which should exceed in Roguery, and so sly and cunningly they carried it, that 'twas difficult to discover them, especially when they all joyned together to cheat or abuse any body; but when they fell out among themselves, they made excellent sport in acting the revenges they took upon one another. My Landlord loved his pleasure and profit so equally, that he made it his business to contrive how to joyn them together; and although he commonly had the best Custom of any house in the town, yet he would practice wayes to gain, and bring in more; among other wayes, he used this for one. He would take his Horse in an Afternoon, and ride out some ten or twelve miles, and so return home again; but he seldome came home, but he brought Guests with him, which he would take up by the way, thus.

If he saw a parcel of Travellers, who he thought to be good fellowes, and fit for his purpose, he would then enquire which way, and how far they travelled; to this they commonly answered, directly; and if they were for our Town, then he would joyn with them; and soon after, his second question would be, to know if they were acquainted at the Town, and at what Inn they would take up their Quarters: If they were strangers, and by that means indifferent of the place where they should lodge; then he told them, that the best Inn in the Town was his House, but not naming it to be his, or that he had any Interest in it, but only that he knew there was a good Hostess, who had a handsome Daughter that would use them well; and he seldom missed with this Bait to win them to agree to go thither with him, and accordingly to bring them home with him. But if they would not agree upon the place, and he saw there was no good to be done, then he would pretend some excuse to stay behind them, & would wait for such company as would at all points be for his turn; and with them would he enter the House as a Stranger: indeed he would call the Chamberlain, Hostler, and Tapster, by their Names; but they, who knew their Duties, would in no case shew any Duty to him. Then would he, as being acquainted in the House, tell his Fellow Travellers what provisions there was for Supper, and would be sure to draw them up to the highest Bill of Fare he could. If the Hostess, or her Daughters company were desired, he would be the forwardest to call them, and only treat and converse with them as of some small acquaintance; after supper, he would endeavour to draw on the Company to drink high, and use all possible means to enflame the reckoning; and when he saw they were well heated with wine, and the fury of their expences was over, he would pretend, out of good Husbandry, to call for a Reckoning before they went to bed, that they might not be mis-reckoned, or staid from the pursuit of their Journey in the Morning; to this they would commonly agree, and the Sum total of the reckoning being cast up, he would be the first man that would, without scruple, or inquiry into the particulars, lay down his share, and by his examples, the rest would follow; if any did question the dearness of the Victuals, or the quantity of the drink, he would by one means or other take them off, protesting that the Hostess was too honest to mis-reckon them, and that he had kept a just account himself, and was well satisfied; or else he should be as cautious from parting from his money as any of them; and then they, not distrusting him further, would by his example pay the shot. Thus would he many times, by his Crown or six shillings share, mis-reckon on them sixteen or twenty shillings; especially if they came to high drinking: and then the reckoning being paid, they went to bed, he retiring with his wife, and he would lye abed in the morning, and let them march off alone; but if they, in the Morning, did fall to drinking again, taking a hair of the Old Dog, then would he up, and at them again, make one at that sport, and many times put them out of capacity to Travel that day, and so keep them there to his profit, and their expences; he shifting his Liquor, and in the end, shifting himself out of their Companies, when he has seen his Conveniency, leaveing them to pay roundly for their folly. If they enquired after him, my Hostess would pretend he was a Chance Guest, as they were, only, she had seen him the last year, or such like; and thus he would force a Trade, and enjoy his pleasure and profit, by joyning them together; and this course did he frequently use when Guests came not in of their own accord; so that our house was seldome empty.

As mine Host, who was the Head and Chief of the House, had his tricks, so had the rest of the Family theirs, even the least in the House; for there was an unhappy boy, who was sometimes with the maid in the Kitchin, sometimes with the Tapster, attending Guests in their lodgings, and other times, with the Hostler and Horses in the Stable; this boy, though he was little was witty; and seeing that every one had their tricks, he cast about how he might have his, and have some profit in the Adventure; so that one day, mine Host being abroad, and the Tapster out of the way, he drew the drink; and not only the Beer, but carried bottles of wine to the Guests, & seeing them in a merry vain, he thought to try his skill at mis-reckoning them; and for six bottles which he carried into them when they came to pay, he reckoned them eight; and though there was some questioning of the truth, yet he justified it, and stood to it, that he had the reckoning he demanded.

This being his first considerable attempt in this Nature, for he had gained two shillings for himself, he was resolved to keep the prize for himself; and therefore putting that up in his Pocket, he delivered the rest at the Bar; the reckoning being wiped out.

But the Company falling into discourse, in short time called for more wine, and then the Tapster being returned, he officiated in the boyes place, and turning him into the stable; more wine they had, and staying longer than ordinary, and falling again to drinking, they quaffed off the other half dozen bottles of wine, and then calling to pay, the Tapster, thinking to put his old trick of mis-reckoning in practice, told them, there were seven bottles to pay; but one of the company who was more cautious than the rest, had made his observation, and every bottle that was brought in, he unbuttoned a button, and so was able to aver and justify that there was but six; and withal, the rest of the company believing him, they all fell a ranting, vowing that they would pay for no more, and farther alledging that they were mis-reckoned one or two bottles in the last reckoning; the Tapster, although he was guilty as to himself, yet he did not believe them as to the other reckoning, because he could not imagine, that the boy would be so bold as to attempt to cheat them, and therefore he huff'd as high as they in justification of the boy and himself; and such a noise they made, that the Hostess went in to know the cause of that clamour: they at first were so hot on both sides, that they would not hear her speak, neither did they speak reasonably themselves; but in the end she understood the matter, that they were wronged of one or two bottles by the Boy, and one by the Tapster; she hearing the matter, did not so much stand to justifie and vindicate the Tapster, whom she did imagine was guilty, but as for the boy, she was very confident, that he had not wronged them, and when the heat of their anger was somewhat over, she examined particulars enquiring how many bottles they paid for, they said eight: she who had not so soon forgotten what she had received, averred that she had but six *shillings* for wine, and therefore it was a mistake; they still aledged *eight*, and she *six*, till now nobody could end the controversie but the boy, who was sought after, and in short time found in the hayloft asleep, or meditating how he should bestow his purchased Treasure; but being found, he was without any questions there immediately led away before the Gentlemen and his Mistress, who were to be judges of this matter of fact. The question was soon stated to him, and he too well understood the matter, which he stoutly deny'd, but there was quickly such clear evidence appeared against him, that he was found guilty; for he not dreaming or mistrusting any such matter, had not conveyed the money away, so but that the pockets being searched, there the two *shillings* were found, to the great shame and confusion of the small delinquent: this was to the great amazement of the Guests, his Mistress, and the Tapster; but the money being laid down, and two bottles wine being brought in for it, the Gentlemen were well enough pleased, and made no further enquiry into the other bottle, which the Tapster had likewise mis-reckoned them; so that he scaped without shame or punishment, so did not the boy, who was not only ashamed, but was ordered to be severely punished, and therefore the next morning was fetched up by the under Hostler, (one who was not so wise as the boy, though in growth he was much biggar) with a Cat of nine tailes, which gave so great an impression on the poor boyes buttocks, that he was resolved on a revenge, which he effected, as I shall presently tell you. This boy was now looked on as an errant cunning Rogue, and one who without good looking to would be too wise for them all, for he had presumed to mis-reckon two *shillings* in six *shillings*, and put it all into his own pocket, whereas the Tapster who was a proficient in cheating, and licensed therein (but with this *proviso*, that half of what he gained thereby was to be paid to his Mistress) only endeavoured to mis-reckon one *shilling* in six; so that, I say, the boy was narrowly watched, and had many a blow on the back, and box on the ear, more than formerly; he who knew he had deserved it, for he was guilty of many petty waggeries, was forced to bear, but however he made provision against it, for his Mistress using to pommel him on the shoulders with her fist, he one time took a paper of pins, sticking them with the points upwards, placed them between his Doublet and Cassock; and his Mistress striking him, as she was wont to do, did light upon the pins, pricked her hand till the blood ran down her fingers ends, and the boy running away, she could not imagine how this was done, for she saw nothing upon his coat, that should cause it; so the boy getting away, removed the paper with pins, and there was an end of the matter for that time. The Mistress finding she had suffered by striking him on the shoulders, would come no more there with her bare hands; but used a cudgel, if it were near her, and if not she would use to slap him on the mouth with the back of her hand; and one time, he being in the Kitchen, and she running after him to strike him, he claps a knife, which lay near him, into his mouth, with the edge outwards, she not minding that, but endeavouring and intending to give him a great blow did so, but to her cost, for she cut her knuckles in such pitious manner, that the blood ran down abundantly, and now it was no fooling matter, but Chyrurgions work, wherefore one was sent for, and the boy ran away to his wonted dormitory, the hay-loft. The Mistress took her Chamber, and towards Evening the Master came home, and bringing with him some Guests, he soon missed his wife, and thereby knew the occasion of her retirement, and it was not long ere he saw the boy, the Authour of the harm; he therefore took up a cudgel, and ran hastily after the Boy, who fearing the danger, betook him to his heels, and ran cross a dunghill in the yard; the Master being eager to pursue the boy, did not take the same course the boy had done, who had passed over a board he had laid there on purpose, but the Master missing of that, went on one side, and fell into a great filthy hole, which by reason of much wet and rain, was there slightly covered; and had he not been helped out by the Hostler, he might have stifled; he having recovered his feet, left the pursuit of the boy, and was forc'd to be conducted to bed, which was to his great grief and dammage, for he had spoiled his cloaths, wet himself, and which was worst of all, he by this means was disappointed of his purpose in making a prey of his guests he had brought in with him to that purpose. But the Tapster and others, did their best in that behalf, and the Boy was again committed to the disciplination of the under Hostler, who by the command of his Master, almost flead the poor boys buttocks.

The Boy was now revenged of his Master and Mistress, who finding him so unlucky, had no great mind to meddle with him, neither did the Boy studdy any revenge upon them; but so often as he saw the under-Hostler, who had now twice been his tormentor, his blood would boyle at him, and all his study was to be even with him; and thereupon he watched for all opportunities, and it was not long ere he found one. There was meat at the fire to be roasted, and he was ordered to look to and wind up the Jack, which was made to go by a stone weight, which was fastned to pulleys, and when the Jack was woond up, the stone weight being on the out-side of the house, was drawn up two storyes high, to the eves of the house; the boy observing this, and that the Jack-weight was down, and seeing his Enemy the under Hostler in the Yard, just by the jack-weight he lifted that off from the hook, and conveighed it under the girdle of the Hostler, just behind, he not perceiving it: when he had thus done, he ran into the Kitchin, and woond up the Jack, the Hostler being none of the wisest, wondered what it was that first of all held him by the back, and afterwards drew him up from the ground; but it was too late ere he discovered the truth, for he was now hanging in the aire; his girdle was of strong leather, with a great brass buckle and thong, which he could not possibly undo; neither durst he attempt it for fear of falling, and therefore he was in short time drawn up to the top; the boy not thinking this revenge not enough, seeing no body came, proceeded further, and taking a parcel of wet horse-litter, and some dry hay, he placed it just underneath the Hostler, and set fire to it, which made such a smother and smoke, that the poor Hostler was almost choaked, wherefore he roared out most hideously; the boy having done all he intended, said, *Now remember the Cat with nine tayles*, and so ran away; by this time the Hostler made so much noise, and the jack together, being forced by weight to go faster than ordinary, that at the noise all the houshold ran to see what was the matter, when, in short, there was found the poor Hostler hanging between heaven and earth, and with coughing and roaring he purged forwards and backwards, but most backwards; in regard his girdle forced it downwards by pressing and gripeing his stomach, so that he was in a most lamentable pickle; and so great was the astonishment of all the beholders, that he was come down almost to the bottom, ere the smoaking hay was removed, or he relieved; but at length down he came, and thus ended this adventure.

CHAP. VIII.

The Boy learns, and practises Vaulting and tumbling, the maid servant attempting to do the like, is intangled, caught in the manner, and laughed at: she puts a trick upon a Puritanical Church-Warden, and makes the boy by another trick, to lye in bed, and lose his dinner; he is revenged on her by a Gunpowder plot.

Mrs. *Dorothy* putting a stop to her discourse, gave us conveniency and leisure to express our satisfaction by our laughter, in which we continued for some space, and then rehearsing and commenting on what she had told us, we again renewed our laughter, she joyning with us in the same exercise, when we had put a stop to our mirth, she thus continued.

Truly, Friends, I did think I might a little divert you by my relation; but I see you are pleased much better than I expected, and if you are so well contented with this which is but a taste of what I can tell you, I am sure the rest would be much more delightful; but being desirous to put an end to my discourse, by relating to you such matters as only concern my self, till my arrival here, I therefore beg your excuse. Nay, replyed I, and Mistress *Mary*, you must not refuse us the request we both make you, of proceeding in these pleasing Adventures of your houshold; and, continued I, it is enough to know and find you are here with us, we are satisfied in that, and hope you will give us the other satisfaction we desire; and I pray be as full and free in your recital as you can, for we cannot think any thing to be tedious that is so pleasant; she hearing my desires, after few excuses, agreed thereto; and thereupon she thus reassumed the discourse.

The poor under Hostler being thus descended from his place of Torment, was almost in as pitiful a plight as one taken down from the Gibbet half hanged to be quartered; he had as little motion or sense; for he was almost suffocated with the smoak that ascended and flew up his nose, and down his throat; and as Malefactors do (as they say) piss for fear, or some other cause, so had he done; and not only so, but we could perceive somewhat else, of a yellowish colour, that had soaked through his breeches, run down his stockings, so that few would touch him; but at length, the Hostler, his superiour, considering his condition and former good service, took him up, and carried him to his bed adjoyning to the Stable; where, with the assistance of *Aqua vitæ*, he was soon brought to his former senses. Our young Rogue in the mean time lying in the Hay-loft over him, laughing at the roguery he had done, and the groans he heard the poor fellow fetch, were as so many instruments of musick to raise his laughter to the higher pitch.

This Rogue, who wanted nothing so much as Roping, or a good Cat of nine tailes, now escap'd with out either; there being no body in the whole house that had any mind to meddle with him; he was threatned by some, whilst others only laughed at him, and he went merrily about his business: and to conclude, much company coming that day to the house, and the particulars of the Adventure being told them, they sent for the boy and Hostler; and after several questions, and much laughter, they made them drink to one another, and become Friends.

The boy being thus freed from punishment, set his wits at work, how he might employ his time to the best advantage, and be getting of money as well as the rest of the Family did; and soon after there being a fair at our Town, among other fooleries that attended it, there were a parcel of Rope-Dancers, and Tumblers; our boy was Master of so much money, as to see them two or three times; and having very much affection to that quality, he purchased acquaintance with such another Crack Rope as himself, who was a very nimble and active youth at the Art of Vaulting; him he invites to our house, and treating him with such as the House afforded, by all means desires his instructions in that nimble mistery; he soon assented, and our boy being ingenuous, and very willing to learn, soon attains to the knowledg of this mistery, and taking all opportunities of practising, could soon leap through a hoop, vault over two or three joynt stools, tumble on the ground in various manners; and being a pretty proficient, had money several times given him by Guests that came to our house, for shewing his tricks; by vertue of his money he would brag and vapour as well as the best in the house; and the rest of the servants seeing his gain would attempt to do the like, but many times came off with the breaking of their shins; amongst the rest, the Cook maid had a mighty great itch to learn and practise some of these tricks belike, supposing that if he, who was a boy, did get so much money by them, that then she might gain much more being a maid; and that she might as well do them as he; the obstacle of Petticoats she removed by, resolving when she had learned, to have a pair of Breeches and Doublet for that purpose, and that she questioned not, but to get money enough, it being a greater Novelty to see a woman in breeches; but before she purchased them, she resolved to practice in her ordinary Habit, her Petticoats, and did so when she had convenient time and place; so that she likewise could perform somwhat in that practice. One time most of the other servants being abroad, she was sent into the Cellar to draw a Gallon Pot full of Claret Wine; she believing it would be some time ere it were full, by reason it ran only through a small Cane whilest the Pot was filling, she lies down on her back, and resolved now to try whether she could put her feet in her neck, in order to practice some new trick of tumbling; shee soon put one there, and with some difficulty likewise put the other, when she had so done, she could not possibly undoe what she had done, her feet were as fast to her neck, as if they had grown there; and though she tumbled and tossed, yet it was all to no purpose, for she could not by any means disentangle, or disengage her self from the posture she was in; she finding her self in this condition, knew not what to do, for the Pot was now full, and the Wine ran about the Cellar, and with tumbling about she had made her Coats to fly about her ears; at length she resolved to cry out, hoping her Mistress, or some other of the females of the house might hear her, and come to her rescue; this resolution she put in execution, and cryed out amain, help, help; we were all in the Room over her, and therefore soon heard her voice, but not knowing whose, or what was the matter; mine Host at length said to the boy, sirrah, run down into Cellar, and see what is the matter there; the boy did so, and after some little stay came up again, and cryes out, Oh Heavens! Master, I think our Cook-maid is murthered for I went down, and there lyes her body without a Head, and a great deal of blood about her (which was the spilt Claret) but, said his Master, are you sure her head was off? yes, yes, said the boy, come see how it is cut of from the neck; and yet, continued he, I cannot think she is yet dead, for she moved her hands, and still cryes out, but her head I cannot find. Mine Host hearing of this strange matter, soon ran down into the Cellar, which was not so dark, nor he so dim sighted, but he presently discovered how the matter was. The only thing he did, was to stop the Wine from running out, by putting the spiggot into the faucet, and so returned up to us, and told us that the boy was a little mistaken; but such a sight had he seen as was very unusual; and thereupon desires us to desend into the Cellar, and see what he had done; no sooner had he said so; but our curiosities likewise induced us to go down, where in short time we likewise had the satisfaction of seeing this strange sight: how said I, this is some Monster, and it would do well to keep it in this manner till the next fair, and then we may gain more by it then all the Tumblers did. A pox of Tumbling, said mine Hostess, I believe this came from that Exercise.

We thus having spent our Verdicts, helped the wench to disingage her self, and put her in her wonted natural posture; but when she was so, she was not come to her self, so much was she spent with strugling, and her joynts were so out of order, that we were forced to lead her up stairs, and put her to bed.

She was mightily ashamed at this mischance, so that we could hardly perswade her to be seen by anybody; but the boy was as well pleased, as she was troubled; it was honey and nuts to him to tell the guests, how the Cook-maid could do some feats of activity, as well as he, and then relate to them, in what posture he found her. Much sport was made upon this account; and although the Wench was shy at first in being seen, yet in time she bore it out bravely, when the guests gave her money to talk with her about this Adventure.

By this means the wench became a great Enemy to the boy, and did him many shrew'd turns, but durst not meddle with his body politick, dreading the danger she should run into by the harmes of others who had been his persecutors; wherefore she was forced to let him alone as to matter of action, only now and then she would exercise her wit upon him, in which she seldome came off but with the disadvantage. She was famous for this her trick of activity, by which she got money, but much more by another, which she soon after effected, and came more clearly off with it: It was then in time of rebellion, and all observations of *Christmas*, *Easter*, *Whitsontide*, or any Holy-days, were by the Factious accounted superstitious, especially any observation of *Christmas*; and therefore, the more to cross the desire and humour of those who would observe the feast of *Christmas*, the men then in power commanded a strict fast to be on that day kept and observed, with penalties on all those who should dress any victuals; and althorough the Town, and especially our house, was of another perswation, yet such was the prevalency of the Faction, that it, was strictly observed; & it was given out that the Officers of the Town would search houses, to find and punish Offenders. Our Cook-maid hearing of this, was resolved to put a trick upon the Officers; who about the middle of Sermon time came attended with a Guard, to see and examine our Kitching, where they found not the Jack a going, yet they found a good fire, and the pot a boyling: *How now*, said Master Church warden, *How dare you break the Lawes, by dressing victuals on this day? What have you in the Pot?* Quoth the Maid, *Nothing but plumb porridg? How*, said the Church-warden, *Superstitious Porridg? this is a very great offence, and deserves as great punishment, to do thus in contempt of the Laws; I will see your Master fined for this, and severely punished. Well,* replyed she, *but I pray, Master Church-warden, be not so angry, but be pacified; which I know you will be, when you see further what is in the Pot, and with what the porridge are made; and lest you should mistake I will shew you*; whereupon she went to the Pot and took out a large pair of Rams-horns, and said, *Look you*, Master Church-warden, *this is the meat; how like you it? I hope so well, that you will tast of the broath your self without scruple of conscience?* The case was so plain, and Master-Church-warden was so sensible that he was jeer'd, that he made all possible haste out of the house, threatning what he would do to the Wench, who now only laughed at him, as did some of his attendants, who knew the Church-warden was very sensible of the affront, his wife being one of those who wore cork-heeld shoes, which made her pass for a light Huswife, as indeed she was.

This trick which our Maid put upon the Churchwarden, raised a great noise in the Town and Country, and brought all the Cavileers to our house, who gave her somewhat to her box, so that she was very happy in this project, and our Host had very great Custom.

But still the Boy and Wench could not agree to set their horses together; for his business was to be up in the morning with the first, and help her make her fire, this he could not indure, for he loved his bed mightily well, and would rather want his belly full of victuals, then sleep, he had liberty to lye a bed on a *Sunday* so long as he pleased, because then they had few guests;

wherefore he would constantly lye by it, till dinner time, which he knew by the jack going; for so long as the jack went, so long would he lie by it, but when that was stopt, he thought it was time, to rise to dinner.

The wench observing that he observed this Custome was resolved to put a trick on him, and therefore one *Sunday* though dinner was dressed by twelve a clock, and eaten by one, yet she let the Jack go on till four a Clock afternoon, still the boy lay listning to the Jacks going; and hearing that go still on, gave himself to lazyness, and took many a sweet turn, which she laughed at heartily; at length she stopt the Jack, and immediately the boy arose, and came down stairs (for he lay in a small loft over the Kitchin) to see what was become of the roast; but he found none in the Kitchin, nor Hall, nor no body in the house but the wench; who seeing him search about for his Dinner, and asking her questions about the affairs of the belly, she could not answer him for laughing; but soon after the family returning from Church, he discovered his own mistake, and her roguery; for this, he resolved on a revenge, which he had upon her the next day, when, a considerable dinner being to be dressed; he was called up in the morning to make a fire; he did so, and was more than ordinarily diligent, for he laid a row of Cinders, then fresh Coals, then a row of gun powder, then a row of Cinders, then more gun-powder, and so Cinders, till this pile of building was erected; that done, he slightly kindled it and departed, going on an errand out of the Town. The Wench not knowing, or distrusting the intended mischief, hung on her Pot; and both the Spits of Geese, Capons, and other Fowls; but before they were a quarter roasted, the train of Powder took; with that up flew the Pot; and both the Spits, with all the Fowl, took a second flight; the Wench was amazed, and the Dinner spoiled, for the ashes and Cinders had made all the Fowls of a sad colour: so that the Wench stamped and swore, as if she had been bewitch'd.

CHAP. IX.

The Maid is out-witted by a Country Fellow in an eateing wager, and so is her Master, mine Host; who makes himself whole again by another eating wager. Three Women drink off eighteen Gallons of Rhenish Wine at one sitting, and the manner how.

Mrs. *Dorothy* pausing, and we laughing, gave her the conveniency to consider of what she was to say further; wherefore in short time she thus proceeded.

The poor Wench was at a great loss, to think that the Guests must loose their dinner; and she could not for a long time think how this came about, nor distrust that the boy had been concerned in it; but at length, the mist being removed, her eyes were opened, and she believed the boy to be the Authour of this mischief. But since it was done, and what was past could not be prevented or helped; she bethought her self how to proceed; and therefore, her Mistress coming into the Kitchin, and seeing the state of the matter, they likewise called me and the Daughter, to assist in the remedy; whilst the Wench made the fire good, we fell to washing the Fowls from the fowleness which the Cinders and Ashes had caused; but when that was done, we had a further and more tedious work, to pick out several corns of powder that were fastned into the skins of the Fowls; at length, with many hands, we likewise performed this work, and with an hours loss, the Dinner was in as much forwardness as it had been; and at length, it was dressed and eaten; but the Guests tasting, and seeing some remains of the Gun-powder, my Host excused it well enough, by telling them that those Fowles were shot by an accident.

Thus was the Dinner eaten, and much Wine drank off before the boy returned; but so soon as he came in, mine Host took him by the hand, and led him into the room where the Guests were still a drinking: and first desireing silence, and then their pardon, he told them this was the Gunner, that had shot all those Fowls they had eaten, at one shot; how, said they, he is an excellent marks-man: yes truly, said mine Host, but he had a strange kind of instrument to do this Execution; and I pray, Gentlemen, do you examine him how it was done.

The Guests thinking there was somewhat in the matter that was pleasant, desired the boy to acquaint them with it; he seeing how matters went, and believing no harm would come to him, in plain terms told them all; they were strangely pleased with the boyes discourse; and he having told them the manner how he did it, they desired to know the cause, wherefore; to this he replyed, it was because the maid had cheated him of his Dinner, by letting the Jack to go, as I told you.

The rehearsal of that Adventure pleased them as much as the other; and the maid was call'd in, who confessing all that the boy had told them, the Guests made them Friends, and gave money to each of them; advising the Wench not by any means to fall out with the boy, and so they dismissed them.

Thus had we much pleasure by Adventures, which every day fell out between this boy and some body or other, but I will leave that, to tell you of somewhat else, as considerable and pleasant. Our Cook-maid, though she were pretty cunning and witty; was yet sometimes out-witted; for one day, an ordinary Country fellow came into the Kitchin; and calling for a Flaggon of beer, sate down by the fire to drink it and thus he began with the Wench: Here is good drink at your house, but I wonder you are not as well provided with Victuals; why, said she, so we are, for here is good meat at the fire, shewing him a piece of roast beef, that weighed above a stone; yes, said he again, the meat may be good, but there is but a little of it, there is enough for you, replyed she; no, but there is not, said he; how, said she, can you eat all this? Yes, that I can, said he; I'le lay a wager of that, said she; what you dare, said the man, she would have the wager be a quart of wine (for she was resolved against money wagers) nay, said the Man, a pint is enough for me with this meat, and so much will I lay: She thinking, that the less she layd the less she should lose, if she lost, and being very desirous to see this great wager of eating performed, agreed to his Terms, and thereupon he fell too lustily, and did eat considerably, but far short of all, so that he consented his wager to be lost, and the pint of wine was called for; he seizing on it first, put it to his nose, and drank all off; and throwing down *six pence* for his pint of wine, and *two pence* for his pot of beer, was departing, when her Mistress, mine Hostess, enters the Kitchin, and seeing the fellow departing, asked who must pay for the meat? Not I, said the fellow; Nor I, said the wench, so that a controversie arose between them; but mine Host and some company coming in, ended it, by ajudging, that since the Country-man called for no meat, it was not fit he should pay for it, and he not paying, the maid must, which she presently did it, but was laughed at for her folly. But she was not the only over-reach'd person in the house, for it was not long ere mine Host himself was finely caught.

There came three men, who although they were neighbours, and famous for eating, yet mine Host not knowing them, they thus over-reach'd him: they came to sup, and lye there that night, and therefore went into the Kitchin to see what was for Supper. There was Capons, Pidgeons, and Sparagus: Very good meat, said they: Now, mine Host, what shall we give you a peice for our supper of these three sorts of victuals? He asked, how much they would have drest: they asked him the same question, How much he would dress:

Why, said he, I will dress three Capons, three dozen of Pidgeons, and fifteen hundred of Sparagus. Very good, said they: but if this be not enough, we expect to have more. That you shall, said he; but you shall sup first, and I hope there will be enough for my self and family, when you have done. For that, you must adventure it, said they; Well now, your price? Said mine Host, I will have three *shillings* four *pence* a piece, that is, ten *shillings* in all. Content, said they; Make haste that we may drink afterwards. Thus was the Bargain made up, and the Fowls laid down to the fire. In the mean time the three Travellors fetched a walk, to get them (as they said) a stomack to their Supper; which in convenient time being ready, and they returned, they thus began; each of the three took, each of them, a Capon whole on their trenchers; and cutting them into pieces, they made one mouthful of each wing, another of each leg; and scraping all the meat from the Carcass, into two or three mouth-fuls, the Capons were invisible; then they drank each his cup of Claret, to whet their appetites; that being done, they fell to the Pidgeons, and cutting each Pidgeon into four quarters, they eat them, bones and all, at four bits; and then they drank again, and fell to the Sparagus, which was in short time bestowed where the rest of the victuals was; mine Host seeing them so quick at their work, stared at them, and they calling for another glass of wine drank to him, and told him, that he must provide more victuals, or lose his wager, he being angry at both their propositions, at length thought it was better to let them have more meat, than not to be paid for what they had, and be laughed at into the Bargain; wherefore he replyed, they should have enough; and calling for the Cook-maid, commanded her to dress the same quantity of victuals; she staring on the Guests, they bad her go down, and make haste for they wanted their supper: down she went, and did accordingly; and whilst supper was dressing, they walked and smoak'd, in their Chamber. In time the other course, consisting of three Capons, three dozen of Pigeons, and fifteen hundred of Sparagus was brought up, and in as little time as before it was eaten up, as the former had been to the great cost, loss, and confusion of mine Host; who stared now worse than he had done; but however he again asked them, if they would have any more; to this they readily replyed, *Yes*. He again called, and the Cook maid being come up, was commanded to dress the same quantity again, and that quickly: She replyed, she could not, for all the Fowl that was killed, was eaten; and it would be a great while, ere she could kill, pull and dress the like quantity; besides, there was no more Sparagus then to be had; they told mine Host they must have their bargain, or he lose his wager: he replyed, if he could not furnish them with that, yet they might have of any other sort of victuals: they said, they would have that, or none, or else a third way, come to composition, to this mine Host gave ear, and asked what composition: they told him, that indeed though they could give a dispatch to more victuals, yet they would for once forbear further eating, and exchange their victuals for drink: so they reckoned what their other mess of victuals might come to, which being computed to ten shillings, they desired ten shillings worth of wine. Mine Host shook his head at this and said, they did him too hard, which they confessing, and a little further discoursing on, it was agreed that they should have each of them a quart of *Canary*, in full satisfaction of the wager: this they had, this they drank off, and so went to bed, where they slept more soundly then mine Host, who with all his Family went supperless to bed; and he was extreamly vex'd, that he should be out-witted and over-reached by three Bumpkins; but what could not be cured must be endured; it was but a folly to complain, self do, self have, and now he remember'd the wager between the Cook-maid and Country-man, and had no cause to laugh at her anymore. Night being spent, part in sleep, and part in these cogitations, he arose, and so did his guests, who honestly paid their shot, though not half so much as their reckoning came to; and at departure they told him, that if ever he had occasion for an eating wager, if he would send for any of them, they would do their weak endeavours to assist him as much to his gain as this had been to his loss; and thereupon acquainted him with the places of their dwellings, they departed: and indeed, it was not long ere he had occasion to make use of them; for a Person of Quality, being to travel our Road, sent his boy before to our house to bespeak a Supper; the boy, having mistook his Master in his direction, instead of a couple of Capons, and a dozen of Larks, which he had ordered him to bespeak, he bespeak, a dozen of Capons, and a Couple of Larks, mine Host did somewhat distrust the boy for his directions, when he spake of a couple of Larks, and told him surely he was mistaken, he must have two dozen of Larks; no, said the boy, my Master is but a small eater, and the dozen of Capons and the two Larks will be enough for him and his Company, which is but one Gentleman, besides himself; well, replyed mine Host, however I'le provide two dozen of Larks; and if your Master will not eat them, I'le have them my self; to this the boy consented, and the fowls were ordered to be dressed accordingly: mine Host was very sensible of the mistake, and that the Boy should have bespoke but two Capons, and a dozen of Larks; but however, the boy being so confident that it was a dozen of Capons, he was resolved to dress them, and that his Master should pay for them; but lest they should be left on his hands, and deducted for, he bethought on a way to have them dispatched; wherefore he dispatched away a boy to one of his three Capon and Pidgeon eaters, desiring him to favour him so far, as to come that evening to his house; for he did believe he might do him a kindness in some affairs relating to the teeth and guts. The Country man was at home, and came at his time: but before he came, the Master of the boy came thither, and asking what was for Supper, was answered, a dozen of Capons, and two dozen of Larks; and for whom is all this provision? said the Gentleman. For your worship, said mine Host: how so, said the Gentleman, by whose order? by your servants, replyed mine Host; and thereupon the boy being called, sirrah, said his Master, what orders did I give you about my supper? Sir, said the boy, I believe there is a mistake, and so I told mine Host. For I only bespake a dozen of Capons, and a couple of Larks; and he said, it was too little, and that he would dress two dozen of Larks. The Gentleman and his Friend laughed at the Boyes mistake, and excuse; and mine Host said, that he thought two dozen of Larks was little enough for one dozen of Capons. That is true, said the Gentleman; but I ordered the boy to bespeak only a couple of Capons, and a dozen of Larks. You see said mine Host, It is not my mistake, and I did nothing but was reasonable. I but, said the Gentleman, it is unreasonable to think, that we two and the boy can eat so much as you have provided for us; not so unreasonable neither, as you think, Sir, replyed mine Host; for I'le lay a good wager, that I'le produce one man, that can, and will eat up all the Capons himself; how, said the Gentleman? I'le never believe that, and I'le lay twenty shillings of it, and venture my Supper; done, said mine Host; done, said the Gentleman; and so both their moneys were laid into the other Gentlemans hand. Thus was this wager concluded of and mine Host went to his Teeth and Gut-Champion, who attended the sport; he told him the wager; to that he shook his head, and said it was a hard task; but he would strive to serve him. Supper being ready, it was Ushered in by mine Host, leading his Champion by the hand; who, after due reverance to the Company, sits down; and the meat being placed on the board, the wager was again recited; and it was further agreed, that the Champion might have what drink he would call for; and thereupon he began to use his teeth, and the rest of the Company their eyes, to behold the manner how he made so quick a dispatch of his Victuals. I told you already how, and in that manner he did eat; but now being to do much, he took more time than ordinary; but in time, ten of the twelve were made invisible, being put into our Gut-mongers *Christmas* Cup-board, and the eleventh was on his Trencher, and part of it sent down his belly, when mine Host looked on him with a more than curious eye, and discovered somewhat of discontent, which caused him to cry out, *Come Friend! bear up, and here's to you*; thank you, replyed the Eater; and taking the drink from mine Host, he whispering him in the ear, said; You have lost, I can eat no more. How, said the Gentleman, what sayes he? Nothing, said mine Host, but that he is sure you have lost, for he can eat a dozen more: How, replyed the Gentle-man, but by my faith he shall not, for i'le have this my self for my Supper: and thereupon he seized on the twelfth Capon, and laying it on his Trencher, cuts it in peices, and gives to his Friend. Nay then, said mine Host, I see you agree the wager to be mine: yes, replyed the Gentleman, I had better do so, than fill his belly, and lose my own supper; and thereupon the money was given to mine Host; who now, meerly by his quickness of wit in thinking, and confidence in speaking so contrary to the Eaters saying, won the wager; and, which was most, saving his own credit, and that of his Champion, who clearly confessed, that the wager was in great danger to be lost.

Thus did mine Host get as much as he lost by the former wager, and the Gentleman was well pleased at the loss of his; and all parties being contented, they went to bed, and next day parted.

And now, continued Mrs. *Dorothy*, that my hand is in, I'le tell you one Story more of the like nature, and so conclude with this eating discourse.

It was not long ere some Company came to the House, and in the Company three Women, who were good girls, absolute *Bona Roba's*, they had a great desire to drink *Rhenish* wine, and therefore asked if we had any? Mine Host told them yes, he had a Runlet of eighteen Gallons newly come in, and it was excellent good; the women said that would hardly serve one sitting: no said one of the Gentle-men surely it will: they said no, they would wager that they themselves could drink it off at one sitting. The Gentleman told them that if they would, he would not only pay for it, but also give unto each of them forty shillings, to buy a new Petticoat; this they agreed to, nay, they said they would not rise from their seats e're it was done, provided they might have Anchoves, and Neats-tongues, and such like victuals to intermix: this was agreed on, and that they might the more conveniently do their business, they had each of them an empty Butter-firkin with the head knock'd off, and so taking up their Coates, they laid their bare bums on the firkins, thus they sate, and thus they drank, sometimes eating and other whiles talking, so that in four hours time, all the wine was drank off, and if they had occasion to evacuate, they did that without trouble sitting as they did on butter-firkins.

CHAP. X.

Mrs. Dorothy *discourses of the several cheats of Drawers and Tapsters, inventing bad drink and small measure. The Host carries two men before the Justice, where he came off with the loss. He is out-witted by two Guests, but is revenged on them by the boyes assistance.*

These were the frolicks we daily had at our house, which were commonly to the profit of mine Host; for whoever won or lost he went away with the profit and gain; and indeed his gain was very great both in his victuals and drink, for when wine was to be sold at eighteen pence the quart, we had two shillings or half a crown, and that we might not come within the compass of the law, to every bottle of Wine, a small plate of Olives was carried up, neither was this enough to have the price, but the Wine was generally mixt, and bad; and that the Guests might as well be cheated in quantity as quality, it was commonly sold in bottles, where we many times had two shillings or half a crown for a bottle of Wine that would not hold above a pinte and a half; and for instance, I will relate one little fine Cheat to that purpose: A Company of Gentlemen come to our house and call'd for Wine, which they drank off but liked not, wherefore they called the Drawer, and desiring another bottle told him that there was two faults in the Wine they had drank, the one that it was not so good as they expected, the other, that the bottle was not full measure; they therefore desired him to mend both the quality and quantity in the next, since they intended him, and always gave the best price, half a crown a bottle, he promised an amendment as to both, and so went down, and indeed was as good as his word, drawing the best wine in the Cellar, and that in a Bottle of the largest size; they thanked him and for his encouragement to continue honest to them they gave him a shilling, he pocketed the money and left them, they drank on and finding their wine good, called for more, which they had: But mark the falsness and ingratitude of this rascally Drawer, he in short time first changed their wine, and gave them worse, and not contented with that likewise cheated them of their measure, he carried a bottle of wine and filled a glass out of it, when one of the Gentlemen who was not yet so dim sighted but he could see somewhat of the intended cheat, cry'd hold Drawer, let me see that Glass and Bottle, and thereupon poured the wine into the bottle which was indifferent full but looking on the bottle, and seeing it was very small, he said: surely this Bottle does not hold a full quart, Oh Lord! Sir, said the Drawer, do you think I would wrong you? I do not know; replyed the Gentleman, but I much distrust it, you have no cause replyed the Drawer, for I am sure that bottle is full measure, what will you wager of that said the Gentleman? any thing you will, said the Drawer: But do you think I would put any tricks upon Gentlemen I have so great respect for, no surely? But said the Gentleman I must and will be satisfied, that you may quickly be, replyed the Drawer, for I will fetch a new sealed quart pot and measure it, this was agreed upon, and in short time up comes the Drawer with a quart pot in his hand, being come to the Table he takes the bottle and pours the wine out of that into the quart pot, which when looked upon was full as it ought to be, now said one to the Gentleman who complained, you have wronged the honest Drawer and must give him satisfaction for the abuse, truly replyed he, I was very much mistaken, and my mind still gives me that there is some cunning trick and cheat in this contrivance, and that it is not as it appears to be; truly replyed the Drawer, if you think I have done you any abuse you do me wrong, and besides the great respect I have for you who are my Masters best Customers, I know if I should attempt to wrong you, my Master would be much troubled and would not keep a Servant in his House that should do it; well for all this replyed the Gentleman, I pray let me see the bottle and quart pot, the Drawer delivered him the quart pot freely, but parted from the bottle with much unwillingness, but in fine the Gentleman had them both when presently he takes the quart pot and out of that filled the bottle, and then he found the Cheat, which was this; there was more than half a pint of wine left in the quart pot, how now, said the Gentleman who is wronged now, where lies the Cheat? The Drawer seeing himself found out and fearing he should be beaten replyed, I do not know, and so turn'd his back and left them; great was the admiration of the whole company, of the management of this cheat, but much more at the impudence of the Drawer; now they all perceived that the Drawer when he went down into the Cellar to bring up a quart pot, brought wine in it, and that above half a pint, the acting of the thing it self was not so much as the manner, that this knavish Drawer should be so impudent as to stand in it, and justifie it with language, when as if he had not been too confident, and so soon as he had put the wine into a quart pot had immediately gone away, he might have escaped undiscovered; but it was his fortune so to be found out to the great admiration of the whole company, who although they found themselves cheated, yet were hugely pleased with the manner, and made it their discourse in all Taverns they came into for a long time after; but I believe it was to as little purpose with others, as with our folks, for when any such tricks or cheats have been told in our house, our people would only give them the hearing, and seem to be astonished with the discourse, but be never a whit the better for it, but immediately upon the next opportunity do the same thing or as bad, and this was their constant practice; they would draw wine in glass bottles that were so thick at the bottom that when they were empty they were as heavy as if they were half full, and also batter'd pots that would not hold out measure, and sometimes would fill a pot not above three quarters full, and when the Drawer brought it in, he would presently fill out a glass, and stare them in the face as Juglers do when they are about their *Hocus Pocus*, slight of hand tricks, and so carry it off, and out of pretence to civility to fill the first glasses they would do it, but their end was quite different, it being only to deceive them and to hinder them from seeing the false measure that is brought them, which cannot be discovered when a glass or two is filled out.

Mine Host was finely caught one day with a pot not being filled: Two Old Country men coming to our house in a morning called for a quart of wine, the Drawer believing they were to be choused, brought up a quart pot, but it was little more than half full, he intended they should have it raw, but it being a cold morning, they bad him rost it, that is put it to the fire and burn it; he was now at a loss in not filling out the first glass, but not knowing how to help it, he did set it down before the fire, and I suppose, he intended to fill it up afterwards, but he forgetting that, and the old men being busie in discourse forgot to look to it, when on a sudden they look'd, and the pot was melted almost half way down, which was as far as there was no wine in it; with that the maid seeing it call'd out to them, what honest men do you melt your pot? Not we, said they, it is the fire, but you are like to pay for it, replyed the wench, that is when we do, said they, at this mine Host came up, the maid tells how that these two old men had been telling their *Canterbury* tales so long that the pot was melted, then they must pay for it said mine Host, for it was given to their charge; thereupon the Drawer was call'd, who likewise averred that he gave them the pot with the wine into their charge and custody, and that therefore they ought to look after it, and since it was damaged to pay for it. They replyed, they took no charge of it, neither did they touch it, but only ordered him, to burn it well: mine Host said they should pay, and they said they would not, whereupon he threatened them with a Justices Warrant; they were somewhat unwilling to be troubled, and were content to pay for the wine, and allow six pence more for mending the pot, mine Host replying that would not do, for it could not be mended, and he must have a new one; they seeing him so unreasonable, were content the Justice should decide the Controversie; wherefore before the Justice they went, and mine Host there made his Complaint that those two men had melted his quart pot, and refused to pay for it. The Justice perceiving where the matter lay, and that he told his tale wrong, desired the men to speak, who in plain terms told him they took no charge of the pot, but onely desired the Drawer to cause Wine to be burnt, that he had accordingly set it down by the fire, and without their handling or touching it, the pot was melted. So, said the Justice, and did neither of you drink of the Wine? No, not one drop, replyed the old men, and yet we offered to pay for the Wine, and give sixpence towards mending the pot. This is more than you shall need to do, said the Justice, & then he thuss proceeded to mine Host.

Friend, with what confidence can you demand any money of these men that had nothing of you? since you would not do them justice, I will; I do hereby acquit them from paying any thing for Wine, because they never had any; and for the melting the pot, how did they do it? It was not they, but your servant who drew the Wine, who had he filled the pot full of wine, the fire could not have melted it; for I very well understand that the pot was melted no further than it was empty: And further, continued the Justice, this shall not serve your turn, for I shall Fine you for not filling your pot; Your Crime is very apparent and evident, and so shall your punishment be, and I order you, as a Fine, to pay down Twenty shillings for your misdemeanor, or else I shall make your *Mittimus*, and send you to Prison. Thus was the Case altered, and the Tale was now of another Hog; for mine Host who expected satisfaction, was forced to give it, and that immediatly, or else go to Prison.

This went against the hair, but Necessity hath no Law, and therefore down he paid the money, and came home heartily vexed, not so much for the money he had paid, as for the disgrace he received; for he was now become the Town-talk: But however, since he could not help the disgrace, he was forced to be contented with that; but for his loss, he soon fetch'd it up either in false measures, Over-reckonings, or some such practises as I have told you. And besides these extraordinary gains he made by Drink, he had his ways to cheat in Victuals, he would reckon for a Dish of anchoves that stood him in ten pence, or a shilling, two shillings or half a Crown at the least; and carry them in a large Dish an inch asunder from one another. *Whestphalia* Ham of Bacon he would cut so thin, and make such a large show of a little meat, that he would reckon two shillings for that which stood him in two groats; nay, and sometimes be paid six pence for fouling of Linnen to it. A Neats-tongue of two shillings, he would reckon four shillings, or four shillings six pence for it, nay though they were cheated of part of it, as I remember he was caught in the manner about one. A Neat's-tongue being call'd for, and carried in to the Guests, but first (as the manner is) it was slit down quite through the middle, and not barely so, but mine Hostess her self had gelded it, and cut off from each side a fine large slice, which she intended for some other Gentlemen in the House, to draw down th'other Bottle of wine. This Neats-tongue being carried to the Guests, one of them complained of the cutting it, saying, he had rather have had it whole; for (said he) there is less loss in cutting it in slices cross-ways than this. Why (said another) you may do so still, and thereupon he took the Tongue and clapt it together again, but it would not come close by above half an inch; and they discovered the place, where it had been pared, to look wide like a mouth: they perceiving the cheat, were resolv'd to try a little farther experiment, and therefore called in for mine Host, who with a *Sit you merry Gentlemen* came in: Landlord (said one) I pray what do you reckon for this Neats-Tongue? Not above four shillings, or four shillings sixpence, said he: I but that is too much reply'd the man, this is but a little one, and I think not a whole one. How! reply'd mine Host, not a whole one! that were a good jest indeed; I say tis a whole one, and a large one too. I'le wager a quart of Sack (said the Gentleman) that you are mistaken; Done, said mine Host: whereupon the Neats-Tongue was clapt together, and mine Host quickly saw that he had lost; he began to flounce and fluster, saying, that some of the company had done it; but leaving the Room, and going to his wife in the Kitchin, he soon found that he had lost indeed: the company being good guests to the house he was unwilling to displease them; wherefore he drew a quart of wine, went in and acknowledged his error, and paid for it, excusing the matter as well as he could, and they took all in good part. Thus was he sometimes caught, and paid for it; but not once in twenty times but he caught his guests, and made them pay for it. They would not only cheat their guests, but their own servants bellies; for except they had good trading, that the Servants might feed on the reversione of their guests dinners, they were like to go without, or at least have a poor one: she was very niggardly, and when they had salt fish, which was commonly once a week, she would allow them neither Oyl nor Butter, but only Mustard, but she was broken of that custom in this manner; after they had one day din'd with fish, drest as I tell you, down stairs went one servant, then another, and so one after another they all dropt away and went into the Cellar; where when they were come, the Drawer said, now to our old Custom, that is, since we have had no oyl nor butter, to our fish, we will soak it in sack, my friends, and that of the best, every one his half pint, and so away to our business: mine Host having some business with some of the servants, and finding them all missing, went to the Cellar door, and there he not only heard this proposition made by the Drawer, but saw it also confirmed and executed; whereupon he went to his wife, and commanded her for the future to allow his servants not onely oyl with their mustard to their salt fish, but butter and eggs too if they would have it, and so they had for the future. I have known mine Host sell and take money for one Joynt of meat twice, in this manner: when a Feast hath been above stairs, Joynts of Meat, and Fowles that have hardly been touched, have been brought down and sold to guests below, as fresh brought from the fire, at a very good rate: indeed no opportunity hath been omitted, to gain money. There was a pretty passage hapned about a couple of guests, that upon occasion lay there two or three nights together; thus it was: two men came one night to lodge, and being not well in health, it having been cold and rainy, they desired a good fire in their Chamber, which they had without any supper, or any drink, but a quart of burnt wine, and so they went to bed: the next day proving cold and rainy and their business not being very urgent, they continued there, and kept their Chamber, with little victuals, and as little drink; but however they kept a good fire, and mine Host seeing they had little else but fireing, was resolved he would get sufficiently by that, and therefore the next morning when they call'd to know what was to pay, he reckoned them ten shillings for fireing for two nights and one day: this demand they thought was very unreasonable, but, they knew that they could not help themselves, for he would have what he demanded; and besides, to say truth, firing was very scarce and dear in that Country: the two Travellers paid their shot, and intended to leave the house, but the weather proved so cold and stormy, they could not; wherefore they were forced to stay; but they resolved withall to be better Husbands of their fireing than they had been, but could not tell how, till in the end looking about the house they saw a great old fashion'd Bed-stead, that lay useless in a Hole: they not telling for what use, asked my Landlord the price of it, who not dreaming of their purpose, in few words sold it to them for five shillings; when they had bought it, they hired a fellow for one shilling to cut it in pieces fit for fireing; and now being furnished with fewel, they resolved to keep a good fire which they did, and calling for mine Host, and a quart of wine, bad him welcome to their good Husbandry; for the wood they had bought of the bed-stead was as much agen as they had paid ten shillings for, wherefore they made a good fire, and sung old rose in the gun-room. Mine Host being thus beaten at his own weapons, and his own Goods by himself sold to his loss, was somewhat netled, and discovered his anger to his servants. Master (said the unhappy boy) if you please I'le be revenged of them: do if you can (said the Master) not doing mischief. The boy having a commission, was not long e're he put it in execution; for joyning another Servant in confederacy with him, they went that evening to wait on the two guests, when among other matters they talked of spirits and apparitions; quoth the boy, we are often troubled with them here, and especially in this Chamber: I am sorry for that (said one of our Travellers) for I am very fearful of any such things: and thus the boy possed them with fear of that which he intended and executed; for about midnight he and his confederate took a Calf out of the Cow-house, and tying his four legs together, but so as he might not only stand, but go a little; they put him into our Travellers chamber, and there waited the event; it was not long e're the Calf began to pace it about the Room, making an unusual noise; and in this manner he continued stamping till both our Travellers were awake, who hearing the noise, were possessed with fear and astonishment, supposing it to be a spirit that was told them of: thereupon they shrunk close into the bed for fear; the noise continuing, and no harm or danger coming to them, at length one of them consented to rise and light a candle to see what was the matter; a candle was found, and some remains of fire being still in the chimney, thither he went: and stooping down fell a blowing with his mouth to light the candle, the Calf seeing a light, went thitherwards, and espying somewhat that was pendulous between the Travellers Legs, and taking it to be his Mother Cows Teat, thrust his chaps thitherwards, and seizing it in his mouth, fell full lustily to sucking, the Traveller perceiving himself caught by the Members, and not knowing by what, and being in fear of losing them, fell a roaring very loud, to the great sorrow and grief of his bed-fellow, and as great joy of our unhappy Boy and his Confederate.

CHAP. XI.

Six Country Blades steal a Goose and two Hens; by the contrivance of two of them and the Host; the other four pay soundly for them, and laugh at their Companions. A Traveller by a mistake lies with another mans Wife. A noise of Fidlers are forced to pay for their sawciness.

The poor Traveller, who was thus used by the Calf, still continued his roaring out, and the Calf being hungry, did suck very hard, but to no purpose, our young Crack-rope and his Companion still listening and laughing: but in fine, the noise continuing, and they doubting that there was more than sport, they entered the Chamber, where they saw the Calf close to the Traveller, but could not tell what he did there; but the Traveller still making a noise, they came near, and perceiving the Calfs mistake; they thrust somewhat into his mouth, and thereby disingaged him from the Travellers Bawble: He still lay on the Ground whilst they carried the Calf out of the Chamber, soon returning with a lighted Candle to see what was the matter: the Traveller was by that time somewhat come to himself, and feeling that he had lost nothing, was indifferently satisfied: they being now entered the Chamber, asked what was the matter? and wherefore he made so much noise? he now looking about the Chamber, and seeing nothing but People with a light, whom he knew, could not well tell what answer to give, only he told them, that the Devil, or some wicked Spirit had been there, and he had like to have been mischiev'd by him, but that now he found himself well again: his Fellow-Traveller likewise said that there had been some walking in the Chamber, but what it was, and wherefore his Companion roared out, he knew not: in fine, they who had done the mischief were thanked for their readiness to come and assist them; and so with some perswations our Traveller went to bed again, where he lay till the next morning, although he slept not, so great was his fear of the foul Fiend; but so soon as morning came they both arose, and though the weather still continued cold and rainy, yet they could not be perswaded to stay any longer in our Inn, but paying their reckoning left it, and half their wood behind them; so that mine Host was now no looser by this bargain, it being ready cleft to sell to the next cold Guest that should arrive there.

The last passage hapned in the Winter time, a little before *Christmas*, which soon after coming, we had two or three notable Accidents that befel in our Inn; the first was this: half a dozen of young Country Blades had been abroad a Fowling, or a Fooling rather, and among other purchase that they had, they coming near a Farm-house where there was store of Poultry, at two shots which they made, they kill'd two Hens and a Goose: this with the rest of their Game they brought to our house to be dressed against the next day for dinner: they drank some bottles of wine when they brought them, and being merry (said one) we will to morrow drink a health to the owner of the Hens and Geese: well, that we will (said another,) but I would not for forty shillings that he should know of it, for if he did, I doubt he would make us pay sawce: and truly I am yet somewhat fearful that we shall be discovered: so am I, said another, and so a third; well, if we be found out we can pay for them, and my share shall be ready. This was their discourse, and so for that time they parted; but it was not long ere two of the Company returned, and calling for a bottle of wine fell heartily a laughing; and (sayes the one to the other) I am resolved it shall be so, and with the assistance of mine Host we may carry the matter very closely; and thereupon mine Host was call'd for: he being come, they told him that they must have his assistance in a design, which he promised should not be wanting, and thereupon one of them thus began: mine Host, we have this day, as you know, been a Fowling, and part of what we brought in we plunder'd for, or in plain English, stole; now some of our Company are very conscious of their guilt and are not only penitent, but fearful; now it is our design to increase their fear, and get some money out of them to make us merry; and thus we have contrived it: to morrow when we are towards the latter end of our dinner, I would have you to tell us, that there is a Country fellow, who enquires for such persons as we are, and likewise that he was here as this day to enquire of us, and that he talks of a warrant that he hath against us about some Poultry his Master lost, and that he suspected us to be guilty; and withal you may add, that he is resolved to have the Law against us, and that you have had much adoe to perswade him to be patient till we had din'd. Mine Host having heard the instructions, was no Fool, but soon understood them, and procur'd a Country Fellow to manage the business so well, that they should be all startled, only (said he) you shall allow him half a Crown for his labor, and the rest that he gets of you (for I know you intend a Composition) shall be justly return'd you. Thus was this Affair agreed on, and accordingly the next day managed: for the Guests also came at the hour appointed, and merrily drank about till Dinner was brought in; which being come they fell to eating, and the Goose being well nigh eaten, a Glass of Wine was call'd for to drink a Health to the Owner, and mine Host himself was then call'd for up to make one in the Frolick: he being come, and seeing whereabouts Causes went, thought it now a fit time to begin, and therefore he thus bespeaks the Company: Gentlemen, I understand your Health, and shall willingly drink it, but if I be not mistaken, you will have but little cause to be so merry on this occasion: why? what's the matter, says one? what's the matter, said another? I'le tell you presently, reply'd mine Host, but first let us drink; whereupon up went his Glass, and down Gutter-lane went the Wine, and mine Host being grave in his Countenance, and slow in his Speech, they all, as amazed, star'd either on him or one another, wondring what should be the meaning of mine Host's Speech: At length he spake, and acquainted them with the business, just as he and two of the Company had agreed on; then having done, added farther, That he had endeavoured to underfeel the Fellow that was below, but he found him very obstinate, and doubted very much that he woad make no end but what the Law should: How! (said one) is your fooling come to this! Oh Lord! (said another) we have brought our Hogs to a fair Market: Well (said a third) but what must we do in this case? Truly (said mine Host) if I may advise you, I would have one of you go down to treat with the Fellow, and see what composition you can draw him to: This was in the end thought to be the best way, and thereupon one went down with mine Host; so soon as the Country-man saw him (being well instructed in every thing) he cries out, nay, I am sure I am in the right, for though the man hath changed his Clothes, yet that won't serve his turn: I know you well Sir, said he, by your hair and beard: What do you know replyed the guest? why I know, said the Countryman that you are one of the six that stole my Masters two Hens and Goose; I saw you well enough when you did it, and know you all well enough when I see you again; I follow'd you hither yesterday, & see you hous'd, and able to swear before Mr. Justice that you are the persons; and my Master is resolved to prosecute you, for he hath lost as much Poultry this winter as is worth five pound, and now we have found you you shall pay for all. How! (said the Guest) surely you do not mean as you say; one body may be like another, and you may be mistaken; and besides, if it were so, that we were the Parties, you mean yet a great deal less than five Pound, which I hope will serve the turn for two hens and a goose, which you say is all you lost. I (said the fellow) that is all indeed that we lost yesterday, but I tell you five pound will not pay for all my Master hath lost within this moneth, and my Master and I both believe you had them all, or else you would not so readily have found the way into our yard; and therefore I say, and so my Master sayes, that you shall pay for them. Nay friend, (said mine Host) I pray let me perswade you to be more reasonable in your demands; reason me no reasons,(said the fellow) it was unreasonable for them to come and rob my Master, and therefore I will not be reasonable; I am sure I shall lose my share of Goose and other Poultry this *Christmas*, that I should have had, had not we been robb'd. Nay but come, (said mine Host) let me take up this matter: I say you shall not, (reply'd the Fellow) the Justice shall know the matter, and no body else; but if they be your friends, if you will make an end, and pay me the money, I'le be rul'd by you. Whereupon mine Host took the Fellow by the Arm, and leading him into a drinking room, said, come let you and I talk a little further of this matter, and in the mean time, said he to the Guest, go you up to your Friends and confer with them about it. How, said the fellow, you mean to lead me out of the way while they get away from me. No, replyed mine Host, I'le pass my word for their appearance. Nay, that matters not much, quoth the fellow; for I have such a Warrant in my pocket, as will fetch them again in the Devils name. Having thus said, he and mine Host went to drink a pot of Ale together, and laugh a while; in the mean time our Guest went up to his companions to relate how things were like to go with the fellow, but he needed not tell them, for they being all concern'd, had listned at the stairs head to what the Fellow had said, and therefore knowing in what case they were, they all agreed to contribute to the fellows satisfaction, but they thinking five pounds were too much, grumbled at the demand, but was resolved to give that rather than fail, and have further trouble. One of the two confederates seeing how matters went, and though he was willing to put a trick upon his companions, yet thought five pounds was too great a sum to get by waggery, he therefore made a proposal that he would go down to the fellow and mine Host and treat with them, and he would warrant to get the business of for a great deal less: They were soon content with the proposition, whereupon down he went, and after some time spent with mine Host and the Country man, he returned, saying, Come, come Friends, draw your moneys, for I have ended the Controversie, and I hope to your content; we must be Noble-men, a Noble a piece, in all Forty shillings is the sum agreed upon to compound this brabling Business, and herein we are much engaged to mine Host for his civility, who hath much perswaded the fellow, and indeed the fellow by his perswasions is brought to be so civil, that I have promis'd him Half a Crown for himself. All the Company were all well contented with this Composition, and thereupon readily laid down their money, which one of our Confederates pretended to carry down to the fellow, but he put it up in his own pocket, onely giving him the Half Crown he had promised, and ordering half a dozen of Beer more for managing the Affair so handsomly. And thus was this Adventure ended, and in short time the Company separated, but the two Confederates soon came back again, and shared stakes of the moneys, and there they laughed at the easiness and credulity of their Companions, and mine Host was as merry as they, and had as much cause, for if the Proverb be true, *Let them laugh that win*, he was sure to win most, and therefore might well laugh; for he made them pay sawcily for the Sawces to their Goose, and in the confusion they were then in, it was no hard matter to mis-reckon them several bottles of Wine, and the two Confederates who onely managed this Affair to make sport and not for gain, delivered all their profits, which was 26s. 8d. into mine Hosts hands to be spent two or three days after, when they were to bring more company to laugh at this Adventure, and I remember they then came, and mine Host knowing they came easily by their moneys, was resolved to put in for a share of it, and so he did, and had it; for they had but three Dishes of Fish, but he again made them pay for their Sawce, reckoning fourteen shillings for that and dressing it, although the Fish it self did cost but half so much; these were his Tricks.

But there was about that time such a trick plaid by a mistake, as I have seldom heard of: Several Companies were in the house and lodged there, and it being long nights, much of that tedious time was spent in Gaming, and higgedly piggedly one with another, all Companies mixt in that pastime; but it growing late, those that were weary and sleepy dropt away to bed: Among the rest, one man who had a very handsome woman to his Wife went to bed, and his Lodging was in a Chamber where there was another Bed; the man being in Bed, laid his wearing Clothes, *viz.*, Doublet, Breeches and Cloak upon him, and putting out the candle went to sleep; in short time after, another single man who was to lodge in the Bed in the same Chamber went up, and walking about, a conceit came into his head, that it was probable he might have a Shee-bedfellow, and in order thereto he thus carried his on Design: He put off his own Clothes, and laid them very orderly on the Bed where the man was asleep, first taking off those of his Chamber-fellows, and when he had done, he very fairly spread them on the Bed he was to lye in; having done this, he went to bed and put out his Candle, expecting the event, which happened to be so as he hoped and expected; for not long after up came the woman, intending to go to bed to her Husband, undrest herself, and seeing and well enough knowing her Husbands clothes, believing that to be a sufficient sign of her Husbands being there, not looking on the face which was purposely hid, she put out her Candle & went to Bed to the wrong man, who although he pretended then to be asleep, yet he did her right before morning; for she still supposing it was her husband, gave him free liberty to do what he would. Her bed-fellow, though he had taken much pains and was weary, yet towards morning considering that if this matter were discovered, he might have sower Sauce to his sweet Meat, studied and contrived how to come off as well as he had come on, and therefore turning to his Bed-fellow and kissing her, &c. as a Farewel, he pretended to rise and make water, went out of the Bed; he soon found the way to his Chamber-fellows Beds side, and there took off his clothes, dress'd himself and departed. The woman missing her Bed-fellow, which she thought had been her Husband, much wondred what was become of him, and lay and studied in great confusion, she knew not what to do or say, and she began to distrust that she had a wrong Bedfellow, especially when she consider'd with herself that her Husband was not wont to be so kinde: when she was partly sensible of the mistake, she could not tell how to think of a remedy; if she should arise and go into the other Bed, she might chance to be mistaken again, and therefore in this confusion she knew not what to do: whilest she was in these thoughts a maid with a Candle appeared, who passing through the Room gave her clear sight that her Husband was in the other Bed, she therefore resolved now to rise, take her Clothes, and go to Bed to her Husband; but he who had slept hard all night was now awaked with the noise of the maid passing through the Chamber, and therefore he leaps out of the Bed and felt for a Chamber-pot, at the length he found one, having used it, and going to return to Bed where he had layen, his wife then took the opportunity to call to him, saying, Sweet-heart, whither go you? you mistake your Bed: No sure, said the man, where are you? Here, she said; he hearing her voice soon found out where she was, but could not presently be perswaded that he had layen there all night, you shall see that by and by, replyed she, when you can see your clothes on this Bed: if it be so, then you are in the right said he, and that he agreed to soon after day light appeared and he seeing his clothes on the Bed, was satisfied: and thus was his business done, and he not knew it, and the woman in the morning enquiring for the man who had been her Chamber-fellow, could not finde him; she was earnest in her inquiry after him, and this raised some jealousie in me, but I was soon after resolved of all by the man himself, who came again to our house and told me. This was a fine Christmas Frolick, I will adde one more, and so have done with them.

The Fidlers of our Town haveing had good trading this *Christmas* were grown proud and surly, and had abused some Gentlemen, who told mine Host of it; he who was good at inventing mischief, soon contrived a way to be revenged of them, and in order thereunto, the next day a considerable Dinner was bespoke, and the Fidlers were sent for to attend and play to them, which they did all Dinner. The Gentlemen having dined, the Fidlers had the Remains for their Dinner, and then again they fell a tuning their instruments and played lustily, whilest the Guests drank of their Cups as roundly; at length they fell to Dancing, and many Countrey Dances they had, spending the day in all manner of Jovial and Sprightly Recreations; the night being come, and therefore a fit time to put their plot in execution, they again Danced several Rambling Dances, and anon they all desired and agreed to Dance the Cushion-dance, which they did, and in their humours rambled from one Room to another all over the house, this musick pacing it afore them, and now one dropt away, and anon another, till in the end all the Guests were gone, and none were left but the Fidlers, who still plaid on expecting their Company. Mine Host seeing it was now time came into them, and causing them to cease their playing, asked where are the two guests? they reply'd they knew not: no, said he, if you do not finde them, you are like to suffer; for if you have played away my Guests, you shall pay their reckoning: he was so peremptory in his demands, that it was to no purpose to contradict it; and the reckoning amounting to three pounds, he made the five Fidlers pay ten shillings a man, and told them he was a looser in abaiting them ten shillings of his reckoning; they were forced and could not help it, and therefore paid down their dust, and they who had not money enough were fain to leave their Fidles, and go home without, and end *Christmas* to the Tune of *Lachrymæ*.

CHAP. XII

Mris. Dorothy *discourses of mine Hosts misfortunes, As first how he was cheated of a Silver Bowl. Secondly, of a thirty pound reckoning; and Thirdly, was carried away Prisoner, and forced to pay Fifty pound for his Ransom.*

Thus, continued Mris. *Dorothy*, was this revenge managed by mine Host and the Guests who had the reckoning of thirty pound to pay, came the next day and paid it, and then appointed to come the next week and spend the fifty shillings mine Host had gotten from the Fidlers, which they did accordingly; and thus said she, did we finish our *Christmas*: and now I hope, friends, said she to me and Mris. *Mary*, that you will give me leave to finish my discourse; not so long as you can think of any more of these stories, replyed I, and so did M. *Mary*; and thereupon we both joyned in our desires to entreat her to proceed. Well, replyed she, if I must, then I will alter the Nature and Quality of my discourse, and as I have told you of mine Hosts good fortune, and wayes to get money, so I will acquaint you with some of his misfortunes, and how he lost money; for Fortune was the same thing to him as she hath been to me, and I think to all others; we all have our several turns and changes, sometimes we are on the top, and anon on the bottom of Fortunes Wheel; and as that is, so is the World, round and rouling, and still in motion, and so are our Fortunes various: I replyed, I had full experience of this truth, and could freely subscribe to it; but, continued I, good honest *Doll*, let us be beholding to you so much as to prevent your discourse, and relate all the other transactions that you can remember befel during your stay in this pleasant place, for by what you have told us, I must needs term it so. We, said she, since you will have it so, i'le endeavour to satisfie you, and then she thus began.

I have already told you of one of my Hosts misfortunes in the quart pot, and how he was forced to pay twenty shillings instead of satisfaction which he expected; it was not long before that, that he had a more sensible loss, for one morning in comes a Countryman which calls for a Flaggon of Beer, and desires a private Room, for, sayes he, I have company a coming to me, and we have business. The Tapster accordingly shews him a room, and brings a Flaggon of Beer, and with it a Silver Cup worth three pound; the Countryman drank off his beer, and call'd for another Flaggon, & withal for mine Host to bear him company: mine Host seeing him alone, sate and talked with him about state affairs, till they were both weary & mine host was ready to leave him: well, said the Countryman, I see my Company will not come, and therefore I will not stay no longer, neither did he; but having drank up his Beer, he call'd to pay: A groat, quoth the Tapster; there 'tis, said the Countrey-man, laying it down, and so he went out of the Room, the Tapster staide behinde to bring away the Flaggon and Silver Cup, but though he found the Flaggon, yet the Cup was not to be found, wherefore he hastily runs out and cries, *Stop the man*. The Countrey-man was not in such haste, but that he quickly stopt of himself; he was not quite out of the doors, and therefore he soon returned to the Bar, where when he was come, he said, Well, what is the matter? what would you have? The Cup, said the Tapster that I brought to you; I left it in the Room, said the Country-man: I cannot finde it, said the Tapster: and at this noise mine Host appeared, who hearing what was the matter, said, I am sure the Cup was there even now, for I drank in it; it is there still for me, said the Countrey-man: Look then further, said mine Host; the Tapster did so, but neither high nor low could he finde this Cup; well then, said mine Host to the Countrey-man, if it be gone you must have it, or know of the going of it, and therefore you shall pay for it: Not I, said the Countrey-man, you see I have none of it: I have not been out of your house, nor no body hath been with me, how then can I have it? you may search me. Mine Host caused him to be searched, but there was no Cup to be found, however mine Host was resolv'd not to lose his Cup so, and therefore he sends for a Constable, and charges him with the Countrey-man, and threatens him with the Justice; all this would not do, and the Countrey-man told him, *That threatned Folks live long*, and if he would go before a Justice, he was ready to go with him. Mine Host was more and more perplexed, and seeing he could not have his cup, nor nothing confess'd, before the Justice they went, when they came there mine Host made his complaint, and told the story as truely it was, and the Country-man made the same answer there, as he had done before to mine Host; the Justice was perplexed, not knowing how to do justice, here was a Cup lost, and the Country-man did not deny but he had it, but gone it was, and although the Country-man was pursued he did not flie, he had no body with him, and therefore it could not be conveighed away by confederacy, and for his own part he had been, and was again searched, but none found about him, and he in all respects pleaded innocency: this, though considered and weighed in the ballance of justice, he could not think that the Country-man had it, and therefore to commit him would be injustice; he considered all he could, and inclined to favour the Country-man, who was altogether a stranger, and he believed innocent, especially when he considered what a kind of Person mine Host his accuser was, of whose life and conversation he had both known and heard enough, and cause him to believe that it might be possible that all this might be a Trick of mine Hosts to cheat the Country-man, and therefore he gave his judgement, that he did not believe by the Evidence that was given, that the Country-man had the Cup, and that he would not commit him unless mine Host would lay, and swear point blank Felony to his charge, and of that he desired mine Host to beware. Mine Host seeing which way it was like to go, said no more, but that he left it to Mr. Justice, who being of this opinion I told you of, discharged the country-man, and advised mine Host to let him hear no more of these matters, & if he could not secure his plate, & know what company he delivered it to, then to keep it up. Mine Host thanked the Justice for his advice, and so departed, the Countrey-man going about his business, and he returning home, being heartily vexed at his Loss, and the carriage of the whole Affair, which was neither for his profit nor credit; but he was forced to sit down with the Loss, being heartily vexed to think how he should lose the Cup: he threw away some money in going to a *Cunning-man* to know what was become of it, but all they could tell him was, that he would hear of it again, and so he did shortly after; though it was to his further cost, and to little purpose. He had some occasions at our Country-Town during the time of the Assizes, and there seeing the prisoners brought to their Trials, among others he espyed the Countrey-man whom he had charged with the Silver Cup, by enquiring what was his crime? was told it was for picking a Pocket: Nay then, said mine Host, I may chance to hear of my Bowl again, and thereupon when the Tryal was over, and the Prisoners carried back to the Goal, he went and enquired for the Countrey-man, to whose presence he was soon brought; Oh Lord, master! said he, how do you? who thought to have seen you here? nay said mine Host, who thought to have seen you here? I believe you have not met with so good friends in this Countrey as you did at our Town, of our Justice; but let that pass, come let us drink together, whereupon a Flaggon of Beer was call'd for, and some Tobacco, which they very lovingly drank off, and smoak'd together; which done, said mine Host to the Countrey-man; I would gladly be resolved in one point which (I question not) but you can do; I suppose you mean (said the Countrey-man) about the old business, of the Silver Cup you lost; yes truly said mine Host, & the losing of it doth not so much vex me, as the manner how it was lost; & therefore, continued he if you will do me the kindness, to give me satisfaction what became of it, I do protest I will acquit you although you are directly guilty. No, this will not do, replyed the Country-man, there is somewhat else in the case: well then, said mine Host, if you will tell me, I will give you ten shillings to drink. Ready money does very well in a Prison, said the Country-man, and will prevail much; but how shall I be assured you will not prosecute me, if I should chance to be concerned? for that, replyed mine Host, I can give you no other Warrant but my Oath, which I will inviolably keep: well then said the Country-man, down with the merry Griggs, let me handle the money, and I'le be very true to you; and as for your charging me with it, I fear you not. Mine host being big with expectation to know how this cleanly conveyance was wrought, soon laid down the ten shillings; and then the Country-man thus proceeded: I must confess that I know which way your Cup went, but when you charged me with it I had it not; neither was it out of the room, and I must tell you this, that if you had sought narrowly, you might have found it, but it was not there long after. We who live by our wits must work by policy more then down right strength, and this cannot be done without Confederates, and I had such in the management of this affair, for I left the Cup fastned with soft wax under the middle of the board of the Table where I drank, which place of the Table by reason it was covered with a cloath, as you may remember it was, it could not well be seen; and therefore you and your servants missed of it: you know that very willingly I went with you to the Justices; and whilst we were gone those Friends and Confederates of mine whom I had appointed, and knew the Room and everything else, went into the house, and into the same Room, where they found the silver Cup, and without the least suspition went fairly off with it, and at a place appointed we met, and there acquainted one another with our Adventures, and what purchases we had made, we equally shared them between us. Mine Host at the hearing of this discourse was mightily surprized, although fully satisfied; but yet, said he, I would be resolved one question, which is this, how if we had found it where you had put it whilst you were there? why truly replyed the cheat (for now I may call him so) then you could have charged me with nothing, and I would have put it off with a jest, and if that would not have done, the most you could have done, had been only to have kicked and beaten me, and those things we of our quality must venture: you know the old Proverb, *Nothing venture, nothing have,* and *Faint heart never won fair Lady*; and we have this other Proverb to encourage us, that *Fortune helps the bold*; as it doth commonly those of our quality, and she did me I thank her in that attempt. And there did this Varlet descant upon his Actions, to the great satisfaction of mine Host, who finding there was no more to be had of him, left him, and soon after the Town; coming home, and giving us an account of this adventure; and this was another of his misfortunes, which was soon after followed by another worse than the last, and thus it was. A Company of pretending Gallants one evening arrived at our house, and there was in their company a young lad of about ten years of age, on whom they all waited, giving him respect equal to a Person of Honor, and their Master; they were soon furnished with Lodgings, the best in the house, where they bespake a plentiful supper, which was provided, drest, and sent to them. Mine Host enquiring what, and who the young Gentle-man was, whom he supposed was their Master; they told him that he was the Son of a *French* Marquess, giving him a name to that purpose, and that his Father their Lord and Master, would in few dayes be there; likewise that they being recomended to this house by a Friend of his, who warranted them good usage, they were come thither, and there they intended to stay till their Lord came. Mine Host was highly pleased with this recital, and he questioned not the truth of it, because the young Gentleman could not or would not speak any thing but a little Gibberish *French*. These Guests staid there a fortnight eating and drinking in most plentiful manner; and every day some or all of them did ride out, leaving only one person to wait on their Lord, and they came home very honestly at night. They had now been fourteen dayes and lain at Wrack and Manger, they and their Horses; and their Bill amounted to thirty pounds, which being a round sum of money; he began to try if he could get any, and to that end spake by the by to him that was chief person next to the young Lord, but he was deaf of that ear, and told him that it would not be above two or three dayes e're he was sure their Lord himself would come, and then he should not only be paid, but also rewarded for the care, and respects he had shewed to his Son: Mine Host was satisfied with their reasons, and so went about his business; and so did this Blade about his; for calling a consultation of his Brethren, they resolved to be gone the next day, and give mine Host the go by for his Reckoning, and therefore they so ordered the matter, that that night whilst they were at supper, and mine Host with them; in enters another man, a new face, and enquired if my young Lord such a one, and his Attendants were there? yes said the Hostler, who took his Horse, and then calling the Chamberlain, he was conducted into the Room where the rest of his Acquaintance were, he being entered the Room, made his obeysance to his young Master; and then putting his hand into his Pocket pull'd out a Letter, which he presented to him; and another who sate next him took from him, opened, and read, telling mine Host that the Letter was from their Lord, who promised to be there with them by the next day at noon; glad did they seem to be, and so was mine Host, who thought now he was near the receiving of his money: the company then told him that he must provide a plentiful dinner, and that they would all ride forth in the morning to meet their old Master, only they would leave their young Master behind to his care; to this mine Host was content, and the next morning they arose early, mounted their horses, and away they went, leaving their Lord in Bed. Mine Host provided dinner according to the directions, and noon came, but no Lord, or Attendants; at length dinner was forced to be taken up, or spoiled, and then the young Lord was enquired for, who was still in Bed, and could not rise, for they had taken his fine Clothes with them: in fine, upon search, an old Country Suit was found, which now our young Lord owned to be his, and could speak *English*, saying, they were gone and carried away his fine cloaths. Mine Host hearing he could speak *English*, asked him several questions, which the Boy answered readily enough, and by that he understood that they took him up in those Clothes, and other rare matters if he would go with them, be ruled by them, and learn a few heard words; and so in conclusion mine Host found to his cost, that they were a company of cheats, who came to do that to him, he had done to others, and though his loss was great, yet he was forced to sit down contented; as for the Boy he being absolutely innocent, he was only turned out of the doors to seek his fortune. Thus, said Mistress *Dorothy* you see he had his bitter with the sweet, and to his sweet meat he had sower sawce; and although his loss was considerable enough, yet soon after he had another of worser consequence, and thus it was:

You must note, that it was now in the time of rebellion, and there was a small garrison of Souldiers quartered in our Town of the Round-heads Party, and about ten miles off there was another Garrison of Cavaliers. Now one day there came to our Town two Gentlemen very well mounted and armed, and they had a Pass from a round-headed Collonel our Neighbour, and coming to our Town, and enquiring for the best Inn, they were directed to our house, where they took up their Quarters; they pretended themselves to be Persons of Quality, and therefore spent pretty handsomely at the first, but in their stay there, which was about eight dayes, they had run five pounds on the score; mine Host desiring his money, they told him suddenly he should have it, moneys were coming to them, but if he had not the patience to stay until their money came, then (he knew) that they had two good Horses in his Stable, and he should in lieu of his money have which he pleased, at such a rate as any indifferent person should adjudg the best of them to be worth: mine Host seeing them answer him so fair, was as kind as they, and told them that he did believe them to be Gentlemen of quality, and that he scorned to undervalue them so much as to dismount them, and as they came on Horseback to depart on foot, but that he had rather wait a while longer for the Money, which they said they staid for: they kindly thanked him for his courtesie, and promised him to requite it; and thereupon all Persons rested well satisfied, but no money coming at the time they said they expected, he again asked them for moneys; and indeed it was their desire that he should do so, or else the design they had in hand, and intended to carry on, could not be well executed; and therefore that they might bring their project to execution, they again offered him one of their horses; he had a great mind to one of them, having a Customer ready that would give him a very good price, told them that since they were so willing he was so too, and that they might possibly have their Horse again when their money came: it is all as one for that, replyed the Gentlemen, we had rather go without horses than you should be dissatisfied, and therefore choose which of the two you will have: they being both, said he good, I care not which of them, and to that end if you please to morrow we will all three ride out of the Town a mile or so, and then you may conclude which you like best, and as for the price we will well enough agree upon that; to this mine host consented, and the next day they all three mounted their horses, and away they rode, but to the great sorrow of us all, for these Gentlemen who had lain thus long in our house were Caveliers, and belonged to the adjoyning Garrison, and when they had drawn mine host with them as far as they could willingly perswade him, and that he offered to return, they then drew, and with Sword in one hand, and Pistol in the other, they came up to him and commanded him to stand, for he was their Prisoner, he asked them for what? and would have disputed the case with them but it was to no purpose; they were deaf to all perswations, and he living in a Round-headed Garrison they concluded him to be one, and therefore he was their lawful Prisonor, and as one they would guard him to their quarters; so they said, and so they did, and taking his Sword from him, they caused him to ride on apace, till they brought him to their Quarters; before their Commander they conducted him, who adjudged him to be a Prisoner, and the next day resolved on his Ransome, which he valued at a hundred pounds: the one half he ordered the Gentlemen should have, and the other to be devided among the indigent Souldiers? this was his doom: and now my poor Host was delivered into Custody; he writ away to his Wife to acquaint her with this doleful News, she could not raise so much Money, and therefore he was like to continue; but in the end, by the assistance of some Gentlemen who were Guests to the house and Caveliers, she got one half of the Ransome to be abated, and so the fifty pounds being sent, he was delivered up, and came home to chear his Wife and Family.

CHAP. XIII.

At the execution of a Felon several Cheaters meet, and seeing a Countrey-man draw a Purse of money resolve to cheat him of it, which they do first by a brass Chain, and afterwards by drawing him in to bet at Gameing. They were again cheated by mine Host, and the principal Cheat comically punished.

Mistress *Dorothy* here putting a stop to her discourse, we thereby understood she had finished, wherefore I thus discoursed her: truly now I find that to be true of your Host, which I have experimented in myself, and that we must meet with many rubs & misfortunes, but these were but trivial to him considering his great comings in, by his extraordinary gain in trading: that's true replyed M. *Dorothy*, but as he had considerable gain, so he had many wayes to spend it, and many spenders, his Wife and Children being all as expensive as might be, and what was got over the Devils Back, was spent under the Devils belly: and therefore though much money went through his hands in a year, yet it went through, and little stuck there or staid with him, so that he was seldome Master of any considerable sum of money; and therefore it went hard to raise this sum of money, and some of his Plate was fain to march off to produce it; but that being paid and he come home, we were all well enough satisfied, and he told his wife this was most certainly the fortune of War, but he questioned not but in short time he would fetch it up again; as indeed he did in using those several ways I have told you of; and now I hope (said she) I have told you enough to satisfie your curiosity; truly, replyed I, you have taken a great deal of pains, but if you have any more in your budget out with them, for what you have hitherto related hath not only been pleasant but profitable, and very full of variety. Well, (replyed she) since you will have it so, I will proceed a little further, and recount some passages as considerable as any you have hitherto heard. There was (continued she) not long before this time a bloody murder committed, for an honest Country-man that lived about six miles from us, one market day was driving his Team of Horses and Cart loaden with Corn to our Town to sell, and being come about half way, he was met by a lusty tatterdemallion rascal that was on foot, travelling on the Road, he first asked the Countrey-man to give him something, telling him he was a poor Traveller and had been robb'd: quoth the Countrey-man, friend, I have nothing to give you, for I have no money, being now going to Market with this Corn to make money of it; the fellow seemed to rest contented with this answer, and thereupon walked on with the Countrey-man; but they had not gone far but the Devil entring into this fellow, perswaded him, here he might have a great prize, and therefore still walked on, he at length seeing the Road clear of Passengers, and a convenient place for him to put his purpose in practice, with a lusty Cudgel he had in his hand, he struck the poor Countrey-man over the Head, that down he fell a sprawling, and not content therewith, drew him a little out of the road, and in most cruel manner cut his throat; having this done, he seizes on the fore-horse of the Team, and leads him also with the Team and Cart out of the road to a convenient place, where he stops, and then drawing the body of the murthered Countrey-man to a Ditch-side, he there made a hole, and having strip'd him of all his clothes, buried him, and stripping himself of those Rags he had on, he putting on the Countrey-mans cloathes, buried his own with the Countrey-mans body; and having thus done, he lead the Team into the Road again; this was done one winters morning early before day; and so he had the conveniency to do all this without interruption, and now with Whip in hand, and habited like a Country-man, he drives on to our town to Market; he took up his standing at the usual place, and had the good fortune not to be questioned of any body, but enquiring how the rates of corn went, he accordingly sold his at a good price as any: and he not only made money of his Corn, but hearing there was a horse Fair that day at a Town but three miles off, and having dispatch't betimes he drove thither and soon had a Customer for both Horses and Cart, and there he bought him a saddle horse to ride on, being thus fitted to his purpose, he was not long e're he met with a company of Shirks and Cheats, who intending to chouse him, he was too crafty for them, and enters himself into their society, and by degrees became a Knight of the *Pad*, an obsolute High-way-man, but the Devil who had set him to work, was not long e're he paid him his Wages, for he was pursued for a Robbery he had committed, and so narrowly followed that he was forced to take the water, to cross a River, he leap'd in on Horseback, but the Horse was soon drowned, and he narrowly escap'd to a little Island in the River, where he was still in sight of his pursuers, they getting a Boat came up to him, he being armed attempted to discharge a Pistol, but by reason the powder was wet, it would not off whereupon they coming nearer to him he drew his Sword, and though there were three in the Boat he kept them from landing, and being resolved to sell his life at a dear Rate, he kill'd one of them out-right, and wounded another, but now another Boat with more help coming he was in danger to be lost, wherefore putting his Sword in his mouth he again took the water, and swam away, and they after him, but length seeing it was in vain to resist he suffered himself to be taken, and bound, led away to the Justice, and thence to Prison, where he believing he must dye, grew some what penitent, and not onely confess'd the Fact he was then accused for, but among other mischiefs he likewise acknowledged the Murther, and Robbery I have told you off; and the Assizes being come, and he tryed, and confessing, he was condemned to be hang'd in Chains at the place where he committed the murther; this being not above a mile from our Town, at the day of Execution it drew most of the people out of it to see the end of this wicked wretch, who did somwhat penitently, but his Penitence and Repentance did not work one jot upon others of his quality, who were there present; but as commonly one Wedding-feast begets another Wedding, so one Execution does usually produce another; and they who are Spectators at one Execution, in short time come to be executed themselves: whether there were any persons at this execution that did soon after take his turn, I know not, but I am sure there were present many Cheats, and Pick-pockets, and such sort of people, for our Town was that day pretty well throng'd with them. Among other practises that was used, this was one.

Two or three Cheaters going together saw a Country-man who had a Purse of money in his hand, they had observed him to draw it to pay for some Gingerbread he bought on the way; wherefore they closed with him, and endeavoured to nip his Bung, pick his Pocket, but could not, for he knowing he was in a dangerous place, and among as dangerous Company, put his Purse of money into his Breeches, which being close at the knees, secured it from falling out, and besides he was very sly in having any body come too near him. Our Practitioners in the Art of Thievery, seeing this would not do, set their wits a working further; and having all their tools about them in readiness, taking a convenient time and place, one of them goes before and drops a Letter, another of his Companions who had joyned himself to our Countrey-man, seeing it ly fairly for the purpose, sayes to him, Look you what is here! but although the Countrey-man did stoop to take up the Letter, yet the Cheat was too nimble for him in that, and having it in his hand, said, Here is somewhat else besides a Letter, I cry half, said the Country-man: well, said the Cheat, indeed you stoop'd as well as I, but I have it; however I'le be fair with you; but let us see what it is, & whether it is worth the dividing; & thereupon he breaks open the letter, & there sees a fair chain or neck-lace of Gold: Good Fortune (sayes the Cheater) if this be right Gold: how shall we know that, said the Countrey man? let us see what the Letter says, which being short and to the purpose spake thus:

Brother John, *I have here sent you back this necklace of gold you sent me; not for any dislike I have to it, but my Wife is covetous and would have a biggar, this comes not to above seven pounds, and she would have one of ten pounds; therefore I pray get it changed for one of that* price, *and send it by this bearer to your loving Brother,* N.B.

Nay, then we have good luck (said the Cheater) but I hope, said he to the Countrey-man, you will not expect a full share, for you know I found it, and besides, if we should divide it, I know not how to break it in pieces, but I doubt it would spoil it, therefore I had rather have my share in money. Well, said the Countrey-man, I'le give you your share in money, provided I may have a full share; that you shall, said the Cheater, and therefore I must have of you three pounds ten shillings, the price in all being as you see, seven pounds. I, but said the Countreyman (thinking to be too cunning for the Cheat) it may be worth seven pounds in money in all, fashion and all, but we must not value that, but only the Gold, therefore I think three pounds in money is better than half the Chain, and so much I'le give you if you will let me have it: well content said the Cheat, but then you shall give me a pint of wine over and above; to this the Countrey-man also agreed, and to our town they came, and into our house, and there the Cheat had the three pounds, and the Countrey-man the Chain, who believed he had that day risen with his A--- upwards, because he had met with so good fortune. They drank off their drink, and were going away, but the Cheat not having yet done with him (intended to get the rest of the money from him) offered him his pint of Wine, which the Countrey-man accepted of; but before they had drank it off, in comes another of the same Tribe, who asked whether such a man, naming one, were there? no, (said the Bar-keeper,) our Cheater and Countrey-man sitting near the Cheat, asked of the enquirer, did you not ask for such a man? Yes, said the enquirer, why said our Cheater, I can tell you this news of him that it will not be long e're he comes hither, for I met him as I came in; and he appointed me to come in here and stay for him: well, then I were best to stay, said the Enquirer: but (continued he) we were best to take a bigger Room, for we cannot stir our selves in this; agreed, said the Cheater, so the reckoning was paid, and they agreed to take a larger Room, leaving word at the Bar that if any enquiry were made for them, there they should find them; they went into another Room, and our Countrey-man having done his business would be going; no, said the Cheater, I pray stay and keep us company, it shall not cost you nothing; well, then said the Countrey-man, I am content to stay a little: they being now entred into their Room, call'd for a quart of Wine, and drank it off, what shall we do to spend time, said the last Cheater? for I am weary of staying for this man, are you sure you are not mistaken? no, said the other: one of them then pretends to walk a turn in the Room, and coming to the window behind a Cushion he pretends to finde a pair of Cards (which indeed he himself had laid there) look you here, said he to the Countrey-man and th'other, I have found some tools, now we may go to work, and spend our time, if you will play; not I, said the Country-man, I'le never play; then I will, said the other Cheat, but not for money: why then, said the other, for six pence, to be spent, and the Game Putt; they being agreed, and my Countrey-man being made Overseer of the Game, fell to playing, and the Countrey-mans first Acquaintance had the better of it, winning twelve Games to the others four: come, said he, what shall we do with all this drink? we will play two pence wet and four pence dry; to this the other agreed, and so they play'd, and at this low gaming the first Cheat had in short time won of the second ten shillings in money; the second seemed to be angry, and therefore proposed to play for all money, hoping to making himself whole again; nay, said the other, I shall not refuse your proposition, because I have won your money; and therefore to it they went, and the first Cheater had still the same luck, and won ten shillings more; then the other would play for twelve pence a Game, no, said the first Cheater, I am not willing to exceed six pence a Game, I will not alter what I have begun, lest I change luck, unless this honest Countrey-man will go my halves; I have no mind to Gaming, reply'd the country-man; you need not play said the other, I'le do that, and you see my luck is good, venture a Crown with me, you know both our lucke have been, and I hope will continue good; well, content, said the Countrey-man, and so they proceeded, still our first Cheat had good fortune, and he, and the Countrey-man won ten shillings a piece more of the other, which made them merry; and the other was mad; he therefore told them he would win the Horse, or lose the Saddle, and venture all now; and drawing out about thirty shillings; said, come take it all, win it and wear it; and so they played; but they had now drawn the Countrey-man in sufficiently, and he was flush; but it lasted not long thus, e're he was taken down a button-hole lower, for the fortune changed, and all that he had won was lost, and forty shillings more: He was now angry, but to no purpose, for he did not discover their foul play, and he in hopes of his good fortune ventured, and lost the other forty shillings; and then he said he would go halfes no longer, for he thought he would be merry and wise, and if he could not make a winning, he would be sure to make a saving Bargain, which he reckoned he should do, because although he had lost four pounds in money, & given the Cheat three pounds for his share of the Chain, that yet he should make seven pounds of the Chain, and so be no Loser: they seeing he would not play, left off, and he that had won the money was content to give a Collation, which was called for, but our first Cheat pretending much anger at his Loss, was resolved to venture more; and to playing again he went, and in short time he recovered much of his losses; this angred the Countrey-man that he had not joyned with him, and in the end, seeing his good luck continued, and that he won, he again went halfs, but then it was not long that they thrived, but the Countrey-man was forced to draw his Purse, and in the end lose all his money, which was near twenty pounds: He did not think his condition to be so bad as it was, because he believed he had a Chain worth seven pounds in his Pocket, and therefore he reckoned he had not lost all. By this time several of the rest of the Gang (having been abroad, employed on the same account, Couzening and Cheating of others) now flocked all to our House, being the place appointed for their Rendezvouz, there they acquainted one another of their several Gains and Prizes; and then they fell a drinking, they drank about lustily for joy, and the Countrey-man for anger; and mine Host was called up to make one in the Company; he soon understood what kind of Guests he had, and how they had cheated the poor Country-man; and therefore he was resolved to serve them in the same kind; he therefore put forward the Affairs of drinking, and some being hungry call'd for Victuals; he told them he would get them what they pleas'd; and they being determined to take up their Quarters there, for that night, a Supper was bespoke for all the Company, such as mine Host in his discretion should think fit, he told them they should have it, and accordingly went down to provide Supper, he soon returnes and helps them to drink whilst Supper was dressing; by this time they were all perfectly drunk, he then commands up supper, and they fall too with a Shoulder of Mutton and two Capons, eat and drink hard, and call for more, he tells them it is coming, but they now having sate still a while were all fallen asleep, he makes use of this opportunity, and brings up half a dozen empty foul Dishes, or at leastwise full of bones of several fowls; as Pidgeons, Partridges, Phesants, and all the Remains of Victuals that had been left in the house that day; and strews and places some on their several Trenchers, and thus he leaves them. Some of them sleeping, and sitting uneasily fell from their Chairs, and so awaked themselves; and their companions being throughly awaked, they again fell to eating and drinking; some turning over the bones that were brought, said, How came these here, I do not remember that I eat any such Victuals? Nor I, said another, whereupon mine Host was call'd, and the question was asked him: why surely, Gentlemen, you forget your selves, said he, you have slept fair; I believe you will forget the Coller of Brawn you had too, that cost me six shillings out of my Pocket; how! Brawn! said one, I, Brawn said mine Host, you had it, and are like to pay for it; you'l remember nothing anon, this is a fine drunken bout indeed; so it is, said one of the Company; sure we have been in a Dream; but it matters not, mine Host, you must and shall be paid: Give us the other dozen bottles, and bring a Bill, that we may pay our Reckoning. This Order was presently obey'd, and a Bill brought, which in all came to seven pounds; and I verily believe he misreckoned them for meat and drink, the one half, and told them he used them very kindly; they were bound to believe him, and therefore every man was call'd to pay their shares; my Countrey-man shrunk behind, intending to escape, which one of the Company seeing, call'd him forwards, and said Come, We must tell Noses, and every man pay alike; the Countrey-man desired to be excus'd; and said he had no money; which they knowing well enough, at length agreed to acquit him. This done, they went to their several Lodgings to bed, and it was time, for it was past midnight, they all slept better than the Country-man, who could hardly sleep a wink for thinking of his Misfortunes, and having such good luck in the morning, it should prove so bad e're night; But morning being come, he and they all arose, and the Countrey-mans money being all spent, he knew it was to no purpose for him to stay there; wherefore he resolved to go to the Goldsmith's in the Town, and sell, or pawn his Chain, that he might have some money to carry him home: Being come to the Goldsmith's he produced the Chain, which although at the first sight he thought to be gold, yet upon trial he found it otherwise, and that it was but brass guilt; he tells the Countrey-man the same, who at this heavy News was like to break his heart: The Goldsmith seeing the Countrey-man in such a melancholy dump, enquires of him how he came by it? he soon acquainted him with the manner, and every circumstance: the

Goldsmith as soon understood the Cheat, and advises him to go to the Justice, and get a Warrant for him that had thus cheated him: and the Countrey-man telling him that he had no money, nor friend, being a stranger; he himself went with him to the Justice, who soon understanding the matter, granted his Warrant; and the Goldsmith procured a Constable to go with him to our house, where the first Cheater was apprehended, and carried before the Justice; who upon examination explain'd the Case, and finding the fellow guilty, ordered that he should be led to the whipping post, and there be whipped, and then be sent on a horse back, with his face towards the horsetail, and so led out of the Town; and withal, the Justice sent away the Constable to our house, to apprehend and bring the rest of the gang before him; but he came too late, for the Birds were flown, doubting some such matter; so that only the first Cheater suffered the punishment aforesaid; but I remember he was so impudent that when he came by our house on horseback, with his face to the horse tail, Ah, ha! said one, what is the meaning of this? nothing, said the Cheater, but that this horse is given me, and I am resolved to ride this way to make good the Proverb, *that I may not look a gift horse in the mouth.*

CHAP. XIV.

Two Shoemakers are cheated of a pair of Boots, and mine Host gets another pair of them. Mine Host and one of the Shoemakers find out the Cheater, who is apprehended, and sent to Prison but is released by the Judge for an enterprize of his Companions, who acted wonderful Feats by slight of hand.

Thus was every one a gainer but the poor Countrey-man, who was forc'd to march home by weeping Cross, only with a brass chain worth eighteen pence, instead of above twenty pounds which he had brought out with him. Mine Host gained indifferently well, but the Cheaters more, being fully fraighted; but as they got it easily, so they spent it merrily; and then went to work for more, though they devided the spoil equally between them, yet none had the punishment but the Chain-Merchant, and I believe he had as many lashes on the back as there was links on the chain; he took his punishment very patiently, only when the blow came he would shrink up his shoulders, which a stander by seeing, told him that did him more harm than good; it is no matter for that, friend, said the cheater, you may spare your instructions, for I shall not follow them, and now I am to be whip'd I will do as I List, and when you come to the same sport, and it is your turn to be whip'd, you may behave your self then as you please, thus was he pleasantly roguish when he was in the midst of his punishment, and when he was on horse-back he answered the People as roguishly as I told you; but being come to the Towns end he was dismounted, and sent packing. Thus were we rid of one Crew of Cheats, but truly, if all the Cheats of the Town had been so served as this was, mine Host must also have march'd off, who had he had his due, did as justly deserve it; but it is the little sort of Knaves and Rogues that are punished, the greater scaping Scot-free, as now mine Host did. After this Trick we had another that was altogether as pleasant, and before the finishing of it, there were some pleasant passages, and thus it was.

A Gentleman-Cheater comes to our house, and stays there a day; walks about the Town to finde some purchase, but lost his labor, he seeing there was no money to be had, was resolved to play at small Game rather than stand out; and somewhat therefore he would do if it were but to bear his charges; he had observed that there were but two Shoemakers in the Town, one at the one end, and the other at the other end: he saw they were well furnished with boots and he wanted a pair, he therefore coming home to his quarters, sent our Boy to one of the Shoemakers to desire him to come to our house, to bring a pair of boots to a Gentleman; the Sho-maker in hopes of a good Customer returns with the Boy, and brings two or three pair, our Gentleman trys them on, and at last is pleas'd with one pair, only one of them was too little in the instep, for that said the Shoemaker, it is a small fault, and I can remedy it in an hours time, by putting it on the Last; our Gentleman intending that so he should, asked, what price? eighteen shillings was demanded, but fifteen was the price agreed upon; well, said the Gentleman, carry back the boot that is so defective, and put it on the Last, let it stay on it two hours at least, and then come and bring it, and take your money; very good, said the Shoemaker, and so taking up the remainder of the Boots he departed, not distrusting any thing, and not thinking any man who had two legs could much advantage himself with one single Boot. Our Gentleman being now Master of one Boot, was resolved to have another, and therefore he again calls the Boy, and desires him to go to the other Shoemaker, and wish him to come and bring a pair of Boots: for, said he, the other Shoemaker you brought could not fit me; the boy believed him, not thinking of the transaction, it being done privately in his Chamber: The boy went, and brings the other Shoemaker with him, who likewise brought two or three pairs of Boots; our Gentleman likewise tries them, and chusing that pair that was likest to the other he had, he likewise agreed with the Shoemaker upon price, but made the same exceptions with this last, as he had done with the former, advising him to put the Boot on the Last, for one hour and a half, and at that time to come exactly and receive his money; away went the Shoemaker with the rest of his Boots, leaving the odd one behind, and no sooner was he gone but he draws on his new Boots, and calling for a Reckoning, paid it, and his horse being bridled and sadled he mounted, and away he rode. At the time appointed both the Shoemakers came, so justly together that they met at the Gate with each of them a Boot under his Arm; they both asked for our Gentleman, but hearing he was fled and gone, they both look'd blank upon the matter; mine Host was present, and understanding the story laughed heartily at it; they knew not whether they should be angry or pleas'd, but being both Brothers of a Trade and both served alike, they resolved to laugh too, though it were but with one side of their mouths, and so they sate them down and drank together; one Pot drew down an other, and being of the Gentle Craft they were both good fellows, and at length a Bottle of wine they call'd for; mine Host seeing them in a merry vain, said, Gentlemen, I'le make a proposition to you, faith since the Gent. hath made a pair of two odd boots do you so too and let these as the other two go together, and therefore fillip up Cross or Pile who shall have both; I but said one, I am not willing to hazard my Boot for nothing, therefore thus I propose it; let us have the other Bottle of Wine, and then let us fillip Cross or Pile and take our chance, and he that hath the fortune to have both the Boots shall pay the Reckoning; agreed, said the other, and so they proceeded; and he whose chance it was to have both the Boots, did not only agree to pay the Reckoning, but also called for another Bottle of Wine. Mine Host still kept them company, and helped them to laugh at the Frolick, and now they were gotten into so merry a Vein, they resolv'd to club for the other Bottle, which they likewise in short time drank off. Mine Host having a Design upon them for the Boots, seeing them merry, said thus, Gentlemen, I made one proposition to you, even now and you agreed upon it; I have another to make, which I question not but you will assent to, but in the first place, I pray tell me the just price of the Boots; truly, replyed the Master of them, I was to have fifteen shillings of the Gentleman for them, but they are really worth fourteen shillings, well then, replyed mine Host, my Reckoning comes to six shillings; now if you please I'le venture my Reckoning, which is near half of what your Boots are worth against them, and fillip up Cross or Pile whether I shall have the Boots for my Reckoning or nothing; we'l make no dry bargain said the third person, we'l have some Wine to boot, or no Boots shall be ventured; well, said mine Host, then I will add another bottle of Wine to the Reckoning; and thus all Parties being agreed, Cross and Pile being fillip'd up, mine Host had his Chance, and the Boots; and thus he gained what the other lost, and neither of the Shoemakers could laugh at one another for their loss was equal; and thus was this pair of liquor'd Boots converted into liquor, and that drank up, and this was the end of the adventure of the Boots for the present, but it was not quite finished, for mine Host who again had some business at the Assizes, went to the Country Town where it was kept, and there he met with one of the Shoemakers his Neighbour; he had then the same Boots on that he had in a manner gain'd by chance; and therefore remembring the Jest, they went in to drink at the next Two-pot house; there they were jesting and laughing at the passage of the Boots, when on a sudden mine Host looking out of the Window call'd to the Shoemaker, look you here quickly, and I think I can shew you your Boot-Merchant; the Shoemaker look'd out and saw him, for it was he indeed, with the very Boots on his Leggs; he was walking by, in company of others, who by their Garbs and Mien did seem to be persons of Quality: The Shoemaker would have run out presently and seized on him, but mine Host would not permit it, only advising him to follow him, and see him hous'd; The Shoemaker followed mine Host's directions, and saw his Quarters, and upon enquiry found that he was to continue there for some time; wherefore he returned to mine Host, and acquainted him of his intelligence; they thereupon advised together what most convenient to be done, and concluded that mine Host should go into his company, and acquaint him that the Shoemaker expected satisfaction for his Boots, and it may be he is a Gentleman of Quality, and only did it in a Frollick, and will now pay well enough for it; but, said mine Host, if I finde him to be otherwise, we can soon have a Warrant to apprehend him, and have him punished; this was reckoned to be sober, and the best advice, and accordingly it was managed; for that evening mine Host seeing him walking alone in the Inn Yard, went and spake to him, telling him if he were not mistaken he thought he knew him; our Gentleman surveying of mine Host, reply'd, certainly no, but however if he would go into a Room, he would gladly drink with him; to this mine Host consented, they being come into a

Room, drank and smoak'd together; mine Host again asking him if he were not long since at our Town? yes, said the Gentleman, and I pray you, where did you lodge? at such an Inn, reply'd the Gentleman, and naming ours; why then, reply'd mine Host, I am not mistaken, and if you please to call to mind you may remember me to be the Master of the House; Oh! I cry you mercy, reply'd the Gentleman, now I know you, I did partly remember you, but could not call to mind where I had seen you; but I pray what affair has brought you hither? no great matter, reply'd mine Host, only a little curiosity; that's well, said the Gentleman: but, said mine Host, methinks your Boots and mine look as if they were somewhat of kin together, I pray where did you buy them? Why? that may well be, reply'd our Gentleman, for I bought them in your Town; but Sir, I pray (be not angry) said mine Host, did you ever pay for them? Why do you ask? said the Gentleman, because, said mine Host, if you did, then you are slandered and abused, and what if I did not pay for them? said the Gentleman; why then, said mine Host, you are best to do it, for the men of whom you had them are both my Neighbours; well, well, said the Gentleman, no more of this, for I paid for them as much as I will do: mine Host seeing him so absolute, said no more to him of that matter, but drank off their drink, and club'd for their Reckoning, which being paid he again at parting said thus; Sir, it will be for your Credit to pay for the Boots, I know all the story, and if you will not pay now, one time or other you will be forc'd to it to your Cost, and Trouble; do not you trouble your head with that, replied the Gentleman, let it alone till that day comes; take your own course said mine Host; and you yours, said the Gentleman, and so they parted. Mine Host having had this huffing answer, made further enquiry what this person was, and found that he was no better than a Cheat, and one that came thither for no other purpose, he therefore tells his neighbour the Shoemaker of all passages, and advises him to get a Warrant to apprehend him, and carry him before the Judge; He who was forward enough before, now went directly and made his Complaint to the Judge that evening, telling him all the Circumstance of the matter; the Judge asked him if he had enquired what quality he was of? he answered, yes, he was suspected to be no better than a Pick-pocket, or Cut-purse: well then replied the Judge, bring him hither to morrow morning before I go to the Court; our Shoemaker did not fail in a tittle, but the next morning seized on him in his Chamber, and carried him immediately before the Judge; when they came there, the Shoemaker made his Complaint, and mine Host was there present, not only to justifie it, but to produce the very fellows, which indeed were easily enough to be known to be so, and so they managed their evidence that the Gentleman-Cheat had little or nothing to say for himself, and therefore he was committed to Prison. It happened at this time that the Judge had a Kinsman with him who was somewhat wilde, and only rid about the progress with him to see fashions, and he had one scurvy humor, which was this; he had a good Estate, and was full of mony; and therefore in a prodigal vapouring way, he would carry a Purse with near a hundred pieces of Gold in it, in his pocket, and this he would always carry about with him, and upon all occasions, though never so trivial he would be drawing his Purse, and shewing his Gold, this was his Custom; and the Judge his Unkle knowing it, had oft times chid him for it, telling him that one time or other he would have his Pocket pick'd and lose it; he would not take any warning, but still replied he would warrant none could pick his pocket, so that his Unkle the Judge did wish many times that he might lose it; and so be broken of that foolish vainglorious humor. Our Cheat being now in Prison, his Companions, who were all Workmen in the same Trade, were very much troubled at his loss, because he would have done them much service, and to be so taken up for so trivial a matter as a pair of Boots much vexed them, and they knew there was no recovering him without the Judges favour; they therefore resolved to put themselves in the best Equipage they could, and go to him, accordingly that night they went, and told him they were humble Petitioners to his Honour, for a poor friend of theirs whom his Honour had commited about a pair of Boots, and they hoped his Honour would release him; because they very well knew he was wrongfully accused, being a Gentleman by birth, and of a very good House, &c. To this the Judge gave ear, and told them that he very well understood the quality of their friend; and theirs also, but, said he, for once I shall pass by this business upon one Condition; to this they reply'd, any Condition he pleased; he then being resolved what to do, commanded all his Servants and Attendants out of the Room; and told them he well understood their qualities, and had occasion to make use of them in an Affair, telling them that he had such a one his Kinsman, who carried a Purse of money in his Pocket, now, said he, I would have some of you to follow him, and get it from him, and bring it to me untouch'd, and then I promise not only to pardon you, but also to deliver your friend to you: They hearing the Judges Proposition, star'd one upon another, not knowing what answer to give, wherefore he again told them that this he expected from them, or else their friend should suffer, they thought fit to answer him with silence, and so departed; when they were gone, they consulted together what was to be done, and believing there would be no great difficulty nor harm in the doing it, resolv'd to effect it accordingly: And therefore the next morning they waited at the Judges Door, and seeing his Kinsman, they found means to perform their Enterprize, and got the Purse of Gold without any considerable difficulty, and forthwith pretending business to the Judge, they delivered it to him; he nodded them an answer, advising them to come to him in the evening; they did so, and he gave them a Discharge for their friend; but that he might do equal justice, he commanded them to pay the Shoemaker for the Boots, and gave them a piece of Gold to drink; they very thankfully received it and did accordingly. The

Judges Kinsman being now come out of the Court had occasion for moneys, but seeking his purse found he had lost it; this perplexed him to the heart; but although the loss was considerable, yet the vexation that his unkle must know it was more; he was exceeding melancholly and discontented; and his Unkle enquired and sent for him, yet he would hardly come into his presence: his Unkle knew well enough what disease he was sick of; but however he asked him again and again what he ailed? and what was the matter? he still answered him with silence, and turning away his head. Supper time being come, they sate down together, but the young man would not eat a bit; what will you eat? said his Unkle, nothing, said he: go fetch me a dish of Partridges, said the Judge; it is a dish I know you love: the meat was brought, but the young man could eat nothing: you shall eat, said his Unkle before you rise, and I will have a dish shall please you; and therefore, said he to the waiters, go bring up the Dish I commanded should be last brought up; they thereupon went down, and brought up a dish covered; come Cousin, said the Old man, eat some of this; I cannot said the kinsman, you must and shall, said the Unkle, and I pray uncover the dish and serve me some: the young man seeing his Unkle so importunate, and believing because the dish was covered, that it might be a dish of stew'd apples, resolv'd to uncover the dish, and satisfie his Unkle by eating a little of that; wherefore at his Unkle's importunity he uncover'd the dish; when he beheld instead of stew'd apples there was a better sort of fruit, it was his own Purse of Gold; he no sooner saw it: how, said his Unkle, I told you I would please you before you did rise from supper, and I think I have done so. The young man smiling thanked him, and then reaching to the dish of Partridges, he fell too lustily, and did eat as hearty a meal as ever; thus did the recovery of his Purse of Gold recover his stomack, as indeed I think it would do any others, it being to him and all others as good a Sawce as a Cordial. And now although the young man was well enough pleased that he had recovered his purse, yet he was vexed that his Unkle should thus discover his folly, and studied how he might be revenged on his Unkle; he knew very well that his purse was taken from him by some cunning cheat, and that by his Unkles consent; and it was not long e're, upon enquiry, he found out the manner, and also the People who did it; he gave them therefore a piece to drink, and told them that he would give them twenty pounds more, if they would do him one piece of service; they seeing there was money coming, promised him to do any thing in their powers; he then told them that it was indeed a high attempt, but he would pay them as largely, and save them harmless; and this it was, he would have them pick the Pocket of the Judge as he sate on the Bench: they told him it was both difficult and dangerous; as for the difficulty, said he, I'le make such means that one of you shall come near him, and for the danger, I will take of his anger, and pay you as I have said: to this they at length consented and the next day put in execution; for when the Judge was most busie in examining

Witnesses, he that was the Artist that was to perform this, approaches the Bench: the young Man sitting next the Judge his Unkle, beckons the Pickpocket, and he comes up, and under pretence of whispering the young man in the ear, he pickt the Old Mans Pocket, and carryed off the Purse cleverly; when he had so done he descended, and stood among the other Spectators. In short time after the causes were heard, and one man who had laid long in prison, only for his fees, petition'd the Judge to mitigate and lessen them that he might be able to pay them, where's the Jaylor? said the Judge; here my Lord, said the Jaylor; what Fees do you demand of this poor man? said the Judge; twenty shillings my Lord, if it please you, and it is no more than your what Lorship order'd me at the lowest; then said my Lord, you must have so much; I cannot help it; I must not make Laws one day and break them another, I had rather pay the money out of my own purse than do so. His Kinsman who sate next him, thought this was a very good opportunity to speak, and therefore thus he said; May it please honour; I had good Fortune yesterday as your Lordship knows, and therefore am resolv'd to do some charitable Act, and I think this of releasing this poor Prisoner who lies for his Fees, will be none of the least: wherefore whereas your Honor motions paying all this poor mans Fees, I make this offer, that if you please to pay one ten shillings, I will pay the other, that the poor man may be discharged: a very good motion, said the Judge. The young man soon found the way to his Purse, and pull'd out an Angel; but the Judge although he searched both Pockets, could find neither money nor Purse, he was therefore much surprized not knowing what to say, nor think, but quickly recollecting himself, thus he spake, I am sure, my friends, when I came in hither I had a Purse of money in my pocket, but now I cannot finde it, he that hath taken it from me while I was here sitting, was his Crafts-Master, and very bold, but I question not but I shall find him, I have so good skill in Physiognomy, that I know a Knave by his looks, therefore I desire you all there below to look on me, every one did so, expecting what the Judge would do, who by and by whispering to the Justice that sate next him, at length arose, and said, look you Master Justice, if I am not deceived, yonder fellow with the straw in his beard hath my Purse; all the People stared one upon another, and the Cheat that had the Purse being conscious of his guilt, doubting he was known to the Judge, and that he had a straw in his beard, he lifting up his hand stroaked it to wipe it away, supposing by that means to pass undiscovered, but that discovered him; for the Judge who had a quick eye, and expected that motion, saw, and observed it, thereupon pointed to him, saying, that is he: it was now too late to fly, for the Jaylor soon seized him, and upon search found the Purse in his Pocket. The Purse was given to the Judge, who told out ten shillings to the Jaylor for the Poor mans Fees, and ordered him to discharge him, and in his Room to take away that bold Delinquent that had pick'd his Pocket; he did so, neither did his kinsman contradict him in the open Court, but when he came home he told him all the management, and desired a discharge for the Prisoner; the Judge knowing that it was done but in jest, granted his discharge, and the Kinsmen sent that, and the promised twenty pounds, and Fees for discharge of the Prisoner.

CHAP. XV.

The Hostess's Daughter being courted by an ignorant poetical Lover; he brings a Soldier with him who becoming intimately acquainted with Mistress Dorothy *relates to her; how he by pretending to be a Cunning-man and raising a Spirit, had furnished himself, his Landlord and Landlady with a plentiful Supper, which had been provided at the Cost of another.*

Thus did these Cheats make the best of a bad market, for being at the first obstructed in their designs by their Companions Imprisonment, they were at a loss, and they got little money this bout but what the Judge and his Kinsman gave them, and the people who were present at this bold adventure of picking the Judges pocket on the Bench, were very curious of their own, and for the future had some what more than ordinary to talk of; but mine Host who knew more of the matter than ordinary, made rare sport with this story at his return, and the Shoemaker who hath receiv'd satisfaction for the loss of his Boot, having had money for the other, by mine Hosts appointment sent for the other Shoemaker his fellow Tradesman, and ordinary Charges being deducted, gave him the one half; but mine Host so ordered the matter, that as they began, so they ended in drink, and spent all they had received at our house, and thus ended the adventure of the boots. Mistress *Dorothy* now stopping, and we thereby finding that she had concluded her discourse, we took the liberty of laughing, and wondring at what she had told us, and therefore desired her to give her self the trouble to relate some more adventures to us, but she told us in plain terms that she had done, and that we were to expect no more from her. I hearing her so peremptory in her reply, told her that we had been very much engaged to her, for the extraordinary pains she had taken in these several relations; but yet I must need add this, that as yet she had not fully performed her promise, for she had promis'd to give us an account of all the family, when as, if I am not mistaken she had said little or nothing of two persons, whom I supposed to be very considerable, and that was the Son and Daughter; and therefore I made it my request to her, that she would recollect her self, and relate to us somewhat of them, because indeed they were a little active while they liv'd at home with their father and mother, but after they went abroad in the world they were very remarkable, (and continued she) since their leaving their father and mother, and my leaving the house were at one and the same time, and one the same occasion I shall now give you an account of it, and then she thus proceeded.

One young Man and Maid living in a house where so much roguery was acted, must needs be well enough experienc'd to act their Parts, but they were so warily looked after by their Mother, that it was almost impossible to exercise their Talent at home, and the young man by reason of the danger of the War, and least he should be taken Prisoner and served as his Father was, was enforced to keep home and ramble but little, but his Sister less, not being permitted to go any way out of the Town. And although many Guests who came to our house saw her, and liked her marvellously well, (for indeed she was handsom) and would have made love to her, yet her Mother knowing the danger by her own experience, watch'd her too narrowly to permit it, and was resolved to use her best endeavor to preserve the Jewel of her daughters maiden-head until she should be lawfully married. She being kept up so strictly had few Suiters, only one in the Town, who was a Farmers Son had a moneths mind to her, and having read the famous History of *Tom Thumb*, and from thence proceeding to *Fortunatus*, and then to the most admirable History of *Dorastus* and *Fawnia*, was infected with Poetry and Love both at once, and absolutely believing that all he read was really true, did with himself to be as fortunate as *Fortunatus* himself, and since he could not meet with that blind Lady *Fortune* to present him with such a Purse, he did however resolve to be as absolute a lover as *Dorastus*; and now nothing to that accomplishment being wanting but a Mistriss who should be his *Fawnia*, he found out our Pretty Mistress *Peggy* my Hostess's Daughter (Hers I may boldly call her, but mine Host's I dare not, the Case being doubtful, by what I have already related to you) a Mistress being found for our Swain, he made some addresses to her, and was permitted by the Mother to more freedom than any, because the youth was not only indifferent handsome, but rich, and mine Hostess was pretty free that they should strike up a match together; I was still desired to keep Company with these Lovers, but I had much ado to forbear laughing outright when I heard his Courtship, all his language was Stuff stoln out of the books he had read; and when he was answered by Mistress *Peggy*, or any question propounded by me to him in any ordinary or different Dialect, he was as deaf as a Bell-founder, and was not able to answer us; I being resolved to make sport with him, told him that I thought he would do mainly well if he would apply his fancy to writing of Poetry, and as an essay I advised him to write a Letter to Mistress *Peggy* in Verse, he thanked me for my advice, and desir'd my friend-ship and said that he would go immediately home and exercise himself in Poetry, and so he said, and so he did, for behold the next morning Mistress *Peggy* received a Letter from him, which we both read and laugh'd at, for it was so foolishly forced, conceited, and nonsensical that have I much ado to remember the words, but having often repeated them, I shall now relate them to you.

Madam,

Ever till I saw thee my heart was still at rest,

Little did I think one Female could have pierc't

Either Heart or Bowels, that on thee doth waste,

So sad all faint and feeble grow within my brest;
Alas, it is pity that sorrow to me should come,
For to tell you the truth as yet I am but very young,
And to express my self I want a better tongue;
But I can truly and sadly say that only you
Are she that hath brought me to grief and sorrow too
Brave Vertues that are in this lovely Damsel found
At the first sight gave my poor heart a desperate wound.
You have my sences very much decay'd
With love, that at one time they will be all dismai'd
Long of the tender love that to you I do bear,
Even now I will make and end my only Dear.

Your true Lover,
L. M.

We all laughed heartily at this non-sensical stuff, and I told mistress *Dorothy* that sure she was mistaken in the recital of these verses, and that they were to be said backwards, for that wayes that she repeated them I discovered the humour of our Poetical Lover, and Mistress *Peggy* by my directions returned him this answer.

Amorous Friend,

Tis much you should receive two infections at once, the one Love, the other Poetry, but it is not very strange since they commonly accompany one another, but i'le assure you 'tis dangerous, for you know the old Proverb, *that sad are the effects of* Love and Pease Porridge; *and besides Poetry is commonly attended with Poverty, but after a strict perusal of your poetick Fancies, I find there is no great danger in your poetick infection, for unless you improve your self mightily it will be a long time e're you be a compleat Poet, and since your Poetry and Love came together, it will be as long e're you be a compleat Lover; now if you have still a mind to prosecute these two Designs, of Love and Poetry, I advise you to make use of some other more fit and sublime object that may raise your fancy to a higher pitch of eloquence, or at least wise sense, as you have been in verse. I return this answer to you in prose, and as you like this you may prosecute your Designs of Love and Poetry, with some other Object, but I pray give no more trouble to*

Your Frind,
M. S.

This to the best of my remembrance was the answer to our Lovers poetical Letter, and although what we writ might have been enough to have dashed the designs of any other, yet our Lover came very confidently that evening, and thanked his Mistress for receiving his Letter, and answering it; telling her that he did acknowledge he had not as yet any great Skill in Poetry, but he had written his best, and intended and hoped in the next to mend it, and so he proceeded in his troublesome Love-Suit. Our Cook-maid coming into the room where we were, and having seen the Love Letter, it being made no secret, told us that she had a Love Letter sent her not long since, which in her opinion was better than that; and we believing that there must be somewhat in it worth the seeing, commanded her to fetch it, and giving it into my hands, I read these words.

Madam,

I Hope the Brains of your Beauty being boyl'd in the Kettle of Kindness with the Beef of Bounty, may at length prove a dish for my dyet, so that the Marrowbone of your Maidenhead being crack'd with the Chopping-knife of my Courage, may upon the Trencher of Truth declare how I love you; let not the minc'd meat of Modesty baked in the Oven of Hatred in the Crust of Coyness cause my Denial, lest the Dagger of Death being drenched in the Barrel of my Blood may with the Spiggot draw forth the Liquor of my Life.

Yours more than his own,

T. J.

This Letter pleas'd me more than the former, and I told her that her Sweetheart was ingenious and witty, for he had courted her in her own language, and made use of such words she understood, and that in my opinion it was far better to do so than to be altogether so poetical as to make mocks of their Mistresses by comparing their fore-heads to Alablaster, their eyes to Diamonds, their lips to Coral, and such kind of fantastical similies, our Lover was of my opinion, and was so taken with the Cook-maids Letter that he desired to copy it, and so he did; and while he was thus employed, I remembered that I had a paper of verses that would employ all his senses to understand, and it may be puzzle him; and therefore fetch'd it, and he having copied the other lines, I shewed him these.

I saw a Peacock with a fiery Tail

I saw a Blazing star that dropt down Hail

I saw a Cloud begirt with Ivy round

I saw a Sturdy Oak creep on the ground

I saw a Pismire swallow up a Whale

I saw a brackish Sea brim full of Ale

I saw a Venice glass sixteen yards deep

I saw a Well full of mens tears that weep

I saw mens Eyes all on a flaming fire

I saw a House big as the Moon and higher

I saw the Sun all red even at midnight

I saw the man that saw this dreadful sight.

And most dreadful it was indeed, said our Lover, if it were true, but however (continued he) the Verses are very good, and I pray let me have a copy of them; which I permitted him to take; and he read them over, and over again without understanding the Mystery, but the more he read, the more he seemed to wonder at the strangeness of the several sights, and said, sure this is impossible, not at all, said I, and if you will lay ten shillings to be spent, I will make it out to you before you go, that all that is there written is very true, and that I have seen it all myself. I cannot believe it, replyed he, and I am content to lay the wager, provided Mistress *Peggy* may be the Judge. Content, said I, and so the money was laid in her hands, and then I took up the paper and began to read thus: *I saw a Peacock*, and there I made a stop, and said, do you believe that? If you do not, I can shew you one in the yard: Ay, but said he, the Verse is, *I saw a Peacock with a fiery Tail*, and that is the wager: no, said I, you must stop when you have red *I saw a Peacock*, and then go on, *with a fiery Tail I saw a blazing Star*; and I am sure that I have seen that too, for blazing Stars have all fiery Tails: that is true, replyed he, but I did not mean to read it so: tis no matter how you meant, said I, but what I read is true, and by vertue of that I suppose I shall win the wager, but however I proceeded, and read; *That dropt down Hail I saw a Cloud; Begirt with Ivy round I saw a a sturdy Oak; Creep on the ground I saw a Pismire, Swallow up a Whale I saw a Brackish Sea; Brim full of Ale I saw a Venice Glass.* And so I read on to the end of the Verses, still making a full stop in the middle of the verse, where the sense required it; thus making sense of the impossible nonsense: by this time our Lover saw he was likely to lose his Wager, but however he cavelled at my thus reading it, and said, I ought to stop only where the rhime ended; but all that he said signified nothing, for his Mistress did me the justice to award me the Wager, and accordingly gave me my money, and kept the other twenty shillings to be spent; neither was the Poetical Lover much displeased, for he had a very high esteem of the Lines he had, protesting he would not part with them for forty shillings, and he questioned not but he should win much money by Wagers he would lay about them, and being thus satisfied he left us, promising the next night to return, and then expecting a Colation for the ten shillings he had lost; and so we were rid of our poetical Lover till the time appointed; which being come, he likewise came and brought with him a young man, a Soldier that belong'd to the Garrison in our Town; I knew the man by sight, for he was very remarkable, it being the general report that he was a Cunning-man and could tell fortunes, and our Lover brought him to give his oppinion, whether he should have mistress *Peggy* or not. We gave him the ordinary welcome, he coming in company with our Lover we were the more free with him, who demeaned himself so well that I had a more than ordinary respect for him, and told him he should be welcome at any other time; and so our Colation being ended, we for that time parted; but in short time after he came again, and being as he said, much taken with my company, desired to take all opportunities of waiting on me: I seeing no harm in him, and finding that he was none of the pitifull sort of fellows, but that he was handsom, witty, and above all things that he wore money in his Pocket, permitted him frequently to visit me, and it was not long e're I grew into such familiarity with him, that I obliged him to shew me so much of his Skill as to tell me my Fortune; he was surprized at this proposition and made many Excuses, but I grew to that height in my importunitie that I wearied him; at length he told me that although all the Town had been mistaken in him yet I should not, and that if I pleased he would undeceive me, and in short he told me that it was a mistake to think that he was skillfull either in Astrology or Magick, and although he had gained some moneys by pretending to be knowing in that mystery, yet it was no such matter: I supposing that he only said this to excuse himself, still importuned him in such manner, that I brought him to this: that provided I would promise him secrecy, he would discover his whole secrets to me, and thereby make it absolutely appear that the Town was mistaken: I being desirous of hearing Novelties, engaged to perform all he desired, and thereupon he thus began.

Madam, in the discourse I shall make you, I shall be forced to discover not only my own secrets, but also those of another, the most eminent of this Town, and were it not to you, and onely to you, I should not do it for any consideration whatsoever, for it is the secrets of a woman of the best quality, and therefore you may be justly angry with me for so doing, but my respects, & indeed my love to you is so great, that I shall not stop at any obstacles to perform anything you require; & withal I pray do not think, that since I am so easie to discover one womans secrets, and that of such eminency and one to whom I am so much obliged, that I should, or may at one time or another, serve you in the like manner. No Madam (said he) assure your self of the contrary, for although the woman I am to speak of be so eminent, indifferently handsom, and one to whom I am so much obliged, yet my acquaintance with her began after a strange manner, and it was a kind of necessity that first induced her to permit me the freedom I enjoy with her; whereas on the contrary, the respects I have for you are of another nature, for my inclination and affection induce me to pay you all manner of service, which I am confident will be very lasting. He having made this plausible speech, thus proceeded.

It is not many monethes since I was first acquainted with this place, you know my quality is a Soldier of Fortune, and I may reasonably enough term my self so, being of late some-what favoured by that blind and inconstant Lady; our Commander in Chief thinking it convenient to draw us out of the field where we had been all the last Summer, and place us in Garrisons for the Winter season; it fell to my lot, among other of my Comrades, to be ordered to be quartered in this Town, where when we came, we had our several Billets delivered to us, and mine directed me to the House of the wealthiest Mercer in your Town, where I still Quarter, and who you know is a Person as eminent for Estate, as any in the Town, I need not name him, you knowing where I Quarter: it so fortuned, that the night I came thither first to Quarter, he was out of the Town, as he had been for some dayes past and was to continue for two or three more. It was somewhat late when I knock'd at the door, and therefore the Maid-servant who heard me, ask'd me what I would have? I answer'd that I was appointed in that House to take up my Quarters. The Maid soon called her Mistress, and acquainted her with the matter; which she knowing, thus answer'd me, that she was a young new-married woman, that her Husband was absent, that she had onely one servant, and that therefore she could not with any conveniency entertain any man in her house. I could not be satisfied with this answer, but reply'd that I was sorry I must be so troublesom, but withal that it was too late to seek any other lodging; and that my Comrades were all in their Quarters, and therefore I must unavoidably lye in the street if she did not entertain me; wherefore I pray'd her to receive me into her house, and put me into any place she pleas'd, and I promised that I would be as little troublesome as possibly I could, and therefore I desired her not to deny that fairly and by entreaty, which she knew I could command. The young woman, although she was much troubled (believing that I might hinder a design she had in hand) yet knowing withal that what I said was true, and that I might command where I entreated, commanded her maid to open the door, and shew me my lodging up in the Garret. When I was entred the house, I told her that I was to lodge there, so I desir'd I might sup with her, (not that I would command it, but that I would willingly pay for what I had) because it was late, and I had not eaten any thing all that day. She seemed angry at my proposal, telling me that I was mistaken if I took her house for an Inn, and if I wanted a supper, want I must, for I was like to have nothing there but my bare lodging, and indeed bare I might call it, for it was a most pitiful one, however I was forc'd to make use of it, and go supper-less to bed. Being thus ready to dye for hunger, I had little mind to sleep, and therefore I only tumbled and tossed without so much as closing mine eyes together. After I had lain an hour in this manner, casting mine eyes about the Chamber, I perceived some light which came through a Chink or Crevis in the floor, and my curiosity inviting me to it, I leap'd out of the bed, and laying my eye to the place, I might perceive under me a room very well furnisht, wherein was a great Fire, two Spits, of roasted Fowls, the Maid turning them, and the young Woman, the Mistress sitting in the arms of a young Fellow a Lawyer, who to me appeared to be so by his Gown. How! said I to myself, is this the Woman that in her Husbands absence will not receive a man into her? Oh the unconstancy and subtility of Women! this I thought, but however I believed it was not as yet time to speak out; but being very hungry, I beheld the Spits with some anger, and devoured the Fowls with my eyes; I had the patience to see the Supper dress'd, though I was not to be a Guest; and though I could not taste, yet I could smell the Victuals: I saw the Table spread, the Bottles of Wine brought out, & the Victuals placed on the Table, but just as they were going to sit down, one knock'd at the door; this somewhat startled them, but their confusion was greater, when the Maid asked who was at the door, understood it was her Master. They were all frighted and confounded, not knowing where to put the man, or the victuals, they had but little time to consider: There was but one little Chamber adjoyning where the maid lay, and under her Bed at length they laid him, and the Meat, Drink, and all the Appurtenances were placed in a Closet in the Chamber: This being done, and the Woman sitting down by the fire, the Master who was impatient with calling and knocking, was let in, and coming up stairs, his Wife rises from her seat, and cryes out, Oh dear Husband! Wellcome home, how glad am I to see you, especially in coming sooner than I expected. That is true, said the good man, I made haste and dispatched my Business, which being done, I took Horse and made all possible speed to come home to you, and indeed, I have rid full speed all this day; And very welcome you are, said she: But how come you to have so great a fire? said the Husband: Oh Love, said the Wife, I am troubled with the Belly-ake as passes, and I made this fire to warm Trenchers and clothes, to put to my Belly to ease me; and truely I think that this pain hath taken me with vexing at a paultrey business that happened this night; for here came a Soldier and said he must, and would quarter here, and it hath so angred and griev'd me, to think that a man must lodge here in your absence, that I think truly it hath brought my paine. I hearing this, thought it would be convenient for me ere long to appear, and therefore put on my Clothes, but still I gave attention to the end of their discourse, which was thus continued: Said the Husband, well, let that pass; but I pray let me have some Supper, for I have made such haste to day in travelling to come to you, that I am almost dead with hunger, wherefore I pray give me some Victuals. Victuals, replyed the woman, where do you think I should have it? Do you think I make feasting in your absence? Alas, my maid and I supp'd to night with each of us a Roasted Apple, I am sorry for that, replyed the Husband, and am very loath if I could help it, to go to Bed without a Supper, but what cannot be cured, must be endured. I hearing this, and believing it to be very proper for my design, being already dress'd, went down stairs, and knock'd at the door, which opened, I entred, and saluting my Landlord, prayed him to excuse me for disturbing his Wife, who had indeed refused to entertain me, till I had acquainted her with my Orders, which, lest he should distrust any thing to the contrary, I then pull'd out and shew'd him, and told him that I hoped his Wife could not complain of any incivility I had offered her. No truly, reply'd she. I having satisfi'd him in this, I told him that I understood that he had not supped no more than I, and therefore if he pleased I would give him and his Lady a Supper, for I had it in my power to accommodate them very plentifully. How is that possible? reply'd my Landlord, since it is so late, and nothing is to be had in the Town, and besides that it will be too late to dress any thing. I bid him take no care for that, but if he pleased he should be provided with victuals ready dresed provided he and his wife would both promise me secresie; they told me that they would do so, but he wondred, and she seemed to do so too, at what I intended to do; whereupon I told them I had a correspondency with Spirits, who would furnish me with what I desired, and thereupon taking a piece of Chalk, and making a Circle I Placed myself in it, made certain Figures about it, and taking a Staff in my hand, waved it about my head, and then I uttered many words which were onely conceited fustian stuff, which they understood not, nor I myself neither, and then proceeding I named a Spirit, and told him that he must quickly provide me a Supper for myself, my Landlord, and his Lady. I seemed to listen, and then told them that my Spirit was obedient, and nothing was wanting now but to know what they would have; I asked the question, but they answered, What I pleased: Bring then, said I, a Boyl'd Hen and Bacon, a Couple of Roasted Capons, a Dozen of Partridges, two Dozen of Larks, a Pippin Tart, with Oranges and Lemmons, and Fruit sufficient; Also bring us two Bottles of Canary and two of Claret; this was the Victuals I had seen provided, and therefore this I call'd for; and withal, said I, I charge thee not to appear in any horrible shape, so as to frighten my Landlord or Landlady, but dispatch quickly and set all down in the Closet of this Chamber. Having thus finisht my Inclination and paused a little, now, said I, open the door and there you shall see I am obeyed. The maid readily did as I commanded, and all was there in ample manner ready dress'd, to the great astonishment of my Landlord, but my Landlady, though she seem'd to be amazed, knew well enough that she was discovered, but as yet could not disaprove of what I had done. The meat being produced, the Table was spread and the provision placed thereon, and now all things being in readiness, I desired my Landlord and Landlady to take their places; at my request they did so, but my Landlord was mighty unwilling to eat, until he see me eat and commend the Victuals and Sauce, and I importuning him to taste, he did so, and my Landlady by his example consented to accompany us in the same employment: Having now done with one Dish, and my Landlord finding that to be good, by my example fell to another, and though he was somewhat cautious, yet he made a good Meal; I am sure I did not spare, but fed like a Farmer, and my Landlady was not at all behind hand, she well enough knowing, that though I told them it was dress'd under ground, yet she could contradict me but she durst not; the maid had her part too, and all were well enough content, except the poor Lawyer, who was both hungry and fearful, lest as I had discovered the meat, I would also discover the Caterer, but I minded no such matter, I thought as I had begun well, so to end, and I would not be so discourteous to him to make him fare ill, when by his means I had fared so well. We not onely eat lustily, but drank off our Wine cheerily, which was as good as ever tipp'd over Tongue, and for us three there was enough; and now at last my Landlord did own that the Meat and Sauce, Bread and Drink were all excellent good, and that if the Spirits could command so good Fare, they were more harmless and better company than he thought for: I told him my Spirit was still in his house, and expected my further Commands, therefore I desired to know whether he would have ought else e're I discharged him? He told me, No: Then, replyed I, he shall descend; but since he hath done us so good service, I will, if you please, let you see him. Oh by no means Sir, said my Landlady, fearing I would discover her greatest Secrets. Rest contented, replyed I, for I am Master of more discretion that to disoblidge a Lady; assure your self it shall be otherwise than you imagine: my Landlord too was very fearful, but I assured him there should be no cause, and thereupon for the more easie management of what I intended, I ordered the Servant-maid to open the Street door, and all the other Doors of the House, that the Spirit might have the more freedom to depart, otherwise I told them he would raise a Tempest; and, continued I, he shall not appear in any horrid form, but in the habit of one of your Neighbors; having told them this, I thus began: Oh thou Spirit, who hast been unexpectedly disturbed, but hast so plentifully catered for us, come forth for I now give thee leave to go whither thou pleasest. The Lawyer who was but in the next room, and who had heard all passages, was not so sottish as to neglect this opportunity, but pulling his Hat over his face that he might go undiscovered, came forth of the room where he had been hid, and with a steady pace walked by us, going down stairs, and so leaving the house, whilst my Landlady in a trembling manner sate and beheld what had passed.

CHAP. XVI.

The Souldier is in danger to be caught by his Landlord in his Landladies Chamber, but by her wit he escapeth. Mistris Dorothy *relates that a parcel of Padders having rob'd a Knight of four hundred pounds, two of them are taken, but the Knight will not swear absolutely against them, because he might sue and get his Money of the Hundred where he was rob'd. A Crew of Pick-pockets wanting money, two of them pretend to be drunk and quarrel with the third, wherefore these two are put into the stocks, and getting company, the third had the opportunity of picking many Pockets.*

The Lawyer having thus pass'd by us to the amazement of my Landlord, he then look'd on me with somewhat a distracted countenance, his wife seeing that, and doubting that he had or would discover the matter; to divert him from any questions or considerations, pretended to be so mightily amaz'd & frighted, that she fell into a swoon, and then her Husband, the maid, and I had enough to do to bring her again to her self, neither could we do it so well, but that her Husband was forced to help the maid to carry and put her into her bed, where for that night I left them and went to my own, and now my belly being full it was not long ere I fell asleep; awaking the next morning I began to consider what had passed, and wondred at my self how I had the confidence to manage an affair so difficult and dangerous, but when I considered what I had done I resolved to proceed, and as I knew the secrets of my Land-lady, to make some use of that knowledg, and out of her misfortunes to make my self a fortune therefore I recommended my self, remembring the old saying, *Audaces Fortuna juvat*, Fortune helps the bold, and therefore I would try her favours, considering that she could do me no injuries, I could not be much lower than I was, and I was in great probability to rise higher by the prosecution of this Adventure. I did not question but I should do well enough with my Landlady, for I had not at all disobliged her in betraying her secrets, but rather mannaged them as well as she could wish or desire, and therefore she could not take me for a Clown or Fool, but rather think me worthy of her favour, and into her favour I was resolved to get, or venture all; she was young, and as you know indifferent handsome, her husband was old, and I believe wanting in what most pleases a woman, and therefore she had permitted the young Lawyer to supply that Defect, and considering that I might as well as he pretend to her favor, for I was as young, and (if I am not mistaken) as handsom; indeed he had this advantage, of having more money than I, but I question'd not but she would well enough dispense with that, she being out of possibility of wanting any, but rather able to supply me; and I had this advantage above him, that I was in the house, and likely for some time to continue there, and by that means I might make use of all opportunities, and indeed it was not long ere I had one; for I having spent good part of the morning in these congitations, I could hear my

Landlord rise and go out of the house, wherefore I also arose and made my self ready, and indeed I spruced my self up in the best manner I could; being now ready I went down stairs, and met with the Maid-servant, who could not look on me without blushing, I gave her the Good morrow, & asked her how her mistress did this morning she replyed, something better than I left her last night. Truly replyed I, I am sorry that she was so ill, but more especially to consider that I had been the occasion of it, but I would study how to make her amends, & at present I desired to make my excuses to her, if she would shew where she was: she is not yet stirring, said the Maid; that matters not, said I, and thereupon we went to her bed side; where when I was come, she seeing me turned away her face: but Madam, to make short with my story, I spake to her, and that in such manner, that she not only turned about, but gave me thanks for the favors I had done, in managing her secrets with so much discretion, and that she was, and should be eternally obliged to me, and should study how to make me amends: I replyed, amends was already made in the good opinion she had for me, desiring her to continue in it, and I should endeavour to serve her in all things to my power; and since it was her misfortune to be disturbed by her Husbands unexpected return, and be disapointed in the enjoyment of her Friend, that was a thing I could help, but however, if she pleased to accept of me in his stead, I should give her the best satisfaction I could, she seemed to be angry at this proposal, but I proceeding and telling her that I was a Gentleman born and bred, and it may be in all things equal, if not above her Friend; she was content to let me kiss her, and I finding that I might without much difficulty proceed further, sent the Maid out for a Mornings draught, and in her absence perswaded her to accept of that from me which she should have had from her Friend the Lawyer, had not her Husband disturbed them; and I then pleased her well, that ever since she hath made no difficulty to let me enjoy her Person, and be Master of that as well as I was of her secrets; and being thus possessed of her person, I not only commanded that but her Purse, and have led the pleasantest life in the World. This Adventure, Madam was the occasion of my being accounted a Cunning-man, for my Landlord, though I had enjoyned him secresie, yet he did not absolutely keep it, but acquainted some of his familiar friends with my knowledg, so that I was in short time pointed at as I passed along the street, and gazed at with the eyes of wonder; nay some of the Neighborhood courted me very earnestly to answer them several questions, and being often importuned, did give them such answers as might probably come to pass, which falling out accordingly I gain'd not only the reputation of a cunning man, but my pockets were also indifferently well lyned with Half-crown pieces. Thus had I a handsome enjoyment of money and pleasure; for I was free with my Landlady, and very little suspected by her Husband; but I was one time near being caught by him, and thus it was. He was not only well stricken in years, but by an accident some years past, had lost one of his eyes, or else he would have espyed us; for one day he being abroad, and I being desirous to toy with my Landlady, we in order thereto entred her Chamber and lay down on her bed, we had not long been there but we heard a noise, and the maid-servant looking to see what was the matter, came hastily in to us, and told us that her Master was coming up stairs; she had hardly delivered this unpleasant message, but he was come up stairs and was entring the Chamber, but he was not so quick, but his wife and I were as nimble, and were got upon our feet, and she running to the door caught hold of her Husband about the Neck and cryed out, *Oh Lord Husband, how dearly welcome you are to me! especially at this time, when I so longed to see you.* For what cause, said my Landlord? what is the meaning of this language? Oh dear Husband, replyed she, I have been asleep on the bed, where I had the pleasantest Dream that I have ever had in all my life; nay, (continued she) it is more than a Dream, for it is a Vision, and I hope a true one: well, what is it, said he? Why truely Husband, said she, methoughts you and I were walking along together in a pleasant Field, and we met with a man that begged an Alms of you, which you very liberally gave him, and he being glad of your liberality told you, that he would recompense it by restoring you the sight of your other eye: Methoughts I was very joyfull at this proposition, and desired him to do it, but you were doubtfull of his performance, and therefore unwilling to let him meddle with you, but he promising and assuring us that he would certainly cure you, I perswaded you to permit him to wash your eye with a certain Water he had in a Viol about him, which he had no sooner done, but methoughts you saw very well with your blind eye, at the sight of which I was so over-joyed, that I awaked, and you then came up stairs; and now Sweet-heart I am so confident of the Truth of my Dream, that I desire to experiment the same, and therefore I pray let me put my hand on your seeing Eye for a tryal. My Landlady having done, her Husband replyed, Surely you have not been asleep as you say, but talk idly for want of sleep, or else you would never make so foolish a proposition. I know not, reply'd she, but I must needs desire you to give me satisfaction in this particular, for I long to try it. Well, said he, that you may see how much a fool you are, I am content. She having liberty, clapt her hand on his seeing Eye, and I who waited that opportunity needed no further instructions what to do, but coming from behind the door where I had stood, with long strides and easie, went out of the Chamber, and going down stairs left the House: She seeing me gone, and thereby her business being done, asked her Husband if he saw any thing? No, said he, but if you will remove your hand I shall see a fool; she did so, and told him that she was satisfied, but hoped it had been otherwise: And thus, continued the Soldier, we escaped this brunt, as we did many others. And now Madam, said he to me, I have been very free in relating to you the greatest Secrets of my life, having so much confidence in your discretion, that I shall run no hazard in your knowing it, but hope as I have been free with you, so you will be so generous as to acquaint me with your quality and condition, and permit me to serve you in all I can. To this request I answer'd, That indeed I was not of that Countrey, but another, and upon an urgent affair was some time since come from *London*, whither I have a desire to return; so have I, said the Soldier, and if you please to accept of my service, I shall gladly wait on you thither, for I have so much respect from my Captain, that I question not but he will not onely give me leave to go, but also give me a Pass to secure me thither. I hearing him say so, told him that I would take such order in my affairs, that I hoped in one months time to be ready to be gone, and then I Should be glad of his Company. This was the discourse I held with the Soldier, who was indeed very civil with me, spending his money freely as often as he came into my company. I being resolved to leave this place, took order to get into my hands what moneys I had, which I had lent out to sufficient persons in the Town, which was in short time paid me; but very strange Accidents happened in our house before my departure, which made me hasten it, and which were thus: I have already told you that our house had been a Receptacle for Cheats and Pickpockets, who by degrees coming to be Thieves and High-way-men, they still frequented it, and mine Host who seeing he gain'd moneys, cared not much which ways he came by it, made no great scruple of Conscience to entertain them, who indeed were very good Customers, and spent equal to the best Guests we had, and he might do that with them he might not with others, for they were bound to believe and pay all that he reckoned, although never so unreasonable, so that he had an equal share, if not more, of all the Prizes they made, some whereof were very considerable; for a Knight of *Yorkshire* having occasion to travel our Road was set upon and rob'd by six of our Guests, he had onely Himself, Wife and Daughter, Coachman, and one Horseman, this was his Company, but the Prize was considerable, being four hundred pounds in money, besides Watches, Rings, and other Jewels: Our Crew of Padders, although at first they were severe enough in searching them, and stripping them of all their Money and Jewels, yet dealt civily enough with them (if I may term Thieves to be so) before they parted, for the Knight seeing it was in vain to resist, and being too weak to do so, permitted them to take all from him, but when they came to his Lady and had taken her little Money, and proceeded to take her Rings from her Fingers, he was troubled, and told them, that he hoped as they had found him civil to confess and deliver all he had to them, and which he said was very considerable, so he hoped they would not use any violence to his Wife and Daughter, in taking their Rings from them which were inconsiderable, and might happen to be prejudicial to them, in discovering of them to the Law. They, who knew he said right, not onely desisted from proceeding against the Ladies, but also gave him his Watch and Rings and all the odd Money they had taken from him, contenting themselves only with the four hundred pounds, and giving him an Oath that he, nor none of his company should remove from that place for half an hours time, that they might have leisure to escape; they left him. He was as good as his word and staid out his time, and they with full speed rode to our Town, and at our house took up their Quarters: They no sooner entred the house, but they first deliver'd their Money to the custody of mine Host, and then called for a Trunk wherein was their Clothes, for they had always Change of Clothes lay there, so that in a quarter of an hours time these six Blades of Fortune were so metamorphosed that they were not to be known; he who when he came in had a black Perriwig and grey clothes, now had a white Perriwig and black Clothes, and by that and pulling off Patches and such like Disguisements, they were not to be known; for if a *Hue and Cry* coms out wherein is named the number of the Robbers, they cannot distinguish or describe them otherwise than by their Clothes and Horses; and as for their Habits they thus alter them, and their Horses are presently either sent to Grass, or lock'd up in a private Stable, and their Sadles and other Accoutrements are convey'd away and lock'd up; and commonly if there be six or eight in a Robbery, not above the one half, or three quarters of them go to one house, but divide themselves into Companies untill the *Hue and Cry* shall be over, and then they meet and divide the Booty: This is their common practice when a Robbery is done at any distance from *London*, but if it be done within twenty miles of that place, then away they all flie thither, and enter the City at several ends of the Town, and to several Quarters they at present disperse themselves; this I say is their custom. I told Mistress *Dorothy* that I was very well acquainted with the Truth of what she had said, and therefore desired her to proceed and acquaint me how their Guests came off with their Prize; Very well, said she, for the *Hue and Cry* came not to our Town till the next day; and by that time two of the six were gone, having taken their shares with them, and the *Hue and Cry* having passed about the Town it came to our house, where the Officers failed in their Enquiry, for it nominated six, whereas our Company was but four, and the Description of the Persons and their Habits was so different from what our Guests had, that there was no reason in the world to suspect them, and as for their Horses they were not to be found, so that, I say, our Guests all escaped, and for joy feasted and drank very highly, but in two days time their Joy was lessen'd; for a trusty Messenger came to them and brought sad Newes from the other two of their Companions, which was, that they were taken, apprehended, and upon examination found so guilty, that they were sent to Goal. Our Guests were very much surprized at the news, & upon examination of the perticulars, thus they found it: The Knight who was robb'd having staid in the place the time he promised, that being over, he caused his Coachman to drive on to the next Town, where when he came, he sent for the Town-Officers, and inform'd them of his Loss, and withal told them that he must, and did expect satisfaction from them, and the rest of the Inhabitants of that Hundred, because he was robb'd two hours before Sun-set: They who heard him knew he said right, and that it must be so, unless they produc'd all or some of the Felons, and had them try'd and found guilty at Law, wherefore the Sum being considerable, and the Case so evident and plain to be proved, they presently took an account of the Knight of all particulars of the Robbers in the best manner that he or his servants could direct, and having so done sent out a *Hue and Cry*, directing and charging the Officers to use all possible diligence in the discovery of these Fellons: but they miss'd of their purpose for that day, but the next it was the misfortune of those two of our Guests who had left our house to come thither, and being now again upon the Pad, were accoutred in their Padding Habit; although they were but two, and the number in the *Hue and Cry* was six, yet their Habits and Horses were so remarkable that they were soon suspected, and the officers seized them quickly, hailing them before the Justice, whither when they were come and examined, they could not answer so well, but that they were shrewdly suspected; but to make the matter more clear, the Knight and his servants who were still in the Town, were sent for, and then it was not long ere the matter was but too plain for our two Delinquents, especially when upon search of their Portmantua's their share of the Money was found, however they stoutly denied the Fact; but notwithstanding all that could be said, they were sent to Prison. This News alarmed our Guests, and made them bethink themselves of what should be most necessary for their own preservation, and thereupon they thus resolved, that two of the four should go near the place where the Knight was, and observe his motions, and according to that act their matters as should be convenient, and the other two resolved for the present to stay at our house: but this Case which now at the beginning appeared to be very bad and sad for their two Companions, in the end by the cunning managment of the two Agents came off much better than was expected, and indeed very well; for they understanding that the Knight was engaged by the Justice to prosecute, and that the Countrey would see that he should do so, whereby they might be discharged from payment of the money he was robb'd off; This consideration being had, they resolved by some trusty Messenger to send to the Knight, and therefore they drew up a Letter to this purpose.

That they were Gentlemen of a good Extraction, but the misfortunes of times, and their own Necessities, had put them upon a Course of life far different from their Inclinations; which, although it was not justifiable by Law, yet they thought it not so unreasonable as the World did, and they had plenty of Examples for their Practice, the whole Nation being now engaged into Parties, who under fair and specious pretence made it their business to Rob (which they termed Plunder *) one another, especially the harmless Countrey, and that so often as they should come in their way: This they said was the president by which they walked, and by vertue of this Commission (which they believe as Authentick as some of* *theirs who levyed great Forces,) they had taken up Arms, and their good fortune, and this present mishap, had caused them to meet, where, although he was dispossest of his Money, yet they were confident he had no very ill opinion of them, in regard they had used him and the Ladies in his company with all civility; this they hoped he would not forget, and for that consideration he would deal as civilly with their two Companions, who had the misfortune to fall under the power of the Law. This they thought was reason enough for them to Expect all favour at his hands, but there were also other reasons for him to do it, and that which they thought would be the most prevalent, was, that it was against his own interest to prosecute their Companions; for should he at the approaching Assizes so absolutely charge them with the Fact, as to bring them within the compass of the Law, and it may be take their Lives from them, then he must expect no other satisfaction, but lose his Money: whereas on the contrary if he and his servants spake doubtfully in their Evidence against them, and they were not proved to be guilty, then he might by Law recover his whole Money of the Country. This they hoped would be a prevalent reason with him to order the matter so as to let their Companions escape, which they prayed & hoped he would do: but if (as they thought against all reason) he should rigorously prosecute them, he was to remember that four of their Companions were still left at liberty with swords in their hands, and his misfortune might again bring him under their power, when he might not expect so civil proceeding against him as he had the last time, but that they might revenge their Companions, but they concluded they hoped he would not give them that occassion.* And so they concluded.

This Letter was carefully conveyed to the Knight, who having read and consider'd the Contents, and finding their reasons to be good, and withal considering that if he should by his Evidence cast these two men for their Lives, he was not sure of his own so long as they had companions, (who though at the first he found civil enough) who had swords in their hands, and might be revengeful and bloody-minded enough on that occasion; neither, as they had urged, would it be for his interest, for he must then lose his Money, or the greatest part. These reasons, I say, made him to manage the matter so as that upon Tryal they should be acquitted, and therefore he sent to the Prison a Confident of his, to tell them that he would do so, charging them to deny the Fact & stand upon their justification; And thus the Assizes coming they were indicted, but the Knight & his Servants (who were directed and instructed by him) were all in one Tale, & said, that indeed he was robb'd of four hundred pounds at such a place & time, by six men, two whereof were in such habits, or like such as the prisoners at the Bar had, but that he could not for all the world swear or say that they were any of the persons. He saying no more than thus, and by his example his Servants saying no more or less, & the Prisoners pleading Justification, they were in the end acquitted, had their Money again deliver'd to them, and the Knight now proceeding in his Suit against the Country, recover'd his whole Moneys of them; and thus our two Prisoners with their two Comrades who had attended the Tryall, came home to our house with great joy. And thus did Thieves escape, and the honest Countrey was punish'd, and this I have known is a trick that hath been used familiarly; so that several Countreys have been almost undone with these kind of Robberies.

Soon after this passage, there happened one as pleasant, thought not so roguish, and thus it was: A Crew of Divers, Bung nippers, or Pick pockets came to our house, and there being a Fair in the Town they brought home very good Purchase, and spent their moneys very freely, but their trade did not continue so good as it began, and they in expenses were so profuse and prodigal, that they had out-run the Constable, spent more than they were able to pay, and they were always us'd to pay their Host well, and so they were resolv'd to do now, or set their Wits on the Tenters; many Projects they had, and many Essays they made, some of them going abroad by turns, and then returning and sending others, but our Town was but thinly peopled, and they could not raise any considerable Purchase, wherefore knowing that if they could get any number of people together, they might then have the more convenient opportunity of getting a Prize, they therefore thus laid their Plot; Three of them went out, two whereof were to act the drunken mans part, and so they did very Comically, for they reeling along the streets, tumbled down several people who were in their way. The people believing them to be what they appear'd, *viz.*, drunk, let them pass on without much interruption; their sober Companion seeing that no body else would take them up, he therefore was resolv'd to do it, and thereupon meeting them as by chance, they gave him the Justle, which he not taking so patiently as the other had done, not onely worded it with them, but they proceeded to blows, so that two being against one it was thought unequal, and they having been abusive to others, a great company were assembled, and among them the Constable, who seizing upon all three carried them before a Justice, who hearing the matter, and finding by the testimony of the people who went with them, that the two were wholly to blame, and believing them to be as drunk as they seemed to be, he therefore ordered that they should be set in the Stocks for two hours, and the third be discharged. This his Order was obeyed, and they were conducted to the Stocks, where they behav'd themselves so pleasantly in foolish discourse to the people, that a very great number of people were about them; their Companion who was at freedom seeing his conveniency, and being his Arts-Master in the Mystery of Diving, fished money out of their pockets, so that in two hours time that they were in the Stocks, he plyed his work so well that he had gained near seven pounds; being thus fraighted, he came to our house, and it was not long ere his Companions followed him; when they finding so considerable a Purchase, paid my Landlord the Reckoning and call'd for a new one, where they drank roundly, remembring all those by whom they fared the better; and then having done the business they came for, they paid their Shot and march'd off to the next Town to see if they could fare any better than they had done at ours. And these, continued

Mistress *Dorothy*, were the Guests we now entertained, *Padders* and *Pick pockets*, who as they got their money easily, so they spent it as lightly, to the great profit of mine Host, for he gained at least fifty pounds of the four hundred, and still put in for a share: but as the Pitcher goes not so often to the water, but it comes home broken at last, so in short time not onely his Guests, but he himself was caught and brought to condign punishment.

CHAP. XVII.

The Author relates a Story how he and six other Padders robb'd a Carrier of six hundred pounds, and that one of the company in consideration of an hundred pounds paid him by the Countrey where the Robbery was committed, owned the Fact, and thereby saved the Countrey (who were sued) from payment of the rest, and at length by their assistance gained his pardon. Also how a young Pick-pocket is put on by an old one, to cut an old womans Purse whilest she is at prayers in a Church-yard by a Tomb-stone; the Boy performs the Exploit, but is discover'd and shew'd by the old pick-pocket to the people, who coming to stare on the Boy had their Pockets pickt by the old one and his companions; And also how an old Padder being in danger to be hang'd for a Robbery, a young one for fifty pounds took the Fact upon himself, discharged the old one, and in the end came clearly off himself.

I Finding by Mistress *Dorothy's* pausing that she was somewhat weary of her large Discourse, and being desirous to know the conclusion of her Adventures, desired her to refresh her self with a Cup of Wine which stood by us, and then we all three, *viz.*, Mistress *Mary*, Mistress *Dorothy*, and my self, having drank off a quart of the best, I thus bespake her; Truly Mistress *Dorothy*, you have taken much pains in reciting these pleasant adventures that befel whil'st you liv'd in the Inn, and you must needs have very great experience by what you have related; for although I was well acquainted with knaveries and rogueries enough whilest I lived in *England*, yet all our adventures are very new, being such whose like I have seldom heard; and although I did follow the *Padding*-Trade, especially at that time when I had the good fortune at the first to meet with, and be acquainted with you, yet I seldom knew, nor indeed ever heard of the like escape that your six *Padders* had; it was a neat and cleanly conveyance: but lest you should be tyred with too long speaking, and that I might enable you the better to give us a full and exact account of the rest of your adventures, I will relate to you some of my former Adventures, and especially one, which was somewhat like that of your six *Padders*, and thus it was.

A stout gang of us who were *Knights of the Road*, were one time assembled together at an Inn, from whence we understood a good round Sum of money was to be carryed, and we only waited the departure and motions of the Pack-horses, that we might put our project in execution, the Sum was six hundred pounds, and we knew it was to be carried in a pack, but which pack and which horse was to carry it, we were ignorant of, and that we doubted would be a hindrance or at leastwise a trouble to our design; for the Carrier having such a charge of money was resolv'd to travel only by day light, and not in the night time, whereby if it should happen he were robb'd, he might not bear the loss; and we knowing this, and doubting that he would keep in as much company as he could, we fear'd it would be troublesome and dangerous to rob him of that money, unless we knew in what pack it was; for it would take up much time to cut up and examine all the rest of the Packs, which were near twenty in number; wherefore one of our Comrades made it his business to discover that matter, but although he was watchful, yet the Carrier and Owners were as shie, so that he could not possibly attain to his desires; wherefore he was resolv'd to under-feel the Hostler, who upon a little acquaintance and a Reward given him, and more promised if the project should take, engaged to give him a certain Token how he should know the Horse and Pack, and to that end directed him to wait the next morning early when the Pack-horses went out: Our Companion did so, sitting in a Drinking-room in the Yard where he could see all passages. The Horses being loaded, went out one after another, and the Moneyed-horse in the middle, when he came the Hostler lifted up his hand, and gave him a Clap over the Buttock, saying, *Goe thy ways* Dun, *for thou wilt never be sold to thy worth*: This was *Item* enough to our Companion to mark, and know what he had to do; so that the Horses being all gone, and he having dispatcht his drink, came up to us who attended him; And then he telling us that he knew how to execute our Design, and that he had knowledge enough, we rested contented, neither did we leave that Inn till noon, although the Carrier went out in the morning early, and this we did that we might not be suspected to have any design upon him, but soon after we had din'd we all mounted and away we rode. It was not many hours before we over-took the Carrier, or at least came near him, and then we sent one of the company to scour the Road, and discover in what condition the Carrier was in, and as occasion serv'd to come back to us and acquaint us; one hour before night he came to us, who were not far off, and told us, that then was the opportunity, for the Carrier had engag'd company all the while before, but now the night coming on, and the Company being to travel further than the Carrier, they had newly left him, and then he was alone, onely with his man and two or three passengers; we being eight in number, quickly made up to the Carrier, and one with Sword drawn and Pistol cock'd seiz'd on him, another on his man, and the rest of our Companions on the rest of the Passengers; he of our Companions that knew the Horse and Pack onely went to him, singl'd him out, cut his Girts, ripp'd up the Pack, and took forth the money, without medling with any thing else; we the rest of his Companions in the mean time had dismounted the Carrier, his man, and the Passengers, and having tyed their hands, we left them to shift for themselves, and six of us taking each of us a hundred pounds, and the other two riding one in the Van, and the other in the Rere, away we march'd, but at that rate that in two hours we were got thirty miles from the place where the robbery was committed, and we had so cross'd the Country to prevent discovery, that it was almost impossible to overtake or finde us. We took up our Quarters at an Inn where we were very well acquainted, and for joy of our purchase wanted for nothing that money could produce us, and there we spent some time in all manner of delights, till being weary of the place, and some of the Company having a desire to depart and separate, we accordingly did so; and one of our Companions who had occasion to ride that way where we committed this Robbery performed one of the boldest exploits that I have ever heard of, and thus it was.

He had an Uncle who kept an Inn in the Town near to the place where this Robbery was done, to whose house he came & was welcom'd; he pretended he was a Soldier, and was newly come from the Garrison at *Bristol*, and with such kind of imaginary Stories he discours'd his Uncle, and telling him the best news he could, and his Uncle likewise acquainted him with the news of the Town, and as the chiefest told him that there had lately been a great robbery done, for a Carrier was robb'd of six hundred pound, and therefore it being done in the day time, that Town must pay for it, and truely Cousin, said he, our Town hath been so mightily pestred with Soldiers that we are very poor and not able and my share comes to thirty pound of the money: but said our companion, can you not meet with the thieves? no replyed his Uncle; we have offered a hundred pound, to any that can discover them, but hitherto all hath been in vain. This was the Hosts discourse with his Kinsman, who very well knew he was one of the number; and a conceit came into his head, that it was possible that as he had got almost a hundred pounds already by this robbery, so he might get another whole hundred pounds; and therefore being resolved what to do, he thus discovered himself to his Uncle: it is now said he, three years since I left my Father, and ever since that I have led a troublesome life, so that I am almost weary of it; and it is not long since that for a misdemeanor I had done in our Garrison, I was condemned to be hang'd, but I thank my stars I escaped it, and being so near death and escaping, I soon after came acquainted with a cunning man, who telling me my Fortune, told me that I had lately escaped a danger, which I very well knew; and he withal added, that I should run into many other dangers, and should escape them; and that he was certain I was not born to be hang'd: and now therefore Uncle said he, I will once again tempt my fate, and being assured that I shall not be hang'd, I care not, if I may be ensured the hundred pounds you spake of, if I take upon me and own the Robbery; and I think it will be no difficult matter to do, for as I remember one of the Gentlemen Padders who did that feat was habited and mounted just as I am. His Uncle having heard his discourse, stared at him, and asked him if he were mad? no, replyed he, but if you will warrant me the money I'le undertake the matter: his Uncle seeing him thus resolved, began to consider a little more seriously of the matter, and told his kinsman, that if he would do the one, he would not only ensure him of the other, but also endeavour his pardon, and thereupon he sent for some of the Neighbors whom he might trust; and told them that there was a wild young man his kinsman, who would save them five hundred pounds, and told them the manner how, they were well enough satisfied with the proposition, and not only promised him the money which was agreed on, should be presently put into any friends hand, but also that they would undertake his pardon, or at least-wise a reprieve that he might sue out his pardon; this being agreed upon, they next proceeded in their discourse how this affair was to be managed, and after several propositions made, it was concluded, that as he came into the Town, so he should go out, and the next day he should re-enter the Town when the Officers who should be then appointed to search for suspitious persons should seize on him, and he should at the first deny the fact, but upon examination should so vary and waver in his discourse, that he should give just cause of suspition; they having agreed on this, and several other particulars, and the money being deposited in a young maidens hand, who was his Uncles Daughter; he took horse and privately left the Town. The next day the Officers of the Town being charged to keep strict watch, and search all suspitious places; they did so, and as they had been a little way out of the town, and were returning our Adventurer overtook them; who rides here says one, sure that man is cloathed just as the Carrier described one of the Padders were? he hearing them say this, made some stand, and offered to turn his back, they therefore imagining that he might be suspected, asked of him what he was? and came near to encompass him, he still withdrawing drew his pistol and fired at them, they then staring on each other, and seeing that none of their company was kill'd or wounded, were encouraged to make up to him; and although he drew his sword yet they being armed adventured upon him, and seizing on him, pull'd him from his horse back, he then asked them, what was the matter, and what they would have? they told him that he was a high-way man, and that they were very certain of, or else why did he shoot at them, and were glad they had caught him, he should pay for all the trouble he had put the Town to; some railed at him in this manner, whilst others disarmed him and bound his hands together, and then they led him away to the Town, where with great noise they carried him before their Justice of the peace; he strictly examined him and absolutely charged him with the former Robbery, advising him to confess, and inform against his companions, and then he told him he would endeavour to get him a pardon: our adventurer gave him the hearing of all, but denyed all knowledge of the robbery, but so faintly and with such faultering and uncertainties, that the Justice committed him to prison. In few dayes after the Carrier came that wayes, and he was conducted to the Thief, were after a light sight and discourse with him, he and his servant remembred him, and the Owner of the money was sent for who was also carried before the Justice; and there he, the Carrier and his Servant were all bound to prosecute the Felon, which was much in the vexation of the owner of the moneys, who expected the next assizes to have a tryal against the Town, and to recover his money of them, whereas now he saw he was like to lose that, and only have an Endictment against the Felon, when as if he should find him guilty, it would be a little satisfaction for such a sum of money as he had lost. And as he expected, and as the plot was laid, so it fell out; for the Assizes being come, an Endictment was brought in against our Delinquent, and although he buss'ld to defend himself, yet he was found guilty, and then he made an ingenious confession to the Judge of the manner of the Robbery, only concealing as much as he thought convenient, alleadging that indeed he was guilty, but it was his first fact, but he was drawn in by chance being overtaken on the way by the Robbers; he being coming to the Town to visit his Unkle, and therefore he pray'd mercy of the court, the Judge told him that if he would discover his companions somewhat might be done, but not else, he replyed, that truly he was not in their company, above eight and forty hours in all, and therefore knew not of their haunts, but if his honor would spare his life he would if ever he met them, cause them to be apprehended; to this the Judge made no Answer, so that our Adventurers Uncle presented a Petition to the Judge in behalf of his Kins-man, and the other Chief men of the Town pretending for his Unkles sake to do so assisted him in it, and they drew the Petition so pitifully, that the Judge at their importunity granted him reprieve for the present, leaving him to sue out his pardon as fast as he could: and thus all Parties were content except the owner of the moneys, who went away with a Flea in his ear: and our Adventurer so plyed his business, wanting for neither money nor friends, that in short time he gained his pardon, and he was set free: and I will add this further of our companion, that after this he turned honest man, for by virtue of the money he had gained in this robbery, and what was given him, he first set up an Ale-house, and soon after an Inn, and hath born all Offices in the Parish. And this story, said I, Mistress *Dorothy*, somwhat resembles yours, for your Thieves cheated the Country who paid the Knight what he had lost, and here on the contrary, the Country outwitted the Party rob'd, and saved their purses; and truly I have known several of these transactions, and sometimes the guilty escape, and the innocent are punished. And now, continued I, Mistress *Dorothy*: you see I am acquainted with these kind of stories and as I have already related one of a Padder, which do somwhat equal yours, I will now also tell you another of a Pick-pocket, which shall be much like yours of that nature, and thus it was.

    A Crew of Blades of that Profession came to a Countrey-town on a market day, and finding there was little good to be done without some occasion to draw the People together more than ordinary, they therefore went to an Ale-house to consult on what was necessary to be done, and there after several debates held, it was concluded as follows, that whereas they had lately taken up a boy of about ten years of age, who was very desirous of learning their mystery, and whereas they had instructed him sufficiently in the theory thereof, that it was now time to put him in practice, and therefore the gravest man in the company was to walk out with him, shew him what he was to do and help him if he stood in need thereof, and the rest of the society were to be at hand to do as occasion should offer; this being agreed upon, the old fellow took the Boy by the hand, and leads him through the Market, but there was no probabillity of a prize; and the Boy having promised to do much, the old man sought out for some what that might be worthy his undertaking, and so going out of the market they entred the Church-yard and there they saw an old woman with a great pouch of mony by her side, kneeling by a Tombstone and doing her devotions: Our old fellow seeing this, said to the Boy, Sirrah, you see that old woman with the Pouch; yes Sir, replyes the Boy, go thither said he, and bring away her Purse and money; the boy was not at all daunted at the boldness of the undertaking, but went up to the woman, and so soon as he came near her, he likewise fell on his knees, and fell a mumbling as if he were also at his devotions; the old woman seeing him so devout, permitted him to continue by her, but he putting down one of his hands by virtue of a Knife and Horn-thimble cut off her Purse: The old man stood not far off and saw his carriage which was so cunningly contriv'd that he could not forbear laughing at it, but bethinking him of a further Design, he was resolved to discover the Boy, whereupon stopping some passengers that were going by, he said to them, I pray friends behold yonder Boy how devout he is, do you not think he will be a good one in time that is so religiously given already? yes surely, said the people, Oh the cunningness of the young Rogue! said the old fellow, and how much you are all mistaken for I have stood and seen that young Rogue cut the old womans Purse, and thereupon he went to his young practitioner in Roguery, and took him by the hand causing him to arise, and bringing him to the people, shewed them the Purse he had thus purchased; the old woman was not so intent at her devotions, but she casting her eyes aside likewise saw a Purse in the Boys hand, missing her own soon knew that to be it, wherefore she and all the people came nearer the Boy, who stood still as a stock and said nothing to them, and all the people, not only they that went by, but also at their report most of the people in the market came thither to see this young Rogue, admiring at the boldness of the fact, but they had been better to have staid away and minded their own Affairs; for our old Rogue seeing his opportunity, and that now there was a great many people together, he fell a diving into their pockets, and got good Pillage, and his Companions who were not far off at the noise came in to the sport, and all laid about them so lustily that there were few who escaped without their pockets being pick'd, onely the old woman had her purse again, but in exchange of that our old Rogue and his Companions had twenty others better fraught with moneys; in fine, they being weary with looking on the boy, & the Pick-pockets thinking they had done sufficiently for that time, the old fellow came to the boy, and told him that as he had first of all discovered him, so he should go along with him; the boy who had learned obedience to his Superiors, consented, and so they march'd off, and went a little way out of the Town to an Ale-house, where they divided the plunder of the field, which amounted to above twenty pounds. And thus having told my Tale, I said to Mistress *Dorothy* that I thought this was somewhat like her discourse of the Pick-pockets. She told me she must needs confess it, and that both my Tales exceeded hers, and therefore she desired me to remitt her promise of proceeding any further in her discourse; for, said she, I shall be able to acquaint you with nothing but what you know already; as for that, said I, I must hear the conclusion of your story, but since you seem to prove of what I have told you, I shall proceed a little further, and relate a Story to you somewhat like my first, and thus it was.

A High-way-man who had used the Trade for a long time, was at length catch'd, and the evidence was so clear against him that he was likely to be cast, and then he was sure to go to pot, for he had been singed on the Fist already, and the Judge who was to try him was very severe on that account; wherefore he was very melancholly, and much perplexed, and all the friends he had could not comfort him; however he was one day drinking with some friends in the Jayl, and telling them the sadness of his condition, and several ways were propounded for his safety; they told him that it would be best to compound the fact with the Prosecutor; I have offered that, said the Felon, and though I did not take above twenty pounds from the party, yet I have offered him fifty pound for composition if he will forbear prosecution; but he will not hear of any thing but the Law, and will make no end but what that shall, and if it comes to that, then I am certain sorrow will be my Sops; how, said one that was present, will he not take fifty pounds for twenty? sure he wants no money, for if he knew the want of it so much as I do, he would not make so slight of fifty pounds; but I pray, continued he, what is the reason he is so outragious against you? what is the cause of his violent proceeding? Truly, reply'd the Thief, it was my misfortune to be one of those two that met with him one night, and he having twenty pounds and a Watch about him we eas'd him of them, my Companion escaped, but I was seized the next night on suspition, and having besides my share of the twenty pounds the watch about me which we had likewise taken from him, it was as he said, a clear Testimony & evidence of the Fact, he earnestly enquired for the ring which my companion had for his share; & because I cannot help him to the ring he is thus obstinate, well then, I see said the other, you have confess'd the fact, & therefore there is no hope of saving you: truly replyed the Padder, I never yet confessed it to any one that I think will do me any prejudice, but much less to him; but instead of confessing I have always stoutly denied it, alleadging that I bought the Watch that Evening of one in whose company I was; nay then, replyed the other, your case is not so desperate as I thought it, and how say you now, continued he, are you willing to be as good as your word, and give the fifty pounds you speak of to be discharged of this matter? yes with all my heart, said the Padder; well then said the other, if you will deposite the money into another mans hands that I may be sure of it when you are discharged I will undertake you shall be acquited; content, said the other, but I pray acquaint me with the manner how you will manage this affair; our Undertaker replyed, that he had considered of what was to be done, and was resolved so he might be sure of the money, to venture his own neck to save the others, and that he would take upon him the fact, and thereby discharge him. The Padder was content to part with his money, but withal he desired to have some cleer demonstration how he intended to manage the business; to which our undertaker replyed, it must be your care not to be tryed till the last day of the assizes, and then still deny the fact very stoutly, continuing your allegation that you did buy the Watch of a stranger, but one whom you knew if you again should see him, and then I must borrow your Clothes, and the Perriwig you wore when you committed the Fact, and then I purpose at that time not to be far from you; and when I see a convenient time I wil appear, & the manner shal be thus: I will attempt to pick a mans pocket, but I will do it so unworkman like, that if he be not a very Dolt he shall discover me, I being discovered must presently be brought before the Judge for the Fact, and when you see me there you shall cry out as amazed and surprized, that I am the very man of whom you bought the Watch, and you shall then see that although I deny it a little at first, yet I will at last confess my self guilty, and so you shall be discharged: This, said our Undertaker is my proposition, and now if you can contrive it better, do, and I will follow your directions. The Padder and all his friends were hugely well satisfied & pleased with the Undertakers discourse, and could not find any fault in any particular, wherefore their Agreement was quickly perfected, and the fifty pounds were delivered into the custody of one whom they both knew and entrusted, to be kept by him until the Padder should be discharged. Several persons then present asked of the Undertaker how he intended to come off himself? as for that, replyed he, I have it in my head, and I will venture that, and keep it safe enough too I hope: this business being thus agreed on they at present parted, and the Undertaker had the Clothes and Perriwig of the Padder delivered to him; and the Padder did put himself into a habit quite different from that; Thus Affairs stood when the Assizes began, which lasted two days, onely the first day was past, and our Padder had by his endeavours kept himself from being called; the second day was come and forenoon past, when in the after-noon this Cause was to be heard; the Judges servant were some of them gone out of the Town to make provision for their Master at another Town, whither he was that night to follow, so that there was a necessity for his removal; & then about three of the clock this prisoner was brought to the bar, his Indictment was read, which was for robing the Countrey-man, of 20l. in money, and a silver watch, and a gold Ring, to this the prisoner pleaded *not guilty* and so put himself upon his tryal, according to the ordinary form;

then was the Countryman called, who did alledge that the prisoner at the Bar was the party, who with another his companion did rob him as aforesaid; the prisoner denyed the fact, and desired the Judge to ask his accuser what habit he was then in, to this the Countrey-man replyed, that indeed his habit and hair were then different from what he now had, but that was an easie thing to alter, but he was sure he was the man, for he had his very watch in his pocket, to this the prisoner replyed as formerly, that he bought it of a person who indeed was habited as the Country-man had described. He was come to this part of his tryal when a noise was heard in the Court of crying out a pick-pocket, a pick-pocket, and soon after our undertaker was haled into Court; the Judge seeing him, said, Sirrah, how durst you be so bold? I shall talk with you by and by, set him by at present; the prisoner at the Bar seeing it was now a fit time, cryed out, O my Lord! I pray let him stay here now, for indeed my Lord that is the very person of whom I bought the watch, and whose just fate hath brought him hither at this time, that my innocency may be cleared, therefore I beseech you my Lord, let him be examined, and I question not but you will soon find my innocency. The Judge hearing the exclamations of the prisoner, and supposing there might be somewhat in the case, and withal being desirous to execute justice caused the Undertaker to be brought to the bar, and then he thus began: now, you who are the prisoner at the bar, and upon your tryal, what do you say to, or charge this man with; my Lord replyed the padder, I say and alledge that this Person who now stands here by me, is the very person of whom I bought the watch, and I gave him fifty shillings for it, let him deny it if he can, and my Lord I further say, that I suppose he is the person who committed the robbery, for he is habited just as this Country-man described one of them to be: what say you to this: said my Lord to the Country-man, truly my Lord, said he, I am somewhat at a stand, for indeed one of those who robb'd me was habited as this fellow is, pointing to the undertaker, but I finding my Watch in the custody of this other did verily believe and was very confident that it was he that robb'd me, but I must leave all to your Lord-ship and the Jury: Now, you Sir, said my Lord to the undertaker, what say you for your self? did you sell a Watch to this man here? my Lord, replyed he, I have never a Watch, no, I know that now, said my Lord, but did you not sell a Watch to this man? my Lord said the undertaker, I am an honest man, that's a sign of your honesty, when you pick a pocket in my presence, my Lord it is a mistake, replyed the Fellow; I believe, said my Lord, we shall not be mistaken in you by and by, having thus said the Watch it self was produc'd, and shew'd to the undertaker; and he was asked if he knew it, yes, my Lord, said he, I had such a watch as this; and where had you it? I know not said the undertaker: at this the Padder cryed out, O my Lord, he hath said enough to discharge me and accuse himself, for he ownes he had the Watch, and I am sure I bought it of him, therefore good my Lord do me Justice? acquit me, and punish him; all in due time said my

Lord, we must not condemn him before he be lawfully indicted, but I think he hath confess'd enough against himself, and therefore he shall be committed, and since I cannot stay now any longer he shall be indicted the next Assizes, till then he must lye by it and have time to repent: but I pray my Lord, said the Padder, let me be discharged; I cannot discharge you reply'd my Lord, now you are upon your tryal, except the Jury find you not guilty: I put myself upon them, said the Padder, whereupon the Jury only asking the Undertaker some questions which he doubtfully answered, the Jury gave their Verdict, *Not guilty*, and thus was the Padder discharged, but however he was bound to come in evidence the next Assizes against the undertaker, and so was the Country-man, but he had been better to have taken fifty pounds than thus to have troubled himself about the Ring, for in the end he lost all, and no hanging was in the case; for when the next Assizes came, and our Undertaker was indicted, the Tale was now of another Hogg, he denyed all knowledge of the Watch, and as he had owned any thing before, he now again denyed it, bringing witnesses to prove where he was at that hour, and all the time of the robbery, and saying, he told them it was a mistake the last time, that he was then only surprized; and indeed he spake so well, and to the purpose, that he was acquitted of the robbery, and only whipt a little for picking the pocket, and so he march'd off with fifty pounds; and the Padder who did not appear at the Assizes as witness against him, let the recognizance go against him, leaving the law to find him where they could catch him.

CHAP. XVIII.

Mistress Mary *relates a notable story of a Countrey-Gentleman's cheating a Gold smith; another much more remarkable, of a Gentlemans Boy by assistance of his Master, who put a notable trick on a Goldsmith: afterwards going for* France, *is notoriously robb'd by way of retaliation, the manner how, <u>with</u> his accompanying a seeming Gallant to a Feast who steals a piece of Plate.*

Having now finished my discourse, I desired Mistress *Dorothy* to proceed in hers, and put an end to her Adventures, to which she replyed, that since I was so well acquainted with these passages, and could recount things so various and wittily-pleasant, which far exceeded anything she could say, she desired to be excused from any further recital; I told her I must needs however, hear what she could further say, for all she had hitherto said was various from what I had related to her; and Mistress *Mary* likewise joyned with me in this request, telling her that she must needs proceed in her Narrative, for she longed to hear what was the end of the Host, and Hostess, and how she left them and came to *London*, and what else had hapned to her till the first of their Acquaintance. Truly replyed Mistress *Dorothy*, I shall give you satisfaction to all these particulars; but methinks you were but short in your Narrative and might have enlarg'd; and since you did as I believe, omit many passages of your Life that were considerable, I pray let us hear some of them from you. I must confess, said Mistress *Mary*, that in the recital I made you of my actions, I only recounted to you those things which did pertain to my own story, as thinking it impertinent to relate any others; but if I had thought it pleasant, I could likewise have told you of some such Robberies and Cheates, as some of my acquaintance were engag'd in. It is not too late to do it now, said I to her; and seeing Mistress *Dorothy* is not yet pleased to continue her story, I pray you therefore to let us know some of your experience in this nature. I shall not deny your request, replyed Mistress *Mary*, and therefore after some little pause to recollect her self of what she had to say; she thus began.

I must confess that I had several of my Customers whilest I liv'd publickly at *London*, who although they come to me full, return'd empty, and then necessity put them upon unlawful courses, and when they could not live of themselves, then they liv'd by shirking upon others; this was their first step, and when this would not do, and they began to be angry and discontented that they could not wear money in their pockets, they then fell to gameing, and all the Cheats of that Mystery were put in practice; when that course left them, the next was to pick pockets, steal Cloaks, and a hundred such kinde of shirking tricks, till from one degree to another they came to the high pad, and from thence to the Goal, and so to the Gibbet; many I say, of my acquaintance did run through all these Courses, and beginning, as they say, with a pin, proceeded to a point, and so to a biggar thing, till the rope held them; but I always made it my business to leave them off when they began these Courses. Among others that came to me, I had a Country Gentleman who designing to deal honestly with a shop-keeper, had occasion to out-wit him, who intended to cheat the Country-man. The Countrey Gentleman when he came to me had his Pockets well lined with Half-Crown Pieces, but he loving his pleasure I made him pay for it so considerably, that his Pocket was well near emptied: he had twenty Pieces of Gold and several Rings, part of which I design'd to be Mistress of, but he was to wise and wary to part from any such precious Commodities: but an urgent occasion happening, and mony being wanting, he was resolved to sell a Diamond Ring that he had, which was worth fifty pounds, wherefore he keeping a Servant took him along, and to *Lombard-street* they went, when he came there, pitch'd upon a Goldsmiths Shop where he intended to sell it; he therefore drew off his Ring, and ask'd the Goldsmith what it was worth? The Goldsmith looking on him, and then on the Ring, did hope to make this Ring his own for a small matter; and seeing our Countrey-man in a plain Countrey Habit, did believe that he had little skill in Diamonds, and that this came accidentally to his possession, and that he might purchase it very easily, wherefore he being doubtful what to answer as to Price, told the Countrey-man that the worth of it was uncertain, for he could not directly tell whether it was right, or counterfeit; As for that, said the Countrey-man, I believe it is right, and dare warrant it, and indeed I intend to sell it, and therefore would know what you will give me for it: Truly, replyed the Goldsmith, I believe it may be worth ten pounds; Yes, and more money, said the Countrey-man; Not much more, said the Goldsmith, for look you here, said he, here is a Ring which I will warrant is much better than yours, and I will also warrant it to be a right good diamond, and I will sell it you for twenty pounds: This the Goldsmith said, supposing that the Countrey-man who came to sell, had no skill, inclination, nor money to buy; but the Countrey-man believing that the Goldsmith onely said thus, thinking to draw him on to part from his own Ring the more easily, and by that means cheat him, resolv'd if he could, to be too wise for the Goldsmith; wherefore taking both the Rings into his hands as to compare them together, he thus said: I am sure mine is a right Diamond: and so is mine, reply'd the Goldsmith: and said the Countrey-man, shall I have it for twenty pounds? Yes, reply'd the Goldsmith; but said he, I suppose you come to sell, and not to buy; and since you shall see I will be a good Customer, I will give you fifteen pounds for yours. Nay reply'd the Countrey-man, since I have had my choice to by or sell, I will never refuse a good Penny-worth, as I think this is, therefore Master Goldsmith, I will keep my own and give you money for yours: Where is it? said the Goldsmith hastily, and endeavouring then to seize on his Ring; Hold a blow there, said the Countrey-man, here's your money, but the Ring I will keep. The Goldsmith seeing himself caught, flustered and flounced like a mad man, and the Countrey-man pulling out a little Purse, told down twenty Pieces of Gold, & said, Here Shop-keeper, here's your money; but I hope you will allow me eighteen pence a piece in exchange for my Gold. Tell not me of exchange, but give me my Ring, said the Goldsmith: It is mine, said the Countrey-man, for I have bought it and paid for it, and have witness of my Bargain. All this would not serve the Goldsmith's turn, but he curs'd & swore that the Countrey-man came to cheat him, & his ring he would have; & at the noise several people came about his Shop, but he was so perplexed that he could not tell his Tale, and the Countrey-Gentleman could; at length a Constable came, and although the Goldsmith knew not to what purpose, yet before a Justice he would go: the Countrey-man was content, and therefore together they went; when they came there, the Goldsmith who was the plaintiff, began his Tale, and said, that the Countrey-man had taken a Diamond Ring from him worth one hundred pounds; and would give him but twenty pounds for it, have a care what you say, reply'd the Country-man; for if you charge me with taking a ring from you, I suppose that is stealing; and if you say so, I shall vex you farther than I have done, and then he told the Justice the whole story as I have related, which was then a very plain case, & for proof of the matter, the Countrey-Gentleman's man was witness. The Goldsmith hearing this, alleadged, that he believed the Countrey Gentleman and his man were both Impostors and Cheats: to this the Countrey-man reply'd as before, that he were best have a care he did not make his case worse, and bring an old house on his head by slandering of him, for it was well known that he was a Gentle-man of three hundred pounds *per Annum*, and liv'd at a place he nam'd but twenty miles from *London*; and that he being desirous to sell a ring, came to his shop to that purpose, but he would have cheated him; but it prov'd he only made a rod for his own breech, and what he intended to him, was fallen upon himself: thus did the Country Gentleman make good his discourse, and the Justice seeing there was no injustice done, dismiss'd them; but order'd that his Neighbour the Goldsmith should have the twenty pieces of Gold for twenty pounds, though they were worth more in exchange; and this was all the satisfaction he had. The Country Gentleman went presently to a Citizen, an acquaintance of his, to whom he deliver'd the ring he had so purchased, desiring him to sell it for him which he did; for being known to be a Citizen, the Goldsmith that bought it offered him at the first word Ninety five pounds for it, and in the end gave him forty shillings more, with which money he returned to the Countrey-man, and he giving him the forty shillings for his pains, returned with the rest to me, relating all the matter as it had passed. I was as much pleas'd as he, because I question'd not but I should partake with him, and so I did; for he gave me ten pound to buy me a Gown; and thus was our Goldsmith well enough serv'd. And it was not long after, before another Goldsmith had a considerable loss, and thus it was.

Amongst the other Customers that came to me, there was a Gentleman, a Blade of fortune, who although he was of a good Family, yet being a younger Brother, had but little besides his wits to live upon; but as he was a Gentleman, so kept himself in a Garb according to his Quality, and had a foot boy in a Livery to attend him: this boy was a notable young Rogue, and had assisted his Master in many an exploit, and was privy to most of his secrets: this young man (continued Mistress *Mary*) coming to visit me, and we falling into discourses of wit, I related to him the adventure of the Countrey-Gentleman with the Goldsmith; he was much pleased with the relation, and told me the Goldsmith was well enough served, and that above all trades, he had a greater picque or anger against them than any; for (said he) it grieves me to the heart to walk through *Cheapside* or *Lombard-street*, with little or no moneyes in my pocket, and see so much jingling of money in their Shops, and so great a quantity of *Jacobus'es* and other Gold, either lying in their Glass-cases, or telling on the Compters, and methinks when I see it my fingers itch to be handling of some of them; but I believe if a Gentleman should starve they would not part from any without very good Security; but (said he) I have now thought upon a way how to get some of them without much hazard; and I being desirous to know, he told me thus: my boy and I will walk along; and Sirrah, said he to the boy, when I make a small stop, do you go into the Goldsmiths Shop where you shall see them telling of money; and laying your hand upon a heap, catch up a handful, but so soon as you have taken it up, let it fall down again and leave it where you had it, and come after me and leave the rest to my management; the boy promis'd to do as he was directed: but, said I, what advantage can you make by your boys handling of money and leaving it behind him? as for that, said he, I question not before I have done I shall make a good business of it, and thereupon he left me, and went immediatly to put this his project in execution; he returned that evening and told me all was well yet, and it would be better in time: I desired to know his meaning, whereupon he told me, that according to his appointment the boy went into the Goldsmiths shop, took up a handful of money, laid it all down again and ran away to him, that he was no sooner come to him, but the Goldsmiths Servants were at his heels, that he looking about and seeing them, ask'd what the matter was? they reply'd, his boy had stollen some money: he answer'd he knew it was false, they said it was true; and he should go back with them to their Master: the boy was content, and so was the Master, when coming to the Shop, the Goldsmith himself said that that Boy, if he were his, had robb'd him. The Boy and his Master both denyed it, and they fell to hot words, so that the Goldsmith call'd me (said the Gentleman) Shirking Fellow, and that he would have me sent to *Newgate* for robbing him: for if the boy did it, it was by my appointment: I (said the Gentleman) told him that he did abuse me, and that in conclusion must, and should pay for it: but first I desired to know with what Sum they charged the boy; they said they knew not, but that he had taken money from a heap which they were telling of, which heap was a hundred pounds; hearing them say thus, I told them I would stay the telling of it, and then they might judge who had the abuse: they were content with it, and accordingly went to telling: half an hour had dispatched that matter, and then they found that they had all their money right to a farthing. The Goldsmith seeing this, asked my pardon for the affront: for, said he, it is a mistake: I answer'd, that he must pay for his prating, and that I was a Person of that quality that would not put up the affront, and that he must hear further from me; he seeing me so hot, was as chollerick as I, and so we parted, and thus far (said he) I have proceeded. But all this while (said I) I do not see where is your gain: that is to come, said he, and so it was, and did come in, and that considerably too; for the next day he caused the Goldsmith to be arrested in an action of Defamation, and the Sergeant who arrested him being well fee'd by the Gentleman, told the Goldsmith that he were best to compound the matter, for the Gentleman was a Person of Quality, and would not put it up, but make him pay soundly for it, if he proceeded any further. The Goldsmith being desirous of quiet harkned to his counsel, and agreed to give 10*l*. but that would not be taken; but twenty pounds was given to the Gentleman, and so the business was made up for the present. Our Gentleman who had some of the Goldsmiths money, was resolv'd to have more, or venture hard for it; wherefore having again given instructions to his Boy what to do, he made several Journeys to the Goldsmiths, walking by his door to watch an opportunity, at length he found one; for he seeing the Servants telling of a considerable quantity of Gold; he gave the sign to his Boy, who presently went in and clapping his hand on the heap, took up and brought away a full handful, and coming to his Master gave it him; neither did the Boy make such haste out of the Shop, but that he could hear a stranger who was in the Shop receiving money, say to the Apprentice, why do you not stop the Boy? no, said the Apprentice, I do not mean it, I know him well enough, my Master paid Sauce lately for stopping him; and so they continued telling their money, which I am sure did not fall out so right as formerly; for that evening the Master and Boy both came to my lodging, and not only told me how they had sped, but I saw the effects of their enterprize; for this young rogue had brought off with him between forty and fifty brave yellow pieces; we all three rejoyced at our good fortune, for I was concerned, having five pieces of it given to me, I then told the Gentleman that he had run a very great hazard, and that I did not think he had practis'd these tricks; no truly, replyed he, this is the first I ever did in *England*, but I have been abroad in *France* and other Countreys, where I was acquainted with rare ingenious fellows at these tricks, and they had notable inventions to get moneys; and sometimes I would put in as a Party with them, and from them it was that I learned this confidence: I then desired him to relate to me some of his practises in those Countreys, he soon granted my request, and began as followeth.

I had not been long in *Paris* but I had some tricks put upon me; the first was this, I endeavoured to appear brave, made a rich Sute and Cloak, and with this strutted about the streets to shew my self, hoping and expecting that some *French* Madam or other would fall in love with me, but instead of that, some of these Gentlemen *Divers* fell in love with my Cloak, and were resolved to have it, wherefore they watched me one evening and as it growing late I was going home to my Quarters passing through a blind Lane where was nothing but back doors of Gentlemens stables; three fellows seized on me, one dives into my pockets, whence he fish'd out all the little money I had about me, which amounted to above thirty shillings *English*, another draws his knife and cuts the Neck-button of my Cloak, and the third takes off my hat; I had not lost all my spirits, so that I told them they did very uncivily by me to take away my hat, and leave me to walk without one; they begun to swear at me and forc'd me to entreat for my hat, and withal considering that the loss of my Cloak would spoil my Suit, I told them that I hoped as they were Gentlemen, so they would hear reason, and offered if they would put any price upon the Cloak I would redeem it; they thinking money would do them more good than the Cloak, told me that if I would give them five pounds, I should have it: the Cloak stood me in ten pounds, and therefore I was resolved to give them five pounds, therefore I desired them to name the place and time when I should meet them with the money; they answered me the next evening about that time, and in a place there adjoyning in the street; but they told me that if I thought by that appointment to bring any with me to catch them, that then they would mischief me; I promis'd them that I would not, and so we departed, but withal they were so civil as to give me my Hat along with me; I went home to my Lodging, and though I was vexed at my misfortune, yet I was forced to rest with patience till the next evening when putting the promis'd money in my pocket, went at the time to the place appointed; I had not staid there long but I heard the noise of a Coach, and on a sudden two men came out at the boot, and seising on me muffled me in one of their Cloaks and put me into the Coach; this done, the Coach-man did drive on apace, and I was in but bad taking to think what a case I was in, and did verily believe that those fellows who had the last night taken my money and Cloak from me, had now a Design upon my life, and therefore were come themselves, or had sent some of their Companions, to rob and kill me, I had not continued long in these thoughts but the coach stopt, and I was taken out of it, and being carried into a Court-yard, was unmuffled, and led into a great Hall, where I was met by those three who had the night before Dis-cloak'd me; they told me I was wel-come, and that what had been done to me that evening was only to prevent their being out-witted and discovered by me, and withal, as I was a stranger, to treat and entertain me amongst them; I hearing that it was no worse Pluck'd up my Spirits and answer'd them, that I was resolv'd to be in every thing as good as my word, and therefore came alone to the place appointed, and had brought my money with me; they then led me through the Hall into an adjoyning Wardrobe which was full of Cloaks, Gowns, Hatts, Swords, and all such kind of Habiliments, and among the rest I saw my Cloak, wherefore I told out the money and took my Cloak, put it on, and went into the Hall amongst them, there I was welcomed by several of the Gang and they had women amongst them, who all looked on me with a cheerful countenance, & treated me very civily. This they all desired of me that if I intended their friendship and my own safety, I must not take any notice of them before any company, or if I met them abroad; I promis'd to perform this Injunction, and so we went to supper, after that to dancing, and spent three or four hours in very pleasant manner, and then several of them departing I thought it was time for me to do so too, but I believed it would be convenient to ask leave before I went; wherefore I told those whom I best knew, that I was amind if they pleas'd, to go home; they told me that I might do so, but it must be in the same manner as I came; I consented to it, and two of them going into the Coach with me, hid my face for a short space, and then let me see; but I quickly perceived that I had gone through several By-lanes and passages, and at length came to the place where I had been taken up, and there they set me down, and the Coachman whirling about left me in a moment; I therefore went the ready way home to my Lodging, where I went to bed and consulted with my self about this Adventure, not having known or heard of the like; but it was not many days before I was engaged in another which was as strange as the former. Although I was in a strange Countrey, yet I had some acquaintance whom I visited sometimes; One day being solitary a walking, I met with one of these of my acquaintance, he saluted me very courteously, and told me he supposed I was minded to break off the friendship we had lately contracted because I had been so great a stranger at his house: I replyed, that I intended suddenly to give him a visit; I pray then, Sir, said he, let it be to morrow, the sooner the better, for I have a great desire to converse with you; and Sir, said he, if you have any friend bring him with you, and for your sake he shall be as welcome as your self; I replyed, it was very likely that I should wait upon him, and thus we parted: I remember since that about the time I met this friend, I was overtaken by a gentile fellow, who had followed me like my shaddow, and during the time of this converse he waited as I did, and now I being parted from my friend, and having walked a little faster than before, I had dropt my Gentleman who sauntred behind. The next day about the time that mortals whet their Knives on Thresholds, and Shooe-soles, I prepared to go to dinner to my friends, and again by the way I was accosted by this gentile fellow, who had the day before followed me, and now he did so again; and when I came to my friends house and entred, there he did so too, and with as much confidence as if he had been of great acquaintance with the Inviter; he sate down among other Guests that were there, Dinner was soon after brought in, and there being several Guests much victuals, and much variety was served at the Table, my strange Gentleman did eat as heartily and talk as boldly as any there, and I thought him to be one of the Inviters acquaintance, and he supposed he was my friend which I had brought with me; but he proved to be very no good friend to the man of the house, for waiting his opportunity he went to the Cupboards head which stood in a convenient place, and clapping a piece of plate worth ten pounds under his Cloak, he walked off *incognito*. I soon after missed him, and my friend missed my friend as he told me, but it was not much longer e're the Plate was missing, and although private search was made, yet it was not found, and our friend being gone, the Inviter missing none of the Guests but him, asked me for him, but when I told him he was no friend nor acquaintance of mine, he soon knew which way his Plate went. Thus (said he) he thinking him to be my friend, and I thinking him to be his, this fellow had the conveniency of doing this injury; but, continued he, I soon understood that it was a usual matter to play such pranks and that more considerable, and that withal a very bold confidence, unusual with other Nations, and upon second thoughts I remember I had seen this fellow among those who had my Cloak, but it was too late now to remember it, and it had been unsafe then to have taken any notice of him, remembring the Charge had been given me.

CHAP. XIX.

Two notorious Rogues robb'd a Church by the help of two Fryers habits they had murther'd; afterwards they robb'd a Merchant of Silks, Plate, &c. By a notable stratagem they laid for the purpose in an Inn next adjacent, they ransack'd a Linnendrapers Shop in the night by conveying a boy into it being enclos'd within a supposed Bayl of Goods, who proved the Key to let them in to perfect their design; by counterfeiting a Gentlemans key, they stole from him six hundred Crowns, and murdering him flead his face that he might not be known, but were notwithstanding by a miraculous providence discovered and executed, who being penitent at their death, confest many notorious villanies. A notable trick a Gentleman puts upon a Pick pocket.

Thus (continued Mistress *Mary*) did this Gentleman finish his two stories of the Cloak, and the piece of Plate. I told him I wondered at the boldness of those *French men*, and that they exceeded our Countrey men in confidence; yes, (said he) if you knew so much as I, you would have reason to say so, for it is a usual thing for them to seize Gentlemen if they can light upon them in any convenient place: and carry them some miles out of the Town, and make them pay money for a ransom, neither dare they contradict it lest worse befal them, and they are bloodily minded, for if they cannot get money, they will do any murder. Not far from *Paris*, continued he, two of these Rogues had been hunting for Prey, and because they could not meet with any purchase, they were resolved rather than fail to commit some murder; the next that met them were two Fryers, these having no money to redeem their lives they dispatched into the other world, and having so done, they stript them; and put on their Fryers weeds; being thus habited they march'd further into the Country, and coming late to a Countrey-town, went to the Parsons house, who entertained them; as they came in late, so they went out early, pretending necessary occasions, and the Parson not being up nor willing to rise so soon, they desired the Key of the Church (which was adjoyning to the house) that they might go it to do their devotions before they went? the Key was accordingly delivered, and they went in, but instead of saying their prayers, they made a prey of what they met with, the silver Chalices, and all the Ornaments of the Church they took with them, and so went on their wayes to do more mischief, but not having the conveniency to execute their designs in the habit they were in, they therefore went to the place where they had hid their own, and there putting them on, they march'd to *Paris*, where they walked about the City to espy what mischief might be done; being now both weary, hungry, and thirsty, they went into a drinking house, which being full of Guests below, they were conducted up one pair of stairs, and there they had both victuals and drink such as they desired, when their bellies were full, their eyes did wander about the Room, to see if they might espy any thing to make a purchase of; but although they could see nothing in that room, yet they could discern that in the house opposite to them, there was much rich Goods, fine Silks, and Sattins; their fingers itch'd to be handling of them, but at present they knew not how, however resolving that they would attempt it, but not finding any means how at present to do it, they therefore were resolved to try if they could take up their Quarters at the house they were drinking in, and then they did not question but they should in short time find out some means to execute their Design, having taken this resolution, they therefore call'd for more drink, and their Landlords company, and being frolick, and expensive, that they might be accounted good Guests, they asked of the Landlord whether they might not have a Lodging there? he believing it would be to his profit, told them they might, but they must lodge one pair of Stairs higher; they were well enough content with that, and therefore drank on till it was night, and then to bed they went; and laid their plot how to rob this Merchants house, which they did in few days after: In order to which Design of theirs, they went out and purchased Ropes, and a Pully, and seeing a large Chest to be sold at the second hand, they likewise bought that, and putting in their Ropes and Pully, and a great quantity of Raggs and stones, and such like Trash, that it might seem heavy, they caused it to be carried to their Lodging: Their Host seeing so large a Chest, and so heavy, did believe that his Guests were rich, and that a considerable quantity of Treasure was therein enclosed, and therefore gave them a greater respect than formerly. They every day when they went out, carried out part of the Rubbish which they had bestowed in the Chest, so that in short time it was empty, or at least, nothing but the Ropes and Pully was in it: They only now waited for a convenient opportunity to execute their design, which they considered must be done when both the houses, as well that where they lodged, as the Merchants house they intended to rob, were empty; and no day was so likely to leave them so, as a Sunday; wherefore that they might have the better pretence for staying at home, they both pretended some indisposition in their bodyes, for which they said they thought it convenient to take Physick, they had been so good Guests to the house, that the Host was willing to accommodate them in anything; however, when he and his Family went to Church, they lock'd the Street-door: No sooner was that house clear, but they were resolved to attempt the other, and knowing that the Master and Mistress, and most, if not all the Family, was likewise gone out, they were resolved to kill the rest, if they found any single person that should oppose them: They intended to make their way into the house by going down the chimny, and therefore they had provided Ropes and a Pully, and there was no great difficulty to get to the house top, for they ascended to the Garret of their Landlords house, got out of the window to the top of that, and the other house joyning to that, to the street side, they soon got to the Chimny they intended to descend. The house where they lodged, and this Merchants house were joyned together in the Front, but backwards there was an Ally of about six foot wide that seperated them, and a cross this Ally it was that they first saw the Room wherein the Silks were placed; they being gotten to the Chimny's top, laid a piece of Timber across, and fastening their Pully to that, and putting their Rope in the Pully, the one who was to descend the Chimny, took hold of one end of the Rope; and his companion holding another part of the Rope, by degrees he was let down into the Room he desired: It was two pair of stairs below the Garret, and in regard the Silk might be soild and spoil'd if they were drawn up the chimny, they did not take that course but a more easie one, for he that was on the house top, went into their lodging the same way he came up, and going down into the Chamber that was even with, and opposite to that where his Companion was, he opened a Casement, and his Companion doing the like, they could without much difficulty reach to one another, and so in short time the richest, and best of the Merchants Silk was conveyed into their Quarters. Our Thieves seeing they had gained this prize with so little danger and difficulty, were resolved to get more if they could; and therefore he that was in the house ransack'd it all over, and finding a considerable quantity of Plate and money, he likewise conveyed it to his Companion; and now having done all this, he went into the Shop, intending to leave the street door open, that the Merchant when he came home might suppose that the thieves who had robb'd him did come in that ways, but the street door was double lock'd, and therefore it could not be opened, wherefore he undid the bolts of one of the Shop windows, and leaving it loosely open, he went up agen, and telling his Companion what he had done, and that there was no more to be done, he ordered him to go to the house top, and as he had assisted in letting him down the Chimny, so to help to draw him up, which the other did accordingly. There was one scruple came into their minds, that although the Shop-window was opened, and the Merchant might reasonably enough imagine that the Thieves who had robb'd him, had come in that way, yet they were very sensible, that with descending and ascending the Chimny they had thrown down much soot, which might cause a jealousie, that they who robb'd the house might come in that way, and so they might be discover'd; wherefore to prevent all such suspition as much as they could, they tumbled down two or three Brick-batts that lay on the top of the Chimny, which might be supposed to be blown down by the wind; and having thus done they retired to their Quarters, disposing all their Silks, Money, and Plate unto their Chest, and that there might be the less suspition of them, the Landlord soon returning, one of them pretending to be very ill, and the other very dilligent in attending his Companion; their Landlord furnished them with strong waters, and such other cordials as were at hand; and the Merchant coming home found his Shop-window open, and his house robb'd, it being so apparent as he thought that the Robbers came in, or went out at the Shop-windows; he had no suspition of any other contrivance, all that he could do, was, to have all suspitious places search'd, his neighbours house escaped, being too near home to be suspected: the host only thinking he had escap'd a danger being so near, and telling them that it was not good to leave a house empty, and although all his folks went with him to Church, yet he had left two honest Guests in his house, and besides they were locked in fast enough. Thus, continued the Gentleman, was this Robbery committed, and they who were guilty went away unsuspected. The next day they conveyed part of their purchase away to a place where they hid all their prizes, and by degrees getting the most part away, they continued not long in those Quarters, but made another Remove. These fellows were notable cunning Rascals, and had so many ways to bring in Purchases, that they gathered much goods together, but covetous of more still attempted further Projects, till in the end they were caught and deservedly punished.

The next Project they had (said the Gentleman) was this, they had a boy who oftentimes served and assisted them in their undertaking, and he was now very useful; for one day intending to steal, they pretended to buy some Linnen cloath; and a conceit coming into their heads, they did buy some considerable quantity; they left it at the Drapers where they bought it, paying a small matter of money in part at present, promising to come the next day and fetch it away, and pay the rest of the money: the next day they came and brought a Porter with them loaden with a Bayl made up, as they said, of Woollen-cloath which they said they had bought, and intending to send that, and what they had bought of him into the Countrey, the Carrier was gone before they came, and therefore they could not send away either till the next day; when, they said, another Carrier was to go to the place they intended to send to; and therefore they desired the Shop-keeper to let them leave that Bayl of Cloth in his Shop till the next day, when they intended to fetch them both. They having been Customers to the Shop, he did not refuse them so small a courtesie, but permitted them to set it in a convenient place in the Shop; but his entertaining of that Bayl of Cloth, was almost as fatal to him as the *Trojans* entertainment of the wooden-horse; for at midnight when the Draper was asleep, these Rogues were wakeful, and having conveyed this Roguish Boy I told you of, into this Bayl, which they pretended was Cloth, he taking out his Knife cut his way through, so that he came out the Bayl, and not finding the Key of the Shop-door, he opened the Shop-windows and did let in his two Masters, who waited there for that purpose; they being within the Shop were not idle, but having seen by day-light where the finest Cloth was plac'd they now removed it, and breaking open a Desk wherein they had observed the Draper did put his money, there they found four hundred *French* Crowns, so taking that money, and as much of the finest Cloth as they could carry, they march'd off; neither did the boy stay behinde, but leaving an empty Bayl covered with Canvas, and stuff'd round about with Cotton, he also loading himself, went with his masters, the same way he had let them in, and so they carried this purchase to the rest. The next morning the Draper, and his Servants were soon sensible of the Robbery, and seeing the hole cut in the Bayl, they quickly discovered the manner how, but it was such a Novelty as had not been heard of; and he was forced to rest himself contented with his loss, for notwithstanding all his endeavours, he could not for the present hear of his Customers, who indeed were safe enough in their Quarters. These Rogues who now had money enough put themselves in a gentle habit, and kept company with the best, but still they waited to do all the mischief they could, and to that end they ingratiated themselves into the company of Countrey Gentlemen, such as were best acquainted with the Customs and Humors of the Town; many they met with, and few escaped them, but that they either got them into play, cheated them, or pick'd their pockets or made some other prize of them: Among others they met with a young Country-Gentleman, who had been unfortunate enough already, for he having had a quarrel about a mistress, and fighting with his Rival, had the Fortune, or Misfortune rather, to kill him; Divine vengeance seldom misses to pursue, and overtake those who are guilty of murther; & although these kind of murthers, which are the most excusable, being as they term them, fairly done, pass rather for pieces of gallantry than otherwise; yet some great misfortune always attends them, as I have observ'd by several Precedents, but more especially by this Gentlemans misfortunes; for no sooner had he made his Enemy to fall in the place where they had fought, but he was forc'd to fly away for his own safety, doubting else he might fall in to the hands of Justice; he therefore with all speed retired to a place, six miles from thence, where he had fought, to a friends house, and not thinking himself safe, being there provided with money enough for a long journey, he travelled on towards *Paris*, being a place whose large Circuit, and number of inhabitants might hide him from all pursuers; in his way thither he was met by Thieves, who attempted to rob him, but they being but two and he valliant enough, as he thought to oppose them, drew and defended himself, he here likewise had the fortune to cause one of them to drop down by him, which the other seeing, fled, but not so far but that he soon returned with three more in his company; The Gentleman seeing this, and doubting that now he should not onely be robb'd of what he had, but also believing that they would kill him to revenge their fellow; he therefore takes one Purse of money and threw it into a Hedge near him, hoping that if he did escape, he might have that for a reserve. By this time the thieves were come up to him, and all drew upon him, he (knowing that odds did overcome *Hercules* and might do him) therefore told them, that if it were his mony they wanted, he would deliver it to them; although they were very angry for the loss of their Companion, yet it being money that they came for, they accepted of that; he giving them another Purse of money which he had about him; but in regard they had suffered so great a loss as the death of one of their Companions, they stripp'd, and ty'd our young Gentleman, and taking away their Companion with them, they departed. He lay not long there but was unty'd, and reliev'd by some Passengers, who furnished him with an old Coat, and he taking up his Purse of money, where he had laid it, went along with them to the next Town; there he furnished himself with Cloaths, and so travelled on towards *Paris*; but before he came thither, he was again met with by Thieves, who then robb'd him of all his money; so that when he came into the City he was in a sad condition, being a Stranger, moneyless, and friendless: however these last Thieves being so civil as to leave him his Cloaths, he took a lodging in a convenient place of the Town, and presently sent away to his friends, acquainting them with his misfortunes, and desiring them to send him more money: Although it was a great way he had to send, yet in a little time he received an answer according to his expectations, and although till then he was forc'd to run on the Score, and keep house, yet now he honestly paid his Host, and putting himself in a very good Garb, he now went abroad, & light into the company of our two thievish Rogues who dealt Roguishly with him; for perceiving him to be a stranger, they took him up, and became his companions; and that they might be able to do him the more mischief, they so far ingratiated themselves into his company, as to take a lodging where he lay, and then finding that he was pretty well furnished with moneys, they tryed several ways to get it from him, they tempted him to gameing, but he was not guilty of that hazardous vanity, and would not play; he carried but little money in his pocket, but he left the rest in his Trunk which was also lock'd up in his Chamber; and the Landlord of the house being an honest man, was very careful of it; however they were resolved to be Masters of it by one means or other: but they delayed it a while longer by an occasion that fell out; he had written for more moneys, intending to pass from *France* into the Low-countreys; and thereupon a Letter came one day to his hands, which acquainted him, that within fourteen days he might receive six hundred Crowns of a Merchant in *Paris*, to whom a Bill of Exchange was directed; this Letter he dropt by accident, and one of these Rogues met with and read it, but knowing that it would advantage him nothing to keep it, he soon gave it to the owner. He acquainted his Companion with the News, and how he did believe that the Gentleman would, when he received that money, bring it home to his Lodging, wherefore they would stay until that time & then they would rob him of it all; this resolution they both continued in, and that he might not distrust them in any particular, they kept him company very much, seldom permitting him to be in any other company; they also carried him abroad with them to several of their friends, who treated him very well for their sakes: In the mean time, they being often with him in his Chamber, one of them took the Key out of his Chamber-door, and making an impression of it upon Wax, put it in there again; his Companion keeping our Gentleman company in the mean time: The fourteen days being come, he went and received his money, and bringing it home lock'd it up in his Trunk;

And now being furnished with money, he was resolv'd to fit himself with Clothes, and proceed on his intended Journey; but he was prevented; as I shall presently tell you, for these two Rogues having now got the key of the Chamber-door made, and having tryed it, were resolv'd to delay no longer, but catch the Birds before they were flown, as they would be in few days, if they did not prevent it; for this cause they invited him one evening to go out with them to supper, he distrusting nothing went with them, where was better cheer than Company, for all the Entertainers were as very Rogues as these two, however they treated him very civilly, and after supper fell to drinking, he being desirous to return to his lodging, requested his companions to be going; but they knowing it was yet too early to execute their Design; desired him to stay longer, and so long as he had their companies, they told him he would be safe enough; he seeing them resolv'd to stay, was content, and so they drank on till about eleven of the clock at night; and then, he not being willing to stay longer, they agreed to go with him; and to the end they might not be stopp'd by any Watch, they agreed to go a back-way, which was somewhat about; this they pretended was the reason of their going that way, but it was indeed, that those who were his entertainers, and who were to assist them in their Enterprize might by going the nearest way, meet them; which accordingly they did, for at the place appointed by all, but our Gentleman, they met, and pretending themselves drunk, jostell'd one another so, that their swords were soon drawn, and they assaulted one another, our Gentleman seeing that those who met them were but four, and he and his Company were three, did not question but he might have the better on it, or at least defend himself, and therefore being perfectly valiant, he so prosecuted one of the two who assaulted him that he laid him at his feet; the rest thinking that those two who assaulted him would have performed their Enterprize well enough had hitherto only plaid with one another, in clashing of their swords, but now seeing one of their Companions fall, and doubting more mischief, they all four, as well those whom he thought were his friends as those whom he knew to be his Assaylants, left their jest and fell all upon him in earnest, and he being thus over-match'd, was soon kill'd. The Rogues who were left alive, seeing him, and one of the Companions dead, knew not what resolution to take, but after a short consultation, they resolved to carry off their dead Companion, and leave the other there; but the two who were his Companions, fearing he might be known before they had finished their Project, and they might be prevented; they therefore drew their Knives, and like bloody Butchers fley'd all the skin from the poor Gentlemans face, and so taking the Key of his Trunk out of his pocket, and all his Letters, that they might leave nothing about him to cause him to be known; they and their Companions parted: the two Rogues went home to their Lodging; where when they were let in, they were asked where the Gentleman their Companion was? they reply'd, they left him presently after they went out; and this answer serv'd for the present: they then went into their own Chamber, but soon after with their false Key they got into his, and opening his Trunk they took out all his money, and lock'd it up in a Trunk in their own Chamber; and this being done, they went to Bed: The next morning they went out, and carried the money with them to the place where all their other Treasure lay; returning again, intended to get away all their other things that were of any value, in the Trunk; purposing to be gone, and leave that behind them, for they knew it would cause suspition if they remov'd Trunk and all, so suddenly; in their removal of their money, they had carelessly left their counterfeit-key of the Gentlemans Chamber-door in their Chamber-window, wherefore the Landlord coming in there, and seeing a Key, which although it was new yet he believed he had seen it, or one like it; he therefore comparing some other Keys with that, found that it was like the Key of the Gentlemans Chamber-door; he therefore try'd it, and found that it would open it as well as the other: he was in some kind of amaze to think of this, and the Gentleman not coming home, he began to suspect that all was not well: About noon he went in again into the Gentlemans Chamber, and knowing that he had lately received a considerable Sum of money, which he believ'd he had put in his Trunk, he therefore lifted up the Trunk in his hand to poize it, and feel if it were heavy; but it was light enough; they having already taken out all the money; he having set it down again saw lying by it a pocket-handkerchief, which, he being now grown curious, dilligently looked for the Marks of it, which he found not to be marked with the two Letters of the Gentlemans name, but two others, which were the name of one of the others: These things raised further scruples in his minde, wherfore he was resolv'd to observe his two Guests with a more curious eye; and one of them soon after returning, he watch'd him, and saw that he went to his Trunk, and made up a Bundle which he carried out; no sooner was he gone out, but he heard the report which had gone about the Town all that day; that a Gentleman in such a place was barbarously murthered, and was so much a Stranger that no body knew him; the Landlord hearing this, his heart leap'd and he was in a very great perplexity, so that he could hardly stand on his leggs; so soon as he was come to himself he took a Neighbour with him, and went to the place where the Gentleman lay murthered: It was to no purpose to think to know him by his face, for that was quite disfigured; his skin being fley'd off; but although his Cloathes were bloody, yet he could by them know that it was his Guest, who lay there murthered; he then told his Neighbour what were his thoughts, and withal, that he believ'd he knew the Murderers, and thereupon having acquainted him with all his Doubts and Jealousies of his two other Guests; he and his Neighbour both were of the oppinion that they had hand in this Murther, and therefore they hasted home to see what might be further discovered; Just as they came in, one of the two went out with a bundle under his arm, which the Landlord seeing, he caused one to follow him, and dilligently to observe all he did. He that was sent was so careful, that he soon after returned, and told him, that certainly there was some matter of great consequence between his two Guests, and three others, who were dividing and telling of moneys, and he heard one of the two say; that now all was well, for he had brought off every thing, and intended to go no more; where are they? said the Landlord; they are at such a house, naming it, said the Messenger: but I followed your Guest to another place first, where he left the parcel he carried out, and waiting some time, he came out of that house, which was a private house; and went to the other, which was a Victualing-house; I, said he, following him thither, was permitted to go in there, as he did, to drink; he went to his Companions, and I took a Room next adjoyning; where I heard, said he, what I have told you, and several other discourses, which makes me think, that these persons have lately been upon some Design; but what, I cannot at present imagine. But I can, reply'd the Landlord, I doubt, what I have imagined is true; wherefore Neighbours, said he, what is best to be done? I pray advise me; they told him the best advice they could give him was to go to the Magistrate, and acquaint him with what had happened; he did so, and they at his request went with him; being come before the Magistrate, the Landlord told him, that not long since a Gentleman came to his house to lodge, and soon after him, two more who being well acquainted together, went out (said he) to supper; the two returned home; but it was somewhat late, and the third not coming home, raised in me some suspition, which hath fallen out too true; for, said he, the poor Gentleman is barbarously murdered, and lies in such a place, I have been to see him, but, although I cannot know him by his face; for they have fley'd off the skin, yet I believe it is he by his Cloathes; and, continued he, I very much suspect my other two Guests are guilty of the murther, for I have found a false Key of the Gentlemans Chamber-door in their Chamber: and so he proceeded in telling the Justice all the particular observations he, and the person he had Sent, had made: the Justice was of their oppinion, that these two men had murthered the third; and therefore sending for Officers, and a Guard, sent immediatly to the place where they were all together, and securing them, they were brought before him, he examined them severally, and so finding them in Several Tales, he gathered so much from their Examinations and Confessions, that he found them guilty; and then being inform'd that one of them had left a parcel at a private house; he caused that place to be search'd, and there was found a great deal of wealth and goods; there was the Merchants Silks; the Drapers Cloth; the Challices, and other Church utensils, and the two Fryars weeds, and much other goods, Commodities, and Disguises; all which was seized on, and the report of this murder, and the other particulars, running about the City, it came to the ears of the Merchant and Draper, and many others who had been lately robb'd;

and they coming, knew and owned their Goods. Our Rogues who were now fast enough for commiting any more Roguries, and seeing that they were discovered, for they were told of all things that had hapned; now saw it was to no purpose to deny those several facts that would be too plainly proved against them; wherefore they confess'd all this that I have told you of, and several murders they have committed, among others that of the two poor Fryars; and robbing the Church, wherefore the Parson, and the Church-wardens of that Parish hearing of this confession, came to *Paris*, and the Felons executed, they and the Merchant, and Draper, and all others whom they had robb'd of any thing, had their goods returned them; and thus said the Gentleman, was the end of these wretches; and I came to be thus particularly acquainted with this story, because when I was at *Paris*, I lodg'd at the same house where they had done, and my Landlord acquainted me with all these particulars.

The Gentleman having finish'd his discourse, said Mistress *Mary*, I told him that these two were cruel, and bloody minded Thieves, and that I did not care for hearing any such stories, for that I was much troubled, and methought sensibly concerned in his relation; he replyed, that indeed this was bloody and horrible, but that it was usual to have such murthers committed in *Paris*; and that very frequently, and continued he, both the Thieves and Pick-pockets, are far more cruel and bold than in *England*; and although I have given you examples of both, yet I could tell you many more, and enlarge very much upon this Subject, for it is usual for Pick-pockets there, to perform their work in an extraordinary manner, for they are furnished with Arms, and Hands made with Wax or Wood; and by vertue of these, they will frequently and without suspition, pick pockets in the Church; for they will hold two hands with a true Arm, and a false one, that is an Arm of Wax or Wood up, and in their hands they will hold a book and seem to be busily employ'd in turning over leaves, at their Devotions, when as the third Arm and hand is picking of pockets; and People standing by, nay, the Parson himself whose pocket is pick'd, will have very little cause to suspect him that does it: also if they get a man out of the way, and are minded to rob him, they will put a piece of Iron or Brass into his mouth, like unto a Pear, which they call a *Choak-pear*; and that properly enough; for the party who hath it in his mouth, endeavouring to get it out cannot, for there being a Spring within it which forceth it open, it is impossible to get it out without a Key to it, which they have; therefore they who put this Choak-pear into the mouths of any, after they are first robb'd of what they have about them, they are told, if they intend to be rid of that Pear, they must go and fetch more mony, which they must bring to a place they appoint, or else they are like to chew upon the Pear, without any other Victuals, which is like to be hard Dyet to them. But continued he, I shall tell you one of these wax or wooden-handed-fellows, and so conclude.

A Gentleman having had his pocket several times pick'd of moneys and Watches, was much troubled and resolv'd if possible to find out, and catch one Pick-pocket that should pay for all; wherefore he advises with a Smith, an ingenious fellow of that quality, to make him a band of Iron or Steel, with some prickles about the side of his pocket, and a spring towards the bottom, which when it should be touch'd, would cause the band of Iron or Steel, at the top to close together, so that if a Pick-pocket should come there, it would catch and hold him fast by the hand: this he had made to his desire, and then he went to the next Assembly, which was at a tryal of causes, and it was not long e're his project took; he heard his Engine discharge, and the fowl was caught; he knew which Pocket it was, and therefore lookt on that side one stood with hat off, and both his hands were upon his Hat, which were held up as high as his face; he therefore wondring whose hand he had caught, and seeing the man in that posture, doubted that his Engine had deceived him, and had given false fire, but putting his hand towards his pocket he found a hand there, which was in vain strugling to get out; wherefore that he might know who this hand belonged to, he got out of the press of people, and the man who held his Hat in that posture went with him; when they were gone a little to the one side, the poor fellow cryed out; I pray Sir, let me have my hand; how! replyed the Gentleman, I see you have two already, and therefore if you have a third, you may well spare me that to guard my pocket for the future: the fellow saw that he was caught, and therefore replyed to the Gentleman; truly Sir, it is but a tryal of skil, a new invention, and I hope you will not be angry with a piece of ingenuity; but if you are, rather than fail, if you please to let me go, and not discover me, ile give you any satisfaction; what security shall I have for that said the Gentleman? all that I can give, said the Diver; and thereupon he drew out a purse of money from his own pocket, which it is like had an another owner but lately, but now it helped to make his composition, for the Gentle-man and Pick-pocket going to the Tavern they clapt up an agreement; he not only receiving satisfaction for what he had formerly lost, but also discovered to him the Nature, Use, and quality of a Wooden hand.

CHAP. XX.

Mistress Mary *continues the story of the young Gentleman; relates how a Cheat (with two more) pretending to be a Countrey man, performed a very profitable but most comical exploit on a Shop keeper; she is interrupted by the Arrival of her comrades;* Meriton Lattroon *enters into a Pleasant Dialogue with her; his* Indian *wife falls in love with Mistress* Mary *and Mistress* Dorothy, *disguis'd in mans apparel: and a pleasant Adventure there upon.*

Thus (said Mistress *Mary*) did the Gentleman discourse of the *French* manner of Thieving and Cheating, which was after a more confident and bold manner than that of our Countrey-men; and their manner of picking pockets was, I told him a great Novelty; he replyed that he could relate many such tricks that were done at his being there; two more whereof, continued he, I will tell you, and so conclude.

Three Cheats intending a piece of roguery, had aparelled themselves like Countrey-men; and two sauntring in the Street, one of the other went into a Shop-keeper, whom they saw was alone in his Shop, and tells him that he was a Countrey-man, and had born all offices in the Parish where he liv'd: and was now Church-warden, and that he was come to Town to lay out a little money for the use of the Parish; but more especially to buy a Cope for the Parson; and, said he, I would buy a good one though it cost me the more money: and thereupon fetch'd several and shew'd him: he turn'd many of them over, but still desired to see better, at length one was brought which he seemed to like: but, said he to the Shop-keeper, I doubt it is too short: no, said the Shop-keeper, it is long enough of all conscience, and thereupon measured it upon the Country-man: who said, I cannot tell by this measuring, whether it be long enough or no: but our Parson is a man much about your pitch, and therefore I pray do you put it on, and I shall be better satisfied, the Shop-keeper to satisfie his Customer, did so; and our cheating Church-warden did assist, and help him to put it on; but in doing it, he clapt his hand into the Shop-keepers pocket, and drew from thence a purse of money, the Shop keeper perceiv'd it, and caught hold of his Customer, but he slipping out of his hand, shew'd him a fair pair of heels, and the Shop-keeper without putting off the Cope followed him; in the mean time the other two of our cheats Companions acted their parts, for the one went into the shop, and taking the next bundle of goods that came to hand went away, and the third doubting that if the Shop-keeper kept his pace he might overtake his Companion whom he pursued; he therefore having plac'd himself in the way on purpose, catches hold on the Shop-keeper, and says, O Lord Master Doctor! what makes you thus distracted? as to run in the streets in this unseemly manner: the Shop-keeper told him that he was mistaken, he was no Parson, and that he was in pursuit of a fellow that robb'd him; by this time our Cheat who was pursued, had turned a corner of a Street, and was out of sight; and the Neighbors coming out to see what was the matter, perswaded the Shop-keeper to go home again and put off that Garment, and then go look for the Cheater; he did so, but there he found that he had a second loss, which made him more angry than before, especially when he considered that he was without all remedy, not being able to discover who they were that had shown him this clenly conveyance.

Another time said the Gentleman, a couple of these bold rogues understanding that a Gentle-man was newly come from travel; and having enquired into and been acquainted with many particulars in his Journey, were resolved to get money out of him; and therefore waiting a time and place convenient, and seeing him walking with another Gentleman, one of these bold rogues thus accosts him: Sir, your very humble servant, I am very joyful to see you after your return; although you have travelled several Countries since I saw you last, yet you are not one jot alter'd: but you are, replyed briskly the Gentleman, if ever I saw you before, for to the best of my remembrance this is the first time: I shall bring you, reply'd the Confident, to be of another mind when I tell you that my name is *Mounsieur Brisack*, and that you and I travell'd many a mile together, and were very merry at such and such places, naming them; I hope Sir, continued he, that you do remember that we staid three dayes at such a place, and then departed, having very bad way, and a tedious Journey to such a place, still naming the places, and there we met with such and such Gentlemen, who continued in our companies a fortnight, all the while we staid there; and we came to such and such a place. All this reply'd the Gentleman, and all those Persons I very well remember; but indeed *Mounsieur Brisack*, if your name be so, I do not at all remember you; but since you give me so good an account of my Journey, I must needs believe you to be acquainted with me in those parts; and since you are so, I pray how doth *Mounsieur Langone*? very well, reply'd our Cheat; he intends to be here in short time, and then I will bring him to you that we may renew our acquaintance: I shall be glad of the opportunity, reply'd the Gentleman, and so good *Mounsieur Brisack*, said he, till then I shall be your humble Servant; yours Sir, reply'd the Cheat; but I pray, Sir, do you now remember me? yes, yes, reply'd the Gentleman; then I hope reply'd the Cheat, you will also remember that I did you a small courtsie in the time of our acquaintance; what was it? said the Gentleman, that I may acknowledge it; and thank you; no great matter, Sir, said the Cheat, it was but a friendly office, we ought to do so for one another at such a distance; I do not understand you, said the Gentleman; you are very forgetful, said the Cheat, but I hope that as now you remember me, so you will remember to pay me that little money you borrowed of me at such a place; I know nothing of it, reply'd the Gentleman; I lent it to you replyed the Cheat, by the same token, that your Horse was taken lame in one legg, and you were forc'd to leave him behind you, and take another: truly, replyed the Gentleman, the token is good, but I do not remember the other matter; but I hope you will, reply'd the Cheat, and pay me for your Credit-sake before it comes to the hearing of our Fellow-travellers; how much do you say it was, reply'd the Gentleman; but twenty Crowns, a small sum, and soon paid; I know you are not without so much money about you, and if you please to pay it me now, it will do me as great a kindness in receiving it now, as it did you when I lent it; well replyed the Gent. if it be so, when *Mounsieur Langone* returns I will pay you, which you say will be in short time; I hope Sir, replyed the Cheat, you will not injure me so much as to put me to stay so long, when you promised me to pay it at our next meeting, and besides, Sir, it will not be for your Credit to let him or any of our Fellow Travellers know that you boggle at the payment of such a driblet as twenty Crowns: and thus did he importune the Gentle-man for payment, by telling him that he had now acknowledged it before witness, and that if he would not quietly pay, he would compel him to it: so that the Gentleman to purchase his quiet gave him what he demanded, lest, as he said, he should shame him.

Whilst Mistress *Mary* was busied in the recital of what was afore delivered, and intending to have proceeded in the same discourse; she was interrupted by the return of the Captain, *Drugster*, and *Scrivener*, and *Gregory*; and her looks and colour discovered to the Capt. that she had play'd the extravagant in the use of that liberty & freedom which he freely gave her, and could not contain himself from expressing some resentments thereof: and addressing his discourse to me in a fleering manner, come Master *Meriton Latroon* (said he) I shall know you better by degrees, and do fear I shall find you too much guilty of the humour of the *Turks* and *Italians*, who unaturally delight in the society of young men: they are pretty Smock-fac'd Lads, how do you like them, Sir, if you could procure a change of their Sex, would not either of them serve for fine play-fellows.

I think (said I) they are best as they are, without any change; nay, with your pardon, good Captain, I know it an undeniable truth, which your own frequent experience doth, or must acknowledge; their unsuitable habits, I confess at first muffled up, or quite darkned all former knowledge of them: but you must excuse them, if they did unmask themselves to be known to one, they once preferred before their own safeties and reputations. Your sweet *William* was once my little wanton *Mally*, whom with many more, I first beguiled by hiring my self in womans apparel, as a Servant maid in a boarding School. This other whom you call *George*, was a Country-girl, whose beauty and good feature disarm'd me in the road, as I went on the Pad, and although I had never seen her till then, I was so passionately in love with her, that I never rested till I had obtained my desires on her, which effected, I ungreatfully left her.

This said the Captain, is a thing I was wholly ignorant of till now, although from our friend *Gregory* I have been informed of the most remarkable passages of your life: such wonderful and unheard of transactions in one man's life, that in his relation I thought him reading to me some Legend of incredibilities.

I replyed that I had reserved this secret with some others, to be discovered as occasion should serve, and that in time, nothing should be hid from him. And now Sir, said I, you nor the rest of your friends must not entertain a jealousie that I participate and share with them in your Mistress's affections; to be plain if your belief of that raise in you any anger or revenge, you will discover thereby your folly most egregiously; for can you expect a constancy from such, who know they cannot live, but by being inconstant; they are like such who are upon a trading Voyage, it is not one Port, but a great many that makes up their market; neither are they like some Merchants who particularly trade to one place, as to *Guiney, Hambrough*, &c. They are generally trucking, or vending their commodities through the Universe: *Mal*, said I, you must not be angry that I thus plainly and boldly disclose the naked truth; pray on, Sir, said she; I shall exercise my patience in hearing your rallery, but I pray tell me when you are out of breath, that I may inform you of the infirmities and frailties that belong to your more noble Sex, and spare not ours; you will not be so unjust to deny me that liberty you take your self; a match, quoth I, and therefore I shall proceed. When you were but fourteen, you began like a Nut to grow brown at bottom, which you know will then drop or fall of it self, or I might more properly compare you to forward Summer fruit, which proves mellow in the non-age of the spring, but rotts by too soon falling, when more sollid fruit shall deny the nipping frosts of an approaching Winter. There is a *Queen-apple*, and a *Bitter-sweet* so call'd, you resemble the one in the lovely colour, the other in the distasteful *Gusto*: but since I speak of fruit, the most common resemblance is a *Medlar*, which is never good till rotten; such are you, never finer drest than in your winding sheet. Several of your Sex when married are but a parcel of *Crab trees*, wall'd in at a great charge. As for thy part, thou art like a honeycomb with a Bee in it, which infallibly stings him that tastes thereof: to be short, ye have fair tongues and false hearts; fine faces, but foul Consciences; pride prompts ye to all manner of prodigality, and lust leads ye to that loosness, which ruinates thousands in the destruction of yourselves. To conclude, I could love thee, but that thou art female, and would never have married, but that I thought it best expedient to bring me to repentance. Now Sir said she, I believe it is my time to speak, for I find by your straining, you are very needy; you have but little water left by the sucking of your Pump; I see where your plot lies clearly, by undervaluing me and our Sex, you would put our friends out of conceit with us and others, that you might make a Monopoly of our Sex; be advised Sir, your Patent will not be worth the procuring, if we are so variable and wavering, as you would falsly make the world believe, you have Marshall'd up a fair company of Metaphors, that your wit might flutter in our disparagement. Our sailing from port to port to advance our profit, is not so discomendable as you would have it, since it is rather our misfortune to meet with such Bank-rupts, Broken-merchants, who have neither stock nor credit to barter with us for our wares. Surely your wit is mightily improv'd (since your poor Poetry you writ to my friend *Doll*, which she related to me was almost all the reward she had for her lost Virginity) it skipt so nimbly from Pole to Pole, from Sea to Land, to fetch a Lean starvelin of a conceit, and that was the comparing of us to ripe Nutts, or Nutts brown at bottom as you well know; for all we are slip-shell'd were it not for truanting-waggs who rushing into our Thickets shake us down; we might hang long enough, not like your Crack-ropes: and for your likening us to fruit soon ripe, and as soon rotten, I dare confidently aver that we might remain a long time on the tree, did not such unhappy Boys as you are throw stones at us. Lastly, you say our sweets are accompanyed with stings, I know not what you mean, but I am sure you stung this Gentlewoman and my self in that manner that the swelling lasted nine moneths, and by a Mid-wife was at last delivered of our pain. To conclude, with what force can you condemn us for inconstancy? when every new face you see shall change your affection, variety shall be as so many winds to blow your amorous pretences to more points than are contained within a Compass, and when you have had, after a long Seige, the Town (you sate down before) surrendered, you fall a plundring instantly, and it may be, after this, ingratefully set the Garrison on fire; if not, at leastwise curse the time and money you spent in your Conquest, throwing it off as a thing not worth the managing and keeping: No more (dear *Mall*, said I,) no more, what hitherto I have express'd, was but a tryal of thy wit, which since I find so pregnant, thy better parts, thy mind, I will endeavour to enjoy hereafter.

All the Company was greatly pleas'd with our Drollery, and now said I, Gentlemen, without trifling the time away too much, since we know one the others past lives, and present intentions; let us enter into a serious consultation, how we may advantage each others interest here, in order elsewhere. Although you, Sir (speaking to the Captain) have been in these parts twice or thrice before, yet I question not but the knowledge I have of this Country will prove as serviceable to our design, as any others that have been here a longer time besides the advantage of my projections; the Captain with all the rest readily consented to be advised with me in every thing, as giving me the priority in all manner of Roguery. Gentlemen, said I, the love I bear my own Countrey (although all Countries indeed, should not be such strangers to us, as not to make them absolutely our own, when necessity compels us thereunto) I say, having a longing desire to see *Europe*, and return for *England*, having now gotten something considerable for a future maintenance, I shall make it my whole business to take up what commodities I can on trust, and with what I have, and my self, I resolve to accompany you homewards; and that I may be the better wellcome among you, I will be assistant to you in the buying your commodities, and procuring you a credit withal.

These proposals commanded both their thanks and embraces, and to work we went immediately. But before I proceed to tell you how, and in what manner we enrich'd our selves by cheating and deceiving the Countrey: I must give you an account, that my she-black divil, my wife, had a moneths mind to no less than a brace of white *Josephs*, I mean my two Girls in mans apparrel; I confess the temptation was great enough to have deluded any other woman of more Christian principles; when I heard of it, I thought I should have dyed by the excess of laughter, and that I might have the more sport, I ordered my two Females not to discountenance her amorous desires. I have heretofore inform'd you that she was for feature and stature as handsome, and as proper as most *Europeans*, and had a natural genius, her Sex is not ordinarily endued withal: in the time of my living with her, I had taken considerable pains to teach her *English* of which she hath a competent understanding and utterance. Seeing me go very gentile and gallant, she disserted her own Country fashion, and thought herself obliged to be cloathed in mine, which I condescended to, not so much to please my eye, as to sport my fancy, for they became her as well as a Hat and Feather, Sword and Belt, with a Red-coat would become a *Jack-an-apes* riding before the Bears.

We had not many *English*-women among us, however she imitated every one of them in some thing or other, so that she seemed when drest to have borrowed of at least twenty women, and those Habiliments look'd as if they had been thrown on her with a pitchfork. She being extreemly smitten in love with these 2 handsome young men, as she thought them, began now to be less careless in her dress, but what disorders she endeavoured to rectifie and amend, she made a thousand times worse; she consulted her glass, and imagining her face was not naturally fair enough, that is, not black (for blackness is esteem'd by them as beauty, and tawniness the contrary) I say to correct that natural defect by Art, she got some Lamp black, or some thing like it, by which paint she resolved to be devilish fair.

I wondred to see my pretty sweetings face, all of a sudden so strangely chang'd, but I concerning my self but little with her, never demanded how it came, but according to my usual Custome went to bed, and not long after my wife followed me: I had drank very excessively that day, by which means I slept profoundly and was not sensible what her petulancy prompt'd her to when I was asleep; but certain I am, she did so all to bekiss me, and so rubb'd the black paint off her face upon mine, that none could tell which was the blacker of the two in the morning when I arose.

I got not out of bed till an hour after all the rest of the People in the house were up, and staying somewhat longer above than I usually did, she came up into the Chamber, and perceiving my face to be black, she was at a stand, not knowing what to say, or do; but at length concluded (as she confess'd afterwards) that her God was angry with her for loving any other white besides her Husband, and therefore had taken away his white face, and had given him a black one in the room: she retired down with much more reverance than usual, and was so amazed, that she spake not a word to any below. The Captain and his friends, with several of my own acquaintance were attending my coming down, who seeing my face thus discoloured, knew me not, yet knew my voice and clothes, and though I bid them good morrow, they returned me not the like civilty, but instead thereof, ask'd me whether I was not an impudent fellow to counterfeit another voice and wear his clothes? Gentlemen said I, are ye all mad, or have ye eyes that ye dare own? I am the man I was the last night I am very certain; you may have the same body, said the Captain, but the foul Fiend stole away thy head last night for being drunk, and left his own in its room; hereupon a Looking-glass was fetcht, and put it into my hands, but I no sooner saw my face in it, but it dropt out of my hands breaking all in pieces, and with the amazement of this sudden alteration, I was just ready to expire; now did all my former roguries come fresh into my memory, believing that they, with what I was now about to act, had rode poste to the Devil to inform him what I was; that he was come to fetch me away alive, and that he had lent me this hellish face, that I might be the fitter for his company in his Journey homeward.

The Company seeing me stand so like a changeling, could not forbear laughing till they held their sides, at length one of them came, and with a wet cloth rubbing my face, restored it me again, I could not imagine who should serve me this trick, or how it should be done, but at last recollecting my thoughts, I remembered that my wife of late seemed to me to be more than usually black; whereupon I call'd her to me, and with the same cloth I made her blackness vanish too. She perceiving I was inflam'd with rage and fury, fell upon her knees, and begging my pardon, she told me every circumstance of what she had done and design'd, concealing her real contrivance; that she had painted her face in that manner to increase my love, she said, and that in kissing me and laying her face to mine, (not imagining the black would come off) she had thus discoloured my face, and would never do so again: I was so far from being Angry with her, that I could not forbear laughing heartily, which renewed the like in my friends; however I charged her never to make herself fairer than she was again, and if I found her pride extend that way, I would devest her and reduce her to the Clout, it being all the clothes the *indians* wear, an insignificant fore covering; this troubled her more than if I should have gashed her flesh and fill'd the wound with salt, a punishment frequently used among them. Notwithstanding the ill success of her first project, yet she was resolv'd to prosecute her love but which she loved best, she could not tell, if there had been an half dozen more, she had room enough in her breasts to entertain them, and had affection to have scattered plentifully among them all.

CHAP. XXI.

Latroon's Wife *prosecutes her love, the manner of her extravagant Horse-courtship, inviting them to a bowl of Punch, she forc'd them to the Squeak, is discovered in her amours by her Husband and would have poysoned her self to escape his anger.* Latroon *brings his new Comrades into the acquaintance of the* Bannian, *whom by feasting him aboard and ashore, they make their friend in their knavish Design.*

My Wife was none of those puling, whining, lovers, who not obtaining their desires, presently exclaim against the injustice of Heaven in not granting their wishes, and growing sullen to make amends for their Blasphemy, hang themselves, or cut their own throats. She had a certain way of Court-ship peculiar to herself, and a kind of Horse-play in her kissing, which was so strong and eager: that you must have a special care she did not beat some of your teeth down your throat; her embraces were as soft as a Bears, I think fully as strong, she hath made me sometimes in a merry humour, cry Oh: and therefore I cannot see how these striplings will escape with life should they be encirkled in her arms.

What kind of Rhetorick she used to perswade them with, I am not yet acquainted, but I understand she boarded them both at once and put them to the squeak, without uttering a word, and had not they fled for it, she had ransacked their carcasses to have tryed their Manhood, this made them ever after shun being alone with her, which made her so mad, that when she hath seen them in company, if by any means she could come at them, she would have pinch'd them by the arms, or else where, her fingers being as bad as a pair of pincers. She was ignorant of the way of winning them by Presents, or the subtle insinuation of fine words, varnished with love and Service; she was downright with them, if they would not love her, she would see whether she could make them; but that not doing, she was resolv'd to try whether drunkenness would operate any thing upon them. Whilst I and my new Associates were gone abroad to hasten our purposes of marching off together, she had prepar'd a Bowl of Punch, with other excellent Liquors, not omitting several Dishes of Sweetmeats; she strained her self at that time to the utmost to express her civillity and kindness, drinking often to them till at last she perceiv'd that the strength of those several Liquors they drank had elevated them; then did she in as good *English* as she was Mistress of, tell them that she lov'd them, and they must love her, that she had never seen such pretty white men before, with that she caught one of them about the neck, the other fearing they should be now discovered, indeavored to assist her Comrade, and struggled to disengage her hands from about her neck, but she being too strong, would not disengage her hold, but by main strength brought them both down to the ground together with her; just as my business calling me home, I entred the Room wherein I found my Spouse at *Tantum*

Scantum with the two supposed young-men, tumbling all together promiscuously: I knew they could not if they would, and would not if they could make me a Cuckold, therefore I had no cause to be angry with any, but my Christian Infidel, and yet I had but little reason to be so with her, considering the brutishness of her nature, and barbarousness of her education: however so sensible she was of the injury she design'd to do me, that taking a Dagger out of her pocket, which she mightily delighted to carry always about her, she would have stabb'd her self, had I not prevented her, by forcing it out of her hands. I saw nothing but distruction and distraction in her eyes, and therefore, watcht her narrowly she would not mischief her self, or any else; she seeing that seem'd better compos'd, and stepping aside drawing a small Box out of her pocket, which she always made her *Vade mecum*, and was fill'd with the rankest poyson, she conveyed some of it into a Cup, and offer'd to drink to me, which she would have done, had I not dasht it out of her hand: she seeing me so careful of her preservation, imagined I had no evil will against her, she fell upon her knees again, and begg'd of me that I would kill her, for she deserv'd it, or take for my satisfaction as many wives as I pleas'd into the house, and she would not be offended at it in the least; I told her I would have no more wives than she, and that I would forgive her this time, so she would never do the like again.

She now trebled her diligence at home, whilst I exercised my wit abroad, among the *Bannians* I invited one of the principal of them home to a treat, a man of vast sway, and great credit in the Country; and having acquainted my new Correspondents, or fellow Conspirators of the time of our meeting, I ordered them to appear as splendidly as they could, according to the Custome of the Country; and to be noble in their expences, all which they performed so well, that they gain'd a great esteem with the *Bannian*; Moreover I informed him privatly; that the Captain (though an Interloper) was resolv'd not to be behind hand in the lading his Ship homeward, with the best Factor in the company, having Gold enough for that purpose, and that those young men that accompanied him to the *indies* were the sons of *English* Lords, that had brought with them great store of Gold to see this Country, and lay it out in the Commodities thereof: he hearkened to me with much attention, and having always had a very good oppinion for me, believ'd what I said to be no less than truth, and therefore desired me that I would perswade them that he might negotiate their Affairs for them; this was the thing I desired, which I should have offer'd him, had he not so happily prevented me by his own voluntary motion, and to encourage his willingness therein, I whispered the Captain in the ear aside, informing him that the *Bannian* was fully wrought upon, and that now he had not need to fear fraught at half credit, as I shall mannage the matter, I desired him to invite him abroad to morrow, and what friends he should think to bring along with him, which accordingly he did; after that we had been sufficiently merry together in my house, and though he was somewhat elderly, yet he was a very comely old man, and had wit and heat enough in him to play the Good-fellow: We had so liberally entertained him (and had so fitted every thing to his humour, I knowing his humour to a hair) that on his going away, he acknowledged infinite satisfaction in that he had received, promising for these civilities his utmost Service and Assistance; the Captain stopt him in his further acknowledgments, by assuring him they were nothing to what he and the Company intended for him, desiring him that he would favour them with his Company abroad the next day; the *Bannian* gratefully accepted the proffer, for he was a person that lov'd dearly his belly, and therefore the more willing and ready to accept our *English* treatment, which he knew was no niggardly one; but had he known what a stale purgation he should have had after all his feasting, he would have sooner swallowed a *Pagod*, than one single morsel.

About noon I found the *Bannian* at his own house, and telling him that he was expected abroad, he made himself ready to go with me, in our way thither we met with some of his most intimate friends, and some of mine, those which I thought would further our design I singled out, and took them along with us. The Captain had made ample provision for us, and understanding from me that the *Bannian* was obliged to abstain from some sort of meat, he had to be sure provided none thereof; having feasted with all the jollity imaginable, firing several pieces of Ordinance according to Command; now Sir, said the Captain, that you might know we come not into your company empty-handed, or that we will take up any of your Goods and Commodities without paying you for them according to contract, I will shew you something which shall be a Secret to every body else, so unlocking a Chest, he shew'd them a great quantity of his own Gold, and his Undertakers; if this be not enough, see there of this friend of mine fifteen hundred pieces, and of that mans there, five hundred, with a thousand more if occasion should serve.

This made the *Bannian* and his friends admire to see so great a quantity of Gold, however he seem'd to take but little notice, only saying, you have a great deal of money, Sir, and we have a great deal of valuable Commodities, which you shall not want, but trust them to my procurement for you, and you shall not fail in your expectation; he spake *English* good enough to let us understand, that he would be our Servant to do our business, and the Merchant too, to credit us if we so pleas'd. What Goods we took of him at first we paid him ready money before delivered, and by degrees caus'd him to send some abroad, and paid him three or four days after: And to the intent we might not be in the least suspected for any knavery, I advised the Scrivener, Drugster, and *Gregory* (their Hanger-on) to give out they intended to stay in the Country some considerable while, that what goods they bought, they would send for *England*, when the Captain should return thither, and to confirm the truth of this report, they built them an house, befitting the entertainment of them, and the securing what Goods they should procure by way of Merchandize, servants I procur'd them, such as I thought would be for their turn, both Male and Female, but if they intended to have their Victuals well drest, they must not expect the Cookery from them; however they resolv'd to try the ability of their new servants, who handled the matter so scurvily, that when it was brought to Table, there was not one, but was of a different oppinion in giving a name for what was brought before them, not knowing whether it was boil'd, bak'd, broyl'd, or roasted; for the looks thereof seem'd to have a touch of them all; so that it was concluded by all that the Proverb was never better verifi'd than now; *God sends meat, and the Devil sends Cooks*; and so any Stranger would have taken them, they being of his own smoaky complexion. Wherefore to avoid these foul inconveniences of sluttish feeding, it was agreed on, that *Mall* (alias *William*) *Doll* (alias *George*) notwithstanding their Breeches, should officiate as Cooks, their friends should be caterers, and their menials Skullions.

CHAP. XXII.

Latroon in order to his returning to Europe gets a great deal of Goods, most on credit; he suspects his wife of some villanous Design, discovers her wicked inclination, and hints at the common cause of Cuckoldry. She under pretence of loving visit poyson'd one of the supposed young-men, and had like to have dispatcht the other, and afterwards kills her self: her Assistant in this Murther was found not far distant from Bantam torn to pieces by wild Beasts, three days after the Fact.

In this Equipage our friends were in, whilst the Captain, and my self were daily bringing in Grist to the Mill; the *Bannian* according to his promise, with speedy sedulity procur'd us what ever we desired, and to encourage his Industry had daily (almost) encouragements for his quick dispatch. Our business now ran on wheels, neither did the pleasures of our new Houskeepers slacken in their carreer, they had every thing which the Country afforded, and more, for they had two such matchless *European* girls, which all *India* could not parallel, whose luster was the brighter by reason of those dark and dusky foils which were always near them.

But damn'd be that cursed instrument that totally eclipst the light of those two *Wandring stars*, which must ne'er shine more in our Hemisphere. Who would have thought a wife, after so much penitence and submission (being obsequious beyond imitation) should renew her revenge, and prosecute it to death. It is true, the found me remiss in the cooling of her amorous Heats, but that from the first I used her to, that she might not expect it when it came, as a duty, but a courtesie, or a very signal favour, by reason hereof the was void of frequent expectation; had the been as white, and as lovely fair as any of my own Country-women, I would have serv'd her in the like manner; if I intended to make my wife absolutely my own. For in my time I have observ'd at least an hundred Examples of this nature; Women, whom I am confident might have ran the Race of their lives in the way of modesty and honesty, had they not been chafed or over heated at first by the ostentatious humour of their hot brained Bride-groome, striving to out-do himself, that he might purchase the esteem of being a lusty man excelling others in strength and vigour; but when the wife shall finde the satisfaction of her desires dis-continued, she will be apt to think her husband was too prodigal at first, and so became Natures Spend-thrift, and now thinks of no other thing than how she shall be supplyed by others. Others again are like some childish appetites, who feeding on some excellent Dish, they never tasted of before, and being exceeding pleasant, eat beyond measure, thinking themselves never to be satisfied, so getting a surfeit, ever after loath what they lov'd, the very sight thereof will even nauseate their stomachs. I say by stinting my wife after this manner, she could not suspect that by rambling abroad, I disappointed her expectations at home, since custom made her believe me indifferently honest. But her revenge was grounded on the Basis of equity, for since she was so far from being jealous, that she allowed me to make use of others, she judged I could not in reason dis-allow her the enjoyment of one or so, especially of my own complexion.

The removal of these two young men (as she supposed, and in that belief courted them to her embraces) she verily believ'd was occasion'd by me, and design'd that she might have no converse with them. Whilst they were in sight of her, she pleas'd her self in viewing them, but being depriv'd of that hourly happiness, she had not so much prudence as to conceal the resentment of her loss, and the injury was done her by me, but exprest (in her manner) to my very face things that carried with them suspitions of a dangerous consequence.

For the prevention thereof, I seemingly show'd much kindness unto her, giving her a many good words, & granting her with all leave to visit those two young-men, with this proviso, she would not wrong me, and all this was to pacifie for the present, till I was ready to go from the implacableness of of her revengful spirit, which is an Inmate properly not onely in her, but in all the *Indians* her Countrey people. She seem'd hereat to be very well satisfied, but so impatient she was to have a review of them, that she went from me immediately to them, at the sight of them she represented her joy in so many antick shapes, and formes, that all which were present burst out into a great fit of laughter, which she construed in favour of her self, supposing from hence, they were over-joy'd to see her; and what made her believe it the more, was their welcoming her to their new house, in the best manner they could, drinking to her so often (in the best liquors they had) till she was half Sea-over; the heat of the PERSIAN-wine she drank, gave fire to the old train, which should kindle the Magazine of Love, which lay covert in the Cole-pit of her hellish lust; and now breaking like a Hand-granado, the pieces of the shell could not fly faster than her arms did about their necks, there was no warding them, so that they were forc'd to submit to the cruelty of her over-powerful affection. But when she insisted upon the complement thereof, they bade her then desist, for they were resolv'd never to wrong her Husband in that nature, and threatned her, that if she would not be civil, they would acquaint him therewith. Hearing them menace her after that fashion, she retreated and sate down at a distance, and seem'd somewhat pensive, but having spoke some few words to a Black that past by her in the *Indian* tongue (which I would have understood had I been by) to which there was a sudden reply; she seem'd to throw off her melancholly and re-assume her jolly attempt, telling them that the next day she would come again, if they would make as much of her as they had done then; they told her they would.

I visiting them that evening, they acquainted me how welcome they had made my wife for my sake, how she had renew'd her love, and how preposterously she had manag'd it; in recital thereof we had good sport over a Bowl of Punch: to avoid the dangers of going home late I bade them goodnight. In the morning early coming down I found one of their female Slaves close in discourse with my wife, who seeing me vanished; I suspecting nothing, went to the *Bannian* about my business, and that day we had so much business to do, that it was near night, before I could visit our friends, to acquaint them what progress I had made therein, and how near it was brought to consummation. But I had no sooner entred the doors, but my ears were entertain'd with the doleful groans of my two disguised *Amazons*, who lay upon a Matt on the ground, foaming at mouth with the Scrivener & Drugster, & *Gregory* attending them, offering their utmost assistance, which was to little purpose, since they were ignorant of what they ail'd; as soon as I saw them, I knew they were poyson'd, having seen several in the like condition (a common practice among them upon the least suspition of an injury design'd, or an offence already receiv'd) but knew not what remedy to apply, and whilst I was in consultation with myself what was best to do, I saw *Malls* teeth drop out of her head, and *Gregory* going to raise her head, the skin and hair with it came off in his hands like a Perriwig, so did the hair of the other; so strong was the poyson administred, that *Mall* died in less than half an hour after the reception thereof; but *Dorothy* escaped ever to a miracle.

This sad accident had like to have converted the house into a Bedlam, for the three young men which had attended them in this disaster, were so strongly distracted at the sight of what had happened, that I thought the Devil had just then by a reentry took possession of them, or that they had taken the same potion of Poyson, which was very near as bad; believing it would work as subtlely and as nimbly on them as it had already done, (*Principiis obsta*) I ran with might and main for some Sallad-oyl, a Jarr where of I brought in the twinkling of an eye, Drink, drink, said I, to them all, quickly, quickly, one after the other, as fast as you can, which they did, not knowing any reason therefore, but that I commanded them; having even gorg'd themselves with it, and being not able to drink anymore, I poured it down their throats till I had almost choak'd them, or rather drowned them therein, they cried out to me, for the love of God to forbear, or I should kill them, judging me to be mad indeed: as they were evacuating what they had too plentifully received, the Captain whom I had left with the *Bannian* to follow after me, came in, who asking me what was the matter? I told him particularly. He could not but shew something of trouble, but having been acquainted with all sorts of losses and miseries from his Cradle in a manner by traversing to and fro the Universe, he bore this with a patience agreeable to his courage and Man-hood, and now our friends having disembogu'd the Oyl that was within them, shew'd all the appearances of perfect health; now seeing them in a condition to return an answer to what questions I should propound to them, I ask'd what strangers they had entertained at home to day? they reply'd, None; but, said *Gregory*, let us first see whether a certain she-devil of ours be within, and then I shall tell you what I have observed; upon this we search'd for her, but could not find her, it seems the same Black I found in the morning discoursing with my wife, when having done this execrable murder, by the instigation of my other devil at home, was fled, as more plainly by and by will appear. Said *Gregory*, not full an hour since; whilst we were at the farther end of the house busied about our wares, Mistress *Mary*, and Mistress *Dorothy*, commanded some wine to be brought them, which was accordingly done by this female we now miss, and brought in a midling Cocoa-nut bowl; they were just drinking the third time round, as we came in, nay, now said *Mall*, my little merry *Grigg*, here's to the Mistress of thy affections, speaking to me, and drinking heartily, I looking into the Bowl to see how much was left, this Black dasht the Bowl out of my hand, and because there was but little in it, I judged it onely to be an effect of her rude petulancy, and so did the rest, taking no further notice. Presently our two friends grew extraordinary ill, and though we were three to two yet they would have found work for as many more had not death thus bound one of them hand and foot, and the other seemingly dead for the present: I will lay my life, said I, I know where there is another of the Conspirators, so taking the Captain with me only, we made all the hast we could to my own house, and found by the extraordinary number of people therein, that something more than ordinary was the matter, and so there was, for my wife with her beloved Dagger, had with one home stabb made a hole through her heart, wide enough for half a score lives to go out a brest without jostling one the other.

I was not troubled to see her thus weltring in her own blood, but that she had not liv'd to be punish'd suitable to the crime she committed, if any punishment could be invented. The President of *Bantam* hearing of this horrid Murder, sent for me, to whom I gave an ample relation as I could by information, or otherwise, who seemed very much concerned, and immediately dispatcht several in the search of the Coadjutrix to the Murderess, about three days afterwards they found (some ten miles distant from *Bantam*) a female Carkcass, turn all to pieces, the limbs thereof were gnawed in that manner, that there was little flesh upon the bones, onely the head was untouch'd, and some of the company that had seen her before, would have sworn it was the same, and therefore it was agreed upon to carry it to the President, which they did, and presently order'd to be fastned on a long Pole, for a future terror to such like Malefactors, especially the Natives.

CHAP. XXIII.

Latroon and his Comrades about to leave Bantam *and go to* Surrat, *having done lading their Vessel, shew some tricks to prevent suspition of marching off, He sets sail from thence and meets with an Enemy, an account of a most desperate and horrible fight with him. He gives you an exact account or journal of that Voyage from* Bantam *to* Surrat.

Having buried our dead, we resolv'd upon a General Counsel, to see what we had done, and what we had left undone. We found that half our ready money was disburst, and that we had above half as much goods upon Credit, as our whole sum amounted to, and now resolving to make a final and speedy dispatch of all, I got all my Estate aboard not leaving any thing valuable behind me, excepting only what was in the house for the accommodation of my Guests, having an happy opportunity of conveying my own Goods with the Captains, and others that were concern'd with us the *Scrivener*, and the rest did the like.

That very day that we intended to set sayl, we were all merry at my house with the *Bannian*, and promising that the next day we would pay him what was in arrears, and also lay out five hundred peices more ready money; he seem'd highly pleas'd, leaving him, we shew'd our selves through the whole Factory with much Gallantry. The reason that we did not take in our whole loading in this Port, was the great number of *Dutch* Vessels which lately came into the road, and more daily expected, which we knew would not only obstruct our Credit, but raise the Commodities of that place. We were fain to scuffle hard among our Country-men for what we had already, there being at that time at Anchor in the harbour several ships. And having ready money pretty store we resolved to take in the rest at *Surrat*, which place would secure us well enough, and what we had deceitfully got. Having spent most part of the day in shewing our selves in the Town, about Three of the Clock in the afternoon, it being the fourteenth day of *July*, we got aboard, as if we intended to feast it, for there was none of the whole Factory, or our *Bannian* especially would think us so indiscreet to set sayl with half our fraught, that was my policy, and being unsuspected upon that account we might with the greater facility and security march off. Getting all our Anchors aboard in a trice, we loost our Sayls away we steer'd between the Main and *Paulo pan jan*, all the next day till six in the Evening, being then athwart the *South-salt-hill*, we steered *South-west* and by *west*, and *west* and by *south*, but from that hill we steer'd *west south west*, having the wind for the most part at *East south east* with much rain, which afflicted me grievously, for my fears of some pursuing us would not let me quit the Decks till I thought we were out of all danger in being followed. The sixteenth of this moneth at noon we espy'd *Hippins* Island *Eastward* ten leagues off, having steer'd all night *West south west*.

Latitude about 6 Degrees 38 and Longitude from *South-salt-hil* 6 Degrees 44 *West*, the wind at *south-east* with the help of a Currant for twenty four hours, from the sixteenth to the twenty ninth of this month, we had the winds between the *south-east*, and *east north east*, with most intolerable rains at Noon, being in latitude 11 degrees 59 *south*, and longitude 20 Degrees 35 *West*, the variation about 12 Degrees 35 *Westerly*; we sailed this month on several Courses, four hundred ninty six miles.

Mistress *Dorothy* being indifferently well recovered though a bad spectacle to look on by reason of the skin of her body all coming off with her nails, such was the malignity of the Venome; I say, speaking as well as she could, desired me to write some lines on her dearly beloved dead Comrade, knowing that my fancy did ever incline to measure lines, and so to please my self, more than to give her satisfaction, I composed these Verses.

On the death of his *Indian* wife, and his old Wench.

Start not my Muse, *what Paradox is this,*
That the same cause works both my Woe and Bliss?
Here lies my bliss, a more than brutish Wife,
By her own Butch'ring hands bereft of life.
My Woe lies here, my murder'd Joy, Alas!
What Wicked hand *durst bring this* Ill *to pass?*
Hells consistory *sate within that brest,*
Which sent my Love *to her Eternal rest.*
How happy had I been, had the Blest Powers,
Enlarg'd her Minutes, *and have made them* Hours.
Turn'd these short hours into long days, that I
Might dread Deaths *approach, when she should dye.*
But she is gone past all recal; and we
Can only weep and sigh her Elegie.
Though we don't mourn she can no Mourners *lack,*
Each Nature *is at her sad death in* Black,
Methinks they're hoarse with crying, and their votes

(Being sad, and doleful) do befit their Coats.

The Clouds *dropt tears; the* Ayry-Quire *(which flies*

Over our heads) do sing her Obsequies.

Shall we be dumb, whilst Birds do use their Art?

No let's in Sorrow bear with them a part,

When that y've done for Mall, *bereft of life,*

Rejoyce with me, dead, dead's my wicked Wife.

August the ninth, steering *Northerly* forty two Leagues, we found *per observationem* the Ship to run but thirty seven Leagues, which is five Leagues less by reason of the Current which sets us the *South-wards* Latitude at 6 Degrees 24 Longitude 36 Degrees 58 *West* from the *Salthil*. This afternoon we were in the Latitude of the *Changus*, to the *West-wards* of them, not seeing any sign of danger, the variation is good help if heedfully observ'd, finding about 22 Degrees when you are in 7 or 8 Degrees of *Southerly* Latitude, a *Northerly* course will go clear of all danger. The twelfth of this moneth we crost *Æquator*, steering *North, North east*, Latitude 10 Degrees, Seconds 85 Digits *Southerly* Longitude 36 Degrees 51 digits *West*, the wind at *South* and by *West*, the variation 19 Degrees, Seconds 35 Digits *West*.

The twenty-fifth of *August* we lay a try with main course, and mizen our Drift *North* 9 Leagues, the wind at *South west*, a fresh Gale. One of our men taking our main Top-sail, cryed out a Sail, a Sail. In a quarter of an hour by the help of my Prospective, I could discern her to be an Enemy of considerable force, about some forty four pieces of Ordinance. She made towards us with all the speed she could, and we to shorted our way, bore up to her with all the Sail we could make, so that we fetch't up one the other quickly although we had but thirty six Guns, eight less than she carry'd, and having fewer men withal we feared her not, but ran up board and board with her before we fir'd a Gun, and then we poured in a whole broad-side into her, whilst we pepper'd them above with whole Vollies of small shot: they returned us the like kindness, which kill'd us four outright besides what were wounded. Our Captain behav'd himself very manfully, and so bestirr'd himself in the fight, shewing so clear a courage as would have animated a very Coward to fight, as for my own part the meer observation of his magnanimous behaviour, infus'd into me more valour than I thought my self capable to contain, or able to make use of: my Land-water Soldiers, the Scrivener and his two Companions, by the Captains example, and my encouraging, look'd Death as boldly, and as daringly in the face, as if they had intended to look him out of countenance, though at first no shot, either great or small went whistling by them but what made them dap their heads, as if that would secure them; that Bullet which injures man never tattles in his ear the ensuing danger; that Bullet that whistles in the Air, proclames your crown as safe from cracking, as is the Goose after she hath past through the Barn door stooping lest her lofty head should knock the top thereof.

There was not any in the Ship exempted from Service, every man as he was Quartered not budging, but doing the utmost he could to offend his Enemy; a brave young stout fellow (whom I shall never forget) standing by me and my *Bantam* Comrades, a shot came and took away his legg with that fury, that it rebounded from the side; falling, he seemed not a wit daunted, but called out aloud, Courage Captain, I warrant you Victory, if you will but send down this Foot and Legg of mine to the Gunner, and let him send it to them instead of shot, and I shall laugh to see here, how it will kick the Arses of those insolent Rogues; *Gregory* standing by and seeing what had past, though something scar'd, yet would not discover any fright, and to hide it the better, commended the brave resolution of the man, and as he was laughing at the odness of his conceit (poor Fellow) a shot came and took away one side of his face, so dyed immediately, now it may be said, *he could laugh at him but with half a mouth.* This last unhappy Bout so scared the little valor which was in the Scrivener, that he instantly quitted his station, and disorder'd more men in his way to his supposed safety, the Hold, than twenty Troopers could have done in the midst of a Foot-company, a little afterwards the Drugster attempted to do the like, some of the men in the waste, seeing him upon his flight (just as I was moving on the same design) cried out, knock him down, knock down that cowardly fellow with a handspike, thinking they had meant me, being on the motion, I endeavour'd to prove the contrary by giving him a sore pelt over the noddle with my Musquet which laid him a sleep on the Deck; was highly commended by our Captain for so doing, telling me that two such fellows among a thousand men, nay an Army of ten times the number, might by their fear occasion their total overthrow.

The Drugster recovering got to his Quarters, and thought it better to dye fighting than to be kill'd for being afraid to dye, to work he went with a Blunderbuss, and fired it so often that he durst not charge it again till it was cooler, my Musquet was in the like condition. By this time the Enemy began to stand away from us, but we were resolv'd to keep her company, and make her pay for the trouble and cost she had put us to. We perceiv'd she had much a doe to keep herself above water, so that we were not long before we came to bear again upon her, which we did so efficaciously, that by a lucky shot penetrating her powder room she blew up, we being so near her, I verily thought she would have blown us into the air too, as she did her own men, part of which fell down into our Ship, as if you would have scatter'd faggot sticks off a house top: we had not above six men in all kill'd, and about nine wounded, none mortally, which were immediately committed into the hands of an excellent Chirurgion we had aboard, who took such a special care of them that before we came to *Surrat*, they were all perfectly cured.

Our ship receiv'd some dammage which was rectifyed by our Carpenters as well as they could for the present, and sail'd forward in our voyage. The next day we were forc'd to lye a Try again, which we did the thirtieth day, the wind at South-west allowing each days drift. The one and thirtieth we shortned sail all but our Sprit-sail, top-sail because of falling too soon with the Coast of *India*. This month we ran eight hundred fifty two Leagues on several Courses.

From the first to the fourth of *September*, we stood away only with a spritsail top-sail the course and distances, *&c.*, observed having a fair wind Westerly, but the next we steer'd East and by North, with Sprit-sail and foretopsail. The fifth from twelve to six (*per Compass*) East five Leagues, having at four of the Clock had ground sixty four fathome Oazy sand, then set more sail and stood in *North, North-west* till six in the morning, our depth in running the Course of seven Leagues was fifty five, sixty and sixty-four Fathome in Latitude, about 20 Degrees, Seconds 42 and Longitude 30 Degrees, Seconds, 3 Digits *West*. On the sixth day we steer'd *East* and by *North*, till four in the afternoon, at which time we saw Land, it was low and Sandy banks, with some Trees, and a white Tower or Church which may be seen four or five Leagues off. This place was judged by those men of ours that had sail'd often this way, to be fourteen Leagues to the *westward* of *Diu*. This evening we took a small boat not far off *Poramena*, bound to *Chichauho* near *Caule*, they had only three horses in her, having nothing in her worth making prize, we dismist them the next day without taking ought from them. The seventh and eight dayes we stood off and on, expecting to meet with some Jonks. On the ninth we met with a Jonk of *Gogo*, coming from *Mare Rubram*, or the Red-Sea, richly laden, which we took, imagining we now were made for ever, but the Commander soon dasht all our joyes, by producing a pass from the President of *Surrat*, upon sight hereof our Captain durst not detain her. I was on board her and having seen some part of her *Cargo*, I judg'd by that the richness of the rest, and therefore perswaded the Captain to make her prize though she had a hundred president passes, but he would not yeild, knowing better the danger than I did, and so dismist her to my great sorrow.

On the tenth we took a Jonk belonging to the King of *Succatore*, bound as they said, to *Surrat*, (the Devil was in our Captain to believe a word they said if ought might be gotten by them) and had aboard of her little that was considerable, saving six horses, and bast to make Ropes withal, wherefore he dismist her.

On the eleventh we anchored in twenty fathom three Leagues off the shore, to give notice if any Jonks should pass by in the night, they stood to the *Westwards*; and met a Jonk coming from the Red-sea, but this cowardly Hulk seeing our Boat, supposed her to be a Scout from some Man of War not far off, ran and sheltered her self under a Fort some fourteen Leagues to the West-ward of *Diu*-head. This Jonk had some *Europeans* aboard her, which plyed their small shot so that our Boat was forced to leave her, and coming aboard us was sent out again better provided with men and arms to lye as they had done before, to meet with the said Jonk, but in the night came six Sayl of Friggats instead of her and anchored by them. Our desperate daring less than little *Fan Fan*, would not leave them (knowing who they were) till she had spit that little Venom that was in her and then retir'd, this so allarm'd us that we got all sayls loose; and weighing up our Anchor the Cable broke, so our Anchor was lost; we stood in and having spent some shot on the Friggats notwithstanding there was such inequality in the number, they stood away for the shore and left us, however we would not let them pass so, but being some seven Leagues from *Diu*-head, in the night we stood in again amongst the Friggats, but there being little wind and a light night, they crept under the shore, from the twelfth to the seventeenth we plyed to and again, standing off in the day, and in again at night, seeing these Friggats every day, but could not come at them; they lay there to give the Jonks notice of us as we supposed.

The eighteenth we made up to the Land of Saint *John's* fourteen or fifteen Leagues off, near which we took a boat that came from *Danda ja-vapore*, bound for a place near *Diu*, out of this boat we only took two *Mestico's* and a boy, and so dismist her; anchoring at eighteen Fathome Oazy (being high water and little wind) in Latitude 19 Degrees, 48 Digits, about nine Leagues of shore, *Valentines pike*, *East* and by *South*, *per* Compass.

The two and twentieth we saw a Jonk and gave chase to her, fetching her up we found her to be a great Junk of *Surrat*, bound for *Acheen* with Merchandise, having a pass from the President and Councel, therefore he medled not with them; but in the afternoon came to an anchor in two and twenty Fathom, about thirty Leagues of shore. The weather was gusty with much rain, but never did I hear such peals of Thunder, nor see such great and continued flashes of Lightning: at four in the evening the next day we anchor'd at eighteen fathom within six leagues of *Damon*, the wind at *North North east*, and variable, with such terrible claps of Thunder and Lightning, that my friends, the Scrivener and Drugster would have freely parted with all they had to have been at the bottom of a *Cornish* Tinn-mine. They envied now poor *Gregories* condition, accounting his misery a great happiness, for since the Element of Water had received him into the Womb of her protection, the Element of fire might as soon give him a new soul as to detriment his body, theirs being now minutely expos'd to the mercy of its uncontroulable fury.

On the twenty fifths evening we anchored in ten fathom reddish clay, the *Pagod East, North east, per* Compass, and the trees of old *Swalley, North, North-east*, about three Leagues off; the next day the wind being at *North, North-west*, we turn'd up and anchor'd in ten fathom, the Toddy-trees *East* and by *North*, *per* Compass.

Lastly, having laid one buoy on the tonge of the sand and another on the point of the Main, we came over the Barr, the least water is four fathom and half at half flood, so we ran in till the Souther-Toddy-tree bore South and by East *per* Compass, and there anchor'd in eight fathom water. This month we sailed not above one Hundred and seven Leagues.

CHAP. XXIV.

Latroon *and his friends arrive in* Swalley Road, *they go ashore at* Surrat, *are entertained with other Captains of Ships lately come to an Anchor, by the President; he discovers an old Mistress of his and his old fellow servant, waiting on a Captain in a disguising habit; he renews his acquaintance with her; she tells him what befell her after his unworthy shipping her to* Virginia, *and the cause of her coming for* India. *She enters into a League with* Latroon *to cheat her pretended Master, which she did, the manner how. They sail together from* Surrat *homeward.*

The next day after our coming to an Anchor in *Swalley* Road, there came in to us six sail of *Dutch*-ships from *Nova Batavia*; and two days after came in four *English* ships more into the same Port. One of the Captains meeting with a Fleet of Friggats entring in at the Rivers mouth, was boarded by them and unhapily blown up, himself and others of his Company escaped, but were miserably burnt with powder. The ship drave into *Swalley* over the Bar and was tow'd on shore by our Boats and Barges, but all in a manner consumed by the fire; there was a *Dutch*-ship fought with the Friggats this while, which Sunk three of them, and in the fight there was three more surpriz'd, the first by the *Charles* Barge, the next by our Long-boat, which we doubly mann'd, and the last by the *Dutch*: they were but of little value, being laden with *Paddee, Beech-leaves* and other trifles.

Now did our Captain command the Skiffs to be mann'd, and taking me, the Scrivener, Drugster, with some of the Ship, we went ashore, and presented our selves to the President, who wellcom'd us in the best manner he could, and to speak the truth, his entertainment was magnificent; whilst we were frankly drinking Healths to our friends in *England*, there came into us (who came ashore that morning) the Captains of the other three Ships, with their Chief Officers, as also a great many *Dutch* Commanders and their Attendants, we used to say *The more the merrier*, and so found it, for the President as he was a very generous man, so he was prudent, and therefore by his noble deportment towards us, was resolved to oblige us both.

We on the other side, strove to out-vy each other in gallantry of Spirit, and in this manner we continued feasting three days, swimming in an Ocean of Liquor.

In this time of our Jollity I minded especially a young man that waited on one of the Captains; he had a very Sweet countenance, but his Complexion was very much Sun-burnt by travelling; I did verily believe I had seen the face before, and therefore very much eyed it, which he perceiving fixt his eyes as often on me, for I never cast my eye that way where he stood waiting, but I found him still looking towards me.

My heart renewed private intelligence what he was, but my reason could not so much as guess from whence it came; for by the extraordinary motion thereof beating strokes on my brest as nimbly as a Drummer a Travale on his Drum-head; I look'd on him as one I knew, neither was I alone thus, for at that distance I could perceive that the sight of me did put him into a strange confusion.

As I was contriving how to have some private conference with him, his Master commanded him to take some of the Boats Crew and go aboard and fetch him something which he wanted, he had no sooner receiv'd the Command, but casting his Eyes on me he endeavor'd to tell me by them, he had an eager desire to speak with me.

He going out, I withdrew from the Company, desiring their excuse for a while and follow'd him, but coming near him he trembled so he could hardly move a foot forward, seeing him in that agony, I asked him what ailed him? Bade him not be afraid, that I came not after him to mischief him, or injure him in the least. I believe, said he, you intend me no harm now, but it would have been well if you had never done me any. How! replyed I, it is impossible I should be so cruel as to injure a face so innocently harmless as thine appears: yes, Sir, you have, said he, and were it not for something within me I have no name for, I would be reveng'd on thy very soul for the abuse thou hast done me; I have now no longer time left to discourse you, but to-morrow meet me under the Southern Toddy-trees, and there I shall not fail to let you understand the miseries of ——, and there he dropt his tears so fast that he could hardly see his way before him. I was so amazed at what I had seen and heard, that there I stood as a thing immovable, speechless, and almost sensless; staying somewhat too long, the Captain came out to look me, and found me in this posture staring up into the Skie; What's the matter man? said he, what wonders dost thou see there, thou dost so gaze? I tell thee man, said he, this is no proper time nor place to take an observation, we are now at Land; but he knew not what observation I had taken, if he had he would have spoiled the Instrument if he could.

Recollecting my self, Your pardon good Sir, said I, I protest you drink too smartly within, so that I was forc'd to come out to suck in some little airy refreshment. This shall not excuse you, quoth he, therefore come along with me. Coming in he told the whole company in what a rediculous posture he found me, and did so Romance upon it, that he made them all laugh. One while, said he, he was telling the Clouds he saw, pleasing himself with the several monstrous shapes they bore, though I could not see one in all our Hemisphere. Then he turned his ear up to the firmament, as if he were hearkening to the Sweet harmony of the Sphears, and in my conscience, if I had not prevented him, I had seen him madly dance by himself without one stroke of Musick. After this he turn'd his eyes upwards again, and fixing them there awhile, the nine heavens or firmaments were so transparent to his sight, that looking through them, he recounted their particular names to himself in order as they were posited. He would have proceeded but that the company would not let him, for my own part he might have talked till dooms-day without any interruption from me, my thoughts being wholly imployed in searching out the meaning of what the young man lately spake to me.

I observed after his return, he could not or would not look once towards me as long as I staid. That night we parted some staying ashore, others going aboard; but I, knowing what business I had to do the next morning, lay all night with one of the Factors, a true Toper, and one that I had been formerly merry with in *London*. I got up early and went to the place appointed, where I staid not long e're I saw him whom I expected advancing towards me, I arose to meet him, so walking together we chose a place where we sate down, which was both convenient, and secret for our purpose. As I was about to speak he prevented it, by calling me base, faithless, perjur'd man (I starting up, laid my hand on my Sword) Nay hold, Sir, said he, think not to expiate your offence by murdering the person against whom they were committed, so pulling off his Perriwig discovered some short red hair? do you know this colour, said he, which once you told me you lov'd beyond any other? Here is the same Dimple in the Chin, and Mole on the Lip, and the same skin (stripping open his doublet) which you have unreasonably praised for its excelling whiteness; these were the flatteries you used to delude a poor credulous maiden, whom you not onely sham'd but ruin'd. You cannot forget your matchless treachery in seducing me aboard a *Virginia* ship, in whom I was carry'd thither and sold, you hoping by that villany to have been for ever rid of me and mine.

I now saw who she was (my fellow servant when I was an Apprentice) and knowing what she said to be a truth, I ask'd her forgiveness, acknowledging all my unworthyness to her, and protested if she durst trust me once more I would make her amends for all, at which she smil'd (for she ever lov'd me too well to be angry with me) I taking hold of this advantage did so press her to a forgiveness, that she could not deny me, having seal'd it with a thousand kisses: and now dear *Jane*, said I, I have a longing desire to know how you spent your time in *Virginia*, and how you came hither with this Captain; that I shall do briefly, she replyed.

When I saw that you had so cruelly trappan'd me, and that all your love was nothing but a deluding pretence to enjoy what you could, and be shut of me afterwards as I saw you had done, I attempted to fling my Self into the Sea, but being prevented in that, I betook my self to my Cabbin where for grief I lay the whole Voyage so desperately ill that none had any hopes of my life, for my Child dying as I suppose for want of those that should carefully looke after it. Arriving at Virginia, *and anchoring at* Potomack River: *several Planters came aboard of us, and made a quick riddance of all the Passengers but my self, none offering a pipe of Tobacco for me, for I was grown so weak I could not stand, and so lean that I was a meer skinful of bones. The Master seeing me in this condition, and judging I could not live two dayes to an end, commanded me to be carried ashore to dye. A Planters wife that was very antient, seeing me lie in that miserable and deplorable manner, took pity on me, and took me home to her house, where she proved so good a Nurse to me that every day I did sensibly amend. Being well, there was a great contest between the Husband of this good old woman, and the Master whose Servant I should be, a Suit was commenced, and upon tryal the Master was cast he putting me a shore as useless to him, acquitted himself of all future trouble with me. I being clear from him, my good Patron and Patroness discharged me in open Court for having any thing to say to me, for what necessaries they had provided for me during my sickness, being now a free-woman I had a hundred good matches offered me, all which I refus'd; there were some of the great ones too courted me for their lust (for I had now recovered my complexion, and my eyes had shaken off that dulness which had clog'd the swiftness of their motion) but all these temptations prevailed not, the memory of you had too large a power over my heart than to yield to any one else. But length of time began by degrees to extenuate that esteem I had of you, so that I did not behave my self so reservedly as formerly I had, but assumed a great deal of freedome. One day my Master (as I now call him) coming to the house where I was (for his Ship then rode in the River not far off us) took so great a likeing to me at the first sight, that as he hath confess'd since, he was never at quiet but when in my society; So that in a little time he had so won upon my affections, that my carriage towards him sufficiently demonstrated how dearly I loved him. To conclude, he made a perfect conquest of me, and as the earnest of a perpetual tye, he fully enjoyed me, and promised marriage if I would go with him as soon as he came to* Weymouth *in the west of* England, *where stood his Habitation. I greedily swallowed all his perswations (although one would have thought me more wary, having been so notoriously cheated by you before,) & the time coming when he would set sail, I march'd down to his Ship with as many as would have compleated a Regiment which followed me, looking upon me as the most absolute mirror of Chastity which ever arrived in those parts, joyful I was to return to my native Country, and as glad was my overcomer in that he had obtained so pretty a play-fellow to pass away his time in his passage homewards. In seven weeks we came upon the coast of* England, *and was by the stress of weather put into* Plymouth-sound, *where we rode with much difficulty between the Island and the Land. The third day after our anchoring there, the wind ceasing though the weather was somewhat hazy, he went ashore, and taking none with him but my self Coxswain and his Crew. I wondred what he meant by it, my fond hopes prompted me to believe that here he would perform the promise he made me at* Virginia, *but I found my self deceiv'd; for he dismist the boat after he had fill'd their skins full of wine, and commanded them to wait upon him in the morning.*

There being now none left but he and I together; Dearest, said he, be not troubled at what I shall tell you, and it shall be never the worse for you. I have a Wife and Children at *Waymouth*, although to gain my ends of you I pretended to have none; she is the most jealous woman in the world, and well she may, for she knows there is no woman in the Creation much more deform'd than her self, wherefore this I would have you to do that I may continue your company; you shall change your feminine habit for what is masculine, under which disguise you shall pass as a young man I have met with abroad, which for fancy's sake I have chosen to be my Companion in my Travels. *I thought I should have sunk into the Earth to hear him make this new confident proposition to me after so many vowes and promises to make me his wife, but gathering courage, I started out of his hand and would have gone down stairs, but pulling me back, what said I, are all my expectations come to this? must I be only your wandring whore at last? have I left so many wealthy matches at* Potomack *for this? no, I am in mine own Country, in a place where I am not known, & I will wash and scour for a livelyhood rather than submit so basely after so many worthy proffers. Notwithstanding a thousand resolutions I had to leave him; yet such was the subtlety of mans sly insinuation, that he made me unsay all that I had said in less than half an hour; and I agreed to everything he would have me do. Leaving me at the Tavern he went immediately, and bought a suite (which he guest would fit me) with Hatt, Shooes, Stockings, and whatever was requisite to cloath a young man fashionably, and brought them to me upon tryal, they exactly fitted me. Now because we would not give any cause of suspition to the people of the house where we were in changing my habit, it was concluded on between us to walk out of the town somewhere, he being well acquainted with all the places about the town, made choice of* Catdown, *where in the cleft of an hollow rock I unchas'd, throwing my proper habit into the Sea, and although it was somewhat immodest I was forc'd to beg his help in my new metamorphosis; he had procur'd me a very* All-a-mode *Perriwig, but before that would fit me he must play the Barbar himself, which he did by cutting my hair off close to my head. Being now clad with everything requisite from top to toe, we made towards the town again, where entring the former house we were in, we drank and were very merry, having a noise of musick, having supp'd one bed serv'd us without suspition; in the morning came the boat for us with the doctor in her, who asked my Master very seriously for the Gentlewoman, he replyed she had kindred and friends in this place and that she resolv'd to stay with them awhile; then he enquired what that young man was; O, said he, he is of my former acquaintance, who having little to depend on here, is resolv'd to see the world abroad with me. Coming aboard our Master need not make a repetition of what he had already said, the Doctor did it for him: now did we set sail steering for* Waymouth *which we did reach in a little time.*

*I was entertain'd in his house with much civility from his wife, and the servants observing what respect their Master shew'd me, paid me the like. There was seldom a day wherein he had me not to a Tavern, sometimes with company, but most commonly alone, and this life I led for fourteen monoths; at the expiration of which my master being employed by some Merchants in a Voyage to East-*India, *took me along with him by which means we have the wonderful hap to see one another again.*

My *Jinny* having ended her discourse, I endeavoured to endear myself unto her with all the outward demonstrations I could devise or imagine, protesting for the future I would never violate my faith to her, that she and I would run our fortune, live together, and she dying I would voluntarily do so too, to accompany her to the other world.

Fearing lest I should detain her too long, and give her Master any cause of suspition, I dispatch'd her away, and soon after went aboard our own ship, but before I went I appointed her to meet me there two days after. The Captain, my self, and all that were concern'd, went roundly about our business, for since he had gone beyond the bounds of his commission, he was resolv'd not to return home with her, but convert Ship and goods to his own use; this in secret he acquainted me with, as knowing my ingenious rogueship would be very helpful and assistant to him in all his enterprizes; and that I might oblidge him to me in an absolute bond of friendship, I seem'd to make him my Cabinet-counsel in all my affairs, and did really inform him of the truth of the last Adventure, knowing I could not carry on my design without his privity and help.

He did much wonder to hear me tell him that I had here also discovered another of my wenches in man's apparel, but his wonder turn'd into rejoycing when I told him how this wench should enrich our Stock by robbing her or his pretended Master of his Gold and what else he had valuable, and could hardly rest to think how I would effect my design. Fear not, said I, his Gold is all our own, therefore let us lay out our own as fast as we can, in the commodites of this place. The *Dutch* thought we had the Devil and all of mony, to see our goods come tumbling in upon us so fast, so that with what goods we took in at *Bantam*, and what we receiv'd here, our ship wanted but little of her full fraught.

The time was come wherein I was to have another Mess of discourse with my *Jinny*, who was punctual to her time, and there before me at the place appointed. And after some few amorous ceremonies I seriously told her that it was my intent never to part with her during life, she answered that it was her desire, and that she would run any hazard to bear me company; well, said I, make your self ready to go along with us, for we are resolv'd to set sayl within these two dayes; that I shall (she said) and know that I will not come with empty hands; my love shall neither be burthensome to you, nor expensive; how prithee, how said I, why thus, my pretended Master, as I have told you loves me dearly, expressing it in whatever way I desire, and to let me see how great a trust he dares impose upon me, and what confidence he hath of my fidelity, I have the key of his Chest wherein is contain'd 8 hundred Jacobuss's, besides a box of rough diamonds with other stones of price, all of which, or as much as I can carry off handsomely will I bring to thee, so much efficacy hath my first Lover over me that I could be content to undo all the rest to raise thee. I told her the notion was very suitable to our present affair, and that it was the best and easiest course I could propound for our happy living hereafter, and that when she saw any white thing hanging in our shrowd she should then fall to her work, which should be the token of our being all ready; which she could easily do at any time, for the Captain being almost continually a shore and she with him, it was but waiting for the boat (upon the sign given) which at her command would carry her aboard and bring her with the least word ashore. Moreover that having got the prize, she should presently make down to the *Toddy-trees*, over against which we lay at Anchor, and upon the signal of a Handkerchief, we would send our boat instantly ashore to receive her. All which according to instruction was exactly perform'd, the Captain whom she requited in this manner for all his love being at that time dead drunk by an invitation of the Factors of *Surrat*.

Having got my double Treasure aboard, and what lading we desir'd, our Hold shut up, our Anchors weigh'd, and our Canvas spread, away we sail'd over the Bar, with an hundred shot after us, for our Country-men as well as *Hollanders*, concluded there must be some damn'd inexpressible Treachery in this our suddain sailing, neither giving notice some days before, or fairly taking our leaves by fireing of Guns according to Custom; besides they knew we had not taken in our full Lading. Let them fire their hearts out we valued them not, in derision we fir'd a Gun at stern, and so stood to the Southwards.

I knew very well this female confident of mine would effectually do the business we had plotted together, and so to divert my self and make sport with the Captain of the discovery of my Rival, I wrote some few Lines and nail'd them on a Toddy-tree on the shore directed to the said Captain, which I knew would be discovered by some or other, and carried to him the verses were as follow.

Noble Captain.

'Twas a close plot y' faith, but 'twould not hide

From me your wench, *which should have bin my* Bride;

You chang'd her Garb, but could not change her face;

Nor change her heart, where once I had a place

Nere thence to be remov'd although she show'd

Some love to you, the Debt to me she ow'd.

Love *was a stranger to her till I came.*

Whom seeing lov'd, and loving lost her fame.

Sated with her delights I basely prov'd

Th' ingrate that loath'd what I should still have lov'd.

I turn'd her off, well might she then perplex

Herself, and curse th' inconstance of our Sex.
To be reveng'd, with me she did confer,
To do her right on those that wronged her.
I was the first, but me she did forgive,
Because as one, we must together live.
You were the next, whose crimes are manyfold,
Yet have sued out your pardon with your Gold:
Your subtle Wheedlings cheated her belief,
And would have filch'd her heart to play the Thief.
You stole into her Secrets, so that she
May at Loves-bar *charge you with* Felony.
For thus purloyning, stealing hearts away,
And being caught you now shall soundly pay.
She vows to me, she'l spare you not a bit,
But keep intire the Purchase *of her* Wit.
What Protestations, *and what* Oaths *you made,*
Were broke by you as soon as they were said.
Your great pretences and your bouncing Stories;
The idle flashings of your fancy'd glories;
All which she minds not, since she hath requir'd
A Treasure which so long we both desir'd.
 Now we are now almost quits (against your will)
This is the Sum *that must discharge our* Bill:
Imprimis *so much; lying by her side,*
And breaking promise, made her not your Bride.
Item *for changing* Petty-coats *for* Hose,
And doing something, which I wont disclose.
Item *for making such a pretty toy,*
Your wanton Mistris, *and your* Cabbin-boy;

Whom Morning, Noon, and sometimes very late,

Fail'd not to make your constant Trickry-mate.

Thus stands th' Account, and now we're even just,

<u>*Discharging*</u> *you of what we did intrust,*

If not quite broke, for some new Credit *look,*

You ne're shall enter more into our Book.

I shall not trouble you with the particulars of an exact Journal of our voyage from *Surrat* till we came to *Venice*, to which part we were bound, but only give you some light touches by the way.

The last day of *April* we cross'd the *Æquator*, and the first of *May* made a new way by judgement, and by observation our way was four Leagues to the South-wards, having a rowling Sea out of the Souther board. The fourth of *June* in the morning we saw the Island *Mauritius* and a little after three or four small Islands appeared also; we stood in betwixt *Mauritius* and these Islands, and when we were thwart the point of Rocks which lye on *Mauritius* side, we edg'd off towards the Island, giving that point and breach a good birth; our depth was twenty, and two and twenty fathom hard ground, and being within one mile of the westermost rock, we had twenty four fathom, the wind being at south east, we left into the shore about a mile distant from it we anchored that night. Here we rode near ten days, refreshing our selves with what the Island afforded, as Goats, Hogs, and fresh fish good store. It is reported here are many fish rank poyson, we did eat all sorts, as *Mullets, Lantarasks, Whiskers, Rockfish and Garfish*, and many others, but found no harm by feeding on them. We set sail hence and about 28 Leagues distance from *Mauritius*, we pass'd by an Island call'd the *Moschachenas*, near which we sprung a leak, that each hour we pumpt above two hundred and fifty strokes, it being gusty whether and a great Sea out of the South-east, but by our Carpenters it was happily stopt, although it was under the next timber abaft the well near the Keel, which by rummidging the Hold they found it so to be. The next place we anchored at was the Island of *Johanna*, here we had much lightning and thunder, the wind having been out of the Sea in the day, and off shore in the night. This place affordeth very good flesh great quantity of fish and fowl, we had a Bullock for ten long red Cornelion heads; we had also excellent *Oranges* and *Lemmons*, the people are very loving and friendly, having two Governours or Captains among them, the one call'd *Androm Pela*, and the other *Masse Core*, they desired of us no other money for ought we bought than those red heads. Sailing from hence we sprung our main top-mast, which our Carpenters taking down fisht it and got it up again the same day. On the third of *September* in latitude 16. d. 33 the wind at South east, we saw the Island of St. *Helena*, to the west-ward of the Chappel thereof we anchored a mile distant, the Captain caused the skiff to be hoisted out and so my *Jinny*, the Scrivener, Drugster, and Doctor *&c.* we landed at Lemmon-valley. Here with some Guns we carried with us we kill'd Hogs and Goats, otherwise it is hard to take them, running at the sight of us up inaccessible craggy Rocks. In ranging through the Isle, our men found divers Oranges and Lemmon-trees but no fruit thereon, the *Dutch* having been there as we suppose, had gathered them, as appeared by their names on certain Stones and Trees; we caught here *Mackrel*, *Breams* and *Borettoes* good store.

FINIS.

Milton Keynes UK
Ingram Content Group UK Ltd.
UKHW051021250324
439991UK00008B/960